E.C. BLAKE

BLUE FIRE

PRAISE FOR BLUE FIRE

"Great world-building, a fantasy feel with an SF twist, admirable characters, and the themes of courage and truth above all make (Blue Fire) a wonderful YA read. I know my teen will really enjoy it."

— BOOK HORDE

"Though many YA fantasies are coming-of-age novels, this one is different in that perhaps it's time not only for the young protagonists to take on active, responsible roles, but for their communities at large to leave behind old behaviours and interactions . . . In a few images, (Blake) presents the differing communities of his protagonists, making these young people and their surroundings distinct and memorable . . . Anyone who can write with such immediacy about light, rain, and mystic discipline has my attention!"

— PAULA JOHANSON, AUTHOR OF TOWER IN A
CROOKED WOOD

"I really loved this book a whole lot, I fell in love with all three of these individuals...I really loved all three of their relationships...an awesome and fun book to read."

— LORI'S LITTLE HOUSE OF REVIEWS

E.C. BLAKE

BLUE FIRE

SHADOWPAW
PRESS

BLUE FIRE

Published by
Shadowpaw Press
Regina, Saskatchewan, Canada
www.shadowpawpress.com

Second edition
Revised by the author
First published 2016 as *Flames of Nevyana*
by Rebelight Publishing, Inc.

Print ISBN: 978-1-989398-19-7
Ebook ISBN: 978-1-989398-20-3

Cover art by Hampton Lamoureux
Interior design by Shadowpaw Press
Created with Vellum

This book is dedicated to the Western Christian College Grade 12 class of 1976, and especially to those members of it who were the first to read one of my novels, all those years ago.

CABBAGES AND CARAVANS

"Oof!" With a grunt, Petra lifted another basket full of cabbages to shoulder-height, wondering how every basket could be heavier than the one before when they all held the same number of cabbages. He lugged the basket to the storewagon. As he dumped the vegetables into the wagon bed, he gave Cort a glare that should have called down Blue Fire from Vekrin and fried the other boy on the spot. But Cort, his fellow Priest-Apprentice, his roommate, and supposedly his friend, remained disappointingly unfried.

He also remained unhelpful while Petra continued to carry cabbages to the wagon. He didn't even look around to watch Petra work. Cort remained entirely focused on a pretty, brown-eyed, barefoot serving girl, talking to her in a low voice while she smiled at him and twirled a strand of her long blonde hair on her finger.

It seemed that whenever Petra and Cort were sent to the market to bring back fresh food for the Temple kitchens, Petra alone focused on the produce. Cort had eyes only for the girls.

Petra didn't see much future in talking to some servant lass he'd likely never see again. Girls weren't allowed in the Grand Temple of Vekrin. He'd have plenty of time to talk to girls when he turned eighteen in a couple of years. Though still a Priest-Apprentice, he would be allowed to roam the city more or less at will during his free time.

It wasn't that he didn't think about girls—he thought about them quite a *lot*—it was just that there was very little he could do about those thoughts.

He groaned and threaded his way back through the crowded market, sprawled along the east wall of City Primaxis. At the farmer's canvas-shaded stand, he refilled his basket for the umpteenth time. The Temple cooks required cabbages in rather alarming numbers. The wives and servants who bustled through the market shopping for their household needs could just pick a couple of heads off of the farmer's table. Petra, and theoretically Cort, had to buy dozens.

This time, when Petra returned to the wagon, Cort met him with an empty basket. He put it on the ground and held out his hands. "Here, I'll take your cabbages," he said brightly. "You take the empty basket and fill it up again."

Petra stared at him suspiciously. "Are you ill?"

"No, I feel great." Cort kept his arms outstretched.

Petra handed him the full basket, and Cort's eyes widened as his arms drooped. "Hey, these things are heavy!"

"Really? I never noticed." Petra bent over and picked up the empty basket. As he started for the farmer's stand again, he glanced back to see Cort picking up heads one at a time from the basket at his feet and placing them carefully and individually into the wagon, rather than dumping the whole basketful in at once. Petra rolled his eyes and returned to work.

When Petra returned with another full basket, Cort again traded him his empty basket. As he did the time after that. And the time after that. When adding one more cabbage would have caused the wagon to overflow, Petra paid the farmer with silver coins. He returned to the wagon to find Cort standing on the spokes of one of the wheels, fussing over the load. As Petra climbed into the seat and took the reins, the other boy clambered up beside him, giving the cabbages a last searching glance.

Petra looked around. "Where'd that girl go?"

Cort shrugged. "Disappeared!" Then he flashed a grin. "Well, what are you waiting for? Let's roll! These cabbages aren't getting any fresher!"

Petra stared at him for a moment. Then he shook his head and flicked the reins.

The placid grey carthorse started a slow plod down the market's main path, framed by vendors' stands. Despite Cort's strange urgency, they couldn't move quickly through the crowds. The horse, used to the press of humans, was careful not to step on anyone. People got out of the way eventually, but so slowly that foot traffic kept passing them.

At the edge of the market, finally free of the crowds, Petra turned the wagon toward the Great Gate in the north wall, only to find himself facing a new obstacle. A long line of brightly painted wagons trundled straight at him. With no room on the narrow dirt road for two wagons abreast, he urged the long-suffering horse to one side.

"Freefolk!" Cort said. "I didn't know they were due today!"

"Well, it's not like they tell the Priests they're coming," Petra said. "Since they hate us."

Cort looked at the cabbages. "I hope they don't take too long to get out of our way."

The lead wagon approached, driven by a grey-haired giant of a man whose eyes never turned from the path. Next to him sat a girl about Petra's age, wearing black trousers and a dark-green tunic, her long black hair pulled back into a practical ponytail. The blue gem in the hilt of a sheathed dagger at her hip glittered in the sun. So did her blue eyes, which flicked from Cort to Petra, appraising them and dismissing them in the same instant. She turned her gaze forward again as the wagon rolled past.

"Cute," Cort said. He leaned closer to Petra. "I've heard the Freefolk have wanton women who dance naked for City-dwellers," he whispered. "I wonder if she's one of them?"

Petra shot him a skeptical look. "Naked?"

"That's what I heard."

Petra snorted. "Sounds like wishful thinking."

"My cousin says he saw it." Cort scratched the back of his head. "'Course, he might have exaggerated. He does that."

"Doesn't matter anyway," Petra said. "It's not like we'll ever see it. Priests of Vekrin are forbidden from entering Freefolk camps. Our god wouldn't like it."

Cort sighed. "I know. But a man can dream, can't he?" He glanced at the cabbages yet again.

Petra watched the rest of the wagons sway and creak past, red and blue, yellow and green, gold and silver, shining in the sun. Fully enclosed, many had shuttered windows and small chimneys, like small houses on wheels. A few—grim and grey and sealed and locked—must have carried stores, or possibly weapons. And then there were the strangest ones of all, with curving tops completely covered in what looked like sheets of black glass and driven by pairs of stern-looking women in yellow robes.

Petra felt uneasy as those yellow-clad women turned unfriendly gazes his way. Freefolk Wise Women. Priestesses of the goddess Arrica.

Heretics.

Actually, "heretics" was one of the *nicer* things City-dwellers typically called Freefolk. Other popular slurs were "shiftless," "thieves," and "immoral." Yet despite the mistrust the Citydwellers felt toward the Freefolk, Primaxis depended on them. Visiting Freefolk brought news, travellers, and luxury goods to each city of Nevyana from the other cities that were strung like gems on a necklace along the King's Way. Petra couldn't think of them without hearing the sing-song rhyme children were taught even before they could read. It named each city from south to north: "Primaxis, Otraxis, Trexis, Ceturxis, Pentaxis, Saxtixis, Septixis, Octixis, Nonixis, Desmixis, Viandaxis, Divpaxis, these are the god's twelve cities."

Only Freefolk could safely camp after dusk outside the walls of the cities and villages. Each night, as they travelled their secret routes through the woods far from the King's Way, they erected a mystical Fence of Blue Fire to protect them from the depredations of murderous Nightdwellers. Like the Fire Curtain that surrounded the Temple, the Fence would strike dead anyone who touched it. However, the Curtain drew its power from the giant Godstone at the Temple's heart, tons of solid, immovable rock intricately engraved with magical symbols, whereas the Freefolk Fence was portable. The Priests assumed the strange glass-topped wagons had something to do with powering the Fence, but the Wise Women no more told the Priests their secrets than the Priests told theirs to the Wise Women.

Those who didn't travel with the Freefolk could only hope to survive a night on the road through force of arms, and even that was no guarantee. More than one heavily guarded caravan had vanished without a trace. So, too, had every expedition of the Unbound, a strange new cult whose members rejected the authority of king and god and goddess alike. The Unbound claimed they were travelling west beyond the mountains to settle a new land, although what kind of settlement could be made with maybe one woman for every ten men, Petra didn't understand. The cities' rulers let them go—to rid themselves of troublemakers, Petra suspected. He and Cort had discussed it and figured the Nightdwellers killed and probably ate the Unbound before they'd travelled more than a day or two.

"Uncooked Unbound," Cort had joked. "Yum!"

Two armed men on horseback brought up the rear of the Freefolk caravan. Once they had ridden by, Petra urged the horse back onto the road. They rolled north for a couple of hundred yards, the massive city wall looming to their west, sixty feet tall and ten feet thick. City guards stared down at them from the battlements of the giant round tower at the city's northeast corner as they rounded it and turned west into the glare of the afternoon sun.

After four or five hundred yards, the road they followed joined the King's Way, created by Vekrin himself. Paved with smooth, unbroken white stone that had not cracked or discoloured in all the centuries since it was laid, the King's Way led from Primaxis to the destroyed city of Divpaxis, hundreds of miles to the north. For most of that distance, it followed the Great River, which also wound through Primaxis before rolling out the southern end of the city into the farmlands and wilderness beyond.

The King's Way bypassed most of the cities, curving around their walls, but it led directly to the Great Gate of Primaxis. Petra and Cort drove up to that gate, which was flanked on either side by two more giant towers. About a third of the way up those towers, a matched pair of cross-bowmen stood on wooden platforms extending from the stone. They watched the comings and goings below.

The guards who concerned them, though, stood at ground level. They were far from a matched set. The one on the left was tall and stout, the one on the right short and skinny. Both wore red surcoats over silver mail, the surcoats marked with the king's twelve-pointed golden crown. The same crown also gleamed on the towering timbers of the two halves of the gate itself.

"Hi, you two," said the bigger of the pair. "Got your cabbages, I see."

Petra nodded.

"Did you see the Freefolk pulling in?"

"Had to get out of their way on the road," Petra said. "How long are they here for?"

"A few days." The guard grinned. "In fact, I'm looking forward to visiting their show tent later tonight."

"Is it true the girls dance naked?" Cort blurted.

Petra winced.

Both of the guards laughed. "Someone's been telling you tall tales," said the portly one.

"But they *are* a bit scantily clad," the skinny guard put in.

"Too bad you lads won't get to see." He winked at his companion.

Cort's face fell.

The first guard laughed again. "Get on inside, you two. You've got starving Priests waiting for those cabbages." He made a face. "Although personally, I'd rather starve."

Petra shared his opinion of cabbages but kept the thought to himself. It wouldn't do for a mere Priest-Apprentice to criticize the Temple's cuisine. He flicked the reins and drove the wagon through the open gate and up the broad boulevard beyond, which lead straight to the king's palace, atop the hill at the southern end of the city. The Temple lay off to their left, about halfway to the palace, isolated in a vast green field, a visual reminder that the Priests were a breed apart, that they were concerned with the worship of Vekrin and not with the everyday mundane concerns of ordinary Citydwellers.

Shops and houses lined the street. Many were shuttered, and a few in ruins, emptied by the plague that had ravaged Primaxis when Petra was a toddler. His mother had been among the dead. He had no memory of her.

Each of the cities and every village and town in between had similarly suffered, some even more than Primaxis. Some villages had been completely destroyed—not by the plague but by the Nightdwellers, who came howling in as the defenders fell ill.

Petra and Cort trundled up to the gate leading into the Temple courtyard, first passing between the tallest of the sigil-inscribed posts surrounding the entire complex. At night, the Fire Curtain's blue glimmer filled the spaces between all the posts, protecting the Temple from any possible attack. Not that either Nightdwellers or Freefolk could possibly penetrate the city to mount such an attack, but the Great God Vekrin's commandment was unequivocal: every night, the Fire Curtain must protect the Temple. And so, every night, it sprang to blue, shimmering life.

The Temple itself had a few small doors opening directly through the wall into the greensward on three of its sides, making it pretty much impossible to defend when the Fire Curtain *wasn't* active. Because of that, Petra thought the main purpose of the courtyard wall, and the guard now holding up a hand to halt them, was to keep a close watch on wayward Priest-Apprentices.

Petra tugged the reins to stop the wagon. The guard came to his side of the wagon and looked up at him. "You were gone longer than I expected."

"Held up by the Freefolk caravan."

The guard nodded. "Right. Heard they were here." He stepped back. "Well, you'd better get those cabbages to the—"

A muffled sneeze came from behind Petra. Startled, he glanced over his shoulder.

There was no one there.

Petra felt a sudden sinking sensation in the pit of his stomach as the guard, eyes narrowed, stepped forward again. "Who sneezed?"

"Sorry!" Cort sniffed and wiped his nose. "Allergic to cabbages!"

"It wasn't you," the guard growled. "Or Petra." He walked down the side of the wagon and peered into the back. Petra gave Cort another scathing look, but once again, to his great annoyance, Vekrin failed to incinerate his "friend."

The guard reached in and shoved a few of the leafy green balls around. His eyes widened. He reached deeper.

"Hey!" A blonde female head suddenly erupted through the mounded cabbages. "Keep your hands to yourself!"

Petra closed his eyes and clenched his jaw to keep from swearing. He took a deep breath. Then he opened his eyes again and glared at his roommate. *"Really?"*

The girl struggled to her feet, waist-deep in produce. She pulled a green leaf from her hair and tossed it aside. "Are we inside yet?" she said to Cort. "Can you show me all the wonders of the Temple now?"

Cort looked at the guard. "Ummm . . . I don't suppose I could convince you she climbed in on her own, and I had nothing to do with what happened?"

The guard glowered at him.

Cort sighed. "No, I didn't think so."

The guard picked the girl up by her slim waist, pulled her out of the wagon, and swung her to the ground. "Go home," he said. "No women allowed in the Temple."

"Oh." She sounded disappointed. "But Cort said—"

"Cort," the guard said, "made a mistake."

"You can say that again," Petra muttered.

"'Bye," Cort said cheerfully to the girl. "I'll look for you next market!"

The girl gave a tentative wave and then dashed off like a scalded cat as the guard took a step toward her. Then he turned to Petra and Cort. "Deliver your cabbages. Then report to the Master of Apprentices for punishment."

"Yes, sir." Petra flicked the reins, and the carthorse lumbered back into motion. He glared again at his roommate. "Cort, you—"

"'If you don't try, you can't succeed,'" Cort said, quoting an old proverb. He grinned. "Hey, it *almost* worked."

Petra shook his head. Cort would never change. He had a

hard time imagining his friend as a full-fledged Priest. *I hope the Priesthood survives. Be a shame if centuries of traditions came crashing down because of Cort.*

He glanced at the sky. *Well, Vekrin hasn't struck him down with Blue Fire, so I guess He isn't worried.*

Yet.

They rolled forward to face their punishment.

2

THE WISEST

Amlinn watched the bustling market roll past as her grandfather, Clan Leader Dainann, led the Freefolk caravan to its campground outside City Primaxis. Her eyes flicked over two boys about her age, watching from a grey wagon loaded with cabbages. They wore the blue tunics and trousers of Priest-Apprentices. She felt a fleeting pang of sympathy for their sad lives, trapped in the Temple day after day, trapped in the city even after they grew up.

But they disappeared from her mind almost the instant she saw them. With every yard they travelled, the time grew nearer to the premiere of the new dance she had been working on with the Sun Organist, Annjia, since they'd rolled away from City Trexis two weeks before. Last night, in the privacy of the rehearsal tent, he'd told her he'd never seen her dance better. Tonight, she would perform the dance for the first time in front of an audience.

Citydwellers. Like the ones in Trexis who . . .

She shook her head. She couldn't let her anger at what had happened in Trexis affect her performance tonight. She should be thinking only of her dance, not of those who would witness it.

But first, she had to think about chores. Leaving the market behind, the wagons rolled into the open meadow where the Freefolk always camped. Every city had a similar clearing outside its walls, and every clan knew it intimately. The wagons spread out, each to its accustomed place, and the Freefolk set about making themselves at home.

For Amlinn, that meant jumping down and seeing to the horses, freeing them from the shafts of the wagon, giving them a good brushing, and then feeding them the mixture of oats and corn they'd earned. Once they'd been groomed and fed, she would release them to graze in the corral that was even then being made of rope strung between posts driven into the ground.

Grandfather hopped down the moment the wagon stopped moving and headed off to hear the outriders' reports. The outriders ranged ahead, behind, and to each side of the caravan, watching for unusual activity, especially signs of Nightdweller activity. He returned just as Amlinn tugged a heavy feed sack out of the storage compartment in the bottom of the wagon. She let it thud to the ground and then undid the hook holding the hinged compartment open. It banged shut. "There's only one more sack of feed left, Grandfather," she said, looking up at him.

"We're all short because of leaving Trexis so abruptly," Grandfather said. "I've sent Orinn and his boys to the market."

Amlinn pulled at the sack's string to open it. The rich smell from the sticky mixture of oats and corn, laced with molasses, made her stomach grumble. It smelled good enough for her to eat, never mind horses. She took down the first of two nosebags hung on the side of the wagon and the wooden scoop that dangled between them. Then she jammed the scoop into the feed sack with considerably more force than was really required. "I wish we didn't have to buy anything from the market," she muttered. "After what happened in Trexis . . ." She pulled out the full scoop and dumped its contents into the nosebag. "We're supposed to be 'free' folk. But we're dependent on the cities for so many things. Even though they hate us."

"You can't blame all the Citydwellers for a few louts in Trexis," Grandfather said mildly. "And remember, we've got eight wagons full of trade goods from the north that we'll be delivering into Primaxis tomorrow. The Citydwellers depend on us just as much as we depend on them."

"They don't seem to realize it." Amlinn scooped out another helping of feed. The "louts" in Trexis had jumped a couple of Freefolk boys as they'd hurried out of the city at dusk, beating them bloody. The city guards put a stop to it, and her grandfather protested strongly to the city authorities, but the consensus among the Freefolk was that the attackers had probably been let off with little more than a warning.

"King Stobor realizes it," Grandfather said. "The Priests of Vekrin realize it, though they don't like it, what with us being 'heretics' and all. They hate the fact the Goddess's gift of the sunscales and the Blue Fire Fence protects us wherever we go, while they are bound to their clumsy Godstones. But without us, they would not enjoy the wines of Pentaxis or the fine cloths of Desmixis or a thousand other luxuries." He smiled at Amlinn. "And without the cities, neither would we."

Amlinn thought privately that the Goddess Arrica could have done a lot more to set her chosen people free than simply giving them a protective fence. That was its own kind of heretical thought, so she said nothing out loud. They might call themselves Freefolk, free to roam wherever they wanted in all the wide world, but in practice, all they did was travel the length of Nevyana, from Primaxis in the south to Viandaxis, the northernmost city still inhabited.

The Freefolk camped outside the city walls, not inside them. They hunted and fished as they travelled, but their nomadic lifestyle did not lend itself to agriculture, so they had to buy food and wine and horse feed and a hundred other things from the cities. They were not nearly as free as they liked to think.

Still, we're better off than those living inside the walls, she thought, recalling the Priest-Apprentices she'd just seen on their wagon full of cabbages.

"You premiere your new dance tonight, do you not?" Grandfather asked. He probably thought he was changing the subject, but her dancing, though she loved it dearly, was another thing that tied them to the cities, and another thing the attack by the Trexis boys had cast in a new light. In addition to trade, the Freefolk's other source of income was entertainment—jugglers and singers and fire-eaters and acrobats and instrumentalists and, yes, dancers. Amlinn's mother had danced. Amlinn's most precious memories of her mother —and she had very few memories at all—were of her leaping and twisting on the show tent stage to the music of the Sun Organ.

The better-received the entertainment, the more money the Citydwellers would give the Clan, and the more necessities and even, occasionally, luxuries the Clan could buy.

Amlinn loved to dance, loved the way music flowed through her body. But she also knew that the best way to ensure a good reception from the Citydwellers who came to the Freefolk show tent —mostly men—was to wear as little as possible. And so tonight, when she danced the new dance she loved so much, she would do so half-naked, trying not to think about what was going through the minds of the men in the audience as they watched her.

She knew Grandfather would not object if she chose not to dance. She'd had to overcome his resistance in the first place. He had never liked the fact her mother had danced, either. "I don't like to think of men ogling you," he had told Amlinn two years ago when she had first broached the idea.

"Mom danced," Amlinn argued. "I've watched other dancers. Who cares what the Citydwellers think? I want to dance like Mom. It helps me feel closer to her. It helps me remember her."

Grandfather had hemmed and hawed but finally consented.

"Who cares what Citydwellers think?" had proved to be a harder question than she originally thought. She'd been taught how to take care of herself. She could fight, and she always carried a knife when she wasn't on stage, but if she found herself in the wrong place at the wrong time and a group of city "louts" caught her alone . . .

Those thoughts went through her mind in an instant. But all she said to Grandfather was, "Yes. It's come together really well. I can't wait for you to see it."

"And I can't wait to see it." He gave her a small, crooked smile. "You're looking more like your mother all the time, you know. I . . ." His voice trailed off. He cleared his throat. "I'd best go check on the fellows setting up the show tent. There might be some patching to do before tonight." He glanced toward the city. The market, so busy and full of life not long before, had already largely vanished. Only a few vendors still raced to collapse their stalls, load their carts, and hurry inside the sheltering walls before nightfall. The sun had vanished early behind a rising wall of dark grey clouds. "Looks like it's going to rain," Grandfather commented, then headed off toward the centre of the camp.

Fifteen minutes later, with the horses seen to at last and the light quickly fading, Amlinn sought out Samarrind, Wisest of the Wise Women of Arrica.

As she crossed the camp, she glimpsed Grandfather by the show tent, carefully examining the canvas as the crew stood by. Before she reached the yellow-clad Wise Women, who were beginning to set up the Fence, the tent started to rise, its bright colours dimmed by the darkening sky.

Samarrind, shorter and slighter of build than Amlinn but white-haired with age, knelt in the dirt with her wagon-partner, Milla, herself twenty years Amlinn's senior. Milla leaned back to wipe her brow and gave Amlinn a friendly wave before continuing to scoop out a shallow depression. Then she picked up the Fence's keystone, resting at her side, and placed it in the depression. The complex twining shape of the copper-filled sigil carved into the black stone glinted dully in the grey light.

Samarrind slowly straightened her back, grimacing. "Daughter," she greeted Amlinn. "How was your day?"

"Long. Boring," Amlinn said.

Milla climbed to her feet, brushing the dirt from her hands, and helped Samarrind stand, too. The Wisest looked down at the half-buried keystone. "Very good." Then she turned to survey the rest of the camp.

Other pairs of Wise Women worked on either side of them, about fifty steps in each direction. To their right, one of the women waved. A moment later, so did one to their left. Samarrind nodded. "The circle is complete. The lesser Fencestones are in place." She glanced west toward the rain clouds that swept ever nearer. "The sun is almost down. Step aside, Milla, and I will activate the keystone."

Milla took three steps back.

Though the gathering clouds were impenetrable to Amlinn's vision, she knew that whether the sun was visible or not, Samarrind could tell to within a few seconds exactly when it would set each day.

"Almost time," Samarrind murmured. She knelt, and from beneath her robes drew a rod about the length and diameter of Amlinn's little finger, made of copper engraved with delicate, intricate symbols. She closed her eyes. "Almost."

Amlinn might have been imagining it, but it seemed to her that the gathering twilight darkened at the same instant that Samarrind touched the rod to the sigil of the Fence's keystone.

With a crackle, the Fence sprang to life, and a wall of glowing blue light surrounded the Freefolk camp. The hair on Amlinn's head and arms stirred as though alive, and a sharp smell assailed her nostrils. Some Freefolk claimed to hate it, but she loved that odour. It meant the Fence was working. It meant the Nightdwellers couldn't get in.

It meant tonight, no children would lose their parents to the monsters of the forest.

Twelve years ago, Amlinn had awakened to the terrifying sound of grown-ups screaming. Her parents had been just outside their wagon, enjoying wine and conversation with friends around the fire. The Nightdwellers had found a tree loosened by some recent storm and pushed it over. It crashed into the roof of one of the wagons, forming a ramp and opening a gap in the top of the Fence. Even as the tree burst into flames, the Nightdwellers raced up and over it, taking the Freefolk by surprise.

Everyone around the fire, five men and four women, had died horribly, torn limb from limb. Amlinn and four other children were orphaned in that moment. Not far away, three more women had died trying to protect their children, to no avail: three boys and two girls, all under the age of seven, had likewise perished. The Nightdwellers, four furred, screaming beasts, were slain with crossbows and their bodies flung unceremoniously over the Fence as a warning to their fellows in the forest, but far, far too late.

Except for the screaming, Amlinn's only other memory of that night was Samarrind kneeling beside her, wiping her tears, and giving her Sisspeth, the small rag doll she'd kept in her bed ever since. The Wisest had picked her up and told her to close her eyes. Then she'd swiftly carried Amlinn away. That night, Samarrind had cared for and comforted her. Though Amlinn had soon moved into her grandfather's wagon, Samarrind had continued to care for and comfort her ever since.

Now, with the Fence glowing blue, Amlinn moved forward and held out her hand to the woman who had been the nearest thing she had had to a mother for most of her life. Samarrind took it with a small smile and let Amlinn help her to her feet. She squeezed Amlinn's fingers. Amlinn squeezed back before letting go and turning away to look toward the centre of the camp. Her throat constricted strangely, and she seemed to have something in her eyes. Dust, perhaps, from the rising wind beginning to whip the flags atop the show tent. "The east gate will re-open in a couple of hours," Amlinn said, her voice rough. "The City-dwellers will descend upon us."

"I know," Samarrind said. "They will come to watch you dance."

Amlinn heard the disapproval in Samarrind's voice. It wasn't what she needed to hear right then. "Will you?" she asked, not looking at the Wisest. Her voice dropped to a whisper. "Please?"

"Why does it matter to you?" Samarrind said softly.

Amlinn turned to face her again. "Because I don't dance for the Citydwellers," she said fiercely. "I dance for myself. I dance . . . I dance for . . ." Her throat tried to squeeze shut on her words. "I dance for my parents. For Mom, who danced before me. The applause of the Citydwellers means nothing. But . . ." *But if you would applaud, it would mean everything,* she wanted to say. The words would not emerge.

Samarrind's dark eyes studied her face. "You know I disapprove," she said at last.

"I know." Amlinn tried a small smile. "But truthfully, Samarrind, making me a Wise Woman would have been a very un-Wise thing to do."

"On the contrary, I think you would have made a fine Wise Woman," Samarrind said. "You showed great aptitude for learning our lore. You're bright and self-assured." She cocked her head to one side and smiled a little in a return. "It's still not too late."

Amlinn shook her head. "I dance, Samarrind. I'm learning to sing. I'm even writing music. It's what I really love. I appreciate what you do, what all the Wise Women do, and of course, I love the Goddess, but it's not the life for me."

"Ah, well," Samarrind said. "You're still young. I will not give up hope yet." She gave Amlinn's face another searching look, then sighed and gazed past her to the show tent. "I wish I could watch you dance, Amlinn. For you, I wish so much I could. But I cannot." She took a deep breath and once again met Amlinn's gaze, her face framed by the blue glimmer of the Fence. "I have spoken out against this undignified practice of entertaining the Citydwellers, the Vekrin-followers, too often to make an exception. Even for you. And to listen to the Citydwellers' lewd comments as you dance . . . no. I cannot, Amlinn."

Amlinn stared at the ground. "I'm sorry for asking," she said in a small voice.

"No," Samarrind said. Her hand touched Amlinn under the chin and lifted her head. "No, do not be sorry, child. Dance as you have never danced before. Dance for your mother. Dance for yourself. Ignore the Citydwellers and their catcalls." She smiled. "And someday, when we are far away from every city, dance for me. I would like that very much."

Amlinn's heart lifted. "So would I," she breathed. "So would I." She threw her arms around Samarrind. The Wisest's small frame felt almost child-like in her embrace. "Thank you," she whispered. Then a bell rang in the centre of the camp and Amlinn pulled back, clearing her throat. "Dinner. I'll talk to you later and tell you how it went."

Samarrind nodded. "Please."

With a half-smile and a wave at the watching Milla, Amlinn turned and headed toward the fires blazing at the heart of the camp. As twilight deepened, the big tent glowed like a jewel from the sparkglobes within. A few tentative notes rose from the Sun Organ; Annjia, preparing for the evening's program.

Amlinn looked west through the blue shimmer of the Fence to the walls of City Primaxis, little more than shadows in the vanishing light. Soon the city guards would re-open the east gate, which, like the Great Gate, closed at sunset. Crowds would stream toward the Freefolk camp, to sample exotic foods from the stalls being erected near the show tent, to buy goblets of exotic wines from the cities of the north, to buy broaches and earrings and scarves and a hundred other trinkets unavailable anywhere else . . . and, of course, to watch the musicians, jugglers, fire-eaters—and dancers.

To watch me, Amlinn thought. She hurried toward her dinner.

3

THE GAP

The night dripped, and Petra dripped with it.

For the fourteenth time, he passed the gate where the guard had discovered the girl beneath the cabbages. For the fourteenth time, he met Cort marching in the opposite direction. For the fourteenth time, Cort's pace quickened. He didn't look at Petra. Petra looked at him, but somehow the water soaking his friend still failed to burst into steam. Then the night swallowed Cort again, and Petra continued his endless, useless march around the Temple, "guarding" it against entirely hypothetical intruders who would promptly be fried by the Fire Curtain anyway if they were stupid enough to try to get past it. In which case, his and Cort's entire function would be to call for Priests to cart away the charred bodies. Smaller victims, they had to deal with themselves. He'd already picked up three cooked birds and a crispy rat, tossing them into the bins located at each corner of the compound for disposal in the morning. "They take them straight to the cooks," the Priest-Apprentices joked.

At least, Petra hoped they were joking.

If he were to touch it, the Curtain would turn him crispy, too, so he gave it a wide berth. It glowed on his right, a glowing, translucent wall of Blue Fire, hissing and steaming in the rain. Every twenty feet within its ghostly glimmer stood a thick square post of black wood. On the side facing the Temple, each post bore a magical sigil, a complex symbol cut into the wood and filled with gold. From each end of a crosspiece atop each post hung a sparkglobe, a glass sphere containing a bright tongue of Blue Fire. Supposedly, the sparkglobes lit his path around the Temple. In practice, especially in the rain, each illuminated only a small circle of ground, making the shadowed spaces between the posts appear even darker, the Blue Fire of the Curtain itself being far too dim to light much of anything.

Occasionally, the gloom was lit by distant lightning-like flashes from atop the dark bulk of the Temple. All around City Primaxis, magical Hearths took in that Blue Fire and turned it into the light and heat Petra was currently in such desperately short supply of.

As he and Cort passed each other at the gate, the rain redoubled its efforts to drown them. Even through the tin-roof patter of the drops on his steel helmet, Petra heard the Curtain hiss like a giant teakettle. Vast clouds of blue-tinged steam rose from it into the night.

The icy water poured over Petra's helmet and down his neck. Useless and sodden, his blue woollen cloak hung heavy as lead from his mail-clad shoulders. His boots squelched with every step. His damp leather trousers chafed his thighs. He couldn't even feel his fingers; they'd gone numb inside his soaked gloves eleven circuits ago.

They'd be nice and toasty wrapped around Cort's neck. The fact that Cort was equally cold, wet, and miserable made his punishment a little easier to bear. Warming his fingers with a good long squeeze of his friend's throat would have made it a *lot* easier to bear. But the Priests would make him do something even worse than this as punishment for murdering Cort, although he suspected they'd have a great deal of sympathy if he resorted to violence: they all knew Cort, too.

He swiped his sodden arm across his runny nose as he rounded the bin into which he'd earlier tossed the burnt rat, started down the backside of the Temple for the fourteenth time . . . and stopped.

Perhaps a hundred feet away, a patch of darkness interrupted the double line of sparkglobes and the steaming blue wall of the Curtain.

Heart suddenly racing, Petra blinked rain from his eyes. Sparkglobes *did* go black from time to time, the Blue Fire leaking through a flaw in the glass, but the Curtain? Never! Which meant someone must have *deliberately* opened that dark gap, to gain access to the Temple.

Someone who might still be inside.

He wouldn't encounter Cort again until he'd rounded the far end of the Temple's long, dark rear wall. For the moment, he was on his own.

He took a deep breath and started forward again, step by cautious step, grateful now for the rain, whose endless rush would surely mask the squish of his steps from the intruder.

There is no intruder, he tried to tell himself. *How could there be an intruder? The Temple has* never *had an intruder.*

Cort's fault again, putting silly ideas into his head. Once every third fortnight, Cort received two days of leave to visit his parents, who ran the Three Stones Inn by the Great Gate. Last time, he'd come back with his cousin's wild tale of naked dancing girls in the Freefolk camp—and an even wilder tale from a just-arrived traveller.

"Someone robbed the Temple in City Pentaxis," Cort had whispered in the dark as they lay in their hard, narrow beds after lights-out.

"Robbed?" Petra whispered back. "And took what exactly?"

"Nobody's saying."

Petra shook his head. "The traveller was just trolling for free drinks. My father is First Keeper. He hasn't said—"

"He wouldn't, would he? What if a thief stole a firelance? That could start a panic." Cort barely mouthed the words. The walls between rooms in the Priest-Apprentice's dormitory were notoriously thin, and the outrageousness of his words could earn him a beating, or worse.

"You know what I think?" Cort continued, barely audible. "I think it's tied up with that 'Unbound' cult. All those malcontents, packing up and heading off into the wilderness, claiming they're going to start their own city. I figured they'd be Nightdweller food by now, but I'm starting to wonder."

Petra had rolled over and said nothing more, but he'd stared into the blackness for a long time afterward, recalling the day a Priest had demonstrated the use of a firelance on a sheep carcass. He had learned many things about firelances that day. He knew they could only be used within the city walls and a short distance outside those walls, perhaps a quarter of a mile. He had learned one of the great secrets of the Priests of Vekrin: that it was not the blessings of the Priests that made the firelances work, but their careful construction and the magical sigils inscribed on their wooden shafts. Which meant that if someone stole a firelance, that person could not only use it within any city but also make more.

Such a person would not be using the weapons on sheep. The thought of a living man reduced to charred meat the same way that carcass had been was the stuff of nightmares.

There is no intruder, Petra told himself again as he drew almost level with the dark opening. *If the Priests thought there was the slightest chance anyone would break into the Temple, they wouldn't have put me and Cort—of all people!—on guard duty.*

Right?

But even as he thought that, a low moan rose from the night beyond the Curtain.

❆ 4 ❆

A THIEF IN THE NIGHT

Amlinn spun across the stage to the wild, wailing music of the Sun Organ, finger cymbals ringing, bare feet and arms and legs flashing in the light. The ruby in her navel, the coins hanging from her scarlet breast band and head-band, and the silver bracelets on her wrists and ankles glittered with every turn. The wide-eyed faces of Citydwellers spun in and through and out of her vision, pale blotches in the light of the sparkglobes hanging above the stage.

And then, as abruptly as a slap, the music ended.

Amlinn stumbled to a halt, panting, her skin wet with sweat that could not evaporate in the steamy air. In the sudden silence, she heard the steady patter of rain on the canvas high above. She smelled sweat and frying meat and her own musky perfume—and something else: the sharp smell of Blue Fire, the same nostril-stinging scent she had welcomed when Samarrind activated the Fence.

She looked left toward Annjia, who poked futilely at the red, yellow, and black keys of the abruptly silenced Sun

Organ. Then the sparkglobes flickered. Amlinn looked the other way, toward the sunwagon hidden from the audience behind the painted curtain that created wings for the stage. In the uncertain backstage light, the wagon's sunscales glistened like wet stone. But somehow, the sunwagon looked wrong. It took her a moment to figure out why: a black-clad figure, a living shadow, knelt atop it, tugging furiously at a sunscale with both hands. As Amlinn watched open-mouthed, the intruder gave a final wrench and pulled the glass square free.

Blue Fire flashed, and the lights went out.

Men and women shouted and screamed. Almost at once, tiny new flecks of blue light pricked the blackness as Freefolk rushed into the tent carrying lightwands. But only Amlinn had been in position to see the cause of the blackout—a thief stealing a sunscale, the greatest secret of the Freefolk, the Gift of the Goddess Arrica.

The first rule of the Freefolk flashed through her mind: "When you see something that needs doing, do it!" If she took the time to find Grandfather, the intruder would escape. Amlinn leaped off the back of the stage into near-pitch darkness, alleviated only by a faint glow trickling through an opening in the back of the show tent—an opening that shouldn't have been there. With another jolt of outrage, Amlinn realized the thief had slashed through the canvas to gain entrance.

She felt her way toward that opening, half crouched, her hands outstretched to keep from tripping over ropes and barrels and other odds and ends littering the backstage area. Even so, she banged her shin against something that boomed like a drum, carrying above the hubbub of the frightened audience, out of sight beyond the stage. At the same instant, a dark figure blotted out the light in the slashed opening. He —or she—paused as though listening, then darted out into the rain.

Less than a minute later, Amlinn also emerged into the sodden night, shivering as water ran down her bare arms and belly and soaked her thin skirt, which clung to her legs like a second, ice-cold skin. She shoved stringy tendrils of hair back up under her headband as her eyes darted this way and that.

There! Wearing a pack that surely contained the stolen sunscale, the thief—a man, she could see now—hurried toward the blue glow of the Fence. Except, in one spot, there *was* no blue glow. Somehow, he had slashed an opening in the Fence, too, just as he had in the canvas of the tent!

Terrified the gap would close behind him, Amlinn dashed after him, her bare feet splashing through puddles. The intruder had only to turn around and he would surely see her, but instead, he bolted toward the city. Amlinn ran after him, heart pounding. She stumbled once and fell headlong, barely catching herself in time to avoid getting a mouthful of mud. She staggered up and hurried on.

The intruder slowed as he neared the east gate. Again, Amlinn glanced behind her. She could run back, call out to the guards at the portal, to Grandfather, but by that time, the intruder would have vanished into the city, taking the precious sunscale . . . where?

To the Temple, Amlinn thought with a shock of bitter certainty. *To the cursed Priests of Vekrin. Who else?*

To prove her theory, though, she would have to witness the sunscale being delivered. And so, instead of running back to the camp for help, she ran the other way, toward the east gate, a single ironbound wooden door, standing open, framed by sparkglobes.

The intruder entered the city unimpeded. The hidden guards didn't challenge Amlinn, either. With the Freefolk encamped, curfew had been extended, and people could freely come and go. There was no way she would ask the guard for help. Reveal to the Citydwellers that a thief had successfully stolen a sunscale from the Freefolk? Never. Samarrind would skin her alive.

She emerged from the dark tunnel through the wall onto the cobblestoned street beyond. Ahead, the thief passed through the pool of light cast by a sparkglobe atop a tall wooden post. Amlinn ducked into a shadowed doorway, arms wrapped tightly around herself, trying unsuccessfully to suppress her shivering.

The thief paused and looked back.

Amlinn gasped. He couldn't see her while he was in the light and she was in the dark, could he?

For a long moment, he stood staring back in her direction. Then, abruptly, he turned and strode away. Amlinn took a deep breath through chattering teeth and slipped after him.

Don't do anything stupid. Don't get too close. Just watch, see where he goes, then go tell Grandfather.

She hurried on, avoiding the occasional sparkglobes, accompanied by the soft clinking of the coins on her costume, clinking she desperately hoped would not carry through the constant patter of the rain.

Ahead and to the left, blue light flickered. The storm had brought no lightning. Those flashes could only mean she was getting close to the Temple of Vekrin, and that meant her suspicions were correct. *Those damned Priests! When Grandfather finds out . . . when Samarrind finds out . . .!*

She dodged from doorway to doorway, her feet so cold that she couldn't feel her toes, though not cold enough to numb the sharp edges of paving stones. Three blocks farther on, the thief slipped through a pool of light from a lone sparkglobe in front of a dilapidated two-story building. He turned left and disappeared behind the dark, shuttered structure.

Afraid she would lose her quarry, Amlinn abandoned all caution and ran, jingling, as fast as she could. She pulled up short just before she reached the corner. Breathing hard, she cautiously peered around it.

A high wooden fence ran alongside the building and well past it to the end of a short, unpaved street. A final sparkglobe at the end of the fence lit a small patch of green on a grassy field. Perhaps a quarter of a mile beyond that, a long row of lights cut across the darkness. Blue glimmered beneath those lights, and above them flickered the lightning-like flashes she had seen from the bridge. Each flash briefly delineated a hulking black behemoth of a building: the Temple of Vekrin.

And the thief was heading straight for it across the grassy field.

Are they mad? Anger blazed so hotly in Amlinn that it momentarily banished the cold nipping her exposed skin. Priests, stealing the Goddess's Gift? The Freefolk wouldn't stand for it. They'd withdraw into the wilderness, city luxuries be damned. Trade would collapse. Businesses would fail. Citizens would riot. The kingdom could well fall apart.

Amlinn looked south and west toward King Stobor's palace but could see only a faint glow through the mist. More than ever, she knew she'd made the right decision to come after the thief at once, by herself, without seeking help. She couldn't accuse the Priests without being absolutely certain, and if the thief evaded her . . .

She took a deep breath and slipped around the corner of the old building and down the short street, clinging close to the shadows of the fence. Then she made a final dash past the last sparkglobe into the open space surrounding the Temple.

The squish of cold mud beneath her feet gave way to the wet tickle of grass. She wanted to run, but she had no way of knowing what obstacles might lie before her, and so, with agonizing slowness, she walked across the black greensward. Wary of being silhouetted against the lights behind her, she crouched low, slowing her progress even more. All the while, she strained her ears, listening through the patter of rain for the footsteps of the thief, clenching her jaw to try to stop the chattering of her own teeth.

She heard nothing.

Wishing with every step she had the dagger she had trained so hard to use, the dagger she carried everywhere but on stage, she neared the Temple at last, the lights resolving into a row of paired sparkglobes on tall poles. In the wagon-length separating each pole and pair of lights from the next, Blue Fire shimmered, the Priests' protective Curtain, hissing and steaming in the pouring rain.

She stopped just a few steps from that deadly wall. Shrouded in vapour, the Curtain stretched unbroken down the length of the Temple. Where could the thief have—?

Something struck the small of Amlinn's back with bruising force. She cried out in shock as it hurled her from her feet. Her face slammed into the muck. She spat mud and grass, turned her head, gulped a mouthful of air to scream, and then choked on it as a gloved hand clamped her mouth, shoving the scream back down her throat. Sharp knees pressed into her back. Heart pounding like a caged bird in her chest, she waited helplessly for the bite of a knife or the sudden twist that would break her neck. Instead, the weight holding her down shifted, though the hand remained over her mouth. Lips and hot breath tickled her right ear. "I don't kill girls," a voice whisper-growled.

The thief turned her face back into the grass and mud so that even though the hand slid away from her mouth, she could hardly breathe, much less scream. He tore at the hem of her skirt, and she heard it rip. She tried to kick him with her heels but couldn't connect. A strip of cloth raked between her face and the ground, almost taking her nose off. It slid between her teeth and pulled tight, biting into the corners of her mouth. Then the thief pulled her arms back so far that her shoulders ached, and lashed her wrists together. As his weight vanished from her back, and she tried to kick again, but he seized her legs and held them down while he tied her ankles together. Then he rolled her onto her back, face-up in the rain, and disappeared in the direction of the Temple.

She sucked air through her nose, drawing so much rain with it that she almost choked. With a monumental effort, she rolled onto her side. By drawing her knees up and arching her back, she eased the pressure on her shoulders.

She now had a clear view of the Curtain and the black silhouette of the thief walking straight toward it.

The Blue Fire will kill him!

The thief raised his right hand. Something flashed, brighter blue than the Curtain. The glimmer vanished between two posts. Their sparkglobes blinked out at the same instant, and the thief walked through the gap into the Temple grounds.

With the Curtain down, Amlinn could see a deep-set door in the stone of the Temple wall. The thief went straight to it and touched it. Another blue flash, and the door swung noiselessly inward. He disappeared into the darkness beyond, and the door closed behind him.

Violent shivering seized Amlinn. All but naked, she would die of cold if she lay there through the night. She strained against her bonds, but it felt as if she were pulling her shoulders from her sockets. Gasping with pain, she folded herself up again and stared at the opening in the Curtain, trying to make sense of what she'd just seen.

That was no Priest. A Priest would walk through the front gate. Is the thief stealing from the Priests, too? Stealing what? And why?

Amlinn shivered helplessly on the cold ground, fuming at her own fecklessness. She knew how to fight! If she'd heard him coming, he would never have been able to render her helpless so easily. Before being allowed on stage for the first time, she'd been taught six ways to disable a man who made unwanted advances. She could outshoot many of the Freefolk men and handle a knife better than most. But the damned rain had foiled her senses, and that black-clad coward had knocked her down and trussed her like a beast without so much as a struggle.

Footsteps pounded the cobblestones beyond the Curtain. The thief, coming back? "I don't kill girls," he'd said, but maybe he'd thought better of leaving a witness. She twisted her head around as far as she could. A figure in a blue cloak and steel helmet slipped through the light of a sparkglobe.

A Priest!

Her heart raced with sudden hope.

The Priest stopped at the gap in the Curtain. She strained to shout but could only manage a moan against the gag.

Still, the Priest's head snapped toward her. His sword flickered from its scabbard.

Then he stepped toward her through the gap in the Curtain.

THE GIRL IN THE RAIN

Petra found his sword in his hand without remembering drawing it. The moan came again from beyond the gap in the Curtain, and his hand tightened on the hilt.

Someone was out there, hurt. But who? And who had deliberately deactivated a section of the Curtain, and how? Magical keys—short wands inscribed with a golden sigil—could open sections of the Curtain, true, but only the most senior Priests had access to them. This could hardly be their work. Which meant an intruder—a thief—had entered the Temple grounds. Just like in Pentaxis, according to the traveller's rumour Cort had whispered to him.

And where was Cort? Still trudging down the far side of the Temple, oblivious to the Curtain's failure? Or lying beyond it in the dark, moaning, injured after surprising the intruder?

Or did that moan come from the intruder himself? Maybe he'd received a dose of Blue Fire—not enough to kill, but enough to incapacitate.

Petra considered getting help, but by the time he ran back

to the guard station at the courtyard gate, the intruder—if it was the intruder—might recover and escape. And if the injured person was Cort, he needed help now.

Petra stepped through the gap in the Curtain with his sword raised.

The moan came again, close by. *There!* A flicker of blue from the Temple spire illuminated a long, pale shape on the ground. He hurried over and pointed his blade at it. "Don't move!"

The shape remained motionless. As Petra's eyes adjusted to the dark, he realized it was a girl about his age, lying bound and gagged in the wet grass. She wore a short skirt, its colour uncertain in the darkness. The cloth that gagged her and bound her bare arms and legs was apparently torn from its ragged hem. Silver bracelets encircled her wrists and ankles. Silver coins hung from the band of cloth covering her breasts. More coins glinted in her dark hair. A jewel winked from her exposed navel. Wide eyes stared at him.

A Freefolk girl! Had the Freefolk somehow opened that hole in the Curtain? Petra drove his sword into the mud, squished to his knees, reached for the gag, and pulled it free.

"Thank you," she gasped. "My legs . . ."

"You're Freefolk," Petra snapped. "Why are you here? Are there more of you?"

"I'm alone. I followed a thief—"

"Another of your kind?" Petra scrambled to his feet and grabbed the hilt of his sword.

"No!" Her eyes rolled, white in the dim light.

Petra tugged his blade free and stared around into the darkness, heart pounding, expecting an attack at any moment.

The girl twisted her head toward the dark gap in the

Curtain. "Listen to me! He's inside the Temple! He'll be back any minute. He'll kill you. He'll kill us both. Cut me free."

Petra looked down at her again, hesitating. She was of the Freefolk—heretics and thieves, the lot of them—but she was also a girl in trouble. And as a Priest-Apprentice of Vekrin, he had vowed to help the helpless. He swore. Then he shoved his sword back into the muck, knelt again, pulled the Freefolk girl into a sitting position, drew his dagger from its sheath, and cut the twisted cloth tied around her ankles. As he reached for her wrists, she screamed, "He's coming!"

Petra jumped up, dagger in hand, and spun toward the Curtain. A dark figure burst through the gap. The intruder held a long staff topped with a glass sphere, which suddenly blazed bright blue. Petra barely had time to recognize the staff as a firelance before the intruder pointed it at him and—

Blue Fire flashed.

Agony blazed through Petra's body. His muscles snapped rigid. Clutching his knife, unable to release it, unable to move, unable to breathe, he toppled like a felled tree.

The black mud swallowed him whole.

✦ 6 ✦

THE UNEXPECTED PASSENGER

Amlinn's breath froze in her lungs as the flare of Blue Fire struck down the Priest-Apprentice and brushed over her. Roaring filled her ears. A black tunnel swallowed her vision, and then her consciousness fell away completely.

Awareness flickered back. Someone was lifting her, cutting her arms free. She tried to speak, to move, but could do neither. Her head lolled to one side. She glimpsed boots and the edge of a swirling cloak. Then she blacked out again.

The next time she opened her eyes, she found herself looking at a little rag doll, wearing a patchwork dress of red and blue and green. A stitched red mouth and two black button eyes smiled blankly from beneath yellow-yarn hair. "Morning, Sisspeth," Amlinn said sleepily. She reached for the little doll, the one Samarrind had given her the night her parents died, the one that had shared her bed every night since.

Her bed. She was in her bed, in the wagon she shared with her grandfather.

Suddenly she remembered everything: the thief, the

Temple, lying bound and gagged and left to freeze, the young priest, the flash of Blue Fire . . . and now here she lay, dry and warm, in her own bed in Grandfather's creaking, swaying wagon.

They were on the road, but they weren't supposed to break camp for a week. They hadn't unloaded their old cargo or taken on new. And hadn't Grandfather said they'd be escorting a dozen travellers when they left? Breaking camp early meant breaking contracts, disrupting business, fomenting disputes that would dog them for months, if not years.

Freefolk never broke camp early.

What had happened? How long had she been unconscious?

She tossed aside the covers. She wore her warmest nightgown of soft flannel. Who had changed her? She pulled it over her head and then dug out fresh breeches and a tunic from the drawer beneath her bed. Dressed once more in the practical boyish clothes she favoured, she made her way between the benches that ran the wagon's length to Grandfather's bunk at the forward end. She slid over the red wool blanket, opened the half-door above the bed, and stuck her head out into bright sunshine. Grandfather looked down from the driver's seat and smiled, teeth flashing white in the shade of his broad-brimmed hat. "Good afternoon. How do you feel?"

"Sore," she said. "And confused." She clambered up onto the seat beside Grandfather and then twisted around. Down a rutted road, walled in by towering wilderness trees, snaked a long line of Freefolk wagons. Directly behind their wagon trundled the six sunwagons, each driven by two Wise

Women. Samarrind drove the first, Milla at her side. Both raised hands in greeting when they saw Amlinn.

She waved back and then turned forward again. She wondered how far they had come from Primaxis. One stretch of the road through the woods looked much like another, so she had no way to tell. From the length of the forest shadows, she judged that it was indeed after noon, though not long after.

She glanced at Grandfather. "We broke camp early."

He nodded, his smile fading. "No choice."

"Because of the thief?"

"Yes." He glanced at her, his eyes bright even under the shadow of his hat. "You should never have run after him like that."

"I thought I was the only one who saw him," she said. "And you always say, 'We do what must be done.'"

"You *were* the only one who saw him, but luckily, someone saw you leaving the camp through that damnable hole in the Fence and came to tell me. By that time, we knew we had been robbed. I guessed you had followed the thief. We came after you. The guards at the east gate had noted you entering the city, not far behind a black-clad man wearing a pack. A little farther down the street, a passer-by told us he'd seen you running past." His mouth quirked in a half-smile. "You made quite an impression on him in your dancing costume. Apparently, it's not the sort of thing city girls normally wear in the streets at night."

"It's not the sort of thing I normally wear in the streets at night, either," Amlinn said. "Especially not in an ice-cold rainstorm. But I'm glad I did if it helped you find me."

Grandfather's smile faded. "Even so, we would not have looked for you in the Temple greensward had that flash of

Blue Fire not drawn our attention." He shook his head. "Amlinn, you could have been killed. Or taken prisoner by the Priests."

"But you got there first."

"We did. And found you bound and gagged in the grass, with a Priest-Apprentice, stiff as a board, beside you. Some of the more hotheaded wagonmasters thought at first he must have attacked you, but it seemed clear both of you had been struck down by Blue Fire, though he took the brunt of it."

"He was no older than I am," Amlinn said, saddened. She hadn't even really met him, and now he was dead. "He was going to cut me free just before the thief killed him."

Grandfather's gloved hands tightened on the reins, leather squeaking on leather. "We knew the moment we found you that the Priests would blame us for whatever happened in their Temple. Another Priest-Apprentice ran up to the hole in the Temple Curtain as we took you away. In the dark and rain, I don't believe he could have been certain who we were, but of course, suspicion must have fallen at once upon the Freefolk. If we'd stayed, anything might have happened. Priests with firelances, the king's guardsmen—most likely both—storming into the camp, all the forces the worshippers of Vekrin could muster against us. So, we didn't stay. We brought you out of the city through one of our smuggling tunnels and rolled away at first light."

Amlinn blinked. *Smuggling tunnels?* That was the first she'd heard of those. But she pushed her curiosity aside to ask a more pressing question. "Why didn't they come after us?" She twisted around to look behind them. Most of the caravan was out of sight behind a bend in the road. "Mounted forces could easily have caught us if they'd set out at dawn."

"I know," Grandfather said. "I have twenty mounted men

guarding our rear for that very reason, but they've reported nothing." He flicked the reins at the dawdling horses, whose only response was a corresponding flick of annoyed ears.

"Maybe they know we didn't have anything to do with what happened at the Temple. Maybe they know who the thief is," Amlinn said. "Shouldn't we have stayed and talked to them?"

Grandfather took off his hat, wiped his brow, and settled the hat back on his grey head before answering. "There were other reasons. You'll hear them tonight."

"Other reasons?"

"Tonight," Grandfather said firmly. "At a full clan council meeting." He jerked his head toward the door into the wagon. "You'll find bread, cheese, cold meat, and fresh water inside."

Amlinn knew she'd get no more information out of her grandfather, and at the mention of food, her stomach growled, loudly and embarrassingly. She ducked back into the wagon.

They reached the night's campground with three hours of daylight left and encamped with the smooth skill born of years of practice. Sunwagons formed a circle at the centre. Grandfather's wagon and the wagons of other prominent clan members surrounded the sunwagons, and the remaining wagons and a smattering of tents radiated out from there.

Amlinn carried out her usual chores of brushing, feeding, and watering their horses, and then led them across the camp to the rope-enclosed corral. Though she judged sunset still more than an hour away, the Wise Women had already emplaced the Fencestones. As she released the horses into the corral, the Fence sprang to blue, glowing life.

Then she saw something else, something that leaped out

at her like a single fish jumping in a still lake—a lone, canvas-topped storewagon parked between the corral and the Fence.

She glanced at the other side of the camp. All the other storewagons were clustered together in their accustomed place. Why had Grandfather ordered this one placed way over here?

Curious, Amlinn looked around for the wagon's driver. Whoever it was seemed to have abandoned it. She studied the wagon again. What could possibly be in it? Lamp oil, maybe? Had Grandfather decided it was a fire hazard?

Well, one way to find out. She strolled over to the wagon and pulled aside the flap above the closed tailgate. Only a little of the late-afternoon light seeped through the wagon's canvas top, so all she could see of its contents were shadowed shapes: not barrels of oil as she'd suspected, but what looked like bulging sacks of grain.

Then the "sack" in the centre of the wagon bed moved . . . and moaned.

Amlinn jumped back. Then she realized what she'd really seen: not a sack, but a person, someone hurt. She drew the bolts on the tailgate, lowered it, and scrambled into the wagon.

Boots, blue-clad legs, a blue tunic, a blue cloak. Blue. The colour of Priests. Suddenly certain who she would find, she leaned closer.

The boy she had thought killed by Blue Fire lay there, bound and gagged just like she'd been when he'd found her outside the Fire Curtain. Short brown hair framed a thin face. The youth's eyelids flickered. He moaned again.

Voices outside reminded her that the tailgate hung open. She scrambled to the back of the wagon, took a quick look to make sure no one was watching, and pulled the tailgate closed. Then she adjusted the canvas so no one could see in, plunging the wagon interior into even deeper gloom. She returned to the boy's side and leaned over him.

Wide, white eyes stared back at her.

She jerked back so suddenly that the wagon rocked. Then shame and anger surged, heating her face like a flame. This boy had been freeing her when the thief attacked him! Why was he trussed up like an animal?

She leaned over him again and met his gaze. "I'm going to remove your gag. Don't cry out, or someone will hear. Do you understand?"

He nodded once.

She reached behind his head and undid the knot. He spat out the saliva-soaked rag, and a violent coughing fit seized him. She drew back and shot a nervous glance to the rear of the wagon, but no one pulled aside the canvas to investigate.

The coughing passed. Amlinn leaned forward again. "I'm so sorry. I didn't know that Grand—I didn't know they took you prisoner. I thought you were dead."

"You were bait," the Priest-Apprentice choked out. "Bait to draw me out through the hole in the Curtain, so your friends could rob the Temple! How many other Temples have your kind robbed?"

Amlinn's face flushed. "I was not bait. The Freefolk were robbed, too. I followed the thief. He caught me outside the Temple and tied me up, as you saw. I don't know who he was, but he definitely wasn't Freefolk. In fact, I thought he was a Priest." She glared at the boy. "And why aren't you dead?"

"Firelances can stun as well as kill. The one your friend stole must have been set to stun. Lucky me."

"I told you, he's not my friend. And it was lucky for both of us. I got some of it too. I only woke up a few hours ago."

The boy twisted his head to look around the inside of the wagon. "And yet here I am, a prisoner." His eyes snapped back to her face. "If you weren't involved, why did your people kidnap me?"

"I don't know," Amlinn said, letting frustration raise her voice. "I didn't even know you were in here. I just wondered why this wagon was sitting all by itself beside the Fence."

Something thumped outside, like a heavy object hitting the ground. She shot a worried glance at the tailgate, but it stayed closed. The noise didn't repeat. She turned back to the boy. "What's your name?"

"What's yours?" he retorted.

Her hands clenched into fists. She forced herself to relax them. "Amlinn. I am the granddaughter of Dainann, leader of Clan Therra of the Freefolk."

A pause. "Petra," he said at last. "Priest-Apprentice of Vekrin."

Amlinn got to her feet. The wagon rocked again as her weight shifted. "Well, Petra, I'm getting you out of here. Then we'll find out what's what." She went to the tailgate, pushed it open, pushed aside the canvas, jumped down—and looked up to see her grandfather striding toward her.

Two steps behind him, panting as he tried to keep up, came the short, bulky figure of Witten, a wagonmaster whose daughter Amlinn had often played with as a small child, though they'd long since grown apart.

Amlinn drew herself up. "Is this how the Freefolk treat guests, Grandfather?" she called. "Tie them up and dump them into a storewagon like a sack of wheat? This boy has done nothing to us!"

Grandfather stopped and folded his arms, a scowl darkening his face. "Amlinn, you are forbidden to speak to him. He is a follower of Vekrin. The Wisest has commanded that—"

"The Wisest? Samarrind is behind this?" Anger surged. "'Behave toward others as you would have them behave toward you' is one of the laws of Arrica. Is this how she would wish the Priests to treat her if she were taken prisoner?"

"There are things you don't understand about—"

"Then tell me, Grandfather!" Amlinn spoke loudly but controlled her voice. She would not scream like a frustrated child, no matter how much she wanted to. "Tell me what 'things' justify this boy's mistreatment!"

Grandfather's frown deepened. The light of the setting sun turned the lines in his face into dark crevices that made him look old and grim, like a statue carved from granite. "Tonight. In the council meeting. This is not a matter to be discussed in the open, where anyone can hear."

"I only see Witten. Is he an enemy too?"

"Amlinn—"

Amlinn pointed into the wagon. "Are you going to leave this boy tied up until he loses the use of his hands and feet? He needs food and drink and exercise."

"And a latrine." Petra's voice emerged from the shadows of the wagon. "I could *really* use a latrine."

Grandfather's face flushed. Amlinn took perverse pleasure in that.

"I was coming here to untie him for that very reason, Granddaughter, and to prepare him for tonight's council meeting. You would have seen him then. We dared not untie him until we were far enough from the city that he could not try to run back to it before the Nightdwellers emerge." He stopped, took a deep breath, and ran his hand through his thinning grey hair. The red in his face drained away. The sharp, dark lines softened. "I am not a monster, Amlinn. Please don't try to make me one."

Amlinn stepped to one side and pointed into the wagon. "Then untie him!"

Grandfather nodded to Witten. "Do as she says. Get him out. Let him use the latrine. Then bring him and Amlinn to my wagon." He looked back at Amlinn. "There'll be food and drink for him there. And we will discuss this further." He spun and strode away.

Witten climbed into the wagon, which rocked under his weight, and untied Petra's arms and legs. The boy sat up and winced. "I don't think I can walk right away."

"I'll help you," Amlinn said.

"All right, boy, let's get you out of here," Witten said. "Amlinn, if you'll take one arm . . ."

Together, Witten and Amlinn slid Petra forward until his legs dangled over the tailgate, and then eased him to a standing position. He grunted and grabbed Amlinn's arm so hard that it hurt. After a moment, his grip relaxed, and he took a deep, shuddering breath.

As Witten stepped back, Amlinn slung Petra's right arm over her shoulders and put her left arm around his waist. Petra leaned against her, heavy, though not unbearably so. He was perhaps half a head taller than she. "All right?" she asked.

"All right," Petra replied, but his voice remained strained. She took a firmer grip around his waist and helped him toward the latrine.

❧ 7 ❧

THAT WHICH WAS STOLEN

Petra found himself acutely aware of Amlinn's hand around his waist, acutely aware not only of the fact that she was a girl, but that she was a Freefolk girl, a follower of Arrica.

I shouldn't have anything to do with her! His heart pounded harder than sudden exertion after being tied up in a wagon all day could account for. *I'm a Priest-Apprentice of Vekrin.*

But she was smiling at him, blue eyes beneath raven-black hair. "How do you feel?"

He had to swallow before he could speak. His throat was dry. "Stronger," he said at last.

"I thought you were dead when the Blue Fire struck you," she said.

"I thought I was dead too," he said. "I thought you might be dead when I found you in the mud."

"He told me he doesn't kill girls," Amlinn said. "I'm not sure I believe him."

They made their slow way across the camp toward the low tent that presumably hid the latrines. Petra remembered

Amlinn lying there, pale and almost naked in the grass, long bare legs and arms, the jewel winking from her naval. He'd never before seen a girl dressed—or undressed—like that. Even now, she dressed very differently from city girls, who wore long skirts, full blouses, and many-buttoned jackets, and heaped their hair into complex formations held in place by jewelled pins. Amlinn had tied her hair back in a practical ponytail, and she wore tan breeches of soft deerskin, calf-high moccasins, a light-blue, long-sleeved shirt, and a dark-red vest. On her belt hung a dagger, a blue gem sparkling in its hilt.

That dagger!

"I saw you," he said suddenly. "Before last night, I mean. I saw you riding to your campground on the lead wagon. At the market."

She glanced at him. "Oh!" she said in sudden realization. "The cabbage wagon!"

He nodded. The cabbage wagon with a girl under the cabbages. The girl whose presence had gotten him and Cort punished and placed on midnight guard detail last night. *I'm a Priest-Apprentice of Vekrin. I'm not supposed to have anything to do with girls. Not even city girls, much less Freefolk girls.*

The rounded curve of her shoulder felt good under his hand, as did the warmth of her body pressed against his and the light, reassuring touch of her hand at his waist.

She's Freefolk.

He pulled his arm away from her. "I can manage on my own now."

She stopped. "Are you sure?" With her hand still around his waist, she looked up at him. Her eyes, blue as Blue Fire, drew him in.

Blue as Blue Fire, and just as dangerous. He swallowed. "I'm sure."

Her hand lingered for a moment more, then withdrew. He instantly missed it.

"Well, good," she said. "Because I really would prefer not to have to help you in the latrine. Guilty though I feel about you being a prisoner."

Petra's face flushed. "Um, I'll be fine."

"I'll wait here to take you to Grandfather."

"All right."

Petra stumped into the latrine tent. Inside its smelly confines, he did what he needed to do, then adjusted his clothing and emerged into the sunlight, blinking. Amlinn smiled, and the sight went through him like a lance.

Oh, Vekrin.

Amlinn led him to the red-and-gold wagon on which he had first seen her, and its paint glowed like a flame in the sun's final rays. Amlinn climbed up the three steps to the door, turned the gilded handle, and pulled the door open. She called into the interior, aglow with lamplight. "Grandfather, I've brought the Priest-Apprentice."

"Bring him in," came the reply.

Amlinn stepped to one side. "You first," she said to Petra.

Petra climbed inside. Padded benches ran along both sides of the wagon, beneath oil lamps hung in reflectors. Blue drapes hung at the end of the wagon to his right and red to his left, presumably hiding beds. An assortment of breads, cheeses, cold sliced meats, and dried fruit adorned the small table in the middle of the wagon. A bottle of wine and a jug of water waited next to the food. Petra had to swallow to keep from drooling.

Amlinn's grandfather—Dainann, leader of Clan Therra,

Petra remembered—took up a great deal of the wagon's interior himself. He extended a hand that not only enveloped Petra's but clearly could have crushed it. "Welcome, Priest-Apprentice," he rumbled. "Please, sit. I know you must be hungry and thirsty, and I apologize for that. We Freefolk pride ourselves on our hospitality, but as Amlinn so forcefully pointed out, in your case, it has been lacking."

Petra sat on the bench and scooted in behind the table. Amlinn slid onto the bench next to him, which made him absurdly happy.

Dainann swept an open hand above the repast. "Eat! Drink!"

Petra needed no more urging. For the next few minutes, he could think of nothing but what seemed the most delicious meal of his life, though to keep a clear head, he avoided the wine and drank only water.

The edge of hunger finally blunted, he met Dainann's gaze and took a deep breath to bolster his courage. "Thank you for the food and drink," he said. "But it does not excuse taking me as your prisoner. When the Priests learn what you have done—"

"You think the Freefolk robbed your Temple." Dainann looked at his hands, palms-down on the table. "I cannot fault you for that belief, based on what you know." He raised his eyes. "However, there are things you do *not* know that should convince you otherwise. In truth, you and my granddaughter," he nodded at Amlinn, "were attacked by a man who robbed both Freefolk and Temple. I wish I could say that such an outrage was unheard of, but it is not."

Petra chewed his lower lip, remembering the rumours Cort had shared.

"We did not set out to take you prisoner last night,"

Dainann continued. "We wanted only to catch the thief and rescue Amlinn, but when we found you there, it seemed too good an opportunity to pass up." His eyes bored into Petra's. "The truth is, we need a Priest. We have an item we hope you can identify and decipher for us, something that might give us some hint of who is behind these thefts and why."

Petra blinked. "What sort of 'item'?"

"I will show you, but not here." Dainann slid out from behind the table and stood, slightly stooped to keep from hitting his head on the curved ceiling. "We must visit the Wisest."

The Wisest of the Wise Women—the Freefolk equivalent of his father, Pelidor, First Keeper of the Temple of City Primaxis—wanted to see him? "I'm just a Priest-Apprentice," he said uneasily. "You should return to Primaxis, speak to the First Keeper—"

"You are at hand," Dainann said. "First Keeper Pelidor is not. And he would not meet with Samarrind in any event, nor she with him. Both our peoples would rebel, should such a meeting take place. The hostility runs deep."

"But—"

Dainann raised his hand, silencing Petra's protest. "Come to Samarrind's wagon. Let her show you what she has and tell you how she got it, and then we will see what happens. The clan council meets in an hour, and decisions must then be made."

Though his pulse pounded in his ears, Petra met Dainann's gaze directly. "I will do nothing that betrays my oaths."

Dainann did not reply. He nodded at the wagon's door. "Let's go."

The sky now blazed with stars, far more stars than Petra

had ever seen in the skies above the sparkglobe-lit City. Against those distant diamond-like flecks of light stood the spiky silhouettes of trees. The camp, an island of campfire and lamplight within the bubble of the Freefolk Fence, seemed afloat in a dark sea.

The Freefolk's strange glass-covered sunwagons clustered at the centre of the camp, near a large white tent. They walked past the sunwagons to another wagon, larger than Dainann's. A woman, sandaled feet visible beneath a long robe, stood at the bottom of the wagon's steps, in a pool of light cast from two small sparkglobes aglow on either side of the door. Her robe and the wagon were the same golden yellow, the colour of a sunflower.

"Clan Leader. Amlinn." The woman looked Petra up and down as if he were a strange plant found growing in the woods. "Priest-Apprentice."

"Hello, Milla," Dainann said. "We are here to see the Wisest."

"And you are expected," said Milla. She turned, knocked on the door twice, and then swung it open. She stepped to one side as Dainann entered, followed by Petra and Amlinn. Then she closed the door behind them, shutting them inside.

The wagon's interior looked much the same as Dainann's, but with only one screened-in sleeping area. At the other end, on either side of a door that presumably led to the driver's seat, stood chests of dark wood bound with bands of black iron.

At the end of the table closest to the bed sat a woman even shorter and slenderer than Amlinn, although the long white hair hanging loosely around her shoulders and her worn, lined face made it clear she was no mere girl. "Clan Leader," she said, nodding at Dainann. "Sit by me."

Without a word, Dainann slid onto the bench beside her.

Then Samarrind looked at Amlinn. "Daughter," she said. A brief smile took years from her solemn face and made her dark-brown eyes sparkle. "You and your companion sit opposite us."

Amlinn took her place, and Petra slid in beside her on the polished wooden bench.

No cushions here, he thought.

Samarrind's eyes now locked onto him. The smile she had shown Amlinn vanished, leaving her face as still and cold as a frozen pond. "Priest-Apprentice," she said. "The world is upside-down when I welcome a follower of Vekrin to my wagon."

It wasn't my idea, Petra wanted to say, but didn't. Silence seemed by far the safest course of action.

"But the world *has* turned upside-down when thieves steal the sacred secrets of Arrica and Vekrin alike." Samarrind looked at Dainann. "What have you told him?"

"Very little," Dainann said. "I thought it best you handle that."

She nodded and looked back at Petra. "You know what was stolen from your Temple."

"I know a firelance was taken," Petra said. "The thief could have taken other things I didn't see."

Samarrind inclined her head. "And from us, the thief stole a sunscale." She leaned forward. "This was not the first such theft. Did you know that?"

"I've heard rumours." Petra wondered what Cort must be thinking now, with his own Temple robbed and his roommate missing. "Supposedly, someone tried to steal from Temple Pentaxis."

"Someone succeeded," Samarrind said. She slid to the end

of the table, stood, and went to one of the ironbound chests. "That same someone, after stealing from the Temple, tried to steal from Clan Fell, which was then camped outside Pentaxis." She bent and flipped up the latch. "He had a magical key to disable the Fence, as did our thief, but his key was flawed. Blue Fire destroyed him." She took a rectangular object wrapped in white cloth from the open trunk and returned to the table. "He was carrying this." She put the object on the table and folded back the cloth.

For a moment, Petra stared at what lay before him, trying to make sense of it. A book, clearly, edges charred, binding blackened. He leaned forward. A pattern, obscured by soot, was incised in the leather cover.

Suddenly, he recognized it—a stylized tongue of flame nested inside a circle.

In the Temple, where that symbol appeared over and over again, the flame was blue, the circle white. When his father led the High Worship ceremony, he wore that symbol on his black vestments. The circle represented the Priests' holy duty to keep safe the secrets of Blue Fire, represented by the tongue of blue flame. And that meant this book was—

He pushed back from the table so hard his back slammed with bruising force against the wagon wall. "You cannot have that!" he choked out. "You cannot!"

"But we do have it," Samarrind said softly. "So, tell me. What is it?"

What should he say? What could he say, without betraying his vows? None of the Priests' teaching had prepared him for this. Even his father wouldn't have been prepared for this.

"It is . . . a holy book," he said at last. Surely that much was obvious. "Part of the Gift of Vekrin. And that is all I can say about it. My oaths forbid more." But outrage drove him to continue. "Do you know how sacrilegious it is for you to have that book? I've only seen our own Temple's copy once, on the day I took my vows. I was not allowed to open it or even touch it. Only the most senior priests have that duty and privilege!"

"I understand your discomfiture," said Samarrind. "But the thief committed the sacrilege, not the Freefolk. Just as he committed sacrilege against Arrica by stealing our sunscale." Samarrind reached out and gently opened the book's blackened cover. Dark bits flaked from the pages' charred edges. "We will not ask you to read it to us . . ."

Petra's eyes narrowed. Was there an unspoken "yet" in that sentence?

"But there is something else here that perhaps you can read to us without violating your oaths." Samarrind pulled a scrap of paper from the centre of the book, placed it on the table, and pushed it toward him.

Petra recognized the script immediately as belonging to the Holy Temple tongue, the secret language of the Priests, used for all their written documents and spoken only during High Worship. All Priest-Apprentices learned it. Having grown up in the Temple as the son of the First Keeper, he had learned it earlier than most. Against the scorched paper, the ink was barely dark enough to read. He peered closer.

. . . return these things to me, and your reward is assured. Beneath that was a single word: *Denthold.*

Petra's eyes widened.

"What is it?" Samarrind asked.

Petra straightened, schooling his face. "It must be written in code. I can't make sense of it."

"I see," Samarrind picked up the paper, slipped it back

into the book, and wrapped the whole in cloth once more. "Perhaps with more thought?"

Petra shook his head. "I really don't think so."

"Hmm." Samarrind returned the book to the chest. As she placed it inside, she said, "Tell me then, about the stolen firelance. Can it be used outside the city?"

"No," Petra said, and instantly regretted it. Did the Freefolk know that? He'd never been told it was a secret, or had he been told and forgotten? "I mean, I don't know."

Samarrind had turned to face him once more. "You said 'no.'" One white eyebrow lifted. "That is the truth, is it not?"

Petra clamped his mouth shut and wished with all his might he was back in his dorm room with Cort.

Samarrind came back to the table and took her seat on the bench opposite him once more. "No Priest has ever told us so before, but we have long surmised it. If firelances could be used on the King's Way, your Priests would escort caravans themselves rather than leaving the task to 'heretics' like us. Beyond that, we know that although your Blue Fire comes from the Earth through the Godstones and ours from the Sun through the sunscales, it is the same force, and must therefore be subject to the same restrictions. There is a limit to how far away we can set up the Fence from the sunwagons. There must therefore be a limit to how far away firelances can stray from the Godstones. Just how far outside the city walls will the firelances work?" She looked at him expectantly.

He kept silent.

Samarrind's lips tightened. "I see we will get nothing more from you tonight, but we will talk again soon." She glanced at Dainann. "It is almost time for the council meeting." Her eyes flicked to Amlinn. "We have erected a guest tent in the usual place. Please escort Petra there while I speak to your grandfather."

"And then come back," said Dainann. "You must give the council your account of last night's events."

Amlinn nodded. She turned and opened the wagon door, gesturing Petra out. He slipped past her into the cool night air. Milla, still standing guard, glanced at them but said nothing.

"This way." Leaving the sunwagons behind, Amlinn led Petra toward the blue glimmer of the Fence.

8

HOWLS IN THE NIGHT

Petra walked in silence, feeling as though he'd been clubbed. *Denthold* was behind the thefts?

"You needn't be afraid of Samarrind," Amlinn said out of the darkness. "I know she seems intimidating, but you have to understand, her first duty is to Arrica. She's really very kind. She's the closest thing I've had to a mother since . . ." Her voice trailed away.

"Since?" Petra said after a moment, curious.

"Since my parents were killed," Amlinn said.

"Oh!" Petra said. He hesitated. "How?"

"Nightdwellers. When I was a toddler."

"I'm sorry." That didn't seem adequate, so he added, "My mother died shortly after I was born." He glanced sideways at Amlinn. She didn't appear to be upset. He supposed she hardly remembered her parents, just as he did not remember his mother. He pressed further. "If Nightdwellers killed your parents, how can you bear to live out here where they roam?"

"We have the Fence."

"But the Fence failed your parents."

"The Fence didn't fail," Amlinn said sharply. "The Night-dwellers simply got lucky. They are always trying to find a way over it. That night, they succeeded. They pushed over a tree whose roots had been loosened. We learned from that. Our scouts carefully check all the trees surrounding our campsites before the Fence is erected. They'll never do that again."

"But someday they may find another way through your Fence."

"Yes, there is a risk, but at least, thanks to Arrica's gift, we live free in the world, and don't have to cower behind city walls, like the followers of Vekrin!"

"We're not cowering," Petra said. "I'm not afraid of Nightdwellers."

Amlinn snorted. "That's because you've never seen one."

They approached a small triangular tent just a dozen feet from the Fence, its pale-yellow canvas glowing with candle-light, a warm and friendly contrast to the cold glimmer of Blue Fire just beyond.

Petra looked uneasily at that blue curtain separating them from the pitch-dark forest. "Have *you* seen a Nightdweller?"

"Yes," Amlinn said.

"What are they like?"

Amlinn opened the flap on one side of the pole at the front of the tent for him. He crawled in on his hands and knees. A taut rope, stretched from the pole at the front to another at the back, supported the low ceiling. He couldn't stand up, so instead, he turned over and sat cross-legged on the groundsheet, facing the flap. A candle lantern hung from a hook on the pole at his back. A swollen waterskin hung below that. Red blankets, rolled and bound with a leather cord, awaited his use.

Amlinn crawled in after him and sat facing him, face pale in the candlelight, legs tucked up under her. "They're animals," she said flatly. "Almost feline, with blunt muzzles, fur, fangs, long, twitching ears. They wear no clothes. They carry only simple weapons. If not for the fact they can see in the dark and move as silently as ghosts, we could exterminate them. Someday, we will."

"Is it true they can't stand sunlight?" Petra said.

"They are never seen in the day," Amlinn said. "Rumour has it that even the touch of sunlight will kill them. If we could find their lair and open it to the sky . . ."

Unlike Amlinn, Petra had never seen one of the Nightdwellers, but he knew their history, for it was the history of Nevyana. Four centuries ago, the War of the Twelve Gods had devastated the Old Kingdom across the sea, rendering it uninhabitable. Only three Gods had survived: Vekrin of the Earth, Arrica of the Sun, and Ell of the Moon. Together, they had brought their remaining followers to Nevyana to start anew.

In the old land, humans had enjoyed great magical powers, given by the Twelve Gods to their respective followers. Those powers made life a dream—and war, a nightmare. The three surviving Gods agreed they would no longer give magic to humans so freely, but they also agreed that they would each give their followers one final Gift to help them survive in this harsh new place.

Vekrin and Arrica, allies in the War, chose to give their followers Blue Fire, though through different means. Vekrin, God of the Earth, placed twelve Blue Fire-generating Godstones along the length of the kingdom. These were the seeds from which the Twelve Cities sprang. Arrica, Goddess of the Sun, gave her followers knowledge of the sunscales, to harvest Blue Fire from the sun, firejars, to store it for use at night, and the Fence, so they could protect themselves with Blue Fire as they moved across the land, no more bound to one place than the Sun itself.

But the third surviving deity, Ell, Goddess of the Moon, had fought against Vekrin and Arrica in the War of the Twelve Gods. Her Gift betrayed the spirit of the uneasy truce among the three, if not the letter of it. She not only gave her followers their own magic—the histories were clear on that point, though none stated exactly what that magic was—but *changed* them, clothing them in fur, arming them with teeth and claws, providing them with sharp ears that heard things no ordinary human could hear, noses that smelled what no ordinary human could smell, and eyes that saw in the dark.

No longer even truly human, the followers of Ell became the Nightdwellers, spending their days in hidden caverns in the forests of the wilderness, roaming the land at night—and killing any Daydwellers they found abroad after sunset. Their relentless raids drove the followers of Vekrin behind high city walls and the stout wooden palisades of strongly guarded villages. All of those settlements were strung like beads on a necklace along the King's Way, which followed the meandering course of the Great River and defined the entire kingdom.

It was several days' journey from city to city, the length of each day's travel circumscribed by the need to find refuge behind palisade or wall by nightfall. Armed men escorted wealthy travellers and vital supplies. Sometimes, at great need, they risked a night in the open, but even the most heavily armed parties had come under attack at night. Sometimes they simply vanished, wagons, guards, and all.

Perhaps the Goddess Arrica's gift of the sunscales and

Fence was originally intended only to keep out ordinary predators, or perhaps somehow, she had known what Ell planned. Whichever, the Fence protected Freefolk from the Nightdwellers, allowing them to carry trade goods and escort travellers from city to city more reliably than the caravans that followed the King's Way. And more quickly too, since their secret paths cut straight through hills and forests, while the King's Way curved alongside the Great River.

For Petra, living inside the walls of City Primaxis, Nightdwellers had always been little more than the stuff of late-night stories told by boys trying to scare each other in the dark. Now, though . . . now, he was camped in the wilderness, protected not by stout walls, but only by an insubstantial blue glimmer, stretching perhaps ten feet into the air before attenuating into nothingness.

"Why did you become a Priest-Apprentice?" Amlinn asked.

Petra started. Exhausted, he had almost dozed off, lost in his own thoughts.

"Do you love Vekrin that much?"

Petra looked down, away from those bright-blue eyes that both pierced him and drew him in. "Something like that." In truth, his father had given him no choice. But he hadn't yet told the Freefolk who his father was. He changed the subject instead. "Don't you love Arrica?"

"I suppose," Amlinn said. "But not enough to suit Samar-rind. She wanted me to become a Wise Woman. I chose to dance instead."

Petra suddenly felt like an idiot. "Oh, of course. You dance."

"Don't tell me you thought I run around barely dressed all the time? Sorry to disappoint you."

Petra's face flushed. "I didn't mean—"

"I was dancing when the thief stole our sunscale. I saw him slipping away and followed him to your Temple." She cocked her head to one side. "What will be happening there now?"

"It's going to be buzzing like a hornets' nest," Petra said. His father would be incandescent with rage, more furious about the break-in and theft of a firelance than the disappearance of his son, probably. First Keeper Pelidor had never been more than a chilly, impersonal presence in Petra's life. A series of nannies had given him day-to-day care. Sometimes, he didn't see his father for weeks at a time.

Petra suspected his father blamed him for his mother's death. He couldn't know for certain, because they never talked about it. They never talked about anything except how disappointing First Keeper Pelidor found Petra's performance in his lessons.

"Buzzing with fury at us, you mean," Amlinn said. "At the Freefolk."

"Probably," Petra said. *Definitely.*

"Grandfather said he was sure the Priests would blame us. He said another Temple guard saw the men who rescued us, though Grandfather thinks in the dark and the rain he couldn't have been certain they were Freefolk."

"Cort," Petra said. "My roommate. And I wouldn't say I was rescued."

"Grandfather feared the king might even send city guards into the camp. That's why we left early."

"Not a great way to allay suspicions," Petra pointed out.

Amlinn sighed. "I know." She shook her head. "I just don't understand what this is all about. Who could benefit from stealing sunscales and firelances? Or your precious *Book of Vekrin?* Who is there, besides the Freefolk and the Citydwellers?"

Denthold, Petra thought. Out loud, he said, "There are the Nightdwellers."

Amlinn snorted. "I told you. They're beasts. Even if they managed to sneak into the city—which they couldn't—they'd just slaughter people until they were killed. They're too stupid to even think of stealing Blue Fire, much less use it."

She chewed on her lower lip for a moment, staring blankly at the groundsheet. Suddenly she raised her head, her eyes widening. "You don't suppose . . . you've heard of the Unbound?"

Petra nodded.

"It would make sense for the Unbound to try to steal the Gifts of Arrica since they're trying to set up their own free settlements outside the kingdom," Amlinn said. "The Fence would be a literal lifesaver for them. But what would they want with the Gifts of Vekrin? You said the firelances don't even work outside the city walls."

Petra winced at the reminder of his inadvertent betrayal of a Priestly secret. "I don't know," he said. But all the while, that single name ran through his mind: *Denthold, Denthold, Denthold.*

The Heretic. The Mad Priest. More than twenty years ago, Denthold and his followers had sacked the northernmost city of Nevyana, City Divpaxis, murdering Priests and sending refugees flooding south, many of them falling prey to Nightdwellers along the way. Every village between Divpaxis and City Viandaxis, the next city to the south, had been burned to the ground, then Denthold and his followers had vanished northward again.

The king sent a heavily armed expedition after them. Not

a single man returned. The Freefolk were asked to investigate, but the clans refused. "Let Vekrin care for his own," the Wisest at the time pronounced—just another sticking point in the long, prickly relationship between the people of Vekrin and the people of Arrica.

"Maybe I'll learn more in the clan council meeting," Amlinn said. "Which Grandfather will be sending someone to fetch me to if I don't get back." She hesitated, studying him. "Sleep well," she finished abruptly. Then she crawled out of the tent.

Petra allowed himself the enormous yawn he'd been fighting for the last five minutes and then turned to the roll of blankets. He spread them out, took off his boots and socks, and lay down on one, pulling another up to his chin against the increasingly chilly air.

He closed his eyes. His thoughts drifted to the Temple. What would his father be doing with a firelance and his son both missing?

Farspeaking messages, he thought. *Every Temple in the kingdom will have heard the tale by now. Dainann's clan will be confronted wherever it goes. The Priests will rescue me.*

Then, his flare of hope vanished like a snuffed flame. Dainann would be sending messages as well, to the other Freefolk clans. The Freefolk had only to close ranks and make it clear that no Priests or city guards would be allowed to search any Freefolk camp without solid evidence of wrongdoing. If Cort couldn't positively identify the men he had seen outside the Curtain as Freefolk—and remembering how miserable last night had been, Petra doubted he could—that evidence did not exist. Neither the cities nor the king could risk open conflict with the Freefolk and the resulting disruption in trade.

No searches would be made.

Well, if he couldn't count on rescue, maybe he could escape. But then what?

He could tell the Priests that the Freefolk had a copy of their holiest book, and quite likely spark a war. Most Priests would assume the Freefolk had stolen the book and the fire-lance from Temple Primaxis. He'd made that assumption himself. And they would almost certainly reject the Freefolk claim that they, too, had been robbed, seeing it as nothing but a flimsy attempt to cover up the truth.

Even the scrap of paper with Denthold's name on it was unlikely to challenge the Priests' long-held prejudices against the Freefolk. If they believed that fragment of text proved anything at all, they would most likely claim it proved the Freefolk were in league with Denthold. After all, who better to move thieves from city to city for the purpose of robbing Temples? More likely, they would claim it a forgery, or an old scrap of paper found in some Temple rubbish heap and stuck into the book to fool Petra. The priests would see Petra as a gullible boy, most likely kidnapped and fed lies precisely so he could return to them and deflect suspicion.

And meanwhile, the fog of confusion, distrust, and accusation would continue to rise between the followers of Vekrin and those of Arrica. It would hide the machinations of the true enemy, Denthold, who neither followed nor feared Vekrin or Arrica and wanted all Blue Fire secrets for his own.

Petra's eyes flew open. Amlinn had mentioned the Unbound. What if *they* were working with Denthold? What if the Unbound's claim to be heading west to find a new land beyond the mountains was only a ruse? Perhaps instead, they had melted into small groups and moved unobtrusively northward, working their way carefully through villages and cities all the way to Divpaxis. Far from falling prey to the Nightdwellers in the forest, as everyone thought, what if they were now part of a growing army under the command of the Heretic?

Petra thought back to the history classes taught by the droning Father Enik. If not for the constant threat of a painful whack across the back of the head with the old Priest's walking stick, Petra would have slept through most of them. But the story of Denthold's rebellion was too exciting for even Father Enik to drain of interest.

The Priests of Divpaxis had wind of Denthold's rebellion before it began, so they disabled the city's Godstone and destroyed its Temple secrets before he could snatch them. Refugees who survived the harrowing Nightdweller-beset journey to Viandaxis reported that the enraged Denthold burned the Temple to the ground, with the Priests still inside.

If Denthold could combine the secrets of Arrica with the secrets of Vekrin, he could march south, guarded by the Fence every night and armed with the firelances every step of the way, and nothing could withstand his advance. The entire kingdom of Nevyana would burn like the Temple of Divpaxis. What would arise from the ashes would be unrecognizable— assuming *anything* arose from the ashes. And assuming the three surviving Gods did not wipe humanity off the face of the world like chalk from a slate in their disgust at the horrific sacrilege such a scheme entailed.

Petra's instinct had been to keep the Priestly secrets as his vows demanded, to say nothing about Denthold to the Freefolk. But if he held to that course in the faint hope he might somehow escape, he was only granting Denthold more time to bring his plans to fruition.

An army strong enough to fend off Nightdweller attacks night after night might be able to journey north to the lost city and wrest it from Denthold. But there was no such army. Even if King Stobor and his dukes could put aside their internal squabbles long enough to ally with the Freefolk and then scrape together a sizable force, mustering them would take weeks.

No matter how he looked at it, Petra came back to the same unpalatable conclusion. Even if he somehow escaped and reached the Priests, it would accomplish nothing. Convincing the Priests that Freefolk were *not* involved in the theft, and that Denthold *was*, might be impossible, and the attempt could take weeks. Convincing them to actually ally with the Freefolk might take longer than all of recorded history.

Only the Freefolk, able to travel freely and act independently, could realistically get to Divpaxis in force quickly enough to thwart Denthold, or at least discover exactly what he planned. That left Petra only one option: to tell Samarrind and Dainann about Denthold's involvement.

Unlike the Priests, Dainann didn't strike Petra as the sort to waste time talking. Convinced of a threat, he would take action and head north, send scouts, gather solid information. When presented with eyewitness accounts from both Freefolk and one of their own Priest-Apprentices, even the most recalcitrant Priests might be convinced to trust the Freefolk. Surely the king and his Dukes would listen. If the whole kingdom were unified against him, Denthold could not prevail.

Petra could almost see his father's glare. After the dawn service at which Petra took his preliminary vows beneath the stained-glass version of the same Holy Symbol that graced the cover of the *Book of Vekrin*, his father had not congratulated him or expressed pride. Instead, he had gazed at his son unsmiling. Speaking the Holy Temple Tongue to give his words added weight, he said, "Know this, Petra, my son or no, if you violate your vows, you will be thrown out of the Temple and driven from the city to face the night alone."

On that cold morning two years before, Petra had vowed to protect the Gifts of Vekrin. To fulfill that vow, he had to help stop Denthold. If telling Dainann helped him do that . . .

And suddenly, Petra realized he had been placed in the Freefolk camp for a purpose. Awe raised goosebumps on his arms. Great Vekrin himself had arranged this very outcome! Vekrin had given Blue Fire to his followers to protect and serve them. To have that gift instead turned against them would be the greatest sacrilege of all. And he had chosen Petra to prevent it!

Besides, a part of him whispered, *this way I can spend more time with Amlinn.*

He blew out the candle, rolled over on his side, and closed his eyes, trying to ignore that last unworthy thought. But having thought it, he couldn't un-think it. When he found he also couldn't stop thinking about black hair, sparkling blue eyes, soft skin, long bare legs, a bejewelled belly button, a warm body close to his, and a hand around his waist, he sighed, sat up again, and reached for the water skin hanging on the tent pole. As he raised it to his lips, an unearthly howl raked his ears, raising fresh goosebumps on his arms and the back of his neck. He froze. A second, higher-pitched howl sounded from a different direction, followed by a third, lower-pitched and more distant.

Petra held his breath, expecting to hear shouts, running feet, the clatter of weapons. But only unconcerned voices murmured nearby. Hanging the water skin back on its peg, he pushed through the tent flap into the night.

Two Freefolk men stood near the Fence, their backs to him. Petra joined them, the dew clinging to the tall grass chilling his bare feet. "What was that?" he asked.

They glanced at him, their faces lit more by the fires toward the centre of the camp than by the faint blue glow of the Fence. "Well, if it isn't the Priest-Apprentice," said one. "Never heard a Nightdweller before, city boy?"

Petra shook his head. He peered out into the night. "Close?"

"Very," said the other man. "Look off to the right there, about twenty yards." He pointed.

Peering through the Fence's glimmer, Petra saw nothing at first, but then . . . there. Down low, two red dots, close together. They vanished, then reappeared. He stared, puzzled, and then realized what they must be.

Eyes!

"Will they attack?" he asked, breathlessly. He'd heard tales of farmers, too slow to return to the city at nightfall, found the next morning, headless and flayed, staked naked to the ground outside the walls of villages. Some claimed the victims' entrails were scooped out and eaten by the handful while they were still alive. The tales grew more gruesome and lurid the longer Priest-Apprentices sat in the deepening gloom around the dying common-room fire. Petra had always discounted those stories, but standing in the dark wilderness, looking at those eyes, every word rang true.

"Not they," said the guard. "They can't touch the Fence, and they know it. And this campground is properly maintained. They'll find no tree branches to run along and drop down from or tall rocks from which to spring over the Fence."

"They don't attack often, even when Freefolk get careless," said the other. He cleared his throat and spat on the ground, then wiped his hand across his mouth. "They're clever. They know it's one thing to get into the camp, another to get out."

"But they took the chance the night they killed Amlinn's parents," Petra pointed out. The two red eyes of the Nightdweller still glinted in the dark, watching him.

The first Freefolk man gave him a guarded look. "Yeah. Surprised she told you about that."

A new and unsettling thought struck Petra. "What about arrows? We're easy targets here, with the fires behind us. The Fence would set the arrows aflame, but it wouldn't stop them from—"

The first guard snorted. "They may be clever, but they're savages. They don't have bows. They barely have tools. They don't even wear clothes, just crude belts they hang knives and food pouches from. They're little more than beasts, really. Bloodthirsty and deadly, but barely more than a nuisance as long as we've got Blue Fire and they don't."

As long as we've got Blue Fire and they don't, Petra thought, and a horrible thought struck him. What if Denthold allied himself with the Nightdwellers? What would those murderous savages do to the Freefolk if they were given a key to open the Fence, like the thief in Primaxis?

He shivered.

The red eyes blinked, then vanished. Spine-tingling howls rang out around the camp once more, and suddenly the night felt emptier.

"They're gone," said the first guard. "Checked us out,

moved on. They might be by again an hour or so before dawn." He yawned and stretched. "Won't be our watch. But it is now, so we'd better make our rounds." He nodded to Petra. "Good night."

"Good night," Petra said.

He watched them go. They'd been surprisingly civil, considering he was a Priest-Apprentice. But of course, they escorted city travellers all the time.

He looked out into the blackness beyond the Fence again. *Where do they go?* he wondered. *Where do the Nightdwellers go when the night ends?*

If they knew that, they could exterminate them.

But if, instead, Denthold made common cause with them and gave them the secrets of Blue Fire . . .

Petra reached a decision. He would tell Dainann and Samarrind about Denthold.

He glanced at his tent. He felt wide-awake, and with his mind made up, he didn't want to lie down again and second-guess himself. Dainann and Samarrind were meeting with the clan council. Amlinn would be there too. Why wait until morning?

He set off through the camp.

9

THE CLAN COUNCIL

No wagon could hold all of the clan council members, so meetings took place in a special tent of plain white canvas, bearing none of the colourful, intricate patterns the Freefolk usually favoured. Four guards circled it at a respectful distance to ensure no one listened in on the deliberations. One of them trotted over as Amlinn approached, but upon recognizing her, motioned her forward.

Just as she put her hand on the tent flap, the unmistakable howl of a Nightdweller tore through the night. She paused as two more howls echoed the first. She glanced around, reassuring herself that the Fence shimmered blue in every direction. Then she entered.

Grandfather sat at the head of the long, rectangular council table, cleverly made of many pieces, one to represent each council member. Each council member brought his or her respective section to each meeting, and the table was assembled on the spot. If someone were absent, the table could not be built. It was a physical representation of the Freefolk belief that all clan members must both work together and fulfill their individual duties for the clan to stand strong.

Samarrind sat at Grandfather's right, leaving an empty chair to his left. The rest of the dozen seats around the table were filled by the ten most senior wagonmasters.

Grandfather gestured for Amlinn to take the empty chair. Seated, she studied the council members' familiar faces, browned by the sun, weathered by the wind, wrinkled, worn, and worried. She could almost read their thoughts. If the Priests learned how to make sunscales, firejars, and the Fence, the Freefolk would lose the city-to-city trade that provided their livelihood. They would be reduced to begging, or worse, farming.

No, Amlinn thought fiercely. *It can't happen that way.* Samarrind had told her that even if someone were able to copy a sunscale, determining what it was made of and inscribing it with the proper sigil, it would be a dead piece of glass without Arrica's blessing. That blessing could only be bestowed by one of the Wise.

Unless the Priests, with their knowledge of Blue Fire, could somehow get Vekrin to—

She shook her head. *No.* The sunscales were the Gift of Arrica. They could never work for the followers of Vekrin. Arrica would not allow it!

"Amlinn," Grandfather said. "Please tell us exactly what you saw last night."

Amlinn nodded. As simply as she could, she told of spotting the thief, following him out through the hole in the tent and the far-more-disturbing hole in the Fence, trailing him through the city . . . she hesitated. "To the Temple," she finished at last.

Shouts of outrage erupted. Karril, eldest of the wagonmasters, rose wavering to his feet, shaking his black wooden cane like a club. "The Priests! I told you it was the Priests!"

"Fools!"

"We'll starve the cities!"

"Leave them to rot!"

"End the trade!"

Amlinn tried to continue, but the uproar swallowed her voice without a trace. She looked helplessly at Grandfather Dainann. His voice cut through the others like thunder through the patter of rain. "Quiet! Let Amlinn speak!"

In the sudden silence, Amlinn said, "I don't believe the thief was a Priest. He entered the Temple, but not by the main gate. He used something to open a hole in their Curtain, just as he had opened a hole in our Fence and walked through it without peril. Then he slipped inside the building. He came out with a firelance."

"A ruse," said Karril. "He knew he was being followed. He wanted to put us off the scent."

Amlinn felt a flash of irritation. "He struck down a Priest-Apprentice with the firelance! Would one Priest strike another with Blue Fire for a ruse?"

Karril scowled.

Grandfather dropped heavily back into his seat. "Amlinn is right. The Priests are not our enemies in this."

"The Priests are always our enemies," Karril said.

"Not this time," Grandfather rumbled.

Karril subsided. He sucked on his few remaining teeth and mumbled to himself.

"The Priests have been robbed of their most holy objects as well, and not only the firelance. As we confirmed earlier," Grandfather nodded at Samarrind, "when we showed the charred book to our Priest-Apprentice. Our guest. We believe there is another agency at work here."

"What other 'agencies' are there?" scoffed a woman named Filla, the youngest wagonmaster at the table. "Nightdwellers? They're barbarians. Little more than animals."

"I am not thinking of Nightdwellers," said Grandfather.

"Then who?" Karril spoke up again. "There are only Freefolk, Citydwellers, and Nightdwellers. Another clan would not steal from us. You claim it is not the Priests. The Nightdwellers are incapable of it. So, who?"

"We don't know." Dainann sighed. "We hoped the Priest-Apprentice could shed some light on the mystery. But thus far—"

"Halt!" a voice shouted from outside the tent. "Stay where you are!"

"Let me talk to them!" called another voice, a boy's voice, frightened but determined. "I have something to tell them!"

Petra! Amlinn glanced at her grandfather, who had already jumped to his feet. He crossed the tent and swept open the flap with the back of his hand. "It's all right," he called. "Let him come in." He held the flap open until Petra ducked through it, then let it fall closed again.

The Priest-Apprentice still wore his blue tunic and trousers. His feet were bare, and his hair tousled. His gaze flicked uneasily from face to glowering face among the wagonmasters.

"You have something to tell us, Petra?" Amlinn's grandfather said gravely, taking his seat once more.

"Have you decided at last to tell us what was written on the piece of paper in that burned book?" Samarrind asked, her voice stern. "And what that book is?"

"Yes," Petra said.

Samarrind's eyes widened in surprise. *She didn't expect that*, Amlinn thought. *Neither did I!*

Petra swallowed and ran a hand through his brown hair. "The book is our holy book, the *Book of Vekrin*. The piece of paper was the end of a letter. It contained part of a sentence and a signature." He stopped.

"How did the partial sentence read?" Samarrind prompted.

Petra swallowed again. "'Return these things to me, and your reward is assured.'"

A murmur ran through the council.

Samarrind ignored it. "And the signature?"

Petra's eyes flicked around the table, then returned to the Wisest. He pressed his lips together, closed his eyes, and murmured a single word, "Denthold."

Amlinn blinked, puzzled. But the wagonmasters jumped to their feet, shouting in anger. Petra's eyes widened, and he took an involuntary step back.

Grandfather pounded on the table with his fist. "Silence!" he thundered. "Silence!" One by one, the wagonmasters sat down again. With order restored, Grandfather looked around at their furious faces. "And so, we have our answer."

"Do we?" Karril pointed his trembling cane at Petra. "I still say this is all some ploy of this boy, of the cursed Priests!"

"You kidnapped me," Petra said. Anger drove his voice higher. "What kind of a 'ploy' could require you to steal me away from the Temple while I was unconscious? You could have left me there. You *should* have left me there. Now the Priests will never believe that you're not involved in the theft. When they find out you've kidnapped the son of the

First Keeper—" He stopped. His mouth hung open for a second, then his jaw snapped closed with a click of teeth.

But of course, it was far too late. Amlinn and everyone else in the tent stared at Petra.

Son of the First Keeper?

"You are right," Grandfather said after a long moment. "The fact you are the son of First Keeper Pelidor—a fact we were unaware of until now—means we cannot let the Priests know we kidnapped you."

"Cort saw you at the Fire Curtain," Petra said desperately. "The guards must have seen you taking me out through the East Gate."

"'Cort' saw something, but it was dark and raining. He can't be sure we were Freefolk. And no one saw us taking you out of the city." Grandfather didn't explain further. Amlinn knew he wouldn't reveal the existence of secret Freefolk smuggling tunnels to a Priest-Apprentice. He hadn't even revealed their existence to *her* until today! "No one knows you are with us, Petra," Grandfather continued. "And no one in the city is going to find out, not until we can go to the Priests with proof that Denthold is involved. If, in fact, you have told us the truth about that."

"It's true," Petra said. "Show that piece of paper to any Priest. He'll confirm what I—"

Dainann snorted. "A burned holy book and a scrap of paper with the Mad Priest's name on it are hardly proof. Not when presented by 'heretics.' As you well know. Attempting to convince them to work with us against Denthold might well spark open conflict."

"So will kidnapping me!"

"But as I just said, they don't know we kidnapped you.

And they won't find out. Not until we have proof of what you say. And you will be an important part of that proof."

Petra blinked. "How?"

"By testifying to what we see when we reach the gate of City Divpaxis."

The uproar from the wagonmasters in response to that statement made it clear the argument would carry on far into the night. "You'd better go," Grandfather murmured to Amlinn. "Take Petra back to his tent."

Amlinn nodded and got up. She took Petra's arm and led him out into the fresh night air.

Behind her, Grandfather once more bellowed for quiet.

"I wish I'd grabbed my cloak," Petra said between chattering teeth. "And my shoes."

"Just be careful where you step," Amlinn said.

She saw his questioning look even in the dim light.

"Horses," she added helpfully.

He groaned.

She laughed and reached into her belt pouch. "Here, this will help." She took out her lightwand, a wooden tube about as long as her index finger, with a glass plug at one end. Brass, inscribed with a tiny silver sigil, capped the other end. Amlinn twisted the brass cap, and a blue-green light poured through the glass plug. It painted Petra's face the colour of a week-old corpse, but it illuminated the ground.

Petra looked down into its light and gingerly moved his foot a little farther away from the pile of horse dung his toes were almost touching.

Amlinn laughed again.

Petra stared at the device in her hand. "I've never seen one of those before."

"Not something we share," Amlinn said. "It's called a

lightwand. It traps a small amount of Blue Fire from the sunwagons and holds it for release as needed."

"Clever," Petra said. "I'm surprised the Priests haven't thought of it."

Because Priests are cleverer than Freefolk? Amlinn almost snapped, but thought better of it. Instead, she pointed the way ahead with her lightwand. As they walked on, she said, "Could the Mad Priest really be behind all of this?"

Petra glanced at her. They weren't far from some of the big fires around which people still moved, eating, and drinking, and this time she could see his face clearly. "We prefer to call him the Heretic," he said.

"I'm sure you do. But the Freefolk call him the Mad Priest. Which is what he was, after all. Mad. Sacking a city, sending people fleeing south—what could he possibly have hoped to gain?"

"He wanted to seize power for himself," Petra said.

"But he failed," Amlinn pointed out. "Nobody has heard anything from him in more than twenty years."

"Until now," Petra said.

Fires left behind, they moved through deep shadows, their path illuminated only by the lightwand. Above burned the cold stars. Ahead shimmered the Fence and the dark triangle of Petra's tent.

"Everyone assumed that he and his followers died, that the Nightdwellers must have overrun Divpaxis," Petra continued. "No one who has travelled there since has ever returned. But that's why I had to tell your grandfather about him." It sounded as though he were defending himself to an accuser that only he could hear. "If Denthold has kept control of Divpaxis all these years, building it into his own private kingdom, then he may have also built his own private army."

"Oh!" Amlinn remembered their earlier conversation. "You think the Unbound have travelled north to join him?"

"Maybe. And if he arms his supporters with firelances that can draw on your firejars, and wraps them in a Fence every night, he can send that army south at will—and stands a good chance of taking all of Nevyana."

They stopped in front of Petra's tent. He gestured at the blue glimmer of the Fence. "And then there are Night-dwellers. What would happen if he made an alliance with them?"

Amlinn's eyes widened. The monsters that had killed her parents, given the key that had allowed the thief to enter their camp? Worse, maybe armed with the lightning-weapons of the Priests? "They'd wipe us out! We'd have to flee into the cities and—"

"That's one reason I had to tell your grandfather about Denthold," Petra said. "The other is that only the Freefolk can travel far enough north to see what is happening in Divpaxis."

Amlinn glanced back in the direction of the council tent. "Grandfather and Samarrind may not find it easy to convince some of the wagonma . . . maaah . . ." A jaw-cracking yawn took her by surprise, swallowing the last word.

Petra grinned as she snapped her mouth closed. "Long day," she said defensively. "Here's your tent. I suggest you go to bed. That's where I'm headed. We both need sleep. We'll see what's what in the morning." She hesitated, finding herself strangely reluctant to leave the boy's side. Finally, she gave him an awkward half-wave of farewell. He raised his hand in a matching gesture, then turned and crawled into his tent.

As Amlinn made her way back through the camp to

Grandfather's wagon, her mind whirled. Thieves stealing the secrets of Blue Fire? The Mad Priest alive and plotting against the kingdom?

Friends with a Priest-Apprentice?

Whatever the council decided, the world she'd always known had just been turned upside-down.

✤ 10 ✤

THE NIGHTDWELLER

Jin woke to a touch on his arm and sat up, instantly awake. Ket-Ra, leader of his watchpack, crouched beside his sleeping pad. "Early patrol, Jin-Ra," he said. "Freefolk."

Jin yawned, stretched, and got to his feet. Though they were the same age, the watchpack leader stood half a head taller, with broader shoulders and the beginnings of a respectable mane. Ket handed him his watchbelt, black leather marked on the inside with silver sigils.

Ket won't be living here much longer, Jin thought as he buckled on the belt, looking around the crowded chamber of the Ra. Every available space was filled with a snoozing young male, too old to live among the Sa, the prepubescent children, and not yet old enough to be considered one of the Pur, the adult members of the warren. The Pur, in turn, eventually became the Ser, the elders of the community.

Rith-Ra and Rath-Ra, the twin brothers who were the other members of their watchpack, stood at the entrance, stretching and scratching, watchbelts cinched around their waists. Like Jin, the belts were the only things they wore besides their own thick fur. Though most of them had fur that bore black stripes on a tan background, Jin's was a pale silver, shading to black at the tips of his fingers, toes, pointed ears, and snout. Ket's was pure black. Unlike the bare-skinned Daydwellers, they had no need to confine their bodies in cloth.

"Latrine," Jin muttered, and went to find it. When he returned, Ket was handing out flasks of water and rations—disks of dried meat pressed together with berries and nuts. Jin slung his flask over his shoulder and tucked the leaf-wrapped ration disk into the leather pouch hanging from his watchbelt. "Orders?" he asked Ket.

"The usual," Ket said. "Scout, make some noise, test the Fence. If we find a weakness, we summon warriors." He flashed a fanged smile. "May Ell give us such luck!"

Jin said nothing. He knew the others would love the chance to raid and kill inside one of the cursed Fences of the Freefolk. But Jin had no desire to kill the Freefolk or the Daydwellers. Barbarians they might be, and yes, they would kill Nightdwellers if they found them, but in the end, all they really sought was the freedom to live their lives and raise their offspring. Jin saw no particular reason to deny them that desire. A vast, empty land surrounded them, and yet the followers of the Three Gods remained locked in this one valley, struggling with each other as the Gods had struggled with each other in the old land across the sea. That had ended in destruction. Jin very much feared the struggles among the Gods' followers in this land would end the same way.

Such thoughts were unorthodox. Some would say blasphemous. Which was why only Ser Mar, the old Scrollkeeper who had befriended Jin, knew of his doubts.

Jin's mouth quirked. Of course, Ser Mar knew of his doubts. He'd instilled them!

Ket looked around his little group. "All set?"

They nodded, Jin a fraction of a second later than the others. "Then let's go. And may Ell smile down on us."

Ket led the way down the corridor toward the south exit. The twins, side by side as always, followed close behind. Jin brought up the rear.

Half an hour later, after exchanging calls with the others in his watchpack, Jin crouched outside the Freefolk camp. He stared through the glimmer of the Fence at two armed guards and a barefoot young man in blue tunic and trousers. Blue was the colour of the Priests of Vekrin, so Jin suspected what the boy was even before he heard the guards call him "Priest-Apprentice." Ser Mar had always told Jin that the followers of Vekrin and Arrica despised and mistrusted each other. So, what was a Priest-Apprentice of Vekrin doing in this camp of the Freefolk?

Even as Jin kept most of his attention on the puzzling blue-clad youth, he sensed every other person in the camp through the magic of his watchbelt. It limned them in his mind like sparks from a fire. Several of those sparks clustered at the camp's heart, a nest of fireflies around which other fireflies made a regular circuit. A guarded meeting of some kind, he guessed.

He listened to the conversation of the Freefolk and the boy, the Daydwellers speaking far too loudly, as they always did.

"They don't attack often, even when Freefolk get care-less," one said.

Jin grimaced in disgust as the man cleared on his throat and spat on the ground.

"They're clever," the Daydweller continued.

And we also have better manners, Jin thought.

"They know it's one thing to get into the camp, another to get out."

True enough.

"But they took the chance the night they killed Amlinn's parents," the boy said.

Amlinn? The name meant nothing to Jin, but clearly, she must have been orphaned one of the nights Ell granted a watchpack the "luck" Ket had so wished for. He felt a little sick.

The boy asked about arrows. Jin bared his teeth as he heard the guard call the Nightdwellers savages without bows, little more than beasts. Jin himself was an expert bowman: on most hunting trips, he brought down his deer with a single shot, returning with every arrow.

In truth, the only reason Nightdwellers did not use bows to attack the Freefolk was that they were forbidden to do so. They were taught that the Goddess Ell found the presence of Daydwellers in her night offensive, and so had commanded her followers to blot away that offence. However, they could use only the Gifts bestowed by Ell: retractable claws; sharp teeth and even sharper hearing; an enhanced sense of smell; the ability to see in the dark; and the magical watchbelts.

Savages, they call us, Jin thought. *Beasts. But we are not the ones who live in cages of Blue Fire. We run free while they cower.*

Ket howled the signal to regroup, and Jin turned and

loped away from the Fence. Were it not for Ell's law, the Freefolk would see just how well Nightdwellers made and wielded bows. If not for Ell's law, not one person in that camp would survive until morning. The Freefolk should be grateful the Nightdwellers were civilized.

Someday, they might well learn the truth. Ell's law made one allowance for the use of all weapons at the Nightdwellers' disposal—all-out war. If ever the Daydwellers grew strong enough or bold enough to threaten the Nightdwellers' survival, they would quickly discover just how wrong they were to think of Ell's people as "little more than animals."

The positions of his watchmates burned in Jin's mind through the magic of the watchbelt. A moment later, he heard voices and caught Ket's scent. A moment after that, he emerged into the clearing where Ket waited with Rith and Rath. They stood close by another of the Gifts of Ell: a watchstone. It was an ordinary-appearing boulder, grey and lichen-spotted, roughly the size and shape of a sheep. But on its hidden, flat underside, another of Ell's magical sigils had been carved and filled with molten silver. The watchstone, a brilliant beacon in Jin's watchbelt-enhanced vision, both marked the approach to Broken Tree Warren and hid it completely from Daydwellers.

The moment Jin appeared, Ket turned and trotted along the trail, the twins close behind, Jin a score of strides farther back.

Watching the broad furred backs in front of him, Jin wondered if he were the only Nightdweller his age who thought about what life might be like if the enmity between Nightdweller and Daydweller ended. If he could meet the young Priest-Apprentice inside the Freefolk camp and simply talk to him, without being compelled to try to kill him, what might he learn?

He frowned. For one thing, he might learn what a Priest-Apprentice of Vekrin was doing in the camp of Arrica's people.

Fifteen minutes later, after he and the others had reported to the watchcaptain and handed over their watchbelts, Ket, Rith, and Rath headed toward the dining chamber to break their fast. Jin took a far less-travelled tunnel, its colonies of glowmoss so sparse it seemed dim even to Nightdweller eyes. Three chambers opened off its end. Two presented only gaping black mouths, breathing out the dank, chill air of an uninhabited cave, but yellow light streamed through the beaded curtain that hung across the mouth of the third. Jin stopped outside the curtain and called politely, "Jin-Ra stands here and asks to enter the chamber of Ser Mar."

Only silence answered. At such moments, Jin always feared that the old Scrollkeeper had died unnoticed during his long hours of solitude. But then he heard a wheezing intake of breath, followed by the scrape of wood on stone. "Jin-Ra is welcome here," came a thin, cracked voice. "Enter."

Jin pushed through the curtain.

Inside, light from a central fire pit shone through the holes in the screen that surrounded all open fires in the warren, to dim the painfully bright flames. The fire's filtered light flickered over rough-cut stone walls and fitfully illuminated the face of Ser Mar.

The old Nightdweller sat in a padded chair stolen long ago from some unfortunate Daydweller caravan. In the newer, smooth-walled chambers nearer the warren's centre, water-powered fans pushed out smoke and pulled in fresh air. Here, most of the smoke rose through a hole in the soot-blackened ceiling.

Most, but not all. Jin had to quell a fit of coughing before he approached the Scrollkeeper, who chuckled as he let the magnifying crystal drop from his left eye to the end of its silver chain. "You youngsters have weak lungs. Not enough smoke in your fancy quarters." He pounded on his chest with the flat of his hand. "Only reason the ague didn't carry me off like it did Ser Vin and Ser Ain last winter is the smoke. Toughens my lungs."

"Yes, Ser Mar," Jin said respectfully. He'd heard Ser Mar's opinions on the weakening effects of better ventilation and coal stoves and other newfangled luxuries many times.

Many, many times.

Jin rounded the fire pit, picking his way carefully through teetering piles of scrolls, and sat down in his accustomed place on a low wooden stool at the old Scrollkeeper's feet.

"Old," in this instance, was not just a description, though old Ser Mar certainly was, with fur gone white everywhere, and in some places, like the back of his head and his belly, just gone. But "old" was also a title. In a much larger and more comfortably furnished chamber near the Great Hall dwelt the current Scrollkeeper, only a few years Jin's senior, sent fresh from the Great Warren Seminary after Ser Mar's retirement five years ago.

All of the other youngsters had been handed over to the new Scrollkeeper for instruction, but Ser Mar had offered Jin, and only Jin, the opportunity to continue studying with him. Though only ten years old at the time, Jin had already fallen in love with the scrolls and the stories and knowledge they contained. He spent long hours in Ser Mar's chambers reading when the others his age were eating, playing, or in bed.

Ser Mar had made no secret of his hope that Jin might one day journey to the Great Warren and study to become a Scrollkeeper himself. At his next birthday, in half a year's time, at winter's beginning, Jin would be old enough to fulfill that hope. For months, he'd been looking forward to it. He increasingly found he had nothing in common with the others his age in Broken Tree Warren. But for now, he was still Ser Mar's student—and his eyes and ears, since Ser Mar rarely left this remote chamber.

As Jin took his seat, Ser Mar pushed aside the oil lamp with a silver reflector that extended on an adjustable arm from a wooden stand behind his left shoulder. Jin winced as the full brightness of that lamp slid across his face. The redirected light illuminated more scrolls lining the rough wooden shelves along the walls. On a low, round table at Ser Mar's right hand lay a plate holding half a roast bird, the heel end of a small loaf of bread, and a lump of blue-veined cheese. Jin suddenly found he couldn't take his eyes from it. He felt his mouth water.

Ser Mar followed his glance and laughed. "Help yourself, Jin-Ra," he said.

"But it's your breakfast, Master," Jin protested.

Ser Mar waved a hand. "My appetite is not what it was when I was a lad of eighty summers. I will not finish it, so you might as well. Then when the boy comes to collect it, he will think I have eaten it all, and I will not have the healer nagging me to eat more."

"As you wish, Master!" Jin grabbed the plate, almost overbalancing the stool in the process, and tore into the bird. Ser Mar chuckled again, picked up the scroll he had been working on, swung the lamp back into position, and resumed his reading.

For a few moments, Jin could think of nothing but satisfying his hunger, but as he chased the cheese down with the last bite of the bread, he remembered his news. "Master, I saw a strange thing tonight in a camp of the Freefolk."

Ser Mar didn't look up from the scroll. "Hmmm?"

"I saw a Priest-Apprentice of Vekrin."

Ser Mar's head snapped up, and the crystal dropped from his eye again. "Are you sure?"

Jin recounted what he had seen and heard.

"Remarkable," Ser Mer said slowly. He looked down at the open scroll in his lap. "There are strange things afoot, Jin." He tapped the parchment with a gnarled finger. "This letter is from an old correspondent of mine in the Great Warren. The watchstones along the King's Way north of City Viandaxis have detected sizable numbers of Daydwellers travelling north to City Divpaxis."

"Freefolk?"

"No. Citydwellers."

"But surely our people—"

Ser Mar shook his head. "No ordinary raiding party could attack these groups. They're heavily armed and armoured. They set up a defensive perimeter every night and light the night with torches and fires. It would take a large-scale assault to overrun one."

"You make them sound like an army!"

"They are an army. Or at least elements of one. Watchpack reports and watchstone records from the length of the kingdom show they come from every city. No one group is very large. But there must be hundreds in Divpaxis by now if every group we identified arrived intact."

"But you told me almost nobody leaves the cities except in the company of Freefolk," Jin protested. "Because of us."

"So it has been for a long time," Ser Mar said. "Apparently, it is not so any longer." He set the letter aside on the low table that had held his meal. "I do not know what the Daydwellers make of these parties' departures, although I would very much like to." He turned his gaze on Jin. "I would also like to know what you make of it, pupil."

Jin knew a surprise test when he heard one. He thought hard. Only one possibility occurred to him. "Someone is assembling an army in Divpaxis?" he ventured.

"Someone?" Ser Mar said scornfully. "You can do better than that, Pupil."

Jin racked his brain. Divpaxis. Something about a rebellion, and the leader's name had been Dip . . . Dan . . . Ded?

Ser Mar's frown reached a severity that in the past had been an omen of imminent punishment. Last time that punishment had involved scraping a dozen old parchments clean of ink. Jin's fingers ached anew as he remembered it, and the strong desire not to have to do it again jogged his memory. "Denthold!" he exclaimed.

"Very good," Ser Mar said. His frown melted into a small smile. "Although not very quick. Yes, Denthold. The Mad Priest who murdered his fellow Priests, ransacked the Temple of City Divpaxis, and drove out its citizens. Our brave warriors accomplished much glorious slaughter in honour of Ell as those refugees fled south." Ser Mar's tone dripped acid. "Aware of the tensions in that part of the kingdom, the Mother Queen made sure there were plenty of warriors in the woods. Her instincts proved right, if mindless slaughter is your goal."

Jin shot an anxious glance at the chamber's entrance, hoping no one else had heard.

"We never bothered to find out what Denthold did with Divpaxis after he seized it," Ser Mar continued.

"You think Denthold is assembling an army to spread his rebellion south?" Jin asked.

"Do you?" Ser Mer countered.

"Um . . . maybe?"

Ser Mar's expression darkened.

"I mean, yes, Master, that is what I think!"

"And indeed, I agree with you," Ser Mar said. "Which means the followers of Arrica and Vekrin are both under threat. Which could explain the unprecedented presence of a Priest-Apprentice of Vekrin in a camp of the Freefolk. Perhaps the Priests and Wise Women are working together to counter this threat."

"But they're enemies," Jin protested.

"There is hostility between them," Ser Mar corrected. "But 'enemies' is, I think, too strong a word. They are not at war with each other—at least, not yet." His gaze sharpened on Jin. "Pupil. Tell me in brief of the Heavenly War and the bestowing of Gifts upon the people of Nevyana."

Another test. Jin sat up straight. "In the distant past, all of humanity dwelt in the Old Kingdom, far across the ocean, on the other side of the world," he began dutifully, recounting how the Twelve Gods had made life heaven on earth for their followers with their great powers, until they had had a falling out . . .

"Falling out over what?" Ser Mar interrupted him. "What have my studies hinted at?"

"You believe that the Gods fell out over us, Master," Jin said.

"Nightdwellers?" Ser Mar said sharply.

"No," Jin said. "There were no Nightdwellers or Day-dwellers in the Old Kingdom. There were only people."

Ser Mar nodded. "Go on."

"You told me that your study of the most ancient scrolls revealed that some of the Twelve Gods believed they did humanity no favours by treating us like pampered pets. They believed the Gods should withdraw from the world and allow humans to make their own way. But other of the Gods felt that humanity belonged to them, to do with as they willed."

"Very good," Ser Mar said. "You do listen to me. Sometimes. Carry on."

"The dispute grew heated," Jin continued. "Eventually, war broke out . . ."

He continued the grim tale. Only three Gods and a handful of their followers survived. Burned and blasted, the Old Kingdom could no longer support even those few survivors, so the surviving Gods transported their followers across the ocean and placed them in a great fertile valley, which they called Nevyana, which means 'new home' in the Old Tongue.

"The three surviving Gods were Arrica of the Sun, Vekrin of the Earth, and Ell of the Moon. Arrica and Vekrin were allies in the War, and Ell had opposed them. Now they made a truce. They agreed they would withhold from humans the great Gifts of old, from which sprang the weapons that produced the Great Cataclysm. But Ell insisted, and the other two reluctantly agreed, that they would each give their followers a few final Gifts to seal the truce and help their followers in this new land."

Jin paused. Ser Mar's eyes had closed. He couldn't see the

old Scrollkeeper's chest rising and falling. Was he asleep? Or even . . . ?

He reached a tentative hand toward Ser Mar's knee, but the Scrollkeeper's eyes flicked open, and Jin jerked back, startled.

"Why have you stopped?" Ser Mar demanded querulously. "Go on."

"Yes, Ser Mar." Jin regathered his thoughts. He told of the Godstones and the making of the King's Way by Vekrin of the Earth, to keep his followers rooted in one place, and the Gifting of the sunscales and firejars and Fence to the Freefolk by Arrica of the Sun, to allow her followers to move as the sun did across the land. "And Blessed Mother Ell, she of the Moon, changeable as quicksilver, chose to change her followers." Jin touched his furred chest. "We would not need Blue Fire to light the night, for we would live in the night. She made us stronger and faster than other mortals, gave us warm fur, armed us with teeth and claws, dug for us vast caverns in which to live, and provided us with the watchstones and watchbelts to hide us from the Daydwellers and warn us of their approach. Wisely, for though the Gods have not warred since that day, Daydwellers and Nightdwellers have been mortal enemies ever since." Jin stopped.

"You have learned your lessons adequately well," Ser Mar said. "Now, though, I think it is time to teach you something new." He struggled to his feet, grunting, and shuffled across the cavern floor to one of the shelves. He pulled out a particularly ancient scroll, its edges brown and flaking with age. "Have you ever wondered why I live in this remote corner of the warren?" Ser Mar returned to his chair and, breathing as hard as if he had run around the warren, plopped himself down again onto its red-velvet upholstery.

"I have," Jin said. "Every time I have to come down the cold, wet tunnel leading here."

Ser Mar laughed. "That tunnel was abandoned for decades because of a rockfall," he said. "I convinced Governor Nix-Pur to open it by mentioning the possibility of ancient treasures. He lost interest when we found—so far as he knew—nothing but musty, rough-hewn chambers too far from the heart of the warren, and too cold and damp, to make good storerooms or living quarters. Which left me alone to pursue the real treasure." He looked around. "On an old map, I saw that this chamber was once home to Ser Lin, a rather infamous Scrollkeeper: the only Scrollkeeper who managed to lose some of the scrolls in his keeping."

Jin blinked in surprise. "He lost scrolls?"

"Several," Ser Mar said. "There is a considerable discrepancy between the inventory of scrolls in his possession and the scrolls which his successor, Ser Nom, found in the library when he took over after Ser Lin's sudden death."

"What was in those scrolls?" Jin said.

"That is indeed the question," Ser Mar said. "Many discussions have been held among Scrollkeepers ever since, trying to determine what the Lost Scrolls of Ser Lin might contain. The consensus is that Ser Lin scraped them clean and re-used the parchment because they were of no significance."

"But you didn't believe that," Jin said. He felt a surge of excitement, certain he knew where Ser Mar was heading with his tale.

"I did not," Ser Mar said. "I wondered if perhaps the Lost Scrolls were lost because Ser Lin did not want them found after his death. Of course, he could have simply burned them, but he was a Scrollkeeper. It is hard to imagine any Scrollkeeper burning scrolls, no matter what their contents."

Jin nodded. The thought of burning scrolls horrified *him*, and he wasn't even an *apprentice* Scrollkeeper yet.

"And so, after learning that this had once been Ser Lin's chamber, I arranged to make it mine," Ser Mar continued. "For days, I examined every square inch of the stone walls. And eventually, I found something." He pointed to his bed, tucked away into a deep-set alcove in the cavern wall. "A secret compartment so cleverly concealed that I lay in bed staring straight up at it every night for a fortnight before I realized there was a hairline crack in the stone." He returned his gaze to Jin. "Ser Lin had indeed hidden several scrolls he did not want found. The governor and council of his day were more corrupt than most—which is saying something—and some of the scrolls contained details of that corruption, dangerous knowledge in his day but of no interest to anyone but a few historians now. But then there was this." He held up the old scroll he had been reading. "This is the oldest scroll I have ever seen. It recounts the history of this land immediately after the bestowing of the Gifts. It does not tell me, as I had hoped, precisely why the Twelve Gods fought, or confirm my pet theories. But it does tell me something that has been long forgotten, suppressed by Ser Lin either on his own initiative or under orders from that era's Senior Scrollkeeper in the Great Warren." He leaned forward. "There was no enmity among the people of Nevyana immediately after the gifts were bestowed," he said softly.

Jin's breath caught in his throat.

"Citydwellers and Freefolk travelled the night freely, guided by Nightdwellers," Ser Mar went on. "Villages sprang up two, three, even four days' travel from the Twelve Cities.

There was even talk of building new settlements outside the valley, since the only threats Daydwellers faced in the night were wild animals. Their Nightdweller guides kept them safe.

"Why, then, do we hunt Daydwellers in the night and claim Ell commanded us to do so? Why do Daydwellers hide behind walled cities and Freefolk behind Fences? Why are two-score or more people of Nevyana slain every year, on both sides?"

Ser Mar stopped and peered at Jin as if expecting an answer. Jin didn't have one. "I don't know, Master."

"Greed and prejudice, Jin," Ser Mar said. "Greed and prejudice." He held up the old scroll again. "It's all in here. Once, all humans looked like Daydwellers, furless and feeble. Once we were changed, we no longer looked human to the Daydwellers. Instead, we looked like strange, dangerous animals. And it is a very small step from 'strange' to 'evil.'

"When cattle went missing, fire destroyed a barn, or a lone traveller vanished in the night, Nightdwellers were blamed. And somehow, rumours began swirling among the Daydwellers that our warrens held hidden treasure houses full of the great magical Gifts that the Gods provided in the old land but withheld in this.

"On the basis of these rumours, the Duke of City Octixis assembled an army. A Nightdweller—a traitor too stupid and greedy to foresee the consequences of his actions—accepted a bribe to guide the Duke's soldiers through the watchstone's glamour to one of the smaller warrens, Silver Lake. At the entrance, the Duke's men paid the traitorous Nightdweller with a yard of cold steel through his gut, then poured into the sleeping warren. They massacred every Nightdweller within—men, women, and children—but, of course, found nothing of value."

Jin felt sick, imagining Daydwellers racing through the sleeping warren, children waking in terror, screaming, dying, rivers of blood coursing down the tunnels, pooling in the central chamber.

"In their grief and rage, Nightdwellers poured out across the land night after night, tearing Daydwellers limb from limb by the light of their burning farms and villages. The followers of Vekrin fled into the cities and towns, feverishly building walls and stockades, protected by the firelances of the Priests of Vekrin.

"Much of the bad feeling between the Freefolk and the followers of Vekrin dates back to those years. Freefolk were refused entry into the overcrowded towns and cities. But the Freefolk adapted quickly. They had Arrica's gifts of sunscales, firejars, and Fence. Though previously, they had only used the Fence when camped in regions frequented by dangerous animal predators, Blue Fire soon protected every clan wherever it camped at night. Soon after that, the cities realized only Freefolk could guarantee the safety of travellers or trade. And so, over time, things fell into a stalemate. A bloody, useless stalemate that has continued for three centuries."

Ser Mar shook his head. "The waste is appalling! Imagine what Nevyana could be if Nightdwellers and Daydwellers worked together. Imagine how much easier everyone's lives would be today if we had continued to spread out through the wilderness, building new villages and new cities in the unknown lands beyond this valley. Instead, Nevyana has become stagnant as a rain puddle, shrinking day by day. Cities lie half-ruined, many of their buildings empty and decaying, their populations decimated by devastating plagues. The Freefolk, who once roamed where they would and lived freely off the land, play jester to Citydwellers and ferry goods for them. And we . . . we simply survive."

"But the warrens are thriving," Jin said.

Ser Mar snorted. "Thriving? We're the most stagnant of all. Along with giving us fur and fangs and night vision, the Goddess Ell made our women to be less fertile the more crowded the conditions in which they live. That prevents us from breeding like rabbits and overflowing our warrens, but it also means our population will not increase unless we can build new warrens. And we *cannot* build new warrens because Ell decreed there should never be more than the twelve she established, counterparts to the Twelve Cities of Vekrin."

"But surely all of this is the will of the Gods," Jin ventured.

Ser Mar's face twisted as though he smelled something disgusting. "Our 'Gods' are nothing but spoiled brats," he spat.

Jin recoiled as though he'd been slapped. "Master!" He glanced fearfully at the chamber entrance again.

The Scrollkeeper leaned forward. "I have held back my views on the matter of the 'Gods,' pupil, in deference to your tender years. But you are no longer a child, even if you are not yet a man, and soon enough, you will head to the Great Warren. Before you hear the pious fictions of the Scroll-keepers of the Seminary, listen to me.

"I have studied and thought about this for five times as long as you have been alive, and this is what I have concluded: the 'Gods' are nothing of the sort. They did not belong to this world at all, but came from outside, some other plane of existence, perhaps, or the stars, or the centre of the Earth. I do not know. They are—or were—powerful and long-lived, but as mortal as we. The Great Cataclysm is proof of that, since nine of the Gods perished in it.

"At some forgotten time in the far-distant past, these beings arrived in our world and decided to play with humans like a bored toddler might play with ants. We have been suffering from their childish whims ever since."

Jin's mouth went dry, and he shot an involuntary glance at the ceiling, half-expecting Ell to bring it down on their heads.

Ser Mar snorted. "If Ell or Arrica or Vekrin were going to strike me down for insulting the Gods, they would have done it years ago. But Ell is gone. Arrica is gone. Vekrin is gone. The Scrollkeepers of the Nightdwellers, the Wise Women of Arrica, and the Priests of Vekrin are wasting their time praying to the Gods. They no longer care about us. They never did, not in the way our pious make-believe pretends." He thumped his chest. "You call this a gift, banishing us into the darkness, twisting us so we cannot bear the light of day? I call it a curse! Perhaps the followers of Arrica and Vekrin have fared better with their Blue Fire, but they have done little with it. They keep it behind Temple walls or inside wagons, jealously guarding its secrets instead of studying it, learning to use it better, using it to lift everyone up instead of keeping us all locked in this grinding sameness for all eternity!"

Jin hunched his shoulders and swallowed hard, but the ground did not rumble, and the roof did not crack. Ell remained apparently unconcerned by the old Scrollkeeper's astonishing blasphemy, and through Jin's shock and initial fear flowed a welling trickle of mingled excitement and hope. If the Gods were not peering over every shoulder, ready to strike down those who denied them, then anything was possible. Jin felt like a man trapped in a cave-in, parched and choking on bad air, who suddenly saw an opening through which came a fresh breeze and a skin of water as his rescuers found him at last.

Ser Mar's eyes never left Jin's face. "The idea is not so scary after all, is it, lad?" he murmured with a twisted smile. He leaned forward and laid a wizened hand on Jin's knee. "I would not have sprung it on you so abruptly, but in the strange happenings above, I sense—or at least hope for—an opportunity." He sat back and lifted the ancient scroll. "If Denthold is drawing followers to City Divpaxis, then at least one Priest of Vekrin has rejected the authority of his God. If a Priest-Apprentice is travelling with the Freefolk, then the wall of hostility between Freefolk and Citydwellers has begun to crumble. And if those things are true, then maybe, just maybe, there is a chance that we may all yet break out of the roles assigned us by capricious Gods and their stupid, belligerent followers." He scratched his chin. "I think," he said, "that it is time you went to the Great Warren."

Jin blinked. "Master? I am still six months from—"

"With my personal recommendation to the College of Scrollkeepers, that will not matter," Ser Mar said. "Governor Nix will not object to your departure. And in any event, it may be some time before you actually enrol."

"Master?"

"Make your way to the Great Warren, but not directly." Ser Mar pointed up. "Follow the Freefolk. Follow this Priest-Apprentice that travels with his enemies. See where they are going and what they are doing. Write back to me with your findings." He smiled broadly. He had so few teeth left that even though he let them show, no one, least of all Jin, could interpret it as a sign of aggression. "There are no guarantees and no promises, Jin-Ra, but maybe, just maybe, the world is about to change. And maybe, just maybe, you and I can help ensure that change is for the better." His smile faded. "For if we do not act," he said softly, "I fear very much that it may instead be for the worse."

The fur on Jin's back rose, perhaps in response to the chill in the air of the damp chamber.

Perhaps not.

AN UNHAPPY BREAKFAST

Amlinn emerged from the wagon into the misty light of morning and, blinking and yawning, went in search of breakfast. She found Grandfather already seated at one of the trestle tables outside the cookwagon, and with him, to her surprise, was Petra. The Priest-Apprentice looked up at her and smiled. She felt her cheeks redden and ducked her head so he wouldn't see.

She'd enjoyed talking to him the night before. She smiled with her head still lowered, remembering his delight and astonishment at the commonplace magic of the lightwand. He knew so little about the Freefolk and the Nightdwellers, but there were so many things he knew about life in the city and among the followers of Vekrin that she did not. It all made him intensely interesting.

She had nothing in common with the few boys her own age in the clan. Daughter of the clan leader and educated by the Wisest, she found the typical wagon-born-and-bred Freefolk boy about as interesting as a horse apple: they were always around and always underfoot, but she didn't really want to open any of them up to see what was inside.

Petra might be a Priest-Apprentice of Vekrin, but he was also smart, educated, and not bad-looking. Right now, with his sleep-tousled brown hair shining in the sun, which also lit the peach fuzz on his cheeks, he looked particularly cute.

Cute? Now her *ears* turned hot. She hurried past Grandfather and Petra to the cookwagon. With a bowl of steaming corn mush in one hand and a cup of mint tea in the other, she returned to the folding table, hesitated, and then, feeling daring, chose to sit next to Petra instead of Grandfather.

"Sleep well?" Grandfather asked, but he didn't wait for an answer. He nodded at Petra. "We have been talking about Denthold. We were always told that he destroyed the Temple and its Godstone. But now Petra tells me . . ." He glanced at the Priest-Apprentice.

"You can't destroy a Godstone," Petra said.

"But you can destroy the sigilled devices that draw Blue Fire from it," Grandfather continued.

Petra nodded. "And you can do it from the Godstone itself. That's what the Priests of City Divpaxis did. They sent out a massive charge of Blue Fire and destroyed every Hearth, every sparkglobe, every firelance, every device of any kind in the city that used Blue Fire. Then they destroyed their copy of the *Book of Vekrin* and disabled the Godstone. Without the *Book of Vekrin*, Denthold could not reactivate the Godstone. When he broke into the inner sanctum and discovered what they had done, he slaughtered them all."

"But it's been more than twenty years since City Divpaxis fell," Grandfather said to Amlinn. "I suspect most people in the southern cities have forgotten Denthold. And even survivors of the rebellion who settled in Viandaxis have shown no inclination to push northward again. They have new lives. Secure lives. They may not have forgotten Denthold, but they wish they could." He scratched his bearded chin. "The trouble is, if he is behind the recent thefts from the Freefolk and Priests of Vekrin, then none of us can afford to forget him. He is clearly trying to gather all the knowledge of Blue Fire he can, from Freefolk and Priests alike."

"At least he failed to get a *Book of Vekrin*," Petra put in.

"We don't know that," Grandfather pointed out. "He may have obtained one in City Primaxis. He certainly obtained a firelance, as you know only too well." He sighed. "And, from us, a sunscale."

"But surely the sunscale is useless without the secret knowledge of the Wise Women," Amlinn said.

Grandfather looked away, and Amlinn followed his gaze to the sunwagons. He rubbed his chin again, then, turning back to Petra and Amlinn, leaned forward and spoke in a low voice. "Petra shared with us a secret of the Priests of Vekrin. Well, here is a secret of the Wise Women of Arrica: there *is* no secret to making sunscales. Close examination of one could show any sufficiently skilled craftsman how to duplicate it."

Amlinn blinked at him. "But Samarrind taught me that each sunscale must be blessed by Arrica. There are special prayers the Wise Women must say. Without that blessing—"

"Without that blessing," said Grandfather, "a properly made sunscale works every bit as well as a sunscale prayed over by a dozen Wise Women for a week."

Amlinn stared at Grandfather, unable to believe he had just spoken such blasphemy.

Petra pushed aside his half-empty bowl of mush so he too

could lean forward. "It is the same with the devices of Vekrin," he murmured. "The Priests pray over them and ask Vekrin's blessing, but a firelance will work blessed or not, provided it is assembled correctly, the proper sigils are inscribed on the shaft and the rod of copper at its core, and it is within the range of influence of a Godstone."

Amlinn felt like someone had pulled a rug out from under her feet. "But the Gods—"

"The Gods gave us Blue Fire," Grandfather said. "And, yes, they asked us to pray over the devices that use it. But the fact remains, the devices work whether prayed over or not. And that means—"

"That means," said Petra, "that Denthold can make sunscales, firelances, and who knows what else."

Grandfather nodded heavily. "And if that 'what else' includes the Fence, he may soon be free to move wherever in Nevyana he wishes, armed and protected by Blue Fire."

Amlinn hardly heard him. Samarrind had *lied*. Lied to *her*. The thought twisted her insides. "But why?" she cried.

Grandfather misunderstood the source of her anguish; his thoughts were still on Denthold. "That's what Petra was just about to tell me."

Amlinn pushed her bowl aside. She'd lost her appetite.

Petra sat up straight again, his gaze squarely on Grandfather, face pale. "I do not believe I have violated my vows by telling you what I have told you so far," he said. His voice shook. "And I hope I will not violate them by telling you what I am going to tell you now. But I'm not at all sure that my father would agree." He glanced at Amlinn.

For a moment, though still heartsick at Samarrind's deception, she was struck by how his eyes glowed a deep, rich brown in the morning light.

Then he turned those eyes back to Grandfather. "We have always said that Denthold went mad," he continued. "That is what we told the citizens and the Freefolk. But in truth, he acted coldly and rationally. There is good reason we call him the Heretic."

He glanced at Amlinn again, and she remembered how he had made a point of that the night before.

"Denthold denied the Gods," he said, turning back to Grandfather. "In fact, he denied them twice-over. First, he denied that they were Gods. Second, he denied that they play any role in our lives. He claimed our worship of Vekrin, your worship of Arrica, and the Nightdwellers' worship of Ell— assuming they do worship her, and have not forgotten her entirely in their beast-like existence—are nothing but ancient relics of a time when the beings we call Gods took an active interest—'meddled,' he called it—in human affairs.

"He attempted to sway the Elders of Temple Divpaxis to his way of thinking. Rightly, they excommunicated him. Disgraced within the Temple, he began preaching in the streets. He was beaten twice and almost killed, but then he gained followers. Some were highly placed among Divpaxis secular authorities. The Elders should have arrested and executed him, but they waited too long. The ranks of his followers swelled. Among them were traitorous Priests who helped him seize the Temple and almost gain control of the Godstone."

"So, his *beliefs* were mad, but *he* was rational," Grandfather said slowly, while Amlinn was thinking how surprisingly erudite Petra had sounded. *Benefit of a Priestly education, I guess.*

Petra nodded.

"And what did he hope to accomplish?"

"The overthrow of the Priesthood of Vekrin. The elimination of the Wise Women of Arrica. Blue Fire made free for all to use without regard for the wishes of the Gods."

Amlinn shivered. "Sure sounds mad to me!"

"And some secular authorities actually supported him?" Grandfather said.

"Yes," Petra said.

"Including the Duke of Divpaxis?"

"Duke Felkor swore he was not involved. He fled south with the other survivors and still lives in City Primaxis, though he is elderly now. I know the Priests wanted to arrest and question him, but Felkor is a favourite of the Royal Family, and was as close as an uncle to then-Prince Stobor and his fraternal twin, Axel."

"That's troubling," Grandfather said, frowning. "Because I think that means it is all but certain that Denthold *continues* to have secular allies. Which might explain why these Unbound have been permitted to form armed bands and leave the cities without harassment or detention."

Amlinn, still reeling from the revelation about the sunscales, listened without speaking. She knew little about the secular authorities of Nevyana beyond the bare facts. King Stobor ruled from City Primaxis, and a duke ruled each of the other cities in the king's name. She'd also heard about unrest between the followers of Stobor and those who supported the claims to the throne of his twin brother, Axel. Not that long ago, they'd rioted in the show tent of another Freefolk clan, damaging the tent and the precious Sun Organ. But ordinarily, Freefolk had little to do with those who passed laws and kept order in the walled cities.

Petra, a Citydweller, obviously knew more about such matters than she did, and his eyes widened in alarm. "Lord Axel is Denthold's ally?"

Grandfather gave him a steady look. "You tell me."

Petra chewed his lower lip. "It's possible," he said after a moment. "Though Axel always denies he wants the throne and dutifully chides his followers for pressing the case for his reign so forcefully. He claims to be interested only in hunting and sport."

"Hmm." Grandfather frowned. "Who else might want the throne?"

"Potentially every Duke in Nevyana, I suppose," Petra said. "My father could tell you more." He leaned forward, suddenly eager. "Here's an idea. The next time we're near a city, take me to its Temple. The Priests there can farspeak to Temple Primaxis, give my father the information we have, and warn him about the Unbound and Axel's possible involvement. Then we can go on to Divpaxis."

"Farspeak?" Grandfather asked.

"Another Gift of Vekrin. It uses Blue Fire to cast messages long distances through the air."

"And how would your information being . . . 'farspoken,' I suppose . . . to Primaxis help?"

"First, they'll know you didn't kidnap me, that I'm with you of my own free will. That should make my story more believable. Even if they aren't convinced right away that the threat of Denthold is real, the seed will be planted. My father, the Priests, and the king could begin to plan. By the time we return, they will—"

Grandfather slapped the table, cutting him off. "They will do nothing," he growled. "They will assume it is all a Freefolk trick, that you have been duped. They will assure each other that the Freefolk are behind everything and try to turn all the cities against our clans." He stood abruptly. "Thank you for your information, Petra. I am glad you were able to help us without feeling you violated your vows. But I have dealt with your precious Priests and city rulers for too many years to believe they would help us in any way. And I cannot let you tell them what I have just told you about the sunscales or, beyond question, Priests will enter our camps and attempt to steal one, either by stealth or by force."

Petra's face flushed. "You think I want to betray you?"

"No, but I cannot risk the possibility. Neither good judgment nor the clan council would permit it."

Petra opened his mouth as if to protest, but Grandfather cut him off.

"Not only that, the council and the Wise Women would see such an action as asking the Priests for their help in recovering our stolen sunscale. That can never be permitted, for it could well tear apart both the Freefolk and Priests.

"At the heart of your Priesthood and at the heart of our freedom lie the Gifts of the Gods. It is your duty to guard the Godstones, ours to guard the sunscales. Your Priests have made no effort to reclaim the Godstone of City Divpaxis. That is their choice to make. But the people of Arrica will not let the knowledge of making and using sunscales remain with Denthold. It is our duty, and no one else's, to ensure that does not happen. To ask the Priests for help with that task would be seen by my people as rankest heresy. Even if Arrica herself did not strike us down on the spot, infighting would disrupt the clans. And you know the same would happen if some among the Priests actually believed you and truly wanted to help. The hardliners among Vekrin's followers would likewise see it as heresy, and a great schism would erupt.

"So, we will tell the Priests nothing. You will not be allowed anywhere near a Temple, not until Denthold no longer poses a threat to the Freefolk." He looked down at Petra for a moment, then leaned across the table and rested a hand on the Priest-Apprentice's shoulder. "I'm sorry, lad," he said, and Amlinn heard genuine concern in his soft voice. "You have the freedom of the camp, unless you do something to make me regret giving it to you, but you are still a prisoner." Then, without looking at Amlinn, Grandfather straightened and strode away toward the work crews loading wagons and harnessing horses.

Amlinn looked at Petra. His face remained red, and his fists clenched. "I'm sorry," she said.

"Not half as sorry as I am," Petra snapped. He glared down at his fists, but after a moment he took a deep breath and slowly relaxed them, turning them to lay his palms flat on the table. "But as much as I hate to admit it, I think your grandfather is right. The Freefolk can't ally with the Priests. Not yet. Not until the threat is indisputable." He heaved a sigh. "Vekrin and Arrica divided the people of Nevyana when they gave us their Gifts—Ell even more, with what she did to the Nightdwellers. I don't see how we can ever be united again."

Amlinn looked after her departing grandfather, then glanced back at Petra. On impulse, she reached out and covered his hand, still outstretched on the table, with her own. "Perhaps our peoples can't be," she said softly. "But what about you and me?"

Petra's eyes widened.

Amlinn, suddenly realizing what that had sounded like, snatched back her hand. Her cheeks and ears flamed. "I mean friends! We could be friends! That's . . . I could use a friend. Couldn't you?"

"I could," Petra said. His face remained pale, and his voice shook anew as he said, "But how do I know your grandfather hasn't *asked* you to make friends with me to convince me to provide him with even more secrets?" He locked his gaze on hers. "Reading the *Book of Vekrin*, for instance?"

Amlinn chilled as though Petra had thrown a bucket of water in her face. An instant later, though, the flame rushed back to her face, furnace-hot. "How dare—"

"I'm a prisoner," Petra said. "Prisoners can't afford to trust their captors."

Amlinn stood so suddenly the table tipped over, thudding against the wet grass, scattering bowls of mush and mugs of tea. "Then spend the rest of the journey alone and friendless! It's what you deserve." She spun and stomped off.

She hoped he'd call her name.

When he did, she took great pleasure in ignoring it.

12

THE APOLOGY

"Amlinn!" Petra called. He couldn't believe he'd lashed out at her like that. He didn't understand why. Vekrin knew he liked her. He liked her a lot. And, yes, he needed a friend, and he wanted her to be that friend.

But her grandfather had just told him he was still a prisoner. It had clearly angered him more than he'd realized. He stared at Amlinn's stiff, retreating back. *What have I done?*

For the rest of the day, he rode glumly on the seat of the same wagon in whose dark interior he had spent the previous day bound and gagged. He barely exchanged two words with the driver, Witten, as they crawled northward through the endless forest. At lunch, he ate alone, chewing sausage and bread and watching Amlinn out of the corner of his eye. She sat with a young man Witten told him was Annjia, the Sun Organ player. When she threw back her head to laugh at something Annjia said, Petra's stomach churned with completely unfounded jealousy that only worsened when she climbed aboard Annjia's wagon for the afternoon part of the journey.

Meanwhile, he spent his afternoon silently rehearsing his next words to Amlinn. *Amlinn, I am a Priest-Apprentice of Vekrin, you are a Freefolk girl; for the good of the kingdom, we must overcome our differences.*

Too pretentious.

Amlinn, I wasn't really angry with you, I was angry at the Gods for . . .

Too theological.

Amlinn, ever since I saw you lying half-naked in the mud, I've wanted to know you better.

He grimaced. That might be the most honest. He suspected it would also get him slapped.

Finally, he settled on *Amlinn, I'm sorry.* It seemed inadequate, but maybe simplicity was best. He just hoped he'd have the opportunity to find out.

That night, sitting by himself and staring into one of the fires, he heard a complex, twisting rhythm playing on a single drum. He looked up across the leaping flames and saw Amlinn dancing.

She wore the same trousers and tunic she'd worn all day, not the gaudy, skimpy costume in which he'd found her outside the Temple Curtain, but her feet flashed bare. Her black hair, released from its ponytail, gleamed in the light of lanterns hung on four poles to define a grassy stage. Annjia held the drum between his knees, fingers flicking as he pounded the tanned skin of the drumhead. Petra's heart beat in the same rhythm as he watched Amlinn dance. He had never seen anything more wild and beautiful.

Nightdwellers howled outside the Fence, but Petra hardly noticed. One by one, the Freefolk entertainers rehearsed. Strange songs rang through the night—sad songs, happy songs, comical songs—played on harp and lute and fiddle and flute, sung by an old man, a young woman, a bell-voiced little girl, a trio of small boys. Petra, used to the staid hymns and stilted readings that passed for entertainment on Temple feast days, loved it all, but Amlinn's dancing enthralled him most. After the stage lanterns were doused and as the crowd began to disperse, he saw her sitting alone on a boulder. He took a deep breath, swallowed hard, and then circled around her through the shadows. He came up from behind and sat down beside her.

The smile she turned toward him vanished as their eyes met. She jerked her gaze back toward the now-dark makeshift stage. But at least she didn't storm away.

"Amlinn, I'm sorry," Petra said. Three simple words, but the way his heart pounded, he figured it was a good thing he'd spent all afternoon rehearsing them.

Amlinn didn't look at him.

Petra sat in silence, watching people drifting toward their tents. Annjia turned from saying a laughing good night to the young woman singer and saw Amlinn and Petra together. He immediately headed toward them, scowling.

"Amlinn, I do need a friend," Petra blurted before the organist could reach them. "I really do. And I hope you'll be it. Her, I mean. My friend." His words tripped over themselves and stumbled into silence.

Annjia stopped in front of them, glaring down at Petra. "Is everything all right, Amlinn?"

Amlinn looked at Petra for the first time since he'd spoken. For a long moment, she just stared, her expression unreadable. Then she turned back to the organ player. "It's all right, Annjia," she said. "Thank you for your playing tonight and for letting me ride with you today."

"You're welcome." Annjia's frown didn't go away, but to

Petra's relief, the musician did, though not without a final look back.

Petra felt as though a huge weight had lifted from his shoulders, or maybe his heart. "Thank you," he said quietly.

Amlinn stood. "It's late. I'm going to bed." She stepped away, but then stopped. After a moment, she glanced back. "We can ride together tomorrow if you want."

Petra nodded, not trusting himself to speak.

Amlinn nodded back. "Good," she said, and strode off in the direction of her grandfather's wagon.

Petra sat for several more minutes before making his way through the camp to his tent. He looked through the Fence's shimmering blue veil for red eyes glowing in the darkness but saw nothing.

Happier than he had any right to be as a Freefolk-imprisoned Priest-Apprentice who might well have betrayed his vows, he crawled into his bedroll and soon fell fast asleep.

13

JIN'S FAREWELL

An hour after he'd left Ser Mar's small, smoky chamber, Jin left the much larger and better-ventilated chamber of Nix-Pur, Governor of Broken Tree Warren. He clutched his written permission to leave Broken Tree for the Great Warren, where he would enrol in the Scrollkeeper Seminary.

"Bit underage, aren't you, Jin-Ra?" Governor Nix-Pur had boomed as he'd read Ser Mar's note.

"Ser Mar feels I have advanced as far as I can here," Jin said, "and the Seminary is always short of—"

But the Governor had already scrawled his signature across the bottom of the letter and turned his gaze to the next supplicant, a frightened-looking young female with slate-grey fur. The Governor's secretary handed Jin the signed pass and ushered him out.

"Follow the Freefolk," Ser Mar had told Jin. Since the Freefolk moved every day, that meant Jin had to leave the warren at the next sunset. That left him a lot to do and very little time in which to do it.

Getting the Governor's permission had been the first

necessary step. With that in hand, Jin made his way to the warren's Storekeeper, Vel-Pur. The diminutive red-furred Nightdweller scratched the back of her neck as she read the pass, leaning on the wooden counter spanning the opening to her storerooms. "The Great Warren, eh? That means a shadowshelter, and let's see . . . we'll make it six days' food and water to give you some to spare. Wait here." She disappeared from Jin's view, and he took the time to make a list of everything else he needed to do.

It proved to be a very short list. Ser Mar had left him little time to say his goodbyes, but then, he didn't really have anyone to say goodbye to except for the other members of his watchpack. Rith and Rath would wish him good luck and promptly forget about him, and Ket would just grunt and start looking for a replacement.

His mother had died of a fever when he was so little that he had no memory of her. His father had never been very interested in having a child in the first place and had handed him over to the warren's fosterers immediately thereafter. Shortly after that, his father left the warren and never returned. It was generally thought he fell victim to Daydwellers, taking an arrow from some city wall, perhaps, or stumbling into one of the traps that Daydwellers sometimes set along forest paths.

Jin grew up in the care of the fosterers, older men and women who had never had children of their own or whose own children were grown. He'd said his goodbyes to them when he'd left for the quarters of the Ra. They'd bid him a fond farewell, but he could see them putting him out of their minds the moment they turned back to the toddlers at their feet.

In truth, except for Ser Mar, Jin had no strong ties to his

home warren at all. If he could have safely done so, he would have left in broad daylight.

But he couldn't, of course, even with the shadowshelter, which Vel-Pur now reappeared carrying. A tent made of thick black fabric, embroidered with a watch sigil in gold thread, the shadowshelter would protect him from the sun, warn him if Daydwellers approached, and hide him from their eyes even if they passed close by—as long as they didn't actually trip over it.

Vel-Pur also provided him with a sturdy backpack, a walking stick, and food and water—ridiculously heavy food and water, he thought as he shouldered the pack. "What about a watchbelt?" he said, though he knew the answer.

Vel-Pur gave him a withering look. "The Governor would use my hide to make the replacement if I let a watchbelt leave the warren," she said. "As you well know."

Jin grinned at her. "Thanks anyway, Vel-Pur. And goodbye."

Vel-Pur's scowl melted away. "Goodbye, Jin-Ra. Have a safe journey. Perhaps you'll return to us someday as our new Scrollkeeper."

"Perhaps," Jin said, but he hoped very much that would never, ever happen.

At sunset the next day, he stood just inside the entrance to the warren with the heavy pack on his back, waiting for the door to be opened. *The Freefolk fear the night because there are Nightdwellers in it*, he mused. *But at least they can walk about in it behind their Fence. Our great "Gift" from Ell makes us unable to ever go forth during the day. Is that really a gift, or is it a curse?*

The guard at the gate nodded to him and turned the crank that swung open the heavy stone door. It felt odd slipping out through the well-hidden entrance alone, instead of in the company of Ket and the twins. Twilight still lingered outside, bright enough to make him blink. Jin took a good look around at the wooded valley in which he had once played and more recently patrolled for so many nights. He knew every tree and rock in it. He wondered if, after tonight, he would ever see it again.

Then he smiled. *Who cares?*

Without looking back, he loped into the gathering darkness to find and follow the trail of the Freefolk.

14

THE CLAN'S ANSWER

The morning after Petra's apology dawned bright and clear. He helped pack up his tent. Then, hoping Amlinn would honour her promise that they could ride together, he made his way to the centre of the camp and found Amlinn checking the harness of her grandfather's horses.

He cleared his throat. "Good morning?" It came out as a question.

"Good morning," Amlinn replied with a smile, and suddenly the morning seemed even brighter and clearer than before. "Grandfather is riding with Samarrind to discuss a few matters in private, so it's you and me on the lead wagon today."

Now the day positively sparkled. Petra climbed up onto the seat beside Amlinn as the Freefolk prepared to move out. He took a deep breath of the cool, pine-scented breeze and realized he couldn't honestly wish he were back in the Temple, where he supposedly belonged. "Where are we going, exactly?" he asked.

"City Desmixis," Amlinn said.

"The ninth city north of Primaxis?" Petra said. "Why?"

She gave him a surprised look, brushing stray hair from her eyes with one gloved hand while the other held tight to the reins. "Because there are more Freefolk there, of course. Clans Fell and Pirra are camped outside the walls."

"But how do you know they won't be gone by the time we get there?" Petra said. "It must be days away."

"It is. But they spend weeks there, entertaining and arranging business. Even under normal circumstances, they wouldn't leave for another month. And these aren't normal circumstances. The morning after you so dramatically interrupted the clan council meeting, Grandfather sent messengers to the leaders of Clan Fell and Clan Pirra with an urgent request for a meeting." A sudden jerk of the wagon threw her sideways against Petra. "Oof! Sorry!"

With her body warm against his, Petra found himself hoping the road ahead would continue to be bumpy. Best not to tell her that. Instead, he said, "Lone riders? Won't the Nightdwellers hunt them down?"

"They each carry four small Fencestones and a fully-charged firejar," Amlinn said. "They erect a Fence just big enough for their tent and fire each night. With a Fence that small, the firejar holds enough Blue Fire for several nights' protection."

Petra blinked. The Freefolk kept surprising him.

"The riders will report what Grandfather and Samarrind have learned and ask that all Clans join forces to march against Denthold."

Another jerk of the wagon bounced Amlinn against Petra again. This time her elbow caught his ribcage, so the effect wasn't nearly as pleasant. He rubbed the bruise as she pulled herself upright.

"Convincing them won't be easy," she went on. "There is bad blood among the Clans. But we are all followers of Arrica. I think—I hope—the Wise Women will force the clan leaders to work together, however little some of them like it."

"And then what?" Petra said.

"Then they will argue," Amlinn said. "And argue. And argue. But once they agree—and Grandfather will make them agree—then we will march north to take back what is ours."

Amlinn sounded awfully sure of that, but Petra knew all about arguing factions and internal politics from growing up in the Temple. He had hoped that Dainann would be able to scout north quickly. But now it seemed the Freefolk might delay as long as the Priests would have, and Denthold could strike south at any time.

Duty demanded that Petra escape and go to the Priests with all he had learned. He glanced back at the long line of wagons. Clan Leader Dainann and Samarrind rode on Samarrind's wagon directly behind. Amlinn's grandfather gave him a hard stare from beneath bushy grey eyebrows.

Petra hastily turned around again. Escape was clearly impossible. Even if by some miracle he managed to slip away from the wagons, he had no idea where they were, other than "east of the river." If he fled, he would wander the woods until nightfall, and then the Nightdwellers would most likely kill him. It was as simple as that.

And so, Petra waited and fretted.

Day by day, the Freefolk moved through the forest, from campground to campground. The routine never varied. As the sun rose, the Fence vanished, the Wise Women gathered the Fencestones, the cooks served breakfast, tents were struck, and the wagons were loaded. No more than an hour after the sun broke the horizon, the caravan moved out again. In the evening, the glimmering blue Fence reappeared, horses were fed and watered, the cooks served supper, and singing, dancing, juggling, and storytelling followed until bedtime.

That first day on the lead wagon with Amlinn was followed by many more. Her grandfather continued to ride with Samarrind or with one or another of the council wagon-masters, obviously trying to shore up support for whatever course of action he wished to pursue.

Warmer though Petra's relationship with Amlinn had become, she could still suddenly turn cold and aloof. That usually happened when he made some ill-considered comment about the relative merits of Citydweller life versus Freefolk life or the Priesthood's mastery of Blue Fire. But those occurrences became fewer as Petra began to fully realize just how much of what he had been told about the Freefolk was wrong.

For one thing, Freefolk clearly weren't just lazy layabouts who survived only by sponging off Citydwellers. That much was clear. Though they relied on the cities for staples like flour and meal, they lived quite comfortably for long periods in the wilderness, hunting and gathering wild plants.

And culturally, well, he'd already learned the cities had nothing to teach Freefolk when it came to the performing arts, but the level of craft displayed by Freefolk weavers and potters and clothiers and shoemakers also outstripped anything he'd ever seen in the city. Freefolk clothes and boots were better made and more comfortable. Although the swords and daggers they carried had been forged in the cities, their bows and arrows were astonishingly well-crafted —light, strong, and accurate.

Hard as it was for Petra to admit, the life of Freefolk was not inferior to that of Citydwellers. It was simply different. Perhaps even, in some ways, better.

The land became much rougher as they travelled north. The Freefolk path skirted the great foothills tumbling up toward the Sunrise Range that defined Nevyana's eastern border. Around noon on the tenth day they came to a vast clearing where circles of blackened stone marked the locations of old campfires. "This is the Field of Arrica, the central gathering place of the Freefolk," Amlinn explained as they rolled through it without stopping. "It's large enough for all the clans to camp here at once."

"What's so special about . . . oh!" His voice trailed off as he saw the bridge. A massive construction of giant, unpeeled logs braced and bound together, it crossed a great canyon down which roared a tumbling whitewater stream. Petra guessed it must be fed by the snows that lingered even in the height of summer among the highest peaks of the Sunrise Range. Presumably, the stream eventually flowed to the Great River. As they clattered across the bridge, Petra looked down through the gaps in the wooden planks and hoped the Freefolk were as good at engineering as they were at so much else.

About four days after that, just as the Fence sprang to life one evening, a horseman galloped in from the west, raising a cloud of dust that glowed orange in the rays of the sinking sun. Milla opened a portal in the Fence with her key, then sealed the opening behind the horseman as he pounded into the centre of the camp. The rider pulled his lathered horse to a halt and dismounted, tossing his reins to one of the youngsters who came running at the forefront of a gathering crowd. Sweat and dust stained the rider's clothing. As Amlinn's grandfather approached, the rider pulled the broad-brimmed hat from his head and wiped his forehead with the back of his hand.

Petra looked up from pounding in the final peg for his tent. He was too far away to hear the conversation, but he had no trouble recognizing the anger on Dainann's face. The clan leader and the rider went off together toward Dainann's wagon. Petra scanned the camp for Amlinn and made a beeline for her.

"What happened?" he panted as he reached her.

Amlinn wore a look of disgust and fury. "They've refused to meet."

"The other clans?" Petra stared after Dainann and the rider. "Why?"

"I don't know, but I can guess," Amlinn said. She scowled at him. "It's because of you."

Petra blinked at her. "Me? What did I do?"

"You provided the information on which Grandfather's plea for assistance was based," she said. "And you're a Priest-Apprentice. They don't trust Priests, so they don't trust your claim that Denthold is behind the thefts."

"But that was the whole point of abducting me in the first place, wasn't it? So you could find out what was really going on?" Anger boiled up inside him. "And now you won't trust the information because it came from a Priest-Apprentice? Are you saying you abducted me for nothing?"

"*We* believe you," Amlinn said. "My grandfather believes

you. Samarrind believes you. But the other clans . . ." She sighed. "I told you there was bad blood. My grandfather has a reputation for acting first and consulting afterward. The other clan leaders have complained about his 'high-handedness' before now." She glanced at her grandfather's wagon. "My guess is they think Grandfather was playing a dangerous, foolish game by kidnapping you, and they think you're just telling a wild fable to send the Freefolk chasing all over the kingdom."

Petra looked around. The crowd had devolved into small groups of men and women standing among the tents and wagons talking and, in some cases, arguing. He glimpsed more than one angry glance turned his way. He met the eyes of a man who stared at him coolly from a dozen yards away, then spat on the ground and stalked off.

Petra's face went hot. "None of you trust me!" He spun to face Amlinn again. "I risked breaking my vows. I may have thrown away my life in the Priesthood and shamed my father, and you still don't trust me!" Frustration bubbled into his voice. He knew he was yelling, but he couldn't stop. "I started to think it mattered, what happened to the Freefolk. I started to think maybe it was important to help you get back your bloody sunscales. But you won't let me warn the Priests about Denthold, and you don't believe in the threat he poses. Why not just throw me out through the Fence to the Nightd-wellers and be done with it?"

Turning his back on Amlinn, on all of them, Petra stormed off to his tent, aware of Freefolk watching his every step. Finally hidden by canvas from their unfriendly eyes, he sat on his bedroll and pounded his clenched fist over and over on the ground. Damn that thief for breaking into the Temple during his watch! Damn Amlinn's grandfather for stealing him away from the city and stealing his life at the same time! And damn Amlinn for—

The already dim light of the gathering twilight outside suddenly faded even further.

Amlinn stood in the doorway of the tent.

15

TICKLING TROUT

Amlinn glared at Petra's stiff back, retreating across the darkening camp. A Priest-Apprentice of Vekrin, criticizing the Freefolk? How dare he!

How dare he what? Tell the truth?

Her rage vanished. He had been kidnapped. He had decided to help the Freefolk because he believed Denthold had to be stopped. He had risked betraying his vows.

And because the Freefolk wouldn't trust him, it had all been for naught.

Petra disappeared into his tent. Amlinn hurried after him. He looked up as she put her head through the flap. "What do you want?" he snapped.

Her lips tightened at his tone, and her fists clenched. She came within a hair of turning and striding away, but instead, she took a deep breath, pushed down her anger, unclenched her fists, lowered her head, and crawled into the tent's shadowy interior.

She sat on the bedroll next to Petra. "I'm sorry for the way my people have treated you," she said roughly. "Nothing that has happened to you has been fair. I wish I could change it. But I can't. All I can do is apologize."

Petra looked down at his own fists, clenched as hers had been a moment before, then relaxed them and took a deep breath of his own. His dark-brown eyes, almost black in the dim light, lifted and looked into hers. His face had freckled during the days in the sun; it made him look child-like, vulnerable. "Thank you. I'm sorry I yelled at you."

Amlinn smiled. Then she got onto all fours and backed toward the tent flap, holding out her right hand. "Come on," she said. "Let's get something to eat."

He smiled back, reached out, and clasped her fingers. She liked the feel of his hand in hers, warm and strong. She held on to it as she backed the rest of the way out of the tent, and then together, they rose. Petra tried to let go then, but she squeezed his fingers, earning a startled glance. "It's important they see," Amlinn said. "Important they see that at least one member of the Freefolk trusts you."

"And here I thought you just wanted to hold my hand," Petra said.

Amlinn felt her cheeks heat and quickly turned away to lead him toward the cookwagon, hoping he hadn't noticed.

A woman carrying a plucked chicken passed them on the right. She raised an eyebrow at them. Amlinn gave her a sweet smile. The woman frowned and hurried on.

At the wagon, Amlinn reluctantly let go of Petra's hand. They took their bowls of rabbit stew and crusty bread and sat together on the ground at one end of the wagon, hidden in the growing darkness. While they ate, they listened to the conversations of the Freefolk gathered around the dining tables, their faces pale in the flickering candlelight.

"We have to get the sunscale back," a big black-bearded

man at a nearby table said, then belched. *Marrkin*, Amlinn thought. A blowhard, but he had a good heart. He pointed his spoon at a sallow-faced youth across from him. *Larric.* One of the young men close to her own age—just a couple of years older—whom she had long ago decided never to have anything to do with. "We can't let a thief get away with something like that. The dishonour—"

"We can't do it alone," said Larric. His Adam's apple bobbed as he talked. "If the other Clans had agreed to help . . . but they can't. It's too dangerous."

Coward, Amlinn thought. Larric had always been afraid of his own shadow. "It's more dangerous to not act," said Marrkin. "If Denthold—"

"Yeah, well, that's a big 'if,' isn't it?" said a thin-faced woman next to Larric—his mother, Lilla—the reason Larric had always been afraid of his own shadow. "Only evidence we've got Denthold has anything to do with the thefts is the Priest-boy's claim he read the Mad Priest's name on a bit of blackened paper. He could be making it all up. This could be a Priestly plot to get us all killed."

"Dainann and Samarrind believe him," said Marrkin, his face visibly darkening in the candlelight. "Are you questioning the clan leader? The Wisest?"

"Maybe I am," said Lilla.

Larric lifted his beer and took three big gulps, his gaze flicking back and forth from Marrkin to his mother across the rim of the mug.

"Maybe we should all question Dainann and Samarrind," Lilla continued. "Maybe those other clan leaders know something they don't—or something they aren't telling us." She slapped her hand down on the table. "I'm not going north to get killed. Not for Dainann. Not for

Samarrind. Not for nobody." She got up. "Come along, Larric."

Her son hastily drained his mug, wiped his mouth, mumbled "good night" to Marrkin, and then hurried after her. Marrkin muttered a curse word under his breath, tossed back the last of his beer, and disappeared in the opposite direction.

Not good, Amlinn thought.

Clearly, Petra thought so too. "The Clan is divided," he murmured to her. "You may trust me, but some of them clearly don't. Even if they did see you holding my hand."

"Grandfather will put it right," Amlinn said stoutly and with far more confidence than she felt.

Finished with their suppers, they returned the plates to the cookwagon and then walked together back to Petra's tent, holding hands once more. They stopped outside the flap. The glow of the Fence cast a blue glow over Petra's face, turning his dark eyes into black, unreadable pools. She cleared her throat. "Good night."

He looked down at their joined hands, looked back up at her, parted his lips as if to say something—and then cleared his throat and released her hand. "Good night." He turned and plunged out of sight into the tent as though fleeing a potentially dangerous animal.

Smiling, though she couldn't have said why, Amlinn returned to her grandfather's wagon. He wasn't there. She changed into her nightgown, climbed into bed, and blew out her candle.

She fell asleep almost at once. She dreamed Grandfather had come into the wagon, half-woke to realize he really had, slept again, and then came fully and suddenly awake to the sound of the wagon door slamming shut.

She sat up. Daylight streamed through the wagon's small, high-set windows, casting long slanting shafts of illumination through dancing motes of dust. Certain she'd overslept, and the wagons were on the verge of moving out, she jumped out of bed, hurried into her clothes, and threw open the door. The camp still slumbered, though smoke rose from the cookwagons.

Grandfather came around the corner of the wagon. "Oh, Amlinn," he said. "Sorry if I woke you. You can go back to bed if you want. We're not moving today."

"Why?" Amlinn asked.

"There are decisions to be made about our next destination," Grandfather said. "That's all you need to know for now."

She felt a flash of anger. *Don't treat me like a child!* she wanted to snap, but she kept her irritation to herself. "Yes, Grandfather."

He walked off in the direction of Samarrind's wagon. She glanced over her shoulder into her own wagon's cozy interior. For a moment, she considered getting undressed again and trying to sleep, but the cold morning air had thoroughly waked her. She might as well start the day.

Which she did by walking across the camp to Petra's tent. *If I can't sleep in, he doesn't get to either!*

She leaned down and stuck her head through the flap. "Wake up, Petra!" she shouted. "Breakfast!"

He bolted upright, the blanket falling from him and leaving him bare-chested. When he saw her standing there, he blushed, grabbed the blanket, and pulled it back up to his shoulders. "Um . . ."

"I'll wait out here," she told him sweetly. She straightened and turned to look across the camp.

Grandfather emerged from Samarrind's wagon. He didn't look happy. He set off in a different direction, disappearing beyond the sunwagons. Behind her, Petra climbed out of the tent on his hands and knees, dressed, but in sock feet. He'd left his boots outside the tent, and now he sat down to pull them on. "Why aren't we breaking camp?" he asked as he tugged. "And if we aren't breaking camp, why did you wake me up?"

"Because I'm awake, and I wanted company. Hurry up. I'm hungry."

As the day advanced, the Freefolk seemed as unsettled as ants whose nest had been disturbed, even though they had a rare respite from travel. They gathered in small clumps, talking, arguing, and giving Petra worried, angry, or unfriendly looks—sometimes, all three. Nobody smiled at him or even said, "Hi."

"Let's get out of the camp," Amlinn said after Smittik, one of the caravan outriders, muttered a pungent remark as she and Petra passed. She hoped Petra hadn't heard, and if he had, she hoped his Priestly upbringing might keep him from knowing what Smittik had meant. "I've given you the grand tour of every single wagon and told you every bit of gossip I know about the Clan. There's a stream with a pretty waterfall not far away. Let's go there."

"Suits me," Petra said, and from the tone of his voice and the colour of his face, Amlinn guessed he had both heard *and* understood what Smittik had said.

She wasn't supposed to leave the camp without telling someone where she was going, so she looked around for Grandfather. She didn't see him, but fortunately, Witten sat on the steps of his wagon, repairing a harness and soaking up the sun. She told him about their plans. He raised an eyebrow and glanced from her to Petra. That made her blush, but all he said was, "Have fun, and be careful."

The trail led through the woods and down a steep, switch-backing path to the bottom of a little ravine. Amlinn heard the waterfall before they saw it, a gurgling, splashing song of water that lifted her heart. A few minutes later, they emerged from the trees onto the edge of a tiny lake. To their left, the stream leaped from a bluff and plunged, sparkling in the sun, twenty feet into the water, which bubbled and swirled and glittered. A flock of iridescent birds flickered across the lake, dipping so low they ruffled the surface, snapping up insects.

"It's beautiful," Petra breathed. "I've never seen anything like it." He sounded wistful. "There's nothing in the city like this. I mean, the inner Temple garden is pretty, but it's not . . ." He paused as if searching for the right word.

"Wild?" Amlinn suggested.

He nodded.

"There's a whole world out here in the woods you City-dwellers never see," she said. She led him to a big boulder at the side of the lake, and they sat on it together, looking at the waterfall and the lake and the dark trees on the far shore. "This is only one small corner of it. All of Nevyana is beautiful. The whole world is beautiful."

"So are you," he said in a low voice, and her heart skipped a beat. She turned to look at him. His freckled face flushed, but he didn't look away. "I mean it."

"Thank you," she said. And then she looked away again, because if she kept looking at him, something would happen, and she didn't know if she was ready for it. "Oh, look," she said brightly. "Trout! Do you know how to tickle them?"

"Do I know how to what?"

She laughed. "I'll show you."

From previous visits to the lake, she knew trout liked to lie in the shadow of the boulder. She showed Petra how to reach into the water and turn his fingers upward, wriggling like the fronds of underwater weeds, until he found the trout's belly. Then, constantly tickling, she showed him how to move his hand up to the trout's gills, try to grab the fish, and throw it onto the bank. They spent the rest of the afternoon laughing and getting wet and even, to Amlinn's own surprise, catching a few trout, though they were all so small they threw them back.

They returned to the camp late in the afternoon to discover the council had been meeting since just after lunch.

"Did you tell Grandfather where I was?" Amlinn asked Witten, as she stared at the council tent. The guards were posted farther from it than usual, a sure sign the council members didn't want anyone to overhear their arguing.

"I did," Witten said.

"And he didn't ask you to come for us?"

"He didn't," Witten said. He looked from her to Petra. "Did you have a good time?" he said innocently.

"We tickled trout," Petra said.

"Uh-huh," Witten said.

Blushing again, Amlinn pulled Petra away. "I can't believe they didn't want to talk to us," she complained. "Or you, at least."

Petra shrugged. "I've told them everything I can. It's all out of my hands. I'm just a prisoner, remember?"

Yes, Amlinn thought. *But I'm not.*

That night, word spread that there would be a general assembly of the clan at dawn. Grandfather returned to the wagon very late again, long after Amlinn had said goodnight to Petra and gone to bed herself. She stuck her head out through the bed curtains. "What happened at the council meeting?" she said sleepily. "What's going to happen at the clan assembly in the morning?"

"I can't tell you," Grandfather said. He sounded exhausted. "Go back to sleep, Amlinn. You'll find out with everyone else at dawn."

Amlinn pulled her head back through the curtains, lay down, and fumed—but not for long. Within minutes, she dreamed of tickling trout. And then of tickling Petra. The dream left a smile on her face when she woke in the morning to the sound of the door closing. Grandfather went out. She remembered the assembly, got up and dressed in a hurry, and emerged into the growing light.

In the morning mist, she gathered with the rest of Clan Therra, to the last infant in arms, around the wagon into which the council tent had already been loaded. Petra joined her, and she gave him a brief smile. He didn't smile back. He stood with his shoulders hunched as though to ward off the unfriendly glances directed his way.

Grandfather climbed into the wagon and stood on the seat, looking out over the Clan. "By now, you have all heard the news." His voice rang through the silent assembly. "Clan Fell and Clan Pirra do not share my belief that the thefts from Freefolk and Priests presage a serious threat. They dismiss out of hand the notion that the Mad Priest, Denthold, still lives in Divpaxis. They reject the possibility that he is stealing the knowledge of Blue Fire. They do not believe he is planning to use that knowledge to arm his swelling forces and launch an invasion of the south. They claim our young Priest-Apprentice guest has told a mischievous and malicious fiction and the thefts are no more than the work of ambitious robbers.

"Samarrind, the Wisest, does not share their sanguine opinion. Nor do I. But I know some of you do."

Dainann paused, his gaze moving over the crowd, sliding past Amlinn and Petra without pausing. "The Freefolk are free," he said at last. "I lead Clan Therra, in consultation with the council, but I am not a king. You must each decide what is best for you, your family, and your clan.

"We are less than one day's travel east of City Desmixis. Clan Fell and Clan Pirra are even now camped outside its walls. Those of you who do not believe we should continue north may leave us today and join those clans with your personal wagons and belongings. You may rejoin Clan Therra, if you so choose, when we return.

"I ask those of you with children or elders, those too young or old to fight, to send them to Clan Fell or leave with them. I will not lead the defenceless into danger.

"But if you are able and willing, and believe as the Wisest and I do that our duty to Arrica and to ourselves requires us to recover our stolen sunscale—or if we cannot do that, to at least learn what happened to it—we continue our journey at noon. Strike the camp." And with that, Dainann jumped down and joined Samarrind, who waited by the wagon. They walked away without looking back.

In the stunned silence that followed, Amlinn stood frozen. Send the children to Clan Fell? Did that include her?

"Grandfather!" She ran after him, leaving Petra behind. "Grandfather!" she called again. He kept walking. She ran in front of him, forcing him to stop. "Grandfather!"

The stern look he gave her used to quash her into obedience, but no longer. "What do you expect *me* to do?" she demanded.

He sighed heavily. "Go to Desmixis, of course. We go into uncertainty and danger. It's no place for—"

"A child?" Her face flushed. "I am not a child, Grandfather."

"Amlinn, I have no time—"

"This won't take long." She folded her arms. "I'm coming with you."

"You're doing no such—"

"Grandfather, do you even know how old I am?"

Dainann blinked. "Of course, I do. You turned fifteen two weeks before we camped at City Primaxis."

"No, Grandfather," Amlinn said. "I turned *sixteen*. And what does the rule of the Clan say about an unmarried girl of that age?"

Grandfather's face darkened, but Amlinn thought she saw a faint smile flicker across the lips of the Wisest. "Don't quote the rule of the Clan to me, granddaughter!" Grandfather growled.

"I haven't. I want you to quote it to me."

Grandfather pressed his lips together as though to seal in his words, then jerked his head right as Samarrind recited, "At sixteen, a girl is old enough to marry, old enough to bear children, old enough to own a wagon, old enough to trade, and old enough to fight. Thus says the rule of the clan."

Amlinn nodded her acknowledgement to Samarrind, then faced Grandfather again. "To *fight*, Grandfather. To fight as I have been trained to fight, to protect myself when I perform, to protect the Clan if we are attacked." She put her hand on her dagger. "You gave me this blade yourself. Is this a gift you give a child?"

Grandfather glared at Samarrind, then turned his piercing blue eyes on Amlinn. "It seems I cannot stop you. If you are set on this course, then so be it. You and Petra can ride with Samarrind." And then, like snow suddenly melting, his shoulders slumped. "But please be careful, Amlinn. I lost your mother. I won't . . . I can't . . ." Emotion choked him into silence.

Amlinn's eyes stung. "But that's why I have to come with you, Grandfather," she said around the lump in her throat. "So I don't lose *you*." She flung her arms around him, and after a moment, his went around her. She closed her eyes and breathed deep of the smells she knew so well—smoke and horse and cedar and, simply, Grandfather. For a moment, she felt again like the little girl whose nighttime terrors could be vanquished with a hug.

But she wasn't that little girl anymore. She never would be again.

She straightened and released her grandfather and turned to walk back to Petra, and as she turned, caught a glimpse of Samarrind's small, sad smile.

16

THE CLAN DIVIDES

Petra watched Amlinn confront her grandfather, though he couldn't hear what she said. Meanwhile, all around him, the startled, uncertain silence that had followed Dainann's announcement gave way to near-chaos. Amid a hubbub of angry voices, the Freefolk returned to their wagons and began striking camp, though the normal well-ordered routine had been shattered.

Amlinn returned, her face flushed, lips tight. "I'm coming north with you," she snapped. "Come on. I'll help you pack up your tent. We're going to load it into our wagon."

She didn't mention her talk with her grandfather. They worked in silence, unlike the arguing Freefolk all around them. Petra saw one wagon loaded, unloaded, and then loaded again. Amid much heated discussion, the supplies were divided among those who would go and those who would stay. Only the Wise Women's silent collection of the Fencestones seemed to proceed as usual.

By the time Petra and Amlinn slid his tent into the storage compartment underneath Dainann's wagon, adults were urging crying children onto wagons that weren't their familiar home wagons.

It took all morning to sort out the chaos. Of the one hundred and fifty or so members of the Clan, thirty were children under the age of fourteen. They would travel to City Desmixis with their guardians, mostly mothers, elder sisters, grandmothers, and a few old men; another thirty or so in all. Two dozen fighting-age men who were unwilling to accept Dainann's call would escort them. Among them was Larric, the young man whose mother had been so outspoken at the dining table the night before. Four of Clan Therra's six sunwagons would accompany the caravan to provide the Blue Fire and Fencestones that Clan Fell and Clan Pirra required to accommodate the new arrivals.

That left fewer than seventy Freefolk to accompany Dainann. Forty men, fifteen boys, and a handful of unmarried, childless women and older girls, including Amlinn. Twenty-eight regular wagons and two sunwagons would make the journey north.

One of the storewagons was positioned at the end of the caravan. As Petra watched, the driver jumped down and went around back. He opened the doors and lowered the tailgate, and those going north began lining up behind it. "What's in that wagon?" Petra asked.

"Weapons," Amlinn replied. "Stay here."

"Right," Petra muttered under his breath as she left him to join the line of Freefolk. "Because prisoners don't get weapons. They can just die."

Amlinn returned in a few minutes with a heavy cloth bundle. She dumped it on the ground at Petra's feet. It clanked. She unrolled the cloth, revealing a thick leather tunic covered with steel rings, with metal plates set into its shoulders; a sword, scabbard and belt; a crossbow and a satchel of quarrels; and a metal cap lined with leather.

Amlinn pulled on the armour, buckled on the sword belt, slung the crossbow and its quarrels over her shoulder, seated the cap on her head, and drew tight the leather strap around her chin.

When she was done, she looked . . . well, "magnificent" was the first word that came to Petra's mind. Followed by "alarming." While he, meanwhile, was left . . . well, "naked" was the first word that came to mind. Followed by "vulnerable."

He pointed at her sword. "Do you really know how to use that?"

"All Freefolk are trained in the use of weapons," she said, grim-faced—but then she ruined the effect by smiling. It transformed her from stern warrior woman to child playing dress-up. "In truth, just barely. I'm a dancer, not a fencer. But I think I can manage not to cut off my own legs."

"What about the others?" Petra watched the scouts, six men and two women who would range behind and to either side of the caravan, mount their horses. "Just how much experience in battle do they have? I have not heard of warfare among the Freefolk."

"Some have fought Nightdwellers," Amlinn said.

"Often?" Petra said.

"Well, no," Amlinn admitted. "Perhaps once in their lives." She sighed. "The truth is, though everyone learns the basics of wielding weapons—it is a religious duty to Arrica— few have actually done so in earnest. If it comes to fighting, we will all be in the same creaky wagon."

"I've been trained," Petra said. "All Priest-Apprentices are.

It's part of our daily routine. I could give you some pointers if I had a weapon."

Amlinn bit her lip and looked away. "I asked the armsmaster," she said. "But he said Grandfather forbids it. An armed follower of Vekrin inside the Fence of the Freefolk is unthinkable. Not to me," she added, hastily looking back again. "But—"

"But to everyone else."

She nodded.

"Your loss," Petra muttered. "I'm actually considered quite good at swordplay and archery." Which was true, but only in reference to the other Priest-Apprentices his age. He couldn't hold a candle to the apprentices hand-picked by the Temple master of arms to specialize in weapons work. Having seen their amazing displays on Festival days, he knew a mere half a dozen of them, despite their youth, could probably cut through this entire troupe of armed Freefolk like a scythe through ripe wheat. It was foolishness to presume Denthold's followers would be any less well-trained.

"I'm sorry, Petra," Amlinn said. "I'll keep working on Grandfather."

Petra looked across the campground to where Dainann stood beneath a shade tree, talking with the wagonmasters who were willing to follow him north. He had wanted Dainann to act, but with this few men? Seventy Freefolk?

It wasn't enough. It wasn't nearly enough. Not if Dainann actually intended to try to recover the sunscale and not just reconnoitre. The other clans were right. Dainann was too hotheaded.

I wanted action, but this could get a lot of people killed. Including me!

Petra heard shouts and the rumbling and creaking of

moving wagons, and turned to look the other way, toward the trail leading to City Desmixis. With all farewells said and daylight wasting, those who would not be going north had begun their journey west. Wagon by wagon, horseman by horseman, they disappeared from sight into the woods.

"Time for us to move, too," Amlinn said. "Come on."

She led Petra up the line of wagons to the first sunwagon, tucked in behind Dainann's. They climbed up onto the seat beside Samarrind, who nodded. With three abreast on a bench that normally held two, Amlinn, in the middle, was pressed tightly against Petra.

He didn't mind.

A whistle shrilled. Scouts trotted their horses out into the woods. Dainann's wagon began to roll. Amlinn's usual spot had been taken by Witten, who had given up his own wagon to take children to safety.

Samarrind flicked the reins, and the sunwagon jerked into motion.

Much diminished, armed and armoured, grim-faced and mostly silent, the Freefolk of Clan Therra set out to recover their stolen sunscale.

Or die trying, Petra thought, and really wished he hadn't.

17

SCENTS ON THE WIND

By the light of the stars, Jin studied the tracks of the Freefolk wagons. The trail continued north but was much diminished from the day before. He judged about thirty wagons had passed this way, plus a few horses—no more than a third of the former total.

They've split up. Why? Jin scratched behind his right ear as he thought about it. He could backtrack to last night's Freefolk camp and look for clues, but if he did so, he might not reach tonight's camp before morning. And, after all, the wagon tracks still led north to City Divpaxis, and that was the direction that interested him.

He decided to forget about the rest of the caravan and loped on down the trail. He moved much faster than any wagon, but even so, he was surprised how quickly he caught up to his quarry. The orange glow of fires and the blue light of a Fence gleamed through the forest ahead of him with hours of the night still remaining. The Freefolk had broken camp late. Something had clearly delayed them that day, presumably whatever had led to them dividing their clan.

The trees tossed and groaned like restless sleepers in the rising north wind, which also brought to his nose the usual Freefolk odours of smoke and cooking meat, sweaty horses, and unwashed Daydwellers. He tested the air for Nightdweller scent but smelled nothing. He had come across no other of his people since starting to follow the caravan—even that first night when they were still close enough to the warren for Ket-Ra's watchpack to come sniffing around. He suspected Ser Mar had prevailed upon the watchcaptain to send the patrols in a different direction.

Before settling in to watch the camp, he turned his back on the glimmering blue Fence and moved well back into the forest to set up his shadowshelter. With it in place, he returned to the camp and watched the guards move around the perimeter of the Fence.

It must be terrible to spend every night in a cage of Blue Fire, he thought. *But I suppose the sun is our cage during the day.*

But did it really have to be?

The Scrollkeepers said, "Yes." The Scrollkeepers taught that the slightest touch of the unclean rays of Arrica's sun would burn a Nightdweller alive, inflicting unspeakable agony.

Jin looked east, where the sun would climb into the sky in another three or four hours. Just once, he had dared to wait until the last possible moment to take shelter underground. Just once.

It had been a dare, of course. Ket-Ra, always seeking to prove his bravery, to prove he deserved to lead the watchpack, had dared several Ra, including Jin, to wait outside the small eastern entrance to Broken Tree Warren long after they should have gone underground. "The last one to run for shelter loses," Ket had said, and Jin, sick of Ket's endless preening, had agreed. Rith, Rath, and a half-dozen others had followed his lead. As the sky lightened beyond the low ridge to the warren's east, they had stood in the open, tense as frightened deer.

The light grew and grew and grew until the sky was brighter than Jin had thought possible. Sunrise had to be mere minutes away. But Ket-Ra did not move, so Jin squinted his eyes almost closed, gritted his teeth, and held on. And on. And on.

One by one, the other Ra broke and fled into the welcoming dark of the warren, until only he and Ket remained, standing in the shadow of the ridge. Unable to face the glare any longer, even with eyes almost closed, they glanced at each other. By unspoken mutual consent, they turned to face west instead, looking up the low grassy slope above the warren entrance to the trees that topped it. When the first full rays of sunlight touched the tops of those trees, they appeared to explode into eye-searing flame. Jin cried out and threw his arm across his face and heard Ket grunt beside him, but Ket remained in place, so Jin, too, stood his ground.

The only way he could gauge the progress of the sunlight was to flick his eyes open and closed as fast as he could. Dagger-like pain stabbed them with every glance. The impossibly bright light devoured the trees bit by bit, burning them away into a glare in which Jin could see nothing at all. And then the horrifying sun-fire began creeping down the slope toward the warren entrance, swallowing the grass as it had the forest, coming nearer and nearer . . .

The sun's rays would touch the back of his head before that flange of fire reached his feet, he knew. *We have to go in,* he thought. *We have to go in!*

But he didn't move. He would not move as long as Ket stood firm.

So both of you can die together as human torches? a saner part of his mind screamed. *Run! Run now!*

One more minute, he told himself, furred palms sweating. *One more minute and I'll give in. One more minute.*

Thirty seconds after that, Ket swore and dived headfirst into the dark hole of the warren entrance.

Now, run! the sane part of his brain shouted, but Jin stayed where he was, counting for thirty more seconds. Then he, too, scrambled for cover.

In the small entrance chamber, he found all of the other boys except Ket, who had vanished. They looked at him with awe approaching terror.

"Are you all right?" Rith asked.

"I think so," Jin said. He laughed shakily. "Though it seems awfully dark in here." So dark, in fact, he hoped he hadn't permanently damaged his eyes.

"Your head doesn't hurt?"

"No. Why?"

Rith leaned in close and spoke in a whisper. "Nobody else saw this—they were watching Ket-Ra—but . . . but in that last half-minute after he left, I risked a quick blink and . . ." He swallowed. "I thought your head was on fire."

Jin laughed. "My fur wasn't even singed."

The truth was, in the last thirty seconds he had stood under the brilliant glare of the sun, filled with both pride and terror, he *had* felt something—but not the agony Scrollkeepers swore would befall any Nightdweller touched by the unholy rays of Arrica's sun.

No. All he'd felt had been warmth.

A pleasant touch of warmth.

Jin had never told that to anyone, not even Ser Mar. If the Scrollkeepers, if anyone, had truly believed he had been touched by the sun without being burned, they might have cast him out of the warren. That would be a death warrant, for even if his body survived the next sunrise, his eyesight would not. Alone and blind in the forest, unable to feed himself or evade predators, he would not have lasted long.

He shuddered at the thought, then shook his head to bring himself back to the present and returned his wandering attention to the Freefolk camp. The guards spoke to each other only in low whispers as they passed in their rounds, their voices almost lost in the rush of wind through the trees. The only other sound Jin heard from the camp was the occasional clank from the guards' steel-ringed leather armour—a new sound, since Freefolk did not usually wear armour. Tonight, they all carried crossbows as well. Jin moved deeper into the shadows of the trees, so the glow of his eyes would not betray his presence. Freefolk bowman had claimed the lives of unwary Nightdwellers in the past.

After watching the guards make their rounds for a half hour or so, Jin circled around to the north, upwind of the camp. With the smells of the camp behind him, he raised his muzzle and scented the wind. Mostly he smelled earth and evergreens, water and animals; but then the wind shifted, and a new scent came to his nose.

Smoke.

And smoke from a different kind of wood than the Freefolk were burning. The scent of horses too, and people who smelled different from any Freefolk he had ever smelled, and very different from Nightdwellers.

Another camp of Daydwellers. But who?

Jin looked back into the camp of the Freefolk. He had

seen few women and no children. The Freefolk rode armed and armoured. They feared attack, then. Was this other camp filled with their allies or their enemies?

Jin took another sniff of the wind, but it told him nothing more. He stared off into the forest for a long moment, then shook his head and turned back to the Freefolk. After a long, slow circuit of the Fence, he returned to his shadowshelter as the first cold light of dawn glimmered over the eastern mountains.

He ate and slept and rose the next evening eager to follow the Freefolk trail, eager to discover if they had encountered the other Daydwellers he had scented, but he saw no signs the two groups had crossed paths. Indeed, he came across no sign of the second group of Daydwellers at all.

That night, though, Jin smelled the second camp once more, and much closer than before. The next night, he smelled it again, so strongly he couldn't understand how the Freefolk couldn't smell it, yet they seemed oblivious.

They are physically impoverished creatures who do not have Ell's Gifts, he reminded himself.

And to be fair, strong though the scent was, not even his Nightdweller eyes could detect a glimmer of light in the direction from which the camp-smells came. Whoever the other Daydwellers were, they were being very careful not to betray their presence to the Freefolk. But they were so close that the state of affairs could not continue much longer.

He glanced up at the stars. Less than an hour until dawn. He had to return to his shadowshelter.

But as he climbed inside the dark tent and lay down, one thought followed him into sleep: *Tomorrow night should be interesting.*

❧ 18 ❧

AMBUSH

Distant, urgent shouts jolted Amlinn from a doze. Her head lay on Petra's shoulder and, embarrassed, she jerked upright, mumbling an apology, hoping desperately she hadn't drooled. But Petra wasn't even looking at her. He'd twisted around to stare in the direction of the sound, behind the caravan and to their left. Milla, who was driving the lead sunwagon today while Samarrind drove the wagon she and Milla shared, tugged hard on the reins. As the horses came to a stamping, snorting halt, she looked back too.

The shouting ended in a gurgled scream that chilled Amlinn's blood. "What . . . ?"

"One of the scouts," Milla said. She twisted around to the right as she surveyed the forest in all directions. On the lead wagon, Grandfather stood, sword drawn, staring down the line. Witten held his crossbow ready. Amlinn looked over her shoulder. All the wagons were stopped, the drivers already holding weapons or fumbling for them.

There was nothing else to see.

Then suddenly, there was.

A dozen men on horseback burst from the trees like a pack of wolves. Armed with longswords, helmeted, and clad in black-crossed forest-green surcoats over mail shirts, they charged the caravan. Amlinn grabbed her crossbow, but even as she raised it, Milla slapped it down. "Inside the wagon!" the Wise Woman cried.

"What?"

"Inside!" Milla swivelled around to open the small door behind the seat. "Priest-Apprentice, go!"

Petra, weaponless, hesitated only a moment, then ducked inside the sunwagon. Amlinn didn't move. Steel clashed, and men shouted hoarsely behind them. From the lead wagon, Grandfather caught Amlinn's eye. "Get out of sight, Amlinn!" he shouted above the din, then leaped to the ground and ran back toward the fight with Witten at his heels.

"Obey your grandfather!" Milla shouted at Amlinn as Grandfather and Witten ran past. "Defend the sunwagon! They may try to get inside! We'll fight them out here." She threw down the reins, seized the hunting bow and arrows tucked beside her on the seat, and jumped off the wagon.

Amlinn's hand tightened on her crossbow. Her heart pounded. She wanted to help Milla, help Grandfather, but Grandfather had ordered her out of sight, and Milla had ordered her to protect the sunwagon. She knew how crucial that was.

Someone screamed. She turned and scrambled inside the wagon to join Petra and wished that a part of her was not so greatly relieved.

The glistening white surfaces of twenty-four firejars glinted in the dim light. Glazed clay urns about three feet tall, they stood twelve on a side, half at floor level, half on sturdy wooden shelves. In the aisle between them, Petra leaned against the right-hand shelf, his eyes wide and white in the pale blotch of his face. "Who are they?"

"I don't know," Amlinn panted. "Not Freefolk. Not Night-dwellers. And those weren't city uniforms. I've seen them all."

"Denthold," Petra said. "It has to be."

Shouts and screams crescendoed outside. Hooves and running feet pounded past.

Where is Grandfather? Is he all right? Amlinn fingered her crossbow and realized that she'd stupidly left its quarrels, and worse, her sword, beneath the wagon seat. Even her helmet still hung outside. Of all her weapons and armour, only her dagger and steel-ringed jerkin remained.

Cursing herself for a fool, she turned, intending to lunge through the door to seize her weapons, but instead, she stumbled as the wagon shifted sharply sideways.

A shadow fell across the doorway. Someone had climbed into the driver's seat. Milla?

No. She glimpsed shining mail and dark-green cloth. She jerked her dagger from its sheath, but even as she did so, the reins snapped. The horses whinnied and bolted. The wagon jerked forward. Amlinn fell backward against Petra, and the door slammed shut, plunging them into darkness. Flinging out her arms reflexively, she flung her dagger too. It clattered against a firejar, then hit the floor and skittered away.

The wagon turned sharply left, thundering over ground so rough she and Petra shook like dice in a cup. His elbow clipped her jaw. Then she fell on top of him and felt her knee drive into soft flesh, drawing a groan. Reaching out blindly, she banged her knuckles on rough wood and a moment later had a tight two-handed grip on one of the upright posts of the firejar shelves. She pulled up her knees and made herself as small as possible, while the wagon rattled along so fast, she feared for its wheels.

Her dagger was lost in the darkness, and her other weapons out of reach. As a guard, she had failed miserably. And now one of the sunwagons, with all its precious sunscales and firejars, was in the hands of the followers of the Mad Priest.

Or was it someone else?

We'll find out soon enough, Amlinn thought, jaw clenched to save her teeth from the jolting of the wagon. *And how will whoever-it-is react when they find us inside their prize?*

Her heart fluttered. Blind in the thundering, rattling dark, she swallowed hard and gripped the post even tighter.

❧ 19 ❧

THE HERETIC

Thrown off his feet as the wagon left the path, Petra felt his elbow hit Amlinn in the jaw, but he only had a second to feel badly about that before he felt a lot worse. Both of them tumbled to the floor of the sunwagon. She fell on top of him, driving her knee into his groin.

Agony constricted his throat, limiting him to a strangled grunt that hardly did the sensation justice. Stomach heaving, he clung to one of the wooden posts of the firejar shelving with one hand, doubled over, swallowing hard to keep from throwing up, praying to Vekrin for the pain to subside.

Just twenty minutes before, he had been riding through the forest on a beautiful day, Amlinn asleep on his shoulder. He focused on that now, reaching for that feeling of contentment to take his mind off the pain. Even though his right arm had started to tingle ten minutes after she'd dozed off, he wouldn't have moved for the world.

Then had come the distant shouts, the gurgling scream . . . Amlinn jerking awake . . . Milla halting the wagon . . . Freefolk drawing weapons . . . and then the attack.

Petra held on tight in the darkness as the pain gradually subsided to a dull ache. *Maybe they'll just park the wagon. Maybe they won't look inside right away. We can sneak out, slip into the forest, and pray to Vekrin and Arrica that we find whatever is left of Clan Therra before nightfall.*

After what seemed an eternity of bone-shaking, teeth-crashing vibration, the wagon slowed. It didn't stop, but at least he could move without risking bruises and broken bones. Still feeling a little tender in one particular place, he cautiously eased himself toward Amlinn. His right leg touched her left, and he stopped. "Now what?" he whispered.

He felt her hand on his leg and reached out for it.

She squeezed his fingers. "We wait," she whispered close to his ear. Her leg was warm against his, her hand was warm in his, just as her head had been warm on his shoulder earlier. At that moment, a sudden, fierce protectiveness took him by surprise.

Whatever came next, he would willingly die to keep Amlinn safe.

I swear it to Vekrin.

But what immediately came next was simply more of the same—the endless rumble and creak and sway of the wagon. Sweat ran down Petra's face in the dark, and he licked dry lips, wishing for water. The wagon never stopped rolling along paths that seemed to be mostly rocks and ruts. Petra wrapped his left arm around a post to hold himself in place, his right hand clasping Amlinn's, resting in the valley between their touching legs.

They had no way to gauge the passing of time, but at last, the wagon's motion slowed and finally, wonderfully, stopped. Petra took a deep, thankful breath and then pulled himself to his feet with a groan. Amlinn groaned, too, as he helped her up. Still holding hands, they turned to face the back of the wagon.

Petra heard voices—a lot of voices—indistinct and unintelligible through the sunwagon's thick wooden walls and sunscale-covered roof. A moment later, the voices were drowned out by a much louder, much closer groan, the creak and screech of wood on wood. A moment after that, the wagon lurched forward again, forcing Petra to grab onto the firejars' shelving again with his free hand.

Clattering rose beneath their wheels. Cobblestones. A city. He could think of only one it might be. *Divpaxis!* His heart raced.

The wagon halted again. Petra heard more voices. Then, without warning, the wagon's double doors flew open, and the tailgate crashed down. The orange light of the setting sun illuminated the sacred and secret interior of the sunwagon— and Amlinn and Petra, squinting in the glare.

The voices cut off. In the sudden hush, Amlinn's dagger, teetering on the tailgate hinge, slipped out and clattered to the cobblestones. As though galvanized by the sound, armoured men in the same forest-green uniforms as the caravan's attackers scrambled into the wagon, shouting. Rough hands seized Petra and Amlinn, dragged them out, and shoved them up against a stone wall.

Petra found all his attention suddenly taken by the needle-sharp point of the sword held just below his chin by an enormous, bearded soldier. The mountainous man's mail shirt glittered beneath his green surcoat, and his narrowed eyes gleamed on either side of his steel helmet's nose-guard.

Petra dared not move his head, but he tore his eyes away from the threatening blade and flicked them left and right. A gate made of massive, squared-off timbers bound in black iron stood open in one wall of a cobblestoned courtyard. Armed guards peered down from atop the walls that bordered it. Beyond it stretched the King's Way, white and smooth. The fact that it ended at the gate instead of curving around the city was all the proof Petra needed. This was indeed City Divpaxis, northernmost of the Twelve.

A second gate, shorter and thinner but still substantial, remained closed in the inner wall of the courtyard. They stood in a killing ground, Petra realized. Attackers who made it through the main gate would find themselves trapped here, while defenders poured arrows and boiling oil and other unpleasantries down on them from all sides. It was not a standard feature of city defence but, judging by the lichen on the rocks and rust on the iron of the inner gate, it had been there for years.

A Freefolk storewagon stood next to the sunwagon. Perhaps two dozen men surrounded the wagons, muttering amongst themselves as they stared at Petra and Amlinn. Half wore the X-marked green uniforms. Two wore red. *The royal colour*, Petra thought uneasily, remembering his discussion with Dainann about who might want the throne, but instead of the twelve-pointed golden crown of the king, these scarlet surcoats were also marked with black Xs. The rest of the men were unarmed, unarmoured, and nondescript, wearing the usual browns and greys of lower-class Citydwellers. In fact, they were dressed very much like Petra, who wore clothes Dainann had provided so he would not be immediately identifiable as a Priest-Apprentice. "For your good, and ours," Dainann had said.

The inner gate creaked open. Two more soldiers in black-crossed green surcoats over mail shirts emerged ahead of a third, older man, likewise armoured and helmeted, with a close-cropped, steel-grey beard. His uniform bore a symbol. Petra gasped. *The Holy Symbol of Vekrin!*

And it was—but it had been defaced. The white circle enclosing the blue flame, the circle representing the Priests' duty to keep the secrets of Blue Fire safe, had been broken in four places. Jagged bolts of blue lightning speared through the gaps.

Sacrilege! Petra thought. Only a heretic would dare wear such an abomination.

Then he realized what that meant: not *a* heretic, but *the* Heretic.

Denthold!

Amlinn's life and his hung by a thread. Denthold had slaughtered dozens to seize this city. He'd burned the Priests alive in the Temple. If he thought Petra and Amlinn posed a threat, he would surely order them killed. But if he thought they might be valuable . . .

"Hail, Denthold," Petra shouted in the secret Temple tongue.

The grey-bearded man stopped in his tracks. Eyes blue and cold as a winter sky pierced Petra from a dozen strides away.

"Greetings," Denthold replied in the same tongue. He came closer, eyes narrowed. "You look like a Freefolk boy. How do you know my name, and how do you know the tongue of Vekrin?"

Out of the corner of his eye, Petra saw Amlinn's sharp, questioning gaze. He hated leaving her in the dark, but he could hardly take time to translate. "I am a Priest-Apprentice of Vekrin. I was kidnapped by the Freefolk."

"Kidnapped?" Denthold glanced at Amlinn. "Well. I had

thought to throw you to the Nightdwellers, but this sounds like a tale I need to hear." He switched to the common tongue and spoke to the guards holding them at sword-point. "Take them to my palace. Have my servants make them comfortable. Food, water, whatever else they might need. I will question them later." He gave Petra a speculative glance before striding on toward the still-open outer gate.

The big man with his blade at Petra's throat sheathed his sword. Then he grabbed Petra's arm and propelled him toward the inner gate. The other guard followed with Amlinn. Petra imagined her eyes drilling into the back of his head.

I'll tell her what I said as soon as I can, he promised himself.

From where Petra had been held, he hadn't been able to see through the inner gate. But now, as they rounded the corner, the city came into view for the first time. Petra gasped.

Far from being a deserted ruin, City Divpaxis bustled with activity in the golden light of the setting sun. Armed men, most in green but a few in red, moved purposefully along the broad, cobblestoned boulevard. Some marched in formation, drilling beneath the watchful eyes of sergeants. Others drove wagons along the boulevard and in and out of side streets or strode along with obvious purpose.

Then he looked farther, to the end of the boulevard, and his breath caught in horror.

The city's Temple stood as broken and defaced as the travesty of the Holy Symbol Denthold wore. The sigil-inscribed poles, toppled and broken, lay scattered around the shattered outer wall like carelessly discarded sticks. Beyond the wall, only blackened timbers remained of the stables and storerooms. Worst of all, the great dome at the Temple's heart had cracked like an eggshell. The Spire that should have stood atop it, beaming Blue Fire from the Godstone to the Hearths and sparkglobes of the city, had plunged into the Temple's fire-blackened interior. Only its golden tip peeked through the smoke-stained ruin into the dying light of day.

Petra stumbled on suddenly weak legs as the guard gave him a shove. He fell to his hands and knees onto the cobblestoned path. Tears filled his eyes, but they had nothing to do with the pain inflicted by the hard stones. The guard hauled him to his feet by the scruff of his neck and gave him another shove, so hard he barely managed to keep from falling a second time.

As he straightened, he heard Amlinn gasp. He looked up through blurred eyes and, for the first time, registered what stood in the Temple courtyard, surrounded by destruction: a wagon. The largest wagon he had ever seen, two stories in height, resting on six enormous wheels, each as tall as Petra.

The wagon's curved roof glistened black.

Sunscales!

And then fresh horror rose in his throat. A long pole capped with a sphere of black glass protruded from a round turret at the top of the giant vehicle.

Vekrin preserve us. It's a giant firelance!

For one agonizing moment, Petra twisted around and met Amlinn's eyes, wide and white in a face gone pale. Then the guard pushed him again, and he had to face front or fall. The Gifts of Arrica and Vekrin, blasphemously mingled in a single, evil device? Petra wondered why the Gods themselves did not descend from the sky and smite the monstrosity.

As they neared the thing, he noted more strangeness looming just beyond what had once been the Temple's courtyard gate. The wagon had no tongue to hitch horses to, offered no hint as to how it could move on its huge wheels. Two men worked inside an open compartment at the front, perhaps ten feet off the ground, presumably where the driver would sit. One of them climbed down a ladder leading from the compartment to the ground, then crouched and shuffled beneath the wagon's belly, disappearing inside it through a trapdoor. A moment after that, sparkglobes on each corner of the wagon sprang to blazing life, chasing away the gathering gloom as the sun slipped below the horizon.

Petra winced and turned his head away from the painfully bright light, his insides roiling. How could Vekrin permit this? The Priests taught that Vekrin would punish anyone who abused his Gifts. Yes, the Gifts would work with or without prayer—as Dainann had admitted was also true of the Gifts of Arrica—but this was *sacrilege*. This thing, full of Blue Fire, must have been months in the building, and Vekrin had done nothing to stop it. Anger, fear, and bewilderment swirled, sickening him.

Through the glare of those unholy sparkglobes, he squinted up again at the giant firelance. He remembered the charred sheep's carcass from his introduction to the weapon's power. Could even a city wall withstand *that*? And what would it do to ordinary men?

If that thing works, Denthold can conquer Nevyana with ease.

And if Amlinn's grandfather had not been deterred by the attack that morning—or killed—and continued his quest to retrieve Clan Therra's stolen sunscales, Amlinn's clan might well be the first to feel that monstrous firelance's fury.

Petra glanced back at Amlinn again. The horror on her face told him she'd come to that same sickening realization.

Their guards now turned them to the left, parallel to the broken wall and tumbled Curtain poles of the Temple courtyard. They headed toward a large house tucked behind a tall, whitewashed wall. The polished red surface of the only gate bore a golden, twelve-pointed crown: the king's mark.

Petra realized this must be the palace of Duke Felkor, who now lived City Primaxis and swore he knew nothing about the conspiracy to capture his city and had been driven from his home in fear for his life.

And yet his palace isn't damaged, Petra thought sourly as they were marched through the gate and along a long white walkway bordered by immaculate lawns and flowerbeds.

Their guards led them up broad, semi-circular steps and between fat, round columns onto a covered porch, and from thence into the palace. They entered through a double door, painted red like the gate and also bearing the golden twelve-pointed crown. Opposite them, across the green-veined, gold-flecked marble floor of the white-panelled entryway, rose a broad staircase carpeted in rich red. Closed doors lined hallways on either side of the stairs, but the guards shoved Petra and Amlinn through an open door on the right. It slammed and locked behind them. Amlinn immediately moved away from Petra, but her blue eyes bore into him with all the sharpness and warmth of twin icicles while he circled the room, examining it.

It looked like a waiting room, a place where supplicants to the Duke cooled their heels until he was ready to deal with them. A gold-fringed white rug with a low round table of polished black at its centre covered most of the marble floor. A massive, unlit fireplace with a white marble mantelpiece rose directly opposite the door through which they'd entered. A red-upholstered sofa stood in front of the long red-and-gold brocade drapes covering the window. Two scarlet chairs stood on either side of the fireplace, and four more were ranged equidistantly around the walls beneath tapestries portraying historical scenes. A particularly fine one depicted Vekrin himself, in his usual form as an ambulatory thunderstorm wreathed in cloud and lightning. He was hurling a Godstone from on high to its chosen place in a fertile valley.

Petra paused before it, raising a hand to touch the image of the Great God. *With all that power, why hasn't Vekrin acted to destroy Denthold?*

Just to the left of the tapestry, he spotted a small, discrete door and a problem he'd done his best to ignore—an overfull bladder—reasserted itself with unexpected forcefulness as he realized what that door probably hid. Fortunately for both his clothing and the expensive rug, he was right. The marble bench with the covered hole in it was a far cry from the rough wood in the toilets available to Priest-Apprentices, but the smell, unfortunately, was the same.

He emerged from the room much relieved, hands still tingling from the icy cold water that spouted from a pipe in the wall at the turn of a tap. Not even the Priests enjoyed running water in the Temple, mainly because they all agreed that hauling water from the well in the courtyard up several flights of stairs built character in Priest-Apprentices. They also agreed that character was built by the process of emptying the sandboxes underneath the toilets and replacing the fouled sand with fresh. Petra had often thought he'd built just about as much character as he could stand.

Without a word, Amlinn brushed past him. When she emerged from the toilet in her turn, she took four steps, spun, folded her arms, refocused her icy glare, and demanded, "Was that Denthold in the gate yard? The Mad Priest?" Her cold, suspicious voice struck him like a slap.

Petra nodded.

"You spoke to him in a strange language."

"I greeted him in the Temple Tongue," Petra snapped, stung by her tone.

"How interesting," Amlinn said, her voice acid, "that he has no compunction about killing the followers of Arrica, but he apparently feels differently about the followers of Vekrin."

Petra felt as if she'd kneed him in the groin again, deliberately this time. *She still suspects the Priests. She still suspects me!*

Almost at once, shock and pain gave way to anger. After everything he had done, everything he'd risked and given up, she still didn't trust him? "Be thankful, or our corpses might be cooling in the forest!"

Amlinn ignored that. "And what, exactly, is that . . . thing . . . out there?"

"A weapon. Built with the knowledge stolen from the Freefolk and the Priests." Petra glared at her. "Just as we feared."

Amlinn's eyes narrowed. She opened her mouth to respond, then snapped it shut and turned her head sharply left as the door opened.

Petra turned, expecting Denthold. Instead, a girl no older than Amlinn, dressed in a white blouse and green skirt, scurried in, head down. She bore a tray laden with cheese, dried fruit, bread, cold slices of meat, two pewter mugs, and a brown earthenware jug filled with bubbling brown ale. The guards watched from the hallway, their eyes cold, hands on weapons, as the girl placed the tray on the low table in the centre of the room, then hurried out again, never meeting Petra's and Amlinn's eyes. The door closed and locked again.

In an uncomfortable silence, Petra and Amlinn gathered food. They ate and drank on opposite sides of the room, Petra in a chair by the fireplace, Amlinn on the sofa in front of the window.

Petra's anger cooled as he ate. He could hardly blame Amlinn. She had to be sick with worry about her friends and her grandfather. And she'd been raised by a Wise Woman, for Vekrin's sake. She could no more stop being suspicious of Priests than he could stop being suspicious of Freefolk—and for the same reasons.

He couldn't stand the silence any longer. "Amlinn, all I said to Denthold was that I was a Priest-Apprentice of Vekrin who had been abducted by the Freefolk. That intrigued him, as I hoped it would. He said he'd intended to throw us to the Nightdwellers, but instead, he would hear our tale. And so here we are, instead of staked in the woods as the sun sets." He lifted his flagon of ale. "Isn't this better?"

"I don't know," Amlinn said, her voice still cold. "Will you continue to talk to him in your Priest-tongue, so I will not be able to judge for myself whether you are telling him truth or lies?"

Petra's anger surged again, but again he did his best to clamp it down. "He is no ally of mine or the Priests," he said as evenly as he could. "That monstrosity in the Temple court-yard is sacrilegious. In fact, I would have sworn it was impossible."

Amlinn said nothing for a moment. "I would have thought so, too," she said at last, and finally, finally, her voice warmed, if only to the extent a winter's day could be said to be warm when the sun managed to draw a drop of water from the tip of an icicle. "He stole just one sunscale from us, and none of the other clans have reported thefts. He *made* those sunscales. And he must have made them a long time ago. So, I don't understand why the thief stole a sunscale from us at all."

"Or why he stole a firelance from us," Petra said. "He certainly didn't construct that monstrous weapon in the few days since I found you outside the Curtain." He rose from his chair, crossed to her, and sat beside her on the couch. She stared at the floor but didn't move away. "Denthold is a threat to us all," he said softly. "But the threat is even greater than I imagined."

"Greater than Grandfather imagined." Amlinn still didn't look at him. "He was a fool to think we could simply march north and take back our sunscale." She stood. With a violent motion, she pulled her armoured jerkin over her head and threw it, clanking, into the empty fireplace. She sat heavily beside Petra on the couch once more. "We never stood a chance."

Cautiously, he reached out and put his arm around her. She didn't snuggle closer, but she didn't pull away, either. They sat in silence until the door opened again.

This time, it *was* Denthold.

He came in alone, closing the door behind him. He pulled off his helmet, ran his hand through his short-cropped steel-grey hair, then tucked the helmet under his arm and regarded the two of them.

At their first meeting, Petra had barely registered more than the defaced Holy Symbol on Denthold's tunic, the neat grey beard, and the sharp blue eyes. Now he took in the square jaw and slightly crooked nose and stern, lined face. Denthold, he judged, was close to his father's age. They could have been Priest-Apprentices at the same time.

"A curious sight indeed," Denthold said at last. "A Priest-

Apprentice of Vekrin with his arm around a lass of the Freefolk. Foolish lovers, or unlikely allies?"

Amlinn shrugged off Petra's arm. "Why did you attack us?" she demanded.

"Clearly, you intended to attack me," Denthold said. "I acted in self-defence."

"You stole from us. We were coming to reclaim what was ours," Amlinn said. "The sunscales are Arrica's Gift to the Freefolk. For you to use them on that . . . that thing you've built is sacrilege!"

Denthold raised an eyebrow. "Sacrilege? Against Arrica?" His mouth quirked with amusement. "To the Priests of Vekrin, to whose ranks I once belonged, I am already the Heretic. If I am willing to risk the wrath of the God I once vowed to serve, why would I not risk the wrath of a Goddess I did not?"

He tossed his helmet onto one of the chairs and spread his arms wide. "I am indeed guilty of sacrilege, not to mention desecration and blasphemy. More guilty than any man who has ever walked this land. And yet, here I am, alive and well, supremely untroubled by any of the so-called Gods. I have not so much as suffered from a toothache or the sniffles since I built that 'thing,' as you call it, in the courtyard." His smile faded, and his eyes narrowed as he lowered his arms. With his crooked nose and unnerving stare, he reminded Petra of the hawks that often roosted on the roof of Temple Primaxis.

"The Gods have not punished me, because there are no Gods!" the Heretic thundered. "The 'Gods' we worshipped for so long are not Gods at all. Their 'truth' is a lie. And all men should be able to freely use their 'Gifts' of Blue Fire without regard for the wishes of Priests or Wise Women.

That is why I seized this city. I and my followers intend to liberate all of Nevyana from the tyranny of your false and thrice-damned 'Gods.'"

Petra felt the blood drain from his face. Surely Vekrin or Arrica or even Ell would strike down Denthold where he stood!

But nothing happened. There were no peals of thunder, no earthquakes, no lightning from on high. Instead, there was only Denthold's mocking laughter. "I still live, Priest-Apprentice. Proof that Vekrin is uncaring, powerless, or dead. Just like Arrica. Just like Ell."

Amlinn sat motionless as a coiled snake, eyes locked on Denthold. "The Gods do not act in our time," she said softly. "Arrica is only waiting. She has prepared a great fall for you, a fall as great as your heresy."

Denthold chuckled. "Spoken like a true Wise Woman, with all of a Wise Woman's incredible ability to rationalize inconvenient facts. It is a great skill, but one I, alas, do not share." He sat in the chair by the fireplace that Petra had occupied earlier. "Fascinating though theological discussion may be, I am a busy man. So, tell me how a Priest-Apprentice comes to be travelling with the Freefolk." He raised an eyebrow at Petra. "You said you were abducted?"

Petra hesitated.

Denthold's eyes narrowed, and he spoke again, this time in the Temple Tongue. "I command you!" he snapped, using the word used by a High Priest giving sacred, binding instructions to an underling. "Answer, for this mystery is all that keeps me from throwing you to the Nightdwellers. Tell me!"

Petra swallowed. "I will tell you," he said, in the common tongue. "But I will speak so Amlinn can understand." Afraid of what he would see if he looked at Amlinn, he kept his eyes on the Heretic and told him everything that had happened, truthfully and completely. Denthold would surely detect a lie, and while telling the truth might keep them alive, lying would probably get them killed.

It made perfect sense, but it didn't feel very heroic.

"An interesting enough tale, but of little use to me," Denthold said once Petra had finished. "I knew or guessed it all, as you must have surmised since you were so forthcoming. Though you failed to mention that you are not just any Priest-Apprentice, but the son of Pelidor, First Keeper of Temple Primaxis."

Petra's mouth fell open.

"My spies are everywhere," Denthold said with amusement. "Among the king's men, among the Priests, among the Freefolk."

"You lie!" Amlinn whispered.

"Sometimes," Denthold said cheerfully. "But not this time. How do you think you were found?"

"Not one of the Freefolk would ever betray the clan!"

"Yet, one of your precious sunwagons is even now being disassembled by my men, its sunscales and firejars added to my own stores. Yes, one of your Freefolk *would* and *did* betray his clan. For the greater good of Nevyana."

"Then he deserves to die!" Amlinn snarled. "How many of us did you kill when you attacked? When we discover who this traitor is—"

Denthold laughed. "But you won't! You are my prisoners, and my prisoners do not escape."

Amlinn spat a string of insults at Denthold that made Petra stare at her wide-eyed. He didn't even know half of the words, but he could guess what they meant.

Denthold clucked like a city matron shocked by a bawdy song. "The things you Freefolk children learn, dancing naked for drunks. Well, it is a debauched way of life that will soon end." He got to his feet. "As has our conversation. Now you will be put to work. You, Amlinn, will serve in the kitchens. But you, Priest-Apprentice, have been long enough in the service of Vekrin to know much about Blue Fire. You can assist me in the final testing of *Liberator*.

"You will be housed in separate quarters—not to protect your virtue, in the unlikely event it is still intact," he said to Amlinn, making her lips tighten, "but to make it harder for both of you to even consider escaping."

Petra's fury at the insult to Amlinn made him reckless. "*Liberator*? Is that what you call that monstrosity, Heretic? *Enslaver*, more like."

"No," Denthold said quietly. "Whatever you may think of me, Priest-Apprentice, I have never sought personal power. I seek only to free humanity—to liberate it—from the yoke of lies imposed by the so-called Gods and their deluded acolytes." He picked up his helmet and placed it on his head. Its sharply creased silvered nosepiece made him look more hawk-like than ever. "My plans are well-laid and nearing fruition. I will succeed. And by the time you are my age, if you live so long, you will both thank me." He turned on his brightly polished boot heel and went out.

Petra and Amlinn barely had time to glance at each other before the guards strode in and dragged them into the hall-way. They pulled Petra toward the front door. "Be strong!" he yelled to Amlinn, who was being propelled toward the back of the house.

The closing door cut off his words.

20

KNIVES AND TEARS

Amlinn stumbled to the back of the house in the guard's grip. She felt drained, shocked, and horrified. By Petra's willingness to tell Denthold everything. By the news of a spy within the Freefolk. And most of all, by Denthold's casual blasphemy and Arrica's apparent lack of interest.

Petra called after her, but the slamming of the door cut off every word but the first "Be."

"Be" what? "Good?" "Brave?" "Careful?" It didn't matter. It didn't matter what he said or what he thought. Not anymore.

Let him go, she told herself. *He'll serve Denthold well. They speak the same language. They're both Priests. The Priests have been behind this all along.*

Sunscales stolen from Freefolk covered the giant obscenity outside, powered it, and made it possible, but the deadly firelance with which it was armed was a Priestly invention. Denthold held Freefolk in pure contempt. He clearly cared nothing for those who had died at his orders.

He claimed he wanted to liberate people. Amlinn had no doubt that he wanted to liberate Citydwellers from reliance upon Freefolk for trade and for protection in the wilderness. With Arrica's stolen Gifts, Priests could build their own Fences, firelances that could work anywhere, armed and armoured vehicles like Denthold's *Liberator*. City folk would swarm out from behind their walls like locusts, devouring everything, reducing the Freefolk to itinerant harlequins, mere entertainers "dancing naked for drunks," as Denthold had put it.

His scornful words held a core of unpleasant truth even now. The Freefolk had fallen far from the fierce independence Arrica intended, from the days when they traded with Citydwellers only sporadically and carefully and their music and dance were for themselves, not the entertainment of fat city idlers. With his stolen sunscales, Denthold would utterly destroy the Freefolk way of life, killing it just as he had already killed an unknown number of her friends.

And Grandfather? Amlinn swallowed a lump in her throat.

The guard shoved Amlinn through a swinging door into the middle of a black-and-white tiled floor. Heat from a huge iron stove to her right struck her like a blow. Pots bubbled atop it. Shelves to her left held bags of flour, dried spices, jars of preserves. A woman as thin and sharp as a blade turned from butchering a chicken at a long wooden table, a bloody knife still held in one large, knobby hand. Three girls not much older than Amlinn also turned from their tasks, eyes as bright and avid as birds'.

"My name is Kestra," said the woman with the knife. "Can you cook?"

Amlinn looked down at the floor and said nothing. A blow to her left cheek snapped her head to the right. Her ears rang, and she tasted blood. She had bitten her tongue. Raising one hand to her stinging face, she jerked her eyes up to glare at Kestra.

"You will answer when spoken to," Kestra said, and like her knife and her face, her voice was thin and sharp. "You will obey me when I command you. If you do not, I will tell the guards that you are useless in my kitchen, and you will serve instead as a barracks maid. A pretty young girl like you would be very popular there. Do you understand me?"

Amlinn pressed her lips together and nodded.

"Good. Then show me what you can do." Kestra pointed to the cutting table and two piles of vegetables: onions and potatoes. "Lord Denthold is feeding twenty officers tonight. I need the onions diced. Peel and boil the potatoes." She glared at the other three girls. "What are you staring at? Get back to work, the lot of you!"

Amlinn seized a knife. Her knuckles whitened as the cook turned her back. She raised the blade. The guard, eyes narrowed, took a step toward her, his hand on the hilt of his sword.

She turned to the counter and started chopping. Her eyes streamed tears.

It's the onions. It's just the onions.

But she knew that was a lie.

21

THE DOLL

J in set out again the moment the sun slipped below the horizon, and for a second night, he found the Freefolk camp far sooner than he had expected.

It sprawled across a small clearing, really nothing more than a wide spot in the path. The Fence glimmered in place, but the wagons inside it had been pulled up into a haphazard jumble, very different from their usual organization. Worse, large boulders and tall trees stood dangerously close by. Jin's former watchpack would have been over the Fence and inside the camp slaughtering Freefolk in moments. Freefolk were safe enough from watchpacks this far north, but there was no way for them to know that.

What happened to make them so careless?

Jin crept closer. Two wagons were missing, one a sunwagon. There were three—no, four dead horses, being methodically butchered by firelight. And there were five fresh graves.

The Freefolk had been attacked, and on this very spot. They hadn't moved on afterward, which explained the perilous location. But their assailants had not been Nightd-wellers. These attackers had struck by day.

Jin climbed one of the too-close trees and stretched out on an overhanging limb to examine the camp from above. From there, he could see every wagon and watch the Freefolk moving slowly about the camp, some wounded, limping, or bound with bloodstained bandages. The elder of two yellow-clad Wise Women knelt weeping beside one of the graves, and he guessed her companion lay there. But he saw no sign of the Priest-Apprentice or the girl who had been his almost-constant companion. Were they lying beneath two of those piles of freshly turned earth?

He hoped not. If the Priest-Apprentice were dead, Jin's reason for following the Freefolk—to discover why the Priest-Apprentice travelled with them—would end.

He climbed down from the tree and carefully circled the camp, looking for tracks. He found them on the far side—two wagons and at least a dozen horses heading a little west of north. He followed them a short distance to be sure of their direction and then returned to the camp.

An old, grey-bearded man with a broad-brimmed hat sat on the steps of his wagon, head bowed, staring at something in his hands, something he kept twisting this way and that as though hardly aware he was doing it. Through the blue flicker of the Fence, Jin could just make out what it was: a tiny rag doll.

A big man with a bandaged head stood close by the old man, talking in a low voice. Jin crept as close to the deadly blue shimmer of the Fence as he dared and managed to pick out the big man's words.

". . . followed as far as they could, Dainann. The tracks lead north, straight toward City Divpaxis."

"We cannot go there, Witten," the old man—Dainann—said. "We are too few. Fifteen men attacked us. There must be far more in the city." He stood abruptly, squeezing the ragdoll in his right hand so tightly his knuckles whitened. "We head south to Desmixis," he said, voice thick. "If the other clan leaders will not march with us to retrieve our sunscales, they will damn well march with us to retrieve my granddaughter, or I will burn their wagons to the ground!"

He raised the doll, stared into its face for a moment, then tucked it inside his shirt and strode off toward the fires.

Jin didn't tarry. The Priest-Apprentice and the Freefolk girl had been taken north. Clan Therra no longer concerned him.

He returned to the tracks leading into the forest, turned his back on the Freefolk camp, and loped into the night.

22

BLUE FIRE AND BLACK RAGE

A week after he and Amlinn arrived in Divpaxis, Petra crouched behind Denthold in the low tunnel that ran fore and aft, between ranks of firejars, through the belly of the giant war-wagon the Heretic had named *Liberator*. Holding a lightwand between his teeth, Denthold was using a fine brush to paint a silver sigil on the strange box of gears and cables that drove the rear axle of the giant six-wheeled wagon. Petra couldn't clearly see his handiwork, though: his only clear view of Denthold at the moment was of the man's fine-clad buttocks.

Petra had not seen Amlinn since they'd been separated. He spent every minute he was not with Denthold locked in a cell in the old city guard barracks. He knew Amlinn was working in the kitchen of the Duke's old house. He fantasized about breaking out of his cell, finding where she slept, a whispered conversation in the dark, making plans, a daring escape. Unfortunately, his prison cell seemed a lot more secure than those so easily escaped by adventure-tale heroes.

During the day, Denthold kept Petra constantly at hand as

he worked on *Liberator*. Now the Heretic grunted with satisfaction, wiped his brush, capped the pot of silver paint, and backed up on his hands and knees, forcing Petra to squeeze to one side to make way for him. Denthold took the lightwand from his mouth and flashed it on the gearbox. Blue light glinted from the convoluted, twisting sigil he had just completed. Petra stared at it in confusion. It looked like nothing he had ever seen. "Is that a Freefolk sigil?"

Denthold laughed. "Of course not. It is one of my own devising. It directs the Blue Fire to drive *Liberator*'s wheels, allowing it to move on its own with no need of horses. Now, hand me that . . ."

But Petra hardly heard him through the roaring in his ears. His vision darkened. If he hadn't been sitting, he would have fallen. "That's . . . that's impossible! Only the Gods can create sigils!"

"Superstitious nonsense," Denthold snapped. "The sigils simply channel the Blue Fire flowing out of the Godstones, sunscales, or firejars. They catch it, collect it, and direct its use. This sigil," he pointed at it, "directs Blue Fire in here," he leaned forward and patted the strange mechanism, "where it spins a flywheel whose motion is transmitted through a series of metal gears and turns the wheels. In the firelances, the sigil concentrates Blue Fire and pours it out through the weapon's tip. In a sparkglobe, the sigil collects, concentrates, and stabilizes Blue Fire, so that it can illuminate its surroundings. Draw the right sigil, and you can make Blue Fire do almost anything." He frowned. "And if the idiot Priests who held the Temple here had simply let me have the *Book of Vekrin* instead of setting fire to the Inner Sanctum and burning themselves alive, I would have—"

"That's a lie!" Petra cried. "You murdered them because

they would not cooperate with you, because they upheld their vows! Those men were martyrs!"

Denthold sighed. "I murdered no one. Although I admit I sent that story south with my agents among the refugees. The legend of my brutality has proved very useful in discouraging annoying expeditions to Divpaxis."

"You can't deny people died when you seized the city. The refugees said—"

"Of course, there were deaths during the fighting," Denthold said. "You cannot seize a city without violence. But I had no reason or desire to harm the Priests. They chose to kill themselves and destroy the Temple rather than let me have the *Book of Vekrin*. They wanted to deny me the power of the Godstone. They martyred themselves. Heroic, I suppose, but also foolish and futile."

"Futile?" Petra couldn't believe what he was hearing. "Foolish? They disabled the Godstone so you could not use it. They kept you from—"

Denthold laughed. "Is that what you were told? I already knew how to reactivate the Godstone, how to draw Blue Fire from it, and the making of many sigils. I sent agents south, some of them renegade Priests, to obtain what else I needed."

Petra gaped at him. Renegade Priests? Followers of the Heretic inside the Temples of the south? He gathered his wits. "Well, they weren't very good at it," he snapped. "The Blue Fire of the Freefolk killed the thief who robbed the Temple in Pentaxis when he attempted to break into their camp. I saw the charred book he carried and a portion of a note with your name on it. That's how I knew you were behind all this. And Clan Therra knows it too. Your secret is already out. Soon—"

"Soon, I will be ready to move south with *Liberator*. What do I care about what anyone knows?" Denthold said.

"This wagon isn't enough to take the whole kingdom."

"Don't worry," Denthold said. "I have the resources I need." He frowned. "Although I admit the failed theft in Pentaxis, and the theft in Primaxis that landed me with you and the Freefolk girl, were unanticipated. In truth, I had a firelance in short order, a sunscale soon thereafter, a firejar almost immediately. My agent in Pentaxis had been out of communication for some time and did not know that I no longer needed a sunscale, or even a *Book of Vekrin*. It was harder to obtain than the other items, but even that, I've had for a year." He shrugged. "Turned out, I'd already moved far beyond anything it could teach me."

"Moved beyond? How can you move beyond perfection?" Petra cried. "And if all that is true, why did another of your agents break into Temple Primaxis, and rob Clan Therra of a sunscale, just a few days ago?"

"Because he was no thief of mine." Denthold shook his head. "Stadnik. That was his name. Ever heard of him?"

Petra shook his head.

Denthold grunted. "Well, the city guard knew it and cursed it from Primaxis to Viandaxis. He'd robbed dozens of the wealthy, even a couple of dukes, but no city guard could never catch him; he used his ill-gotten gains freely to ingratiate himself with the poor, and they helped hide and protect him.

"Six months ago, he robbed and murdered my agent in Ceturxis, and once again evaded the city guard, fleeing to Primaxis. He must have found my orders among my agent's possessions, found someone to decipher them, and discovered an opportunity. He probably thought I would reward him for bringing me a stolen sunscale and firelance. But I no longer had need of them, and even if I had, I would never have sent an agent to break into the Temple in City Primaxis within sight of the king's Palace. For multiple reasons."

"If this Stadnik was such a great thief, how do you know all that?" Petra said.

Denthold snorted. "Because he came to me to negotiate the sale of the items he'd stolen. Instead, I questioned him to learn who he was and why he had endangered my plans, and then I had him executed. With the very firelance he'd stolen."

Petra shivered. Stadnik had gotten only what he deserved, but Denthold's off-hand account of his brutality shook him, as did the realization that the theft of Clan Therra's sunscale and Temple Primaxis's firelance had been unintended and unnecessary.

I should still be at home trying not to throttle Cort, Petra thought, *not sitting in this sacrilegious monstrosity of a wagon with the bloody Heretic!*

Denthold pointed the lightwand again at the complex sigil on the gearbox. "This is the birthright that has been kept from us by the Priests and Wise Women. I can do things with Blue Fire none of them can match. Blue Fire can be and should be used for far more than it has been all these centuries. Obedience to the 'Gods' is a mental prison. I intend to free all Nevyanans from it." He twisted his body around and crawled toward the front of the wagon. "And now it's time to prove I can do it. Follow me."

Petra crawled after him, head spinning. His father, the entire council of Elders . . . they would have sworn to Petra— they *had* sworn to Petra and all the other Priest-Apprentices —that to alter one of the magical sigils that channelled Blue

Fire was to invite certain, sudden, and complete destruction from Vekrin himself.

Yet here was Denthold, singularly undestroyed.

Denthold disappeared up a ladder at the forward end of the tunnel. Petra climbed after him. As his head emerged through the trap door at its top, Denthold held out a hand and helped him scramble the rest of the way into the rectangular cockpit, ten feet above the ground, from which the wagon and its weapon were controlled. A wheel like the wheel of a river ship dominated the space. To its left were two levers. One was a brake lever, just as there might be on an ordinary wagon. The second was something Denthold called a "throttle," to control the flow of Blue Fire to the gearbox on which he had just painted that outlandish sigil. To the right of the wheel were two smaller wheels with protruding handles that allowed them to be turned more easily. The larger of the two controlled the raising and lowering and rotating of the giant firelance above their heads. The smaller red-handled lever served as the weapon's trigger.

Denthold kicked shut the trapdoor and moved to the left. Petra stepped to the right. Though a bench ran the width of the cockpit, Denthold remained standing, so Petra did too.

While they had finished up in the wagon, Denthold's men had cleared the boulevard. It now stretched empty all the way to the city's inner gate, cobblestones glistening from an early morning shower. About a hundred yards down the boulevard stood a rough wooden tower, two stories tall, made of unpeeled logs.

"Ready?" Denthold asked Petra.

Petra swallowed. He'd been told what would be expected of him this morning, but to his surprise, his hand shook as he reached out to grasp the red lever. "Ready," he said.

Denthold leaned forward, fierce blue eyes locked on the target in the middle of the boulevard. He looked more hawk-like than ever. "Fire!"

Petra pulled the lever.

A searing flash of light made him cry out and throw his arm over his eyes. The loudest crack of thunder he'd ever heard shook the wagon and his very bones. Ears ringing, he jerked his arm down to see smouldering chunks of wood raining down on the boulevard and the buildings all around it. Nothing remained of the tower but a few shattered, blackened logs, a vast circle of glowing flinders, and a rising cloud of blue-grey smoke.

A strange, sharp scent pricked Petra's nostrils: the smell of air burned by Blue Fire.

After a long moment of eerie silence, cheering erupted from the side streets. Men with buckets of sand and water flooded back into the boulevard, shouting with excitement as they doused the burning bits of wood.

Denthold turned to Petra, his face alight in a fierce grin. He clapped Petra on the shoulder. "It works!" he shouted.

"Very impressive," said a voice from the ground.

Denthold and Petra both turned, Denthold so quickly that his elbow slammed painfully into Petra's side. Petra rubbed the place while he stared down from the cockpit at the newcomer. Though mud-splattered, the man's attire spoke of wealth and power. A red surcoat, worn over silver-plated chainmail and belted with black leather, bore the royal crown in gold. A red cape trimmed with white fur, shining calf-high boots, and a sword whose hilt and scabbard glittered with jewels completed the outfit. Intense green eyes watched Denthold and Petra from a thin, sun-browned face framed by long blond hair and a thick blond beard and moustache.

To Petra's astonishment, Denthold bowed his head to the newcomer. "Lord Axel! I did not know you had arrived."

Petra's stomach dropped as his and Dainann's suspicions were suddenly confirmed. *Lord Axel. King Stobor's fraternal twin!*

"I gave orders not to disturb you until the test was completed," Lord Axel replied. "Congratulations on its success."

Denthold inclined his head again. "Thank you, Your Highness. We are making good progress. We will soon be able to conduct the mobility trials. The second machine should come together much more quickly. Next year, when we—"

Lord Axel shook his head. "Not next year, Denthold. This year. We march south within the month."

Denthold stared at Axel. For the first time since he had met the Heretic, Petra saw him at a loss for words.

Axel stared back, expressionless.

When Denthold spoke at last, his voice was tight. "Your Highness, firelance construction is slow and difficult. We have only fifty, and we will not have the materials needed to make more for at least a month, probably longer. Surely we can delay until—"

Axel flicked his hand as though shooing an insect. "Fifty firelances is sufficient as long as we have *Liberator*." He turned to look at the smoking wreckage of the wooden tower. "As long as we can do *that*."

"But I've only begun testing it," Denthold protested to Axel's back. "The motivators for the turret and the wheels still draw a great deal more Blue Fire than I would like. I don't know how far we can travel each day and keep the weapon ready for use. I also suspect we will either have to push the wagon up any hills or find a way to hitch horses to it. With respect, Your Highness, if we maintain our original schedule, we can build at least one, and possibly two, more of these war-wagons, *and* double our stock of firelances. As well, by spring, I believe I will be able to build even better sunscales, which can—"

Axel turned sharply to face Denthold again, like a master bringing his dog to heel. His eyes glittered in the morning light as they locked on Denthold's face. He hadn't so much as glanced at Petra.

"Master Denthold," he said, "whatever your rationalizations are for your work, never forget that you are ultimately my servant, and my only concern is the throne. I have lived my entire life knowing that but for the corruption of a foolish midwife, I would be king and not my brother." He made the last word sound like a curse. "I have lived my entire life working toward the day when I would rectify that injustice. As a youth, I heard of your heretical musings and recognized the opportunity you offered. Never forget that it was *I* who sent spies to contact you, *I* who ordered Duke Felkor to help you, *I* who gave you the support you needed to seize this city, *I* who helped spread the lies about the city being completely destroyed and abandoned, *I* who provided men to ensure no one who ventured this way returned south to reveal the truth, *I* who paid the cost of armed parties to fend off Night-dwellers when you required something smuggled from the south, *I* who recruited the thieves and spies who stole the secrets you needed from the Priests and the Freefolk, and *I* who created the 'Unbound' as a false front for the build-up of our forces here!"

With each repetition of the word "I," Axel's voice rose, and Denthold's hands, which the Prince could not see from where he stood but Petra could, clenched tighter and tighter.

Axel took a deep breath and lowered his voice, though he sounded no less dangerous. "My patience has been immense. I have waited for the people to forget about Divpaxis, for the guards in city after city to dwindle and sink back into torpor as the fear of revolution receded. For more than twenty years, I have kept your work secret." His eyes unfocused slightly, as though he were no longer talking to Denthold, but to someone else—himself, perhaps. "But it is secret no longer. I had a traitor, a bloody traitor, among my men. My brother knows I intend to seize the throne. Fortunately, he does not know how. If I hadn't been warned and fled with as many of my men as I could gather, I would be awaiting execution. But the guards didn't find me when they burst into my room before dawn. The found their informant. What was left of him."

His right fist clenched and lifted. He looked down at it for a moment, then opened it, took a deep breath, and let it fall to his side. His eyes focused on Denthold again. "You claim you wish to liberate the people from the Priests and Wise Women and the fear of the Nightdwellers. The only way to do that is to place me on the throne. As king, I can overthrow the influence of the Gods-botherers."

Petra felt sick. This man, the brother of the king, wanted to destroy everything his father believed in. Everything *he* had been taught to believe.

Petra looked up at the sky, blue and cloudless now that the morning's rainclouds had blown away. *And still, Vekrin does nothing?*

Denthold breathed heavily through his nose, his jaw clenched tight.

"As for the Nightdwellers . . ." Lord Axel ran his gaze over the towering wagon before him. "With this and with firelances, I can exterminate the Nightdwellers wherever they dwell, however they try to hide. Nevyana will thrive, and at last, we will be able to move out of this one valley, this prison of the Gods, to exploit all the riches of the lands, beyond the mountains and down to the sea." His cold green eyes locked on Denthold again. "But we must act. As we speak, my brother is arresting and questioning anyone he suspects of being disloyal to him—anyone loyal to me. The Priests of Temple Primaxis will soon realize, if they have not already, that everything points to City Divpaxis—to the Heretic. If we wait until spring, we will find ourselves fighting in a place and time of my brother's choosing, with guards from every city, the firelances of the Priests, and perhaps even the Freefolk Clans arrayed against us.

"And so, we do *not* wait. We move *now*."

Stiff as a Temple Curtain sigil-post, fists still clenched, Denthold radiated fury like a furnace. But his voice, when he spoke, remained icily polite. "Your Highness," he said. "Again, with respect, I must point out that without proper tests, I cannot guarantee that *Liberator* will perform as hoped. If unforeseen difficulties arise—"

"It is your job, Master Denthold," said Lord Axel, his voice soft but with a core of steel, like a dagger in a velvet sheath, "to foresee 'difficulties' and ensure they do *not* arise. For if *Liberator* fails me, or the firelances you have made fail me—if, in other words, *you* fail me—the throne will remain my brother's. The secrets of Blue Fire will once more be known only to the Priests of Vekrin and Wise Women of Arrica, your life's work will have been for naught, and Nevyana will continue to wither and decline. But neither you nor those loyal to you will see any of that." He glanced at Petra for the first time, and the shock of that gaze struck

Petra like the bolt of Blue Fire that had taken him down outside the Temple Curtain. "For in the hour you fail me, you and all those who follow you will die." His unsettling eyes returned to Denthold. "Do you understand me, Heretic?"

Petra felt as if the very air of the cockpit trembled with Denthold's barely leashed rage, but his voice, though half-choked, remained level. "Of course, Your Highness."

"Good." Axel smiled. There was no warmth in it. He turned toward the shattered target once more. "Congratulations once more on the success of your test! We should celebrate." He glanced at Denthold again, one eyebrow raised.

Denthold cleared his throat. "Please, Your Highness, come to my house. I have an excellent cook, and I have barely touched Duke Felkor's extraordinary wine cellar. Shall we say an hour after sunset?"

"You're too kind. I accept. Until then." Lord Axel spun and strode off, boot heels clicking on the cobblestones.

Denthold turned sharply and stared down the boulevard, as though he could see beyond the gate to the cities of Nevyana strung like eleven pearls on a necklace, waiting to be plucked one by one by *Liberator*.

Then his attention snapped toward Petra. "Stop your gawking," he snarled. "Examine the firejars. See that none of the sigils burned out. Fine fools we'll look if we point *Liberator*'s firelance at a city gate and nothing happens."

"Yes, sir." Petra reached down, opened the trapdoor, and clambered down into the wagon's belly once more. Taking a lightwand from his belt, he bent to examine the first of the firejars, his head still whirling with what he had just learned.

Lord Axel, King Stobor's brother, had been behind everything—the destruction of Divpaxis, the harrying of the villagers, the thefts. It was all a play for power on a massive scale, a breathtaking attempt to remake the kingdom and eliminate the influence of the Priests of Vekrin and Wise Women of Arrica, of the Gods themselves.

More than twenty years had passed since Axel had sacked Divpaxis with Denthold's help. His plans obviously ran deep. Denthold might be known as the Heretic among the Priests of Vekrin, but clearly, Axel was the greatest heretic of them all.

Yet there he had stood beneath the open sky, hale and hearty, ready to march against his brother the king. Ready to overthrow the Priests of Vekrin and the Wise Women of Arrica, and then to turn Blue Fire against the Nightdwellers, the children of Ell, in blatant defiance of all three Gods.

And the Gods had done nothing about it.

For twenty years.

Do they really *care what we do?* whispered a voice inside him, a voice that had been growing louder day by day since he had come to Divpaxis. *Have they* ever *cared?*

Are they even there?

As always, he had no answer.

23

A VALUABLE HOSTAGE

Amlinn chopped six carrots at once into round pieces, scooped the bits into the waiting pot, and reached for another bunch. She welcomed the mindless, repetitive action. It took her mind off everything that had happened to the Freefolk, might have happened to her grandfather, and could be happening in the kingdom.

In the month she'd been trapped in this culinary prison, only rumours of events in the city had reached her. A week ago, lightning had flashed and thunder cracked out of a clear blue sky, startling her into dropping an egg. That had earned her a cuff on the ear from Kestra. Later, the other kitchen maids spoke in awed whispers about the successful test of Denthold's mighty weapon. That evening, they had to prepare a special feast, and she learned from the gossiping servers that Lord Axel, the king's brother, had arrived. As the maids prattled on about the dozens of new men in town and Axel's red-clad army joining forces with Denthold's, the depth of Lord Axel's treachery became clear to her. Every new outrage heated the anger deep within her. It simmered away like a pot on the stove, a stew of fury and sorrow and despair and confusion that made it hard to sleep and hard to think.

She'd looked for the opportunity to escape. The other scullery maids, who called her "Freefolk whore" and worse when they weren't simply shunning her, were free to leave at the end of the day. She was escorted to a locked room in the basement by an armed guard. She ate there alone and returned to the kitchen in the morning. She would not despair—not she, granddaughter of Dainann, leader of the Freefolk Clan Therra—but every day in captivity ate at her spirit like a cancer.

She finished yet another bunch of carrots, reached for more, and then froze, belatedly realizing someone had spoken to her. She turned from the table and discovered Denthold standing behind her in the doorway, one eyebrow raised as he awaited her response.

"What did you say?" she asked, then flushed, ashamed of how foolish she sounded.

"I said, put down your knife, Amlinn," Denthold replied.

She gripped it harder. "Why?"

"Partly so you're not tempted to stab me," he said dryly. "But also, because your work here is done. We head south in three days, and you're coming with us."

She scowled. "Why?"

"Because I say so." Denthold's gaze flicked pointedly to her knife. She realized she now held it like a weapon, not a kitchen tool. She forced herself to lay it on the table next to the half-chopped carrots.

She hadn't seen the Mad Priest or Petra since the day she

and Petra had been taken prisoner. She assumed she'd been forgotten and would likely still be chopping carrots when City Primaxis fell to *Liberator*.

Apparently not. But what was Denthold up to?

"I know nothing of Blue Fire. What do you want with me?"

"You could prove helpful, should we need to negotiate with the Freefolk."

"As a hostage, you mean."

He inclined his head. "Of course."

"And Petra?"

"Petra has been helpful in preparing *Liberator*," Denthold said. "For that reason alone, I would take him with us. But he is also the son of First Keeper Pelidor of Temple Primaxis and therefore potentially even more valuable as a hostage than you."

Amlinn glanced over her shoulder to where the sharp-faced cook and her scullery-maid tormentors stood tucked in a corner, hands folded, heads down, clearly afraid to look Denthold in the face. She smiled. She turned her back on the other women. She removed her apron, folded it neatly, and placed it on the table next to the carrots. Then she very pointedly *did* look Denthold in the face. "So, what happens now?"

"You keep working," the Heretic said. "But now you work to help us prepare for the march." He stepped to the side, and one of his green-liveried soldiers appeared in the doorway. "Escort her to the cookwagons."

"Yes, sir." The soldier turned sideways and gestured for Amlinn to step into the hallway. Holding her head high, she slipped past Denthold and, a moment later, stood in the bright light of day for the first time in a month.

The main boulevard, busy enough when they first arrived, now put Primaxis itself to shame. It teemed with soldiers. As many or more now wore Lord Axel's red as Denthold's green. Heavily laden wagons trundled through the crowds, drivers cursing at their horses and the pedestrians in their path. *Liberator* still stood in the Temple courtyard to Amlinn's left, guarded by a dozen men, half in green, half in red. Late-afternoon sunshine reflected off its glistening sunscales and sparkled brilliantly within the glass ball at the tip of the giant firelance.

Amlinn hated the very look of that bloated, cancerous offspring of the stolen Gifts of Vekrin and Arrica. She hated the threat it represented to her people, to the Citydwellers, to everyone in Nevyana. She hated everything about it, and now, it appeared, she would be forced to accompany it south.

Maybe I'll get a chance to sabotage it.

She turned her back on *Liberator* as the guard led her toward the city gate. About halfway there, they left the boulevard and turned left down a broad, cobblestoned side street. Though at first glance the buildings looked intact, a closer look showed Amlinn streaks of soot above empty windows. Gaping holes in many of the roofs revealed blackened timbers, bearing mute witness to the fires that had gutted the structures.

The street ended in a large square, also paved with cobblestones. Long, low wooden barracks lined each side. Through a thick hedge of bushes and small trees along the square's far border, she caught the glimmer of water. The Great River flowed well to the west of Divpaxis, she recalled, so this must be some other stream.

Wagons and men and a very few women filled the square. In the centre stood six cookwagons, drawn up close together and surrounded by tables and benches. Amlinn's guard delivered her into the charge of a fat, sweaty man with a dirty white apron, who promptly set her to peeling potatoes. Watching him scrape maggots off a piece of meat before throwing it into the stew pot almost made her miss her sharp-tongued mistress from the kitchen—almost, but not quite.

She passed the next couple of hours doing the same kind of work she had done for a month, with the guard watching her the entire time from one of the dining tables. After the evening meal had been served and she'd eaten her own supper of bread and cheese—she wasn't going anywhere near the stew—her guard, lightwand in hand, guided her to one of the latrine buildings. Then they wove through the maze of wagons to a roofed one similar to those of the Freefolk but far smaller, not much longer than the fold-up bunk that hung on one wall. A tiny table that also folded up against the wall hung at one end. There was nothing else.

She heard the guard lock the door from the outside. He had not offered her his lightwand or even a candle, so she felt her way to the bed and lay down in darkness, alone with her thoughts.

Soon they would march south beyond the wall onto the King's Way and through the forest. Again, she wondered what Grandfather would be doing, if he still lived.

He lives. He has to!

Grandfather would never rest until he found Amlinn, but what could he do to free her from this army and its monstrous, lightning-hurling weapon?

The bitter answer was clear. Nothing. He could do *nothing*. Nor could anyone else. Only with the help of the

Gods themselves could the kingdom hope to stand against Denthold, and the Gods, it seemed, were not interested.

Tears started in Amlinn's eyes, and for the first time since she was a little girl, she cried herself to sleep.

24

A CHANGE OF PLANS

For two weeks, Jin lurked outside City Divpaxis, sleeping in his shelter during the day, watching and listening at night. The ancient forest surrounding the city boasted giant trees, large enough to provide a view even over the high city walls. From their towering branches, he watched one night as a flare of blue flame exploded from a long staff held by one of the green-clad soldiers loyal to the man he'd learned was Denthold. Another flare followed, then another. Their brilliance stabbed his Nightdweller eyes like daggers.

He knew at once what it meant. At least some of the soldiers within the city were armed with firelances, the Blue Fire weapons thought to belong only to Priests.

From his treetop vantage point, Jin also kept an eye on the strange vehicle in the courtyard of the ruined Temple. Roofed with sunscales like a sunwagon but far larger than any Freefolk wagon he had ever seen, it loomed like a thundercloud at the far end of the main boulevard from the city gate. A long, thin rod with a glass ball at the end protruded from a turret atop the wagon. He didn't know what it was.

Sparkglobes hung from each corner of the wagon, but that first night, they remained dark. On the second night, while he stared straight at the strange vehicle, those globes suddenly blazed so brightly that he cried out and almost fell off his branch. For several seconds, he could see nothing, and even as his vision returned, purple spots lingered in it for several more minutes. Every night after that, the sparkglobes switched on at dusk, turning the wagon into a miniature sun he could not bear to so much as glance at.

Then one morning, with echoes of a monstrous thunderclap ringing in his ears, Jin scrambled quivering to his feet straight from sleep to heart-pounding alertness. It had been raining lightly as he retired, but a gentle, windless drizzle. He would have sensed any storm powerful enough to produce such an enormous lightning strike hours before it arrived, and there had been nothing. He reached out and touched the black canvas of the shadowshelter. From its warmth, he knew the sun shone. Yet, what but a thunderstorm could have made that sound?

Then, drifting on the breeze from the direction of City Divpaxis, he smelled woodsmoke and the unmistakable, acrid smell of air seared by Blue Fire. Puzzled, he lay down again but slept fitfully. That night, intent on finding out what had happened in the morning, he climbed his favourite tree and peered into the city while light still lingered in the west.

The population seemed to have doubled during the day. More men than ever moved through the streets and crowded around the cookwagons in the centre of the parade ground. Far more horses now grazed in the paddocks. But the new arrivals wore red uniforms instead of green.

Now sorely puzzled indeed, Jin decided to do something he'd never risked before. In a moment when he judged no one on the wall was looking his way, he dashed across the cleared space immediately surrounding the city and pressed himself, panting, tight against the massive stone blocks of the city wall. In its protective shadow, he circled Divpaxis, straining to hear the conversations of the bored guards patrolling the battlements.

Mostly, of course, he heard trivial gossip and coarse jokes. But he also learned at last that the strange rod on the giant wagon was a giant firelance, and it had fired that morning for the first time, blasting a two-story wooden tower to kindling.

As he continued to circle and eavesdrop, he learned much more. That morning had also seen the arrival of Lord Axel, brother of King Stobor, with a sizable force. Axel intended "at long last" to overthrow his brother and seize the throne with the might of the firelances, small and large, that Denthold had constructed.

As he was about to slip back into the forest and to his shadowshelter, with pre-dawn light glimmering in the east, Jin heard something else.

"Axel will have the cities, and that's all well and good," said one guard to another as they leaned on the battlements above Jin's head and stared idly out at the surrounding forest. "But I'll tell you what I want to see Blue Fire used for—to burn those stinking Nightdwellers out of their hidey-holes in the forest once and for all."

"You and me both," the other man agreed. "You know my motto—never volunteer—but that's one mission I'd be the first to step forward for." He hawked and spat, the spittle flying into the air and landing on the grass not a dozen feet from where Jin crouched. "Bloody savages killed a buddy of mine down by Nonixis. I'd like to see them all burn."

Shaking with rage, Jin waited until the men moved on, then dashed across the clearing and back among the trees. He lay in his shadowshelter through the day, mind churning, dozing only fitfully. The Gifts of Ell offered no protection from the power Denthold had assembled in City Divpaxis. With Blue Fire fully unleashed, the Daydwellers would fear nothing in the night. Even the warning and warding magic of the watchstones might not keep Nightdweller warrens hidden.

He could see only one solution. The Nightdwellers had to strike first. They had to destroy the Daydwellers' giant weapon and scatter their army of firelance-armed warriors.

The mystery of the Priest-Apprentice travelling with Freefolk no longer concerned Jin, not with the survival of his race at stake. And so, the moment the sun set that evening, he tore down his shelter, packed it away, turned his back on City Divpaxis, and headed for the Great Warren, four nights away by his map.

Flitting through the moon-dappled trees like a ghost, he ran to save his people.

❧ 25 ☙

REUNION

A serving girl banged a plate of food on the breakfast table rather harder than usual. Petra glanced up, surprised, and with a shock like a spark of Blue Fire, his eyes met Amlinn's. They stared at each other for a moment, and then Amlinn, expressionless, turned and went back to the nearest cookwagon.

Petra looked at the surrounding tables. His increasingly lackadaisical guard was currently engaged in conversation with another of the serving girls, one considerably older and more buxom than Amlinn. Petra picked up his mug and casually walked over to the cookwagon as though to refill it with the hot, bitter tea favoured by the soldiers, though in fact, he could barely stomach the stuff.

Amlinn stood by the open side of the cookwagon, apparently waiting for more food to serve. Gathering his courage, Petra stepped close behind her. "Hello," he said.

She stiffened, and then slowly turned. "Petra," she said, voice and face equally unreadable.

"I thought you still worked in the kitchen at Denthold's mansion," he said.

"Apparently, Denthold thinks I have some value as a hostage. I'm coming south with you." She folded her arms. "Are you still helping him build that obscenity?"

Petra flushed. "It's not an obscenity. It's not like I thought. It's a marvel, an incredible work of—"

"Sacrilege?" Amlinn interrupted him. "Desecration?"

"It's—" Petra bit off his hot retort. This was not the way he wanted the conversation to go. "Never mind. Are you all right?"

"Fine," Amlinn said. "Just wonderful. Food, water, a place to sleep, a chamber pot, and a front-row seat as an army marches south to seize the kingdom in blatant defiance of the Gods."

"There's nothing we can do," Petra said.

Amlinn looked around, and Petra followed her gaze. No one seemed to be taking any notice of them. Inside the wagon, oaths mingled with smoke as the cook berated his assistant for burning the toast.

Amlinn stepped closer to Petra.

Her nearness made his heart beat faster.

"We could escape," she whispered. "All this confusion. There must be sortie gates in the wall, like the east gate in Primaxis. They're unlikely to be watched, just locked. You have access to tools. We could break out—"

"I see you've discovered your little Freefolk friend," Denthold's voice interrupted. Petra spun to see the Heretic at the corner of the wagon.

"Why didn't you tell me she's coming with us?" Petra demanded.

"Why should I? You're both my prisoners." Denthold took a rag from his belt and wiped grease from his hands. "The steering is fixed. But I want you to test all the cables again."

Petra ignored that. "Amlinn says she's a hostage. Is that true?"

"Of course, it's true. As I told her, she could be valuable when the time comes to deal with the Freefolk." He shrugged. "I have no quarrel with them, but they may have one with me. Perhaps with her in hand, I can persuade them not to do anything foolish."

Amlinn pointed at Petra. "And have you told him he's a hostage, too? Or do you think of him more like a pet?"

Stung, Petra shot her an angry look, but Denthold just laughed. "I haven't told him, but unless he's an idiot, he must know that the son of the First Keeper of Temple Primaxis is a very valuable hostage indeed."

Petra, feeling very much like an idiot, gaped at the Heretic.

Denthold sighed. "Lad, when we roll up to City Primaxis, the fact you're my prisoner may spell the difference between a peaceful surrender and a bloodbath. And remember, most of the blood spilled would belong to the Priests and Liberators." His expression hardened. "Now. You've met. You've assured each other you're both all right. Have you hugged? Kissed?"

Petra carefully avoided Amlinn's gaze, but he wondered if she were blushing as hard as he was.

"No?" Denthold said. "Oh, I guess misread the situation." His voice hardened to match his face. "Very sweet, very touching, but that's an end to it. You will not speak to each other again." He pointed to Petra. "You will come with me back to *Liberator*. You," he pointed at Amlinn, "back to work." His gaze flicked to the cookwagon as a platter appeared on the serving shelf. "Your bacon is ready."

Without a word, Amlinn turned, grabbed the steaming platter of burnt-to-a-crisp bacon, and strode off toward the tables.

"Come on, boy." Denthold led Petra toward the street that linked to the main boulevard. They walked in silence for a few moments. Then Denthold said, "I heard you tell the girl *Liberator* is a 'marvel.'"

Petra said nothing.

"You know I'm right, don't you?" Denthold said softly. "*Liberator* is proof that the Gods are gone forever, that everything the Priests and Wise Women teach is a lie."

Petra kept walking, deliberating. When they'd arrived in Divpaxis a month ago, he would never have dared share his thoughts with the Heretic. But he and Denthold had spent a lot of time working together in the weeks since then, and Denthold—Vekrin help him—had impressed him. More deeply than his tutors in Temple Primaxis, truth be told. Denthold answered every question Petra asked about Vekrin and Blue Fire, admitting frankly when he did not know something. He'd also told Petra much about how Blue Fire worked and was controlled, information Petra did not believe even the senior Priests knew—or would have permitted Petra to know if they did.

The more Petra learned about Blue Fire, the more he suspected that, though it might have been a gift from the Gods, the Gods had not invented it. The magical energy of Blue Fire had always been present, in the earth, in the sun, in the air. The truth was, power filled the world, power that could be used by anyone—provided they had the right knowledge and the right tools.

With a strange sense of sorrow, as though someone close to him had died, Petra knew he could never again hold the unquestioning belief in Vekrin that his father and tutors had tried so hard to instill. Even if he were magically transported to City Primaxis in an instant, he could not return to his life as Priest-Apprentice. Temple Primaxis, so large he had once thought it all he needed or could ever need, now seemed as cramped as Wettin's wagon. The whole valley of Nevyana was little better. An entire world lay beyond its mountainous borders, and Denthold wanted to free anyone who wished to explore it.

"All right," Petra said at last. "I admit I'm beginning to see some truth in what you say. I know Nevyana can't go on like it has, with people trapped in the cities every night and the Nightdwellers always lurking, ready to pounce. We're dwindling. City Primaxis has almost as many empty buildings as City Divpaxis, and it's supposed to be the greatest city in the kingdom. Another plague could finish us. We have to get out of the cities, build new settlements, expand. Things need to change. But here's what I don't see." He looked around. They were alone. There was no one coming up the road behind them, no one turning down the road from the boulevard. He stopped.

Denthold carried on another step, then turned to look at him.

Petra stared into Denthold's eyes and hoped he wasn't about to get himself hauled off to prison or worse. "You claim to want to free people from the tyranny of the Priests and Wise Ones. And yet you are working to put Lord Axel on the throne, with Blue Fire in his hands. How can you do that when you know, you *must* know, that you're just replacing one form of tyranny with another?"

Denthold looked around. They were still alone. Then he stepped toward Petra and murmured so softly that Petra could hardly hear him, "Because I will betray Lord Axel at the first opportunity."

Petra blinked.

"He thinks that somehow, when this is all done, he will control Blue Fire instead of the Priests and Wise Women. But he will control nothing. Many of the 'refugees' who fled south from Divpaxis were not refugees at all. They were my followers. As we drive south, I will contact them wherever and whenever I can, passing along the knowledge I have amassed regarding the use of Blue Fire. By the time Axel actually ascends the throne, that knowledge will be so widespread he can never stamp it out. My followers will arm themselves with firelances and sunscales and Fences and more. They will move out into the wilderness, hunting down and exterminating Nightdwellers, exploring, establishing farms, digging mines, starting new villages—villages that will owe no loyalty to Lord Axel."

Petra stared at him. "You're talking civil war!"

Denthold laughed. "There will be no war."

"But Lord Axel—"

"Axel trusts me too much. The fifty firelances in his soldiers' hands will work perfectly until we get to City Primaxis and for some time thereafter, but I can disable them at will."

"He'll make new firelances."

"Not with my help," Denthold said. "And he does not have the knowledge himself."

"The Priests—"

"The Priests' firelances can only draw on the Godstones.

He may use them to hold the cities, but in the wilderness and villages, they will be useless."

"And *Liberator*?" Petra said.

"It is my intention to liberate *Liberator* from Axel's service, along with myself," Denthold said. "And failing that, it, too, can be easily disabled."

Petra stood in stunned silence, contemplating Denthold's vision. "There will still be bloodshed," he said at last. "Maybe a lot of it."

Denthold inclined his head in agreement. "Perhaps. I hope not. But if there is, well, sometimes fires burn vast swathes of forest. But the forest that grows back afterward is greener and healthier. Likewise, the society that will grow back after the Priests, the Wise Women, the Nightdwellers, and Lord Axel and his ilk are pruned away will also be greener and healthier. The suffering I may inflict on Nevyana is small indeed compared to the suffering this kingdom has already endured and will endure in the future if nothing changes."

Petra glanced back toward the parade ground. A dozen soldiers were headed their way. Denthold followed his gaze and then turned toward the boulevard. "Back to work."

Throughout that day, as he and Denthold checked and rechecked every mechanism and sigil in *Liberator*, and then in his wagon that night, Petra thought about Denthold's words.

People had already been killed. More almost certainly would be. Some of them might be people he knew, even loved. A captive Priest-Apprentice could not stop what the king's brother and the Heretic had set in motion, but could the Priests? He did not know all the secrets contained in the *Book of Vekrin*. Perhaps the Priests had powerful Blue Fire weapons hidden away in the Temples, weapons that would make short work of Axel's fifty-firelance army and even Denthold's great *Liberator*.

Through a vow sworn before Vekrin, the senior Priests, and his father, it was his duty as a Priest-Apprentice to loyally defend and protect them and the Temple. That vow demanded he try to escape and get a message to the Temple in City Viandaxis before Axel's army arrived. The Priests there could farspeak the Priests in City Primaxis. His father could warn King Stobor. Every Temple between Viandaxis and Primaxis could prepare its defences. The king could rally his forces, meet Axel head-on along the King's Way at a place of his choosing instead of Axel's, and—

And what?

If the king and the Priests prevailed, nothing would change. The kingdom would continue its slow decline until, one day, the Nightdwellers overran the last plague-decimated city.

With that thought, Petra suddenly sat upright in his narrow bed. Staring into a darkness as black as the future he'd just imagined, he realized he had already made up his mind.

He would help Denthold.

He would join forces with the Heretic.

He would help spread the knowledge of Blue Fire outside of the Temples of Vekrin.

People would receive the knowledge and tools they needed to move beyond the walled cities, beyond the slopes of the valley that had held them for so long, the knowledge and tools they needed to explore the wide world. They could move west to the mountains and beyond, east to the empty sea, perhaps even someday return and reclaim the Old

Kingdom beyond the ocean, the land devastated by the War of the Twelve Gods.

And with that decision, he knew he was finally, irrevocably doing what he had sworn to the Freefolk he would never do:

Breaking his vows.

No, not just breaking them. Shattering them. Crushing them to dust and flinders and letting them blow away in the howling wind of change.

His breath caught in his throat. *Father.*

His father would never understand. His father would disown him, arrest him, execute him if it came to that. First Keeper Pelidor would never break his vows to Vekrin. Those vows defined him. They meant more to him than Petra did.

They always had.

That thought, bitter though it tasted, only made Petra more determined to follow through with his decision.

Perhaps someday, when Nevyana had become a better place, he would be able to explain. But as he lay down again and wrapped his blankets around him and heard the guard outside clear his throat and stamp his feet to keep warm, he couldn't imagine how far away such a day might lie.

26

DEPARTURE

Amlinn tossed and turned on her narrow cot. She should have known better than to trust a follower of Vekrin. Petra had clearly thrown his lot in with Denthold, the man he'd pretended to consider a Heretic. He'd helped Denthold build that monstrous *"Liberator."* He wouldn't help Amlinn escape. He didn't want to escape. And without him . . .

It galled her to admit it, but without Petra, she could do nothing.

When at last she slept, she dreamed of Clan Therra's camp, but in her dream, the Fence had fallen, and Nightdwellers with red eyes and bloody fangs and claws rampaged among the wagons, rending and tearing the flesh of the Freefolk.

A knock on the side of the wagon startled her awake. When she poked her head out into the morning sunlight, she blinked in surprise. Her guard wore full armour. He wasn't the only one. Everywhere, men in mail shirts and helmets bustled, striking tents, harnessing horses, loading wagons.

"We're moving out," her guard said. "No kitchen duty today. Secure your wagon."

Amlinn nodded and ducked back inside to dress. In the kitchens, first in Denthold's home and then in the camp, she'd worn the green skirt and white blouse Denthold had provided, marking her as one of his servants. But a few days earlier, her own Freefolk clothes had been returned to her, the clothes she'd worn when she and Petra were captured. She tugged the white tunic, black trousers, and black boots over her armoured leather jerkin. Missing her blue-jewelled dagger, but still feeling like herself for the first time in weeks, she climbed into the wagon's seat. Her guard gave the harness a final tug and then climbed up beside her.

Nothing remained of the camp. Each soldier now carried his own small tent atop a bulky backpack. They gathered in a large clump, waiting for orders—about three hundred in all, Amlinn estimated. Not a very large army, but their small numbers were more than made up for by the fifty elite troops already positioned four-abreast in a tight column. Strapped over their shoulders, they carried five-foot-long glass-tipped black rods: firelances.

Another fifty men milled around on horses. None of them carried firelances, and Amlinn, who had lived her whole life around horses, could guess why. No cavalryman who discharged a mini-lighting bolt from horseback would still be in the saddle two seconds later.

It took another half hour and a not-inconsiderable amount of swearing to organize the disparate forces into something approaching an organized column. The firelance-armed troops led the way. Behind them rolled several wagons like Amlinn's. Since they couldn't all be filled with hostages, she guessed they were mostly home to various officers.

Behind those came wagons loaded with weapons, then wagons loaded with food and other stores, then cookwagons, complete with cooks and a handful of serving girls, then regular troops, and finally, the cavalry. Once they left the city, she assumed the mounted troops would scout far ahead, behind, and to either side of the column, like Freefolk outriders.

The leading firelancers reached the boulevard, but only the first half of them turned onto it, vanishing around the corner of a burned-out building. The others stopped, as did the wagons.

A moment later, *Liberator* rolled into sight.

No horses pulled it. Nothing pushed it. It moved of its own accord, majestic and silent except for the creak of wood on wood as it swayed from side to side. The sight was so strange, so *wrong*, that it gave Amlinn goosebumps. Then she saw Petra seated in the driver's compartment next to Denthold, and her goosebumps turned to nausea.

Liberator followed the first half of the firelance-armed troops, but still the column in the side street held fast. The six wagons that rolled by next were familiar to Amlinn, but their appearance nauseated her even more.

Sunwagons, with not a Wise Woman in sight!

The first five looked strange to her eyes. Not only were they bigger than Freefolk sunwagons, the shining surfaces of their sunscales glinted deep blue. No Freefolk sunscale showed anything but black. Their roofs were different too, more sharply sloped and peaked. But the sixth sunwagon she recognized all too well as the one stolen from Clan Therra, the one in which she and Petra had arrived.

Her column fell in behind the sunwagons. Hooves and wheels clattered on the boulevard cobblestones and echoed from the buildings all around as they rolled toward the main gate, where the smooth white stone of the King's Way began, leading south to all the cities of Nevyana—and Grandfather.

Please, Arrica, let him still live!

Grandfather would have told the other clans what happened. By now, they might have formed an army of their own, an army of Freefolk, rolling northward—northward to face certain destruction when it encountered the firelance-and-*Liberator*-armed army of Lord Axel.

The thought horrified Amlinn, but the truth could not be denied. Her people would not stand a chance.

I have to escape. I have to warn them, she thought as her wagon rolled out through the gate. She looked ahead to where the broad, cleared area around the city gave way to the dark shadows of the northern forest, a green corridor into which the King's Way plunged. *I have to!*

But escape seemed impossible. As she expected, the cavalry fanned out to patrol, ahead, behind, and to the sides. If she jumped off the wagon and ran into the woods, they would catch her in seconds. Even if by some miracle they didn't, she would be alone in the Forest as night—and the Nightdwellers—closed in.

The trunks of the trees that closed in around them as they plunged into the forest felt like prison bars.

27

SMOKED GLASS

Jin stood at one end of the long stone table in the Mother Queen's council chamber in the heart of the Great Warren, waiting to hear if he would live or die. Smoothly polished walls of black stone rose to a domed ceiling, at the centre of which hung an orb of the same apparent size and brightness as the full moon. To his left sat the Senior Scrollkeeper, Ser Hiv, half Ser Mar's age and twice Jin's size, a grey-furred giant who glared at Jin with smouldering eyes.

"Well, Mother Highness?" Ser Hiv said. "Tell us this Ra lies so I may serve him the punishment he so richly deserves."

From the far end of the table, Mother Queen Sayb glanced at the Scrollkeeper. "Peace, Ser Hiv." Small and sleek, with dark-red fur that lightened to white on her face, neck, breasts, and belly, and wearing only a simple gold circlet set with a single red stone as a sign of her rank, she did not look powerful or dangerous.

Jin knew well she was both.

Her gaze slid from Ser Hiv past Jin to the fourth Nightdweller in the chamber, Watchmaster Kar-Pur, seated opposite Ser Hiv. The supreme commander of the Mother Queen's warriors sat stolidly. Though not as big as Ser Hiv, his silent strength frightened Jin more than the Scrollkeeper's pious bluster.

"Well, Watchmaster?" Sayb asked. "Has Jin-Ra lied to us as Ser Hiv insists, since Ser Hiv assures us that Arrica and Vekrin would never work together in the fashion Jin-Ra describes?"

Kar-Pur kept his eyes squarely on his queen. "He did not lie," he said, his voice a deep rumble.

The Scrollkeeper drew a deep, indignant breath, but a glance from the Mother Queen kept him from speaking.

"Lord Axel has joined forces with the Mad Priest, Denthold," Kar-Pur reported. "Their army is preparing to move out. They have fifty men armed with firelances, between two and three hundred foot soldiers, and another fifty horsemen. The firelance-armed wagon exists as Jin has said, and the scouts counted six sunwagons."

Ser Hiv muttered under his breath.

The Mother Queen turned her gaze to him. "You have something to say, Ser Hiv?"

"I said this is sacrilege," the Scrollkeeper snapped. "Sacrilege and desecration on such a scale that the Gods will destroy them before they have travelled a day. Mark my words."

"I do," said the Mother Queen. "But I also mark that the Gods have had months, if not years, to destroy this force, and they have not acted yet. Perhaps it is best we do not wait for them." She glanced at Kar-Pur again. "You concur?"

"I do, Mother Highness," Kar-Pur rumbled.

"Then proceed as we discussed. Muster your men. Intercept and destroy this force before it can reach City Viandaxis."

"Can't be done," Ser Hiv said dismissively. "By the time you reach the King's Way, Denthold will already have captured Viandaxis, and his forces will have grown with those who choose to join him, as many will. Even if you could reach the King's Way before that, if in fact this force is armed and protected by Blue Fire, the weapons of Ell will not be sufficient to enable you to destroy it." He shook his head. "No. You have no choice but to trust in the Gods to—"

"I think," the Mother Queen said, "that this threat is sufficient that we will not rely solely on teeth and claws. I also think this threat is sufficient that some secrets need no longer be kept."

Ser Hiv's ears flattened, and his claws scratched the tabletop as he clenched his fists. "You cannot—"

"Can I not?"

The Scrollkeeper leaped to his feet. "I forbid—"

"You *forbid*?" For the first time, the Mother Queen raised her voice—only slightly—but even that was enough to make the big Scrollkeeper . . . well, "wilt" was the word that came to Jin's mind.

Visibly trembling, Ser Hiv picked up the chair and seated himself once more. "I will discuss my decision with you momentarily," the Mother Queen said, and though her voice softened, it held within it an edge of steel. She turned once again to Kar-Pur. "You have sufficient horses for the force?"

"Yes, Mother Highness."

"And weapons?"

For the first time, Kar-Pur looked at Ser Hiv. He bared his teeth. "Yes, Mother Highness. Crossbows, swords, and spears aplenty."

"And you are ready to depart?"

"Upon your command, Mother Highness."

"Then depart," the Mother Queen said. She returned her gaze to Jin, who had stood silent, satisfaction mingled with astonishment growing in him with every word spoken. "And take Jin-Ra with you. He has earned the right to fight."

Jin's heart leaped. "Thank you, Mother Highness! Thank you!"

"I obey, Mother Highness," Kar-Pur said. He got to his feet. He nodded at the Scrollkeeper. "Ser Hiv," he growled. Then he turned to Jin. "Come, young one. Let's get you armed and find you a watchbelt."

"Watchmaster," Jin said tentatively as they strode through the broad corridors of the Great Warren to the armouries, "even on horseback, we may be too late. The nights are short."

Kar-Pur grunted. "Wait, Jin-Ra. All will become clear."

They reached the armouries. Even in Broken Tree Warren, Jin had never been in the storerooms where the weapons of war were kept. When he had trained with sword and bow and javelin, the weapons were brought to the training chamber or field. Now he gaped at the ranks of bright swords and tall spears, the quarrels full of arrows and crossbow bolts, the wall covered with bows hung on hooks driven into the stone. Most impressively of all, an entire side chamber was given over to watchbelts, their silver sigils glinting in the light of the glowmoss. Kar-Pur handed him a crossbow and quarrel, a sword, and a watchbelt. "And now," he said, "one more thing."

At the back of the watchbelt chamber stood something Jin had never before seen in a warren of the Nightdwellers: a locked wooden door.

Kar-Pur took a key from his belt pouch, unlocked the door, and pushed it open.

Inside the small chamber, a dozen wooden racks held small leather bands, each set with two ovals of smoked glass. Kar-Pur took one from its place on the rack and held it out to Jin, who turned it over in his hand. The band had a buckle at the back, like a watchbelt. An extra lip of soft leather surrounded the back of each glass oval, which were each bound into the leather with rings of silver wire. "I don't understand," Jin said.

"Don't you?" Kar-Pur said. He picked up a second band and held it up. "Smoked glass," he said softly. "So thickly smoked that even the sun cannot penetrate it."

And suddenly, as Kar-Pur had promised, all became clear. Jin's great secret, the secret he had discovered the morning he had outwaited Ket as the sun rose outside Broken Tree Warren, was no secret at all. The Scrollkeepers knew the truth. The Mother Queen knew the truth. The senior members of the Watch knew the truth.

The sun did not burn Nightdwellers. They could ride by day as well as by night.

And that meant that maybe, just maybe, they could indeed intercept and destroy the monstrosity created by the Mad Priest and the king's brother to seize the kingdom and destroy the Nightdwellers.

Jin loosely buckled the smoked-glass goggles around his neck, hefted his crossbow, and followed Kar-Pur from the weapons chamber to join the raiding party.

The Daydwellers, he thought with grim elation, *are in for a surprise.*

28

OVER THE EDGE

Amlinn's day wore on. The view did not change. Twice, they stopped briefly to tend the horses and to eat their own bread and cheese and dried meat. The day waned, and still they rode. Nervously, she kept an eye on the sun as it sank lower and lower. It was already far later than the Freefolk would ever have risked travelling, and still they didn't stop. Of course, they were a powerful armed force, but still . . .

Finally, as the sun touched the horizon, they reached a ruined village. Chimneys stuck up from the shattered shells of houses and cast long shadows like black, accusing fingers across the rubble-strewn ground. As the gloom deepened, they set up camp in the surrounding fields. Amlinn watched tents being pitched, horses tended, cookwagons opened. The light faded, and campfires sprang to life, but one task remained unperformed.

No one moved around the perimeter, setting up Fencestones. Amlinn felt a chill that had nothing to do with the falling temperature. *They can't mean to camp unprotected. The Nightdwellers will—*

And then the four sparkglobes hanging on the corners of *Liberator* blazed to life. She yelped and raised a hand to shade her eyes. The glare of sparkglobes, brighter than any light she had ever seen except for the sun, flooded the camp and many yards of the surrounding fields with brilliant blue-white illumination. *That's why there's no Fence,* she thought. Light that bright, coupled with watchful guards armed with firelances, would be almost as effective as Blue Fire at keeping away Nightdwellers.

A new guard took over from her driver. He followed her to the latrine and then the cookwagons. He stood by while she ate her dinner of boiled vegetables and crusty bread and drank her cup of weak ale, then followed her back to her wagon. He didn't say a word to her, so she didn't bother saying good night to him. Sparkglobe light shone so brightly through the tiny windows under the ceiling that it might have been daylight, and once again, she had a hard time falling asleep.

The next day passed the same as the first. Again, they camped outside the ruins of a once-walled village. The Great River ran far to their west through a deep ravine, one of many in the rough country between Divpaxis and Viandaxis. A smaller stream, perhaps the same one that had run through Divpaxis, ran through the village and trended away from the river.

As they set out on the third day, the King's Way continued alongside that stream. That afternoon, they rolled down into a narrow valley, one of many they had crossed, though this one was steeper and deeper than most. The stream, now much broader but still shallow, cascaded down the rocks to their right. At the bottom of the valley, it swung sharply left and actually flowed across the King's Way. When Vekrin created the road, he hadn't bothered with bridges for streams shallow enough to be forded, so the road's white stone surface simply dipped beneath the creek, though Amlinn could still see it gleaming through the water. The road rose out of the water again on the far side. To the east, the stream disappeared around a bend in the valley.

Amlinn looked over the side as the wagon rolled along the submerged King's Way. Water foamed white around the wagon's wheels and the horses' legs. She twisted around to see how the men on foot behind them would fare. They waded into the water—swearing about how cold it was—and then the entire column stopped moving, leaving fifty men stranded in the stream. Amlinn thought the resulting oaths should have turned the water to steam.

She twisted around to the front again to see what had caused the delay.

Beyond the stream, the King's Way climbed the steep valley slope and curved around a tall spire of bare rock. The lead group of firelancers rounded that bend and vanished from sight. *Liberator* was struggling. With its unholy use of Blue Fire, it propelled itself across flat land as fast as a horse could trot, but on slopes, it slowed to a crawl. The second group of firelancers had amassed behind it, pushing. Holding back to give them room, the sunwagons had, in turn, brought the rest of the caravan to a halt. Some of the cursing foot soldiers now began to clamber out of the water, breaking formation to step off the King's Way and splash back to the northern shore.

When *Liberator* and the firelancers pushing it were more than halfway up the slope, the sunwagon drivers at last clucked at their horses and started to follow.

A bright spark of sunlight, glinting on metal high atop a rock spire, caught Amlinn's eye. As she looked up at it, a small black object hurtled from the peak, trailing smoke. It plunged to the ground, striking the King's Way in front of *Liberator* and exploding into orange fire and black smoke.

A sharp bang echoed and re-echoed off the rocks. Horses neighed and reared in terror, including the one pulling Amlinn's wagon. She clutched at the seat as the vehicle lurched. The driver leaped to his feet, swearing, and then made a strange gurgling sound. He fell back into his seat, and the reins dropped from his suddenly limp hands. The black-feathered end of an arrow protruded from his throat. Blood poured down his chest. His eyes, wide in shock, stared blankly at the blue sky.

The horse bolted, slamming Amlinn back in her seat. The dead guard rolled sideways and dropped from the wagon as the horse galloped off the King's Way to the left along the stream's southern bank. Amlinn lunged for the reins, but before she could clutch them, they fell out of her reach—and then she had to grip the seat to keep from being bounced from the wagon. Holding on white-knuckled, she glimpsed chaos all around her.

Armed horsemen galloped out of the forest, and she gasped. *Freefolk!*

She spotted familiar faces among them as, swords drawn, they swept past her. Was that Witten? She shot a glance over her shoulder and saw the Freefolk thundering down on soldiers who were still milling in confusion in the stream or bogged down on its muddy bank. Men shouted. Swords clashed.

Men died.

A firelance flashed and cracked thunder. Amlinn's horse, now wild with terror, plunged into the water and fled downstream, splashing fetlock-deep through the icy water, which cascaded over Amlinn, soaking her to the skin. The wagon bucked and swayed on rounded rocks. Still gripping the seat, Amlinn leaned forward and peered down. The reins trailed in the water. She looked up again.

What's that roar?

A flash of light cast every tree around her into stark relief. An instant later, thunder shattered the air.

Liberator had fired!

The horse galloped even faster. The wagon skidded on streambed stones as the horse rounded a bend. The strange roaring sound intensified.

Amlinn recognized the green-glass curve of water falling over a cliff's edge into nothingness bare seconds before they reached it. Gasping, she flung herself out of the wagon just before the maddened horse galloped into thin air and fell, pulling the wagon with it.

Amlinn hit the water with so much force that it drove the air from her lungs. She scrabbled desperately for purchase on the streambed's slimy stones.

She didn't find it. Mouth gaping, with no breath even to scream, she followed the horse over the waterfall.

29

THE RAVINE

"Get out," Denthold said.

Petra didn't argue. *Liberator* had climbed several slopes since they'd left Divpaxis, and he'd grown accustomed to being ordered out of the cockpit as the hum of the Blue Fire motivators deepened and the gearbox started groaning. A rope ladder flung over the side of the cockpit allowed either of them to dismount without having to go through the wagon's interior. He clambered down its swaying length a few rungs before jumping clear.

He landed a little awkwardly, falling to his hands and knees. As he stood and brushed dirt from his trousers, he glanced back. As usual, the firelancers behind *Liberator* had moved forward to push. He turned the other way and climbed up the valley slope after the forward group of firelancers, who were already nearing the bend in the path at the base of the fang-like spire of rock.

Panting, he, too, soon reached the top of the ridge and paused there, leaning against the cliff face with one hand. As he caught his breath, he gazed out over the heads of the now-descending lead firelancers to the seemingly endless forest. He traced the white gleam of the King's Way through the trees to yet more distant, jumbled village ruins. Far off to his right, he caught a silvery glimpse of the Great River. It looked like they'd soon be leaving the smaller stream they'd been following and rejoin the River, which wound close to the ruins.

Something banged behind him. Air slammed his back and shoved him forward. He spun around to see black smoke mushrooming into the sky, orange fire at its base. Had *Liberator* exploded? No. The giant wagon had almost reached the top of the slope and remained intact, though the now-dying flames had blackened its front quarter.

He couldn't see Denthold. No doubt, the Heretic had found cover inside the cockpit.

Behind *Liberator*, startled horses reared and neighed. Drivers dropped from wagons, felled by arrows flying from a stand of trees west of the King's Way. One wagon thundered crazily away to Petra's right. He glimpsed someone in the seat reaching down as though trying to grab the reins.

Horsemen galloped past the runaway wagon, bearing down on the foot soldiers at the bottom of the valley. *Freefolk*, Petra realized with a Blue Fire-like shock. Screams and shouts and the sound of steel on steel shattered the air. Bodies floated in water already turning red. The firelancers who had been pushing *Liberator* now charged toward the fray, but he didn't see how they could fire without hitting their own men. The chaos of milling wagons and frightened horses delayed them.

The lead group of firelancers came back over the top of

the ridge and charged down the King's Way. A sound like swarming hornets hissed over Petra's head.

Arrows!

The two men farthest from the rock spire's face tumbled and fell, firelances skittering across the ground, feathered shafts protruding from their backs.

"Archers on the spire!" someone screamed, and the surviving firelancers turned and scrambled to the cliff against which Petra stood. They struggled to find a way up the spire, but Petra stayed put. On the northern side of the valley, a group of Axel's outriders burst out of a copse of trees and thundered down the slope, slamming into the swirling melee in the stream. One Freefolk rider galloped out of the group and swung his horse around to ride back. In that instant, lightning flashed from a firelancer's staff. The rider and his horse burst into flame. Greasy black smoke billowed upward, and they crumpled into the water in a cloud of steam, the charred horse still twitching. Petra's stomach heaved.

The wagon that had broken out of the column now ran wildly downstream, sheets of water cascading from the horse's churning legs and the wheels of the wagon. The figure he had seen reaching hopelessly for the reins twisted around to look back, and recognition hit him like a bolt from a firelance.

Amlinn!

Forgetting everything else, Petra dashed away from the safety of the spire, flinching as an arrow zipped over his head and shattered against a rock. He ran along the top of the ridge, his eyes locked on the careering wagon and the tiny figure clinging to it.

And then *Liberator* fired.

The flash lit the valley from end to end. Petra's shadow

flicked out in front of him, long and black on grass turned frost-white by the flare. Thunder hammered him to his knees. Ears ringing, he stumbled back to his feet and twisted around. A cloud of black smoke rose above the shattered top of the stone spire. Rocks slammed to the ground at its base—right where he'd been standing moments before.

Petra spun round again and resumed the chase. Below, Amlinn's wagon disappeared behind trees lining the river. Petra turned sharply left and galloped down the slope at breakneck speed. He crashed through the line of brush and burst out of it onto the bank of the stream, so unexpectedly that he overbalanced and fell headlong into the water, gasping at the sudden, icy shock. He staggered to his feet and raced downstream, splashing through the shallows, slipping on rocks, falling to his hands and knees and scrambling up again, searching for any sign of the wagon. Ahead, a sound brought his pounding heart to his throat: the roar of falling water.

And then he saw it: the clear, smooth curve of the plunging stream, gleaming at the lip of the falls. What he didn't see was the horse, wagon—or Amlinn.

His heart skipped. "No!" he cried. He scrambled out of the water and forced his way through the bushes on the bank until he reached the precipice. Hanging onto a tree branch to keep from falling, he peered into the ravine beyond the falls.

The falling water thundered into a deep pool. The horse floated in the red-tinged shallows on the other side of that pool, a bloody wagon shaft rising spear-like from its shattered ribcage. Broken bits of wood bobbed alongside the corpse, but the bulk of the wagon had vanished.

And Amlinn?

There! Half-submerged, she lay on her back on his side of

the river, fifty yards downstream, legs floating loosely in the tossing water.

He felt as if an icy hand had gripped his chest. He couldn't breathe.

Then she moved, coughing and retching, and relief flooded him—so strong and sudden that he almost lost his grip on the tree branch. He tightened his hand convulsively, watching as Amlinn crawled a little farther out of the water and then collapsed.

He had to get down there. He plunged into the woods, following the edge of the ravine, looking for a place where the slope gentled, where there was any slope at all and not just a sheer drop. He had to struggle a good three hundred yards past where Amlinn lay before he discovered a suitable spot. Even then, he had to hang on to branches and roots to keep from tumbling to the bottom and likely breaking every bone in his body. At last, he reached the stony riverbank and rushed upstream to Amlinn's motionless form.

As he bent over her, her eyes flickered. Then she gasped and lashed out with a foot, sweeping his legs out from under him. He thumped painfully onto his rear. She rolled over and tried to scramble up but cried out and collapsed the moment she put weight on her left foot.

"Amlinn!" Petra shouted over the waterfall. "It's all right! It's me, Petra!"

Amlinn rolled over, sat up, and glared at him. "Why should that make it all right?" she demanded. Wet hair hung around her white face in black tangles. "You're in league with Denthold."

"Well, he's not here now, is he?" Petra said. "And I'm not going to drag you back to be locked up again." He got up, rubbing his bruised buttocks, and approached her. She watched him with narrowed eyes, but at least she didn't kick him again. "Let me look at your ankle." He knelt beside her.

"It's all right," she snapped, but she gasped as he raised her leg. He gently slipped her boot off, then the sodden sock. Holding her bare foot tenderly in both hands, he carefully examined her ankle.

"It's swelling," he said. "Can you wiggle it?"

She tried and winced. "Yes. But it hurts."

"I don't think it's broken, then," Petra said. "Probably just a sprain. Good thing the river falls into such a deep pool." He glanced at the dead horse, its legs bobbing in the swirling water on the other side of the stream. The broken wagon shaft that had impaled it swung from side to side like the mast of an anchored riverboat. "You were lucky."

His gaze travelled up the side of the ravine, then downstream. The walls rose steep and high as far as he could see, which wasn't far because the river wound out of sight almost at once, bending to the south. "You'll never be able to climb out of here, even the way I came down," he said. "I'll have to get help—"

"I won't be here when you come back," Amlinn said. "I won't be taken prisoner again. I won't be Denthold's hostage."

Petra imagined himself leading armed men through the forest, hunting Amlinn down as if she were a wounded animal, then carrying her back to the army like a trophy. His insides twisted. Faced with a choice between Denthold and Amlinn, could he really choose Denthold?

Not and live with myself.

"All right," he said. "Then we'll head downstream until we find a place where we can climb out of the ravine."

"Those attackers were Freefolk," Amlinn said. "They may have captured your precious *Liberator* by now."

Petra shook his head. "No," he said. "Axel's cavalry reformed and charged as I came after you. The firelancers were beginning to fire. And you must have heard *Liberator*. It took out the archers at the top of the spire. The surviving Freefolk will have retreated." *If there are any survivors.* He didn't say it out loud. Amlinn almost certainly knew the Freefolk who had attacked . . . who had died.

He remembered the burning horse and rider and the awful way they had collapsed as so much smoking meat into the river, and he swallowed hard. What had happened to Witten, to Dainann, to all the other Freefolk he had begun to know during the journey north?

"People are already dying because of your precious Denthold!" Amlinn flung the words like sharp-edged stones, as though she could read his thoughts. "How many more have to die before you'll stand against him?"

Petra remembered Denthold's words about forests growing back lusher and greener after a forest fire. He didn't share them with Amlinn. "We'd better get moving," he said instead. "We've only got two or three hours of daylight left. There may not be any Nightdwellers in this ravine, but then again, there might. We have to find a place to hide."

"I'll take Nightdwellers over Denthold any time," Amlinn said coldly. She pulled her sock back on and reached for her boot, but it wouldn't fit over her swelling ankle, and the effort made her gasp in pain. "Great," she said. "One-booted." She tied the boot around her neck with its laces instead, and then held out her hand. "Help me up."

They made their way with agonizing slowness along the stony riverbank. Amlinn held on to Petra's arm, but the intimacy carried no warmth. Her hand might as well have been carved from ice. As they rounded the bend that took the river south, the thunder of the waterfall faded until Petra could no longer distinguish it from the ongoing rush of water in the stream.

Above them, the bright sunlight illuminating on the ravine's eastern wall shrank inexorably away.

30

DEATH IN THE NIGHT

From the deep shadow of the woods, Jin watched soldiers and waggoneers circulating through the camp sprawled around the great, hulking shape of the sunscale-roofed wagon they called *Liberator*. They thought themselves safe, those firelance-armed soldiers. Safe inside a heavily patrolled perimeter, safe inside the circle of radiance cast by the sparkglobes on each corner of *Liberator*.

They were about to find out how wrong they were.

Ordinarily, an attack into that brilliant light would have been futile, the light blinding the Nightdwellers and eliminating much of the advantage given by the watchbelts. But the same smoked-glass goggles that had protected the Nightdweller force from the sun on their ride to the King's Way protected them from the glare of the sparkglobes. Under ordinary circumstances, it would have taken them two nights to reach this spot from the Great Warren. Instead, they had covered the distance in one night and one day.

The experience had been surreal. The sky, bright overhead. Distant hills, clouds, birds—all visible through the dark goggles, revealed by the light in a way they weren't at night even to Nightdweller vision. Unaccustomed to long hours in the saddle, Jin had been sore and exhausted when, at last, they'd dismounted in the woods and organized for the attack. The soreness remained, but nervous energy had swallowed his exhaustion. Peering through the smoked glass, he could see everything happening in the camp by the glare of the very sparkglobes meant to keep Nightdwellers at bay.

He could also hear every word spoken. The soldiers made no effort to keep their voices down. They sounded angry and elated at the same time.

". . . see that one burning like a torch . . ."

". . . horse's tail on fire, it galloped . . ."

". . . Sharl never had a chance, bastards shot him right out of . . ."

". . . thought I'd drown before . . ."

Snatches of conversation swirled like leaves in an eddying stream. The army had already been attacked that day.

Not that far away, their Freefolk attackers also camped, licking their own wounds. They were safe behind their Fence of Blue Fire, but they would have been safe even without it. The Freefolk were of no concern to the Nightdwellers with Axel's and Denthold's men on the march. In fact, their earlier attack had made them inadvertent allies.

Ser Mar's dream come true, Jin thought. *Though not in the way he would have liked.*

And then Jin's ears pricked.

". . . Denthold's furious," someone said. Jin spotted the speaker, one of the few green-clad men standing around the nearest campfire among those wearing red. "Bad enough the Freefolk girl disappeared—drowned, looks like; her wagon went over the falls—but then to lose his pet Priest-boy too . . ."

"What happened to him?" said the other man.

"Ran off after the girl." The first man spat into the fire. It hissed like a snake. "Never came back. Cavalry ran a sweep, but no sign of him. He's Nightdweller carrion by now."

He's not the only one, Jin thought grimly. Then he then stiffened as his watchbelt suddenly filled his mind with a warning: *prepare to attack*. He double-checked his loaded crossbow.

Ser Mar might believe there didn't have to be enmity among the followers of the three Gods, but whether enmity *had* to exist or not, exist it certainly did. Without question, the men in the circle of light before him were his enemies. For the first time, he felt some of the hatred Ket had always expressed for Daydwellers welling in his own heart.

He raised his crossbow at the urging of his watchbelt, silently transmitting the will of Watchmaster Kar-Pur, who wore the master belt. He aimed and waited, knowing that all through the woods, his fellow Nightdwellers did the same.

And then, at Kar-Pur's silent command, they all fired at once.

The perimeter guards toppled like felled trees, spinning and falling, spraying dark, shining blood. Jin's bolt and three others, however, struck not flesh and bone but *Liberator's* sparkglobes. Blue Fire flared as the globes shattered, and then darkness swallowed the camp below.

Like the fellow Nightdwellers all around him, Jin ripped off his smoked-glass goggles. As those without bows scrambled to their feet and raced silently toward the camp, Jin slung his crossbow over his shoulder and pulled his sword from its scabbard—or tried to. In his eagerness, he fumbled it. The sword fell from his hand. Hoping desperately no one had seen, he turned back to pick it up.

In that instant, the world exploded with light.

With his back to the camp, it looked to Jin as if the sun had suddenly risen behind him in the west. His shadow, long and black, slashed across tree trunks so brightly lit that light stabbed his eyes like needles. He cried out, dropped his sword again, and scrabbled with frantic fingers for his smoked goggles. Pulling them over his eyes, he spun to see what had happened.

Nightdwellers lay on the ground between him and the camp screaming, clawing at their eyes, blinded by the impossibly bright light pouring out, not from sparkglobes, but through the sunscales of *Liberator* and the five largest sunwagons. Only the sunwagon stolen from Clan Therra remained dark.

No more than a handful of fighters besides Jin had been fortunate enough to be looking away from the sunwagons when the light exploded. Like him, they had pulled on their goggles again, but far too late. The light had shattered the Nightdweller charge. Daydweller swords plunged into writhing furred bodies.

More soldiers charged out into the fields, shouting defiance.

Some carried firelances.

Brilliant blue bolts stabbed through the night. They turned fleeing Nightdwellers into living torches that writhed and screamed and ran for horrible seconds before collapsing into merciful stillness. Others fell to crossbow bolts, tumbling to the ground like puppets whose strings had been cut.

Sickened, furious, Jin raised his sword and charged

toward a firelancer, but the soldier heard him coming and swung the weapon in his direction. Jin gasped and flung himself to the ground, slamming his shoulder into the dirt. The sword flew from his hand as Blue Fire ripped the air above him, so close he could smell its sharp metallic tang and feel its scorching heat. Rolling over, he scrambled back into the forest on all fours and stumbled to his feet as he entered the trees.

An arrow slashed his side open before thudding into the trunk of a tree. Jin gasped, his hand flying to the wound. With hot blood welling over his fingers, he ran deeper into the woods, the useless crossbow banging on his back, his sword still lying where he had dropped it. The lightning flashes behind him drove him deeper and deeper into the shadows that had always sheltered him. He ran because it was impossible not to run, ran even as his side burned with agony, dodging trees, leaping fallen logs, seeking only to put as much of the forest as possible between himself and the terrifying firelances.

His limbs weakened. He stumbled. Roaring filling his ears. His breath came in short, painful gasps. His heart pounded in his chest unsteadily, as though it were trying to break through his ribs.

And then the ground dropped away beneath his feet, and he fell into darkness.

31

THE WOUNDED NIGHTDWELLER

Petra and Amlinn struggled along the ravine, Amlinn white-faced and limping, gasping with pain. The ravine grew shallower as they travelled, but never enough to allow Amlinn to climb out. Minute by minute, the sunlight on the ravine's eastern wall shrank away, until at last, only a thin bright outline of fire touched the tops of the trees high above.

Then it vanished.

In the deepening twilight, Petra stopped and looked around. "We have to find shelter."

"There isn't any," Amlinn said, her voice trembling. "You can't hide from Nightdwellers. They always know where Daydwellers are. It's one of Ell's Gifts. They'll find us. And then they'll kill us."

Petra stared at her. He'd never heard her sound so vulnerable. *She's spent her whole life listening to Nightdwellers howling outside the Fence, the cries of the creatures who killed her parents.* The fear in her voice made him want to protect her, even if she now hated him.

"The Nightdwellers can't be everywhere," he said, trying to reassure himself as much as her. "And it can't be any easier for them to get into this ravine than it is for us to get out of it." He pointed into the gloom. "See those rocks by the next bend in the stream? I think we can get in behind them. At least we'll be out of sight."

Amlinn shook her head. "You can't hide from Nightdwellers," she whispered again.

"We can try," Petra said. "Come on."

He pulled out the lightwand that Denthold had given him as they worked in the dark interior of *Liberator*, but Amlinn grabbed his wrist. "Are you mad?" she gasped. "The Nightdwellers might see it."

You just said magic would tell them where we are anyway, he wanted to say, but didn't. "All right." He looked up at the stars beginning to prick the sky. "At least it's clear."

Their progress slowed as the light faded. By the time they reached the bend in the river, the only illumination came from the band of star-spattered sky sparkling between the walls of the ravine. Ferns, barely visible, grew among the rocks. He pushed through them, discovering an area beyond where the boulders enclosed a space like a roofless cave. He helped Amlinn into it and then glanced up at the glittering stars. "With a night this clear, the temperature is going to drop like a stone down here." He looked back at Amlinn's barely visible shape. "We'll have to, um, share body heat."

"I agree," she said, and his heart leaped with excitement. He'd expected her to refuse outright. "If by some miracle the Nightdwellers don't get us, the cold could." But the frost returned to her voice as she continued, "But don't get any ideas. It's strictly for warmth."

"Of course," he said. "Nothing else even crossed my

mind." *Vekrin, forgive the lie.* "If I gather some of those ferns to for us to lie on and to use as a blanket, we'll be warmer. And maybe more comfortable."

"All right," she said. "But don't use the lightwand."

"I know," Petra said. He felt his way back to the ferns, hands outstretched. Once fronds tickled his fingertips, he reached down to pull up the plants by the roots.

He blinked. For the briefest instant, he'd seen the ferns clearly.

He looked up. A flash lit the eastern wall of the ravine, then another, and another.

The stars still shone. No thunder grumbled in the distance. Absent lightning, only one thing could make a flash like that.

Firelances!

The Freefolk wouldn't attack Axel's army in the middle of the night. Could it be a force of king Stobor's? He didn't see how. Even if the king knew of his brother's treachery, he hadn't had time to muster an army and march it this far north. That left only—

Something slid and tumbled down the ravine, perhaps fifty feet away. It crashed through bushes and stirred up a welter of sliding pebbles that rattled down long after the main bulk of the object lay still.

Silence reclaimed the gully, but only for a moment. A growling, inhuman moan sent a shiver down Petra's spine and made his heart skip a beat. Injured animal? Or injured Nightdweller? And if the latter, how long before another Nightdweller came looking for him?

Unless . . . the flashes. Firelances against savages armed only with teeth and claws. How many Nightdwellers could possibly have survived?

If they were lucky—very, very lucky—maybe only this one.

Petra felt his way back to the enclosed space behind rocks. "Petra?" Amlinn's voice, faint and frantic, came from the darkness. "Is that you?"

"Yes."

"What was that sound?"

"Something tumbled into the ravine not far downstream." Petra hoped he wasn't about to push the already frightened Freefolk girl into a complete panic.

"Something?"

"There's been another fight. I saw the flashes. Firelances."

"Only Nightdwellers would attack in the night." Amlinn's breathing quickened. "Arrica protect us! A Nightdweller fell into the ravine?" She scrambled to her feet, then cried out and stumbled, surprising Petra by falling against him. He barely caught her and barely kept from falling himself. She gripped his arms so hard it hurt. "There'll be more. They'll find us—"

"They may all have been killed. All but this one," Petra said.

"It's alive?"

"I heard a moan."

"We have to kill it!" she cried. "If it's alive, others will come. The Nightdwellers . . . their magic . . . they'll find him; they'll find us . . . we have to kill it!"

"All right, all right!" Petra pulled out his lightwand again and activated it. "This way."

By the pale blue-green glow, they made their way along the edge of the stream until Petra saw broken branches and tumbled dirt and gravel. They edged closer. Above the rush of water, Petra heard shallow, wheezing breaths, and his heart quickened.

The circle of light slid over a clawed foot. Amlinn clutched Petra's arm tighter. He lifted the light. Silver-furred legs and body, a cat-like head. Unclothed except for a leather belt covered with intricate sigils in silver and hung with a silver-hilted dagger, the Nightdweller, a young male, sprawled awkwardly on his back. A leather band hung loosely around his neck. A crossbow and quiver surrounded by scattered bolts lay nearby. In the lightwand's cold illumination, blood as black as oil soaked the creature's right flank.

Suddenly, the Nightdweller's tortured breaths stopped. Dead?

No. After a couple of seconds, he shuddered, then noisily sucked in more air.

Petra had expected something monstrous, hideous, evil. Not this. Yes, the Nightdweller wore no clothes, was covered with fur, had a blunt muzzle and pointed ears—but no mere beast or savage could create that belt. Petra had never seen the sigils that adorned it, but they were intricate, beautifully made, clearly not the work of animals or ignorant barbarians. And that crossbow! He well remembered the Freefolk guards telling him the Nightdwellers were too ignorant to use bows. Clearly, that was a lie.

But if they've had them all this time, why haven't they ever used them to attack the Freefolk?

Amlinn let go of Petra's arm and dropped to her knees. She leaned forward, jerked the dagger from the sheath on the Nightdweller's belt, and raised it to strike. Petra grabbed her wrist in his left hand. "Wait!"

Amlinn tried to jerk free. "We have to kill it!" she panted. "More will come!"

"It's not an it," Petra said. Amlinn pulled harder, but he tightened his grip. "Look at him! He's strange, but he's just a boy. A naked, wounded boy. You can't kill him in cold blood!"

"Do you think *he* would hesitate?" Amlinn snarled. "He's not a boy. He's a *Nightdweller*. A monster. An animal. A vicious killer. His kind has murdered Freefolk and City-dwellers for centuries. They killed my parents."

"Maybe his kind did," Petra said. "But he's young. He didn't kill your parents. He may not have killed anyone."

"He'd kill us right now if he could!" Amlinn tugged again, but Petra held on.

"Freefolk and the Priests of Vekrin have mistrusted each other forever, too," he said fiercely. "But I don't mistrust you."

Amlinn snorted. "*That's* your argument? I mistrust *you*. You helped Denthold!"

Petra pressed on. "This boy is what Ell made him. As your people are what Arrica made you, and mine are what Vekrin made us. But before the Gods divided us, we were all the same—all human. This Nightdweller may be different, but he's still human."

"He's covered with fur! He has claws and fangs! He lives in the dark! He doesn't wear clothes! He's an animal!"

"He doesn't need clothes, because he's covered with fur," Petra countered. "He lives in the dark because Ell changed his people so they can't live in the light. We have claws and fangs too, but ours are blunted. And he's wearing a belt—a magical belt!—and weapons." He lifted her wrist, so the knife was at her eye level, and aimed the lightwand at it. "Look at this knife. Does that look like the work of an animal?"

Green light rippled across the straight, sharp blade, gleamed off the fine silver wire encircling the hilt, and glinted off the multifaceted green jewel in the pommel. Amlinn stared at it. The murderous fury drained from her face, and her arm suddenly relaxed in his grasp. "No," she reluctantly said after a moment. "No. It's one of the finest knives I've ever seen."

The Nightdweller moaned and rolled his head. Startled, Petra let his grip on Amlinn's wrist loosen. She jerked free, pushed him away so hard he stumbled and fell on his rear, and raised the knife again. "No!" Petra cried, raising a futile hand, but she didn't strike. Instead, she stared down at the wounded boy, the blade trembling in her hand. Then she sat back on her heels. The knife clattered on the rocks, falling from her limp fingers. "Arrica forgive me," she said softly, "but you're right. I can't kill him."

"Good." Petra put the lightwand on a handy rock so that it illuminated the Nightdweller from head to foot and then crawled over to him on his hands and knees. He carefully examined the wound in the boy's side. "Arrow graze, I think. He's lost a lot of blood, and he's still losing it." He ran his hands over the fur-covered limbs. It felt just like petting a cat. "No broken bones, though he could have injuries inside. And, of course, he may have hit his head." He looked up at Amlinn. "We need to bind his wounds."

Amlinn shook her head violently. "No! I won't kill him, but I don't see why I should help him, either. We should just get out of here."

"Same thing as killing him," Petra argued. "He'll bleed to death. But go if you want."

"You know I can't. I can't even walk." She stared at the

wounded Nightdweller boy. "Fine. Bind his wounds. But with what?"

Petra straightened, quickly stripping off his light jacket and the shirt he wore beneath that, self-consciously aware of Amlinn's unwavering gaze as he did so, even more aware of the night air chilling his bare flesh. He pulled the jacket back on, then took the Nightdweller's knife from Amlinn and used it to cut his shirt into broad strips about three fingers wide. He tied the ends together to make one long, continuous bandage. "I need you to lift his upper body," he told Amlinn.

Her mouth tightened, but she complied, moving to the Nightdweller's head. Gingerly, as though the very feel disgusted her, she lifted the Nightdweller by the shoulders. Petra wrapped the bandage around the Nightdweller's silver-furred torso as many times as it would go, then tied the ends to hold it in place. By the time he finished, the bandage already showed a dark spot above the wound, but the spot grew no larger.

For the first time, he took a closer look at what hung around the Nightdweller's neck. His eyes widened as he fingered the supple leather and dark lenses and realized what they meant. The "savages" had figured out how to protect their eyes from *Liberator*'s lights—maybe even from the sun itself. *Nightdwellers who can travel and attack by day? There's a thought to give a lot of people nightmares.*

"Petra!" Amlinn cried. Petra jerked up his head and found himself staring into the Nightdweller's open eyes, black pools without a hint of iris. The Nightdweller whispered something, the white tips of fangs appearing as his mouth moved. Petra almost thought the Nightdweller had said "Priest-boy" in the Common tongue, but he couldn't have.

Could he?

Those disconcerting eyes stared at him for a long moment, blinked twice, and then closed again. The Nightdweller's head rolled limply to one side as Amlinn lowered him to the ground.

Shaken, Petra got to his feet. "Now we can go."

"About time," Amlinn said. She shoved the Nightdweller's knife under her belt. "Let's get away from—"

A terrifying yowl rent the night above them, and in a shower of pebbles and small branches, three more Nightdwellers slid down the slope of the ravine, surrounding them in an instant.

❄ 32 ❄

THE THRONE OF BONES

As the Nightdwellers appeared in the dimming circle of light from the fading lightwand, Amlinn made one small, involuntary movement toward the knife she had just placed in her belt. Then she froze. She would never live to draw it.

She didn't expect to live anyway. The three Nightdwellers were big, bigger than Petra. The largest, black-furred and with a jagged lightning-like scar on one cheek below a tattered ear, loomed bigger than her Grandfather. Of the others, one was dark grey, the other silver-furred like the wounded boy. Sleek, muscular, aggressively male in their unashamed nakedness, they terrified her. She suddenly couldn't seem to draw enough air into her paralyzed chest.

The Nightdwellers looked from her and Petra to the boy on the ground. A rapid-fire exchange of weird, yowling speech followed. She couldn't understand any of it; but she wasn't dead yet, and she didn't understand that, either.

The black, scarred Nightdweller raised his eyes. They glowed faintly red in the light of the lightwand. "You are

Freefolk," he growled in the common tongue, his speech strangely accented but perfectly understandable. Her mouth dropped open in amazement.

He turned his smouldering gaze to Petra. "And you are a Priest-Apprentice. You travel with the Freefolk. We know much about both of you."

The fact that somehow these creatures knew them as individuals, rather than just hated Daydwellers, shocked Amlinn almost as much as the Nightdweller's power of speech.

She reached out, almost without thinking, and seized Petra's hand.

His fingers wrapped around hers. "You . . . you know of us?" Petra asked, his voice so much higher pitched than usual that he sounded like a frightened child.

"He who lies wounded here, whom you have helped, is Jin-Ra," the Nightdweller said. "He told us of you, of the Priest-Apprentice travelling with a Freefolk girl. He told us of you being taken to City Divpaxis. And he warned us of the great machine of conquest that we have this night failed to destroy."

The Nightdweller spoke as well as any other man, and better than most. Amlinn felt years of certain knowledge about his race crumbling away like dried mud in a rainstorm.

"You tried to destroy *Liberator*?" Petra said.

"*Liberator*?" The Nightdweller snorted. "*Butcherer*, more like. Yes, we tried. And we will try again. And again. Until we succeed. Because if we do not, it will surely be used to destroy us."

Amlinn dared not turn her head to look at Petra, but she prayed he would not try to defend Denthold to this Nightdweller as he had to her. Their lives hung by the thinnest of threads.

To her relief, Petra said nothing. He squeezed her hand reassuringly, and then hers tightened into a near death-grip as the Nightdweller stepped closer, so close she could feel his breath on her cheek. Her heart fluttered.

The Nightdweller reached down.

Amlinn flinched as his hand brushed her hip and pulled the knife from her belt. "This is Jin-Ra's." He held it by the hilt.

Amlinn waited in terror for him to drive the blade into her belly, but instead, he simply slipped the knife into his own belt. "I will return it to him when he recovers. As he will, thanks to your help." He stepped back. His eyes searched Amlinn's face, then Petra's, flicked to their joined hands, and then lifted again. "Your names?"

"Am . . . Amlinn," she said, voice trembling.

"Petra," he said, his voice no steadier.

"I am Shik-Pur. The two with me are Stin-Pur and Grul-Pur."

Amlinn didn't turn to look at the other two, but she knew they stood close enough behind her and Petra to kill them in an instant.

"Now, Amlinn. Petra. Tell me why you have helped Jin-Ra. Your kind hates Nightdwellers. Why did you not kill him on sight?"

"Like Nightdwellers would if they found us lying wounded in the night?" The words burst out of Amlinn, and she felt Petra's hand tighten even further. She instantly wished she hadn't spoken. Surely now the Nightdwellers would—

"Some would," Shik-Pur said. His voice remained calm.

"Some would not. Jin, I think, would not. I think he would give you aid, just as you have aided him. That alone is enough to convince me to spare your lives this night. Though I do not promise that she to whom I will deliver you will do the same."

"I can't walk," Amlinn said. "Not well. My ankle . . ."

"Then, we will carry you." Shik-Pur glanced over her head at the others. "Bind them, gag them. The boy can walk. Stin, carry the girl. Grul, help me rig a travois for Jin. We must report to the Mother Queen." He looked at Petra and Amlinn again. "She will decide your fates."

Strong hands seized Amlinn's wrists, pulled her away from Petra, and bound her wrists behind her with thin, strong rope. The Nightdweller named Stin—Amlinn guessed that the "Pur" was some kind of title since Shik-Pur had not used it when he spoke to his companions—slashed at the bottom of her tunic. He cut away a piece of cloth that a moment later gagged her into silence.

Petra's lightwand still rested on the nearby boulder. By its light, she saw Petra suffering the same fate. A moment later, propped up against the rocks like sacks of meal, they watched the Nightdwellers rig a triangular frame of large branches. Then they wove smaller branches into a kind of bed within that frame, and on that bed gently lowered the young Night-dweller, Jin. Shik picked up the lightwand. He squinted at it, as though its dim light hurt his eyes, then twisted the brass, sigil-inscribed cap.

The light vanished, leaving them in darkness except for the cold light of the stars. Stin suddenly picked her up—she would have screamed if she hadn't been gagged—and slung her over his shoulder as though she weighed nothing at all.

And then they were off, Amlinn's head bouncing against the Nightdweller's furred back.

He smelled like a wet dog.

Amlinn turned her pounding head, trying to see Petra, but the darkness defeated her. Her anger at the Priest-Apprentice for aiding Denthold seemed like some years-old memory from childhood. Now she longed to hold his hand again, to hear his voice, but she heard nothing more than the Nightdweller's breathing, the constant rush of water to their left, and the sound of the travois dragging over the ground.

They travelled alongside the stream for what seemed hours and then crossed it on a low wooden bridge. After that, they began to climb, and the sound of water faded behind them. When they levelled off, Amlinn guessed they were out of the ravine at last, but the thought brought no relief. Exhausted and in pain, she slipped in and out of a fitful doze, gasping awake from nightmares of monsters only to find herself in the grip of one.

The Nightdwellers paused briefly now and then to rest, each time dumping Amlinn unceremoniously onto the ground, where she lay aching until one of them heaved her up on his shoulder again. At one such stop, hitting the ground woke her from yet another troubled dream. She blinked at blades of grass in front of her eyes and lifted her head. Petra sat against a tree, head back, eyes closed, face pale in pre-dawn light.

Morning!

The Nightdwellers couldn't travel in sunlight. They would have to leave her and Petra—

And then the Nightdwellers pulled on their dark goggles. The journey continued as another of Amlinn's dearly held beliefs crumbled in the harsh light of reality.

They travelled east toward a wooded ridge above which the sun eventually rose. When it neared the zenith, they stopped. The Nightdwellers untied Amlinn's and Petra's hands and removed their gags so they could eat and drink. No one spoke, and Amlinn fell instantly asleep once she had gulped down her dry bread and hard, sour cheese. She woke sometime later to find herself once more bound and gagged and slung over Grul's dark grey back, with a disconcerting view of his furry buttocks working back and forth beneath her. She groaned and closed her eyes again.

The next time they stopped, their shadows stretched long and black in front of them. Panting, Grul swung her off his shoulder and onto her feet. Her ankle seemed less swollen, but the moment she put weight on her sock-clad foot, dagger-like pain stabbed her, and she stumbled forward. Grul's strong furred arms barely caught her before she fell headlong.

On the other side of Grul, next to Stin, Petra stared at her, his eyes wide and worried above his gag.

Grul seized Amlinn's tunic, drew his knife, and cut off another strip of cloth, shortening the garment so much it exposed her belly button to the cool air. An instant later, he wrapped the cloth around her head and tightened it. The blindfold pressed uncomfortably against her eyes, and a hard knot dug into the back of her head.

Furred hands guided her forward and supported her as she limped blindly along with rocks digging into the sole of her one unbooted foot. Something tugged at her clothes, and she cringed away until she realized the "fingers" were really hanging vines. Soft soil gave way to solid rock beneath her feet. The quality of the sound changed as they moved from the open air to an enclosed space, though a fairly large one, judging by the echo of Petra's footsteps. The Nightdwellers' furred feet made no sound at all, and only one of hers did.

They kept walking. From the changing sound and the feel of the air, Amlinn sensed walls closing in. They began to descend, not steeply, but steadily. The temperature rose, and she welcomed the warmth. Finally, the space around them opened out again, and at last, they stopped. She breathed in air so rank with sweat and smoke it made her nose wrinkle.

"Take off the blindfolds," came Shik's voice. The strip of cloth covering Amlinn's eyes jerked away, and she blinked in a dim red glow.

Beside her, Petra made a weird grimace. It took her a moment to recognize his expression as an attempt to smile around the gag. He probably meant it to be reassuring

It wasn't.

They stood at the edge of a vast underground chamber. Huge pillars sprouted from the floor and rose like the trunks of giant trees to the shadowed ceiling. Strange, dim torches, far redder than any Freefolk or Citydweller torch, burned in brackets set at ten-foot intervals in the chamber wall. To her eyes, they cast more shadows than light, and in all those shadows, she saw Nightdwellers.

In the centre of the chamber, a circle of torches made the uncertain light a little bit brighter, illuminating a Nightdweller woman who sat on a throne made of—Amlinn blinked—bones.

Not just bones, but bones of frightening, impossible size. Enormous thighbones formed the sides of the chair, enormous curving ribs formed the back, smaller bones filled out the spaces between, and a huge skull with teeth as long as Amlinn's middle finger loomed like a canopy above the seated woman's head. Yet despite the barbaric splendour of the throne, it was the woman upon it who inexorably drew Amlinn's gaze.

A flowing white robe draped her red-furred shoulders, though beneath it, she was as unclothed as all the other Nightdwellers. On her head, she wore a crown made of fine silver and gold wires woven into a mesh, gems sparkling redly in their midst, like sparks from a fire somehow frozen in place. To her left, the hilt of a sword with an enormous ruby set in its pommel rose above the arm of the throne, ready to her hand in an instant. Though slim and no taller than Amlinn, she exerted a strange, attractive force.

Numerous low-voiced conversations buzzed throughout the room, but everyone, consciously or unconsciously, stood turned slightly toward the throne, drawn to it like iron shavings to a lodestone.

Grul seized Amlinn's arms from behind and propelled her toward the throne of bones. Stin pushed Petra forward. The woman on the throne watched their approach through narrowed eyes.

At the very foot of the throne, Amlinn and Petra were forced to their knees, with the black, empty eye sockets of the hideous toothed skull glaring down at them. Amlinn tried to raise her head, but Grul pushed it down again so that all she could see were the woman's furred feet, each claw-like nail painted gold.

"Daydwellers." Though soft, the woman's voice bore a cold, hard core, like an icicle in velvet. "I am Sayb, Mother Queen of the People of Ell. Your lives hang by gossamer. You still breathe for only two reasons. One, we need to know more about the monstrosity now rolling south along the so-called King's Way. Two, you gave aid to our brother Jin-Ra as he lay injured, rather than slitting his throat—a thing unheard of in the long war between our races.

"I will now have your gags removed. You will address me as 'Mother Highness.' You will answer all my questions truthfully and instantly. I will know if you are lying, and the instant you do so, your blood will bathe my feet. Nod if you understand."

Heart pounding, throat dry as sand, Amlinn nodded. Out of the corner of her eye, she saw Petra do the same.

"Very well. Remove their gags. Let them look at me."

The strip of cloth around Amlinn's mouth slipped away, but her hands remained bound. She raised her eyes to meet the Mother Queen's, two obsidian-black pools with fiery cores glinting in a red-furred face.

Sayb's left hand rested on the rubied hilt of the sword attached to the throne as she looked from Amlinn to Petra, then back to Amlinn. "I will begin with you, female. What is your name?"

"Amlinn, Mother Highness."

"You are of the Freefolk."

"Yes, Mother Highness."

That penetrating gaze flicked to Petra. "Your name, male."

"Petra, Mother Highness."

"And you are a Priest-Apprentice of Vekrin."

"Yes, Mother Highness."

"It is a very strange thing, finding a Priest-Apprentice and a Freefolk girl together," said Sayb. "It is an even stranger thing to find them together in the night, in the forest. Are you a mated pair?"

Amlinn blinked. "No!"

It took Petra a moment longer to answer. "No."

"Then your togetherness is even stranger. But the strangest thing of all is that children of Arrica and Vekrin should aid a child of Ell. So now you will tell me the tale. Begin at the beginning and leave nothing out. Amlinn, speak first."

Kneeling before that terrifying throne and its equally terrifying occupant, Amlinn told everything that had happened from the moment she saw the thief prying the sunscale from the sunwagon. The Mother Queen listened intently, interrupting from time to time to ask a question, each surprising Amlinn with the level of understanding of the Daydweller world it revealed.

How does she know so much of Freefolk and Citydwellers when we know so little of them? she wondered. But, of course, she knew the answer. Freefolk and Citydwellers considered Nightdwellers to be ignorant beasts, animals to be feared, and whenever possible, slain. They'd never tried to learn more about them. But the Nightdwellers hadn't made that mistake. *They watched us, hated us, killed us, but never thought of us as less than human. So, which of us is more primitive?*

What would Grandfather, the other clan leaders, and Samarrind say when they learned the truth?

If they learned the truth. It seemed unlikely that she'd ever have the opportunity to enlighten them.

Amlinn ended her tale with the moment she and Petra were captured by the Nightdwellers. Despite the Mother Queen's stern warning to leave nothing out, she did omit one little fact—her initial inclination to gut Jin with his own knife.

The Mother Queen stared at Amlinn with smouldering eyes for a long moment, then turned that disconcerting gaze on Petra. "Priest-Apprentice Petra. Tell me your version of this strange tale. Tell no lies, or both of you die. Amlinn first. Begin."

Amlinn's breath froze in her throat. *Tell no lies?*

Petra had betrayed her with Denthold. Would he really tell all the truth now?

She waited to discover whether she would live or die.

33

BEFORE THE MOTHER QUEEN

Petra knelt before the Mother Queen in the hellish, Nightdweller-filled underground chamber, his knees aching after Stin's shove slammed him to the stone floor. But then, after the nightmarish journey they'd just endured—part of it by daylight—every inch of him ached.

Amlinn must be in agony, he thought. She knelt beside him, but he dared not turn his head to look at her. At least he had been able to walk on his own feet. For the entire trek, she had been slung like fresh kill over the shoulder of one of the Nightdwellers. The memory enraged him even now. He would gladly have gutted Stin and Grul like fish for their rough handling of her.

I love her.

The thought sprang into his mind full-formed, and he realized it had been building for some time. Now, as they faced what might be their final moments, it could no longer be denied.

I love her. And she . . . she hates me for aiding Denthold.

But even now, he could remember how it had felt when

she'd squeezed his hand, seeking reassurance and protection. *Maybe she doesn't hate me. Maybe someday . . .*

Someday? They might not even have *this* day.

The terrifying Nightdweller woman on the throne of bones introduced herself as "Sayb, Mother Queen of the People of Ell." At her command, Stin pulled the gag from Petra's mouth, and Grul removed Amlinn's. Petra desperately wanted to spit, but that seemed like a really bad idea while kneeling in front of the Nightdwellers' supreme leader. He raised his eyes now and saw her again, slim, fierce, crowned with silver, shoulders draped, the rest of her body, red-furred on limbs and flanks but white as snow on her face and breast and belly, unclothed. The giant fanged skull loomed over them like a threat. *Another* threat. Vekrin knew Sayb herself had issued plenty.

Amlinn gave her name. Sayb's gaze moved to Petra. "Your name, male."

He swallowed. "Petra, Mother Highness."

"And you are a Priest-Apprentice of Vekrin."

"Yes, Mother Highness."

"It is a very strange thing, finding a Priest-Apprentice and a Freefolk girl together," said Sayb. "It is an even stranger thing to find them together in the night, in the forest. Are you a mated pair?"

"No!" Amlinn burst out.

Petra found it harder to answer because, in truth, he wished . . .

He swallowed again. "No."

"Then your togetherness is even stranger. But the strangest thing of all is that children of Arrica and Vekrin should aid a child of Ell. So now you will tell me the tale.

Begin at the beginning and leave nothing out. Amlinn, speak first."

Aching, exhausted, wishing more than anything he could simply lie down and sleep, Petra listened as Amlinn told her version of events, truthfully and completely as far as he could tell. It gave him a long time to decide what he would say. If the Nightdwellers knew how much he had helped Denthold with *Liberator*, or worse, how he had begun to believe in Denthold's cause, he would die where he stood.

Amlinn wound down. The Mother Queen turned her penetrating attention to him. "Priest-Apprentice Petra. Tell me your version of this strange tale. Tell no lies, or both of you die, Amlinn first. Begin."

So, though he did not lie—he did not doubt for a moment that Sayb spoke truth when she said she would know if he did—he left out a great deal. He told the tale of the attack on the Temple, his finding of Amlinn, his abduction; the *Book of Vekrin*; the scrap of paper with Denthold's name. But when at last he reached the part where he and Amlinn came face to face with Denthold . . . "He forced me to work with him," Petra said. "I had no choice. I had to do as he commanded."

All true. But he very carefully said nothing about how much he had come to believe Denthold spoke the truth about the need to spread knowledge of Blue Fire throughout the kingdom to halt its stagnation and decline. After all, from the Nightdwellers' point of view, the stagnation and decline of the Daydwellers of Nevyana meant victory.

Besides, a number of assumptions he had made in deciding to throw in his lot with Denthold seemed highly questionable now, kneeling before the Mother Queen in that astonishing chamber. The Nightdwellers were not mindless, murderous beasts. Different from Daydwellers, yes, but their differences had been imposed upon them by one of the Gods. In the distant past, he and Sayb might have shared an ancestor. As he finished his tale, that thought came with the force of a blow. It should have been obvious, but it had never occurred to him before.

He stopped talking. The Mother Queen gave him a long, hard stare. In the dim light, her eyes looked like polished black gems, each containing a single red spark deep in its depths.

"Your tales change nothing," she said at last. "Whichever faction of Daydwellers wins, the victor will turn this 'Liberator' against us. Daydwellers are our enemies. You are Daydwellers." She lifted her eyes to Stin and Grul. "Kill them."

Petra's heart stuttered, and his breath congealed in his throat. He tried to shout, "No!" but no sound would emerge. Steel slid from scabbards behind them. He wanted desperately to reach out to Amlinn, but his hands remained bound. Eyes closed, he waited for the bite of the blade that would end his short life and that of the girl he would have given anything to protect.

But then someone did shout, "No!" and the voice was neither his nor Amlinn's.

34

JIN OBJECTS

Jin emerged from unconsciousness into pain-filled wakefulness. He blinked up at the stone ceiling sliding by above his head. The Great Warren, at last. He'd been convinced he'd die before he reached it. At times he had *wished* he'd die before he reached it, so agonizing had been the nightmarish journey through the forests, slipping in and out of consciousness with every bump of the travois on root and rock.

At least the floor of the Great Warren was smooth. He managed to lift his head to see the corridor sliding away behind them. Shik-Pur, a Great Warren Watchcaptain who had been part of the catastrophic raid on Denthold's and Axel's camp, looked down at him. "You are awake," Shik said, stating the obvious.

Jin nodded.

"We approach the Great Hall," Shik said. "The Day-dwellers must appear before the Throne of Bones. I will call for a litter, and they will take you to the Healers' Chambers—"

"No," Jin said.

Shik growled. "Jin-Ra, your wounds—"

"I can walk," Jin said.

Shik looked skeptical.

"The Daydwellers saved me," Jin said. "I would see what the Mother Queen says to them."

Shik glanced up. "We're here," he said. The travois settled flat on the floor of the corridor. Shik stepped past it, out of Jin's sight. "Take them in. Present them to the Mother Queen," he heard the watchcaptain say to Stin and Grul. He returned to Jin. "All right," he said. "If you can walk, walk."

Jin nodded. He sat up. Ahead he saw the Daydwellers, Stin and Grul behind them, silhouetted against a red-lit archway. Then they vanished from his sight. The corridor swam around him, but only for a moment. Despite the pain of the journey, his body had had time to replace much of the blood he'd lost, and in fact, he felt stronger than expected. He reached up a hand to Shik, who hesitated but then, with a grimace, took it. With the watchcaptain's help, Jin managed to stand, though he gasped as he did so, the wound in his side stabbing with agony.

"You need treatment. You need rest," Shik said severely.

"I need to see what happens when the Daydwellers meet the Mother Queen," Jin told him. "I have followed them across half the kingdom. They saved my life last night."

Shik snorted. "Maybe. But I doubt they will save their own." Nevertheless, he helped Jin into the Great Hall. He guided Jin to one of the benches carved into the chamber wall, where he slumped, grateful for the hard stone at his back. Shik moved away.

Jin listened as Amlinn told her tale. Then Petra began to speak, and Jin's mouth went dry. He could tell as clearly as if he could read the youth's mind that he was holding back part of the truth. It was obvious from his body language, his voice, even his smell. And if Jin knew it, the Mother Queen, who was far more attuned than he to the prevarications of others—and only a couple of arm-lengths from the Daydwellers—certainly knew it, too.

With enormous effort, Jin got to his feet and staggered toward the throne, heart pounding, ragged breathing roaring in his ears. He came up behind Stin and Grul, who stood directly behind the Daydwellers, just as the Mother Queen said, "Kill them."

But as the two warriors drew their swords, Jin thrust himself between them and shoved them aside. "No!" he shouted. His knees gave way, and he collapsed on the chamber floor right between the kneeling Daydwellers.

"Hold!" the Mother Queen commanded.

Jin lay where he had fallen, his cheek pressed against the stone. His wound burned, and spots swirled in his vision.

"What means this outburst?" the Mother Queen demanded in the Nightdwellers' tongue.

With enormous effort, Jin pulled himself to all fours, then to his knees, so that he knelt before the Throne of Bones like Amlinn and Petra. He raised his head to meet the Mother Queen's cold black gaze. "Mother Highness," he whispered in the same language, "they saved my life. They could have killed me. Most Daydwellers would have. They did not. I owe them."

The Mother Queen's stone-like expression did not soften. "They are still enemies. Their aid to you has earned them a quick death. It has not earned them more."

"Then, Mother Highness, consider instead their value," Jin said, desperate to make her listen. "The boy is a Priest-

Apprentice of Vekrin and assisted Denthold. He knows much about Blue Fire, firelances, and the machine they call *Liberator*. The girl is Freefolk, daughter of a clan leader. She must know much about sunscales and firejars and Fence. Both know much that we do not of how things are inside the cities, of the forces now at play, of what the king, the Priests, and the Freefolk clans and their Wise Women may do—knowledge we may need to save our people from destruction."

"Destruction?" the Mother Queen said. "You overestimate their chances."

Jin shook his head. "No, Mother Highness. How many of us died in our failed raid on Lord Axel's army? A surprise attack, at a place of our choosing, in the night that has always been our friend? With their sparkglobes and firelances and *Liberator*—and if there is one of those monstrosities, there will surely one day be more—they will be able to hunt us down at will. I do not believe that even the glamour of the watchstones will protect our warrens once the forests are full of Daydweller soldiers day *and* night."

The Mother Queen gazed at him. Blood roared in his ears. Warmth spread through the fur on his side. The arrow wound had re-opened. He prayed she'd respond before he fainted.

At last, she turned her glare from him to the Daydwellers. "Priest-Apprentice Petra," she said in the common tongue. "Freefolk girl Amlinn. Jin-Ra begs me to spare your lives so that you may be of use to us. Very well. I offer you this one chance. Vow now, before your Gods and ours, before me, that you will help us without reservation to remove this threat to our existence. You have aided one Nightdweller. Will you aid more? Or will your blood warm my feet?" She stood, swirling the white cape aside. She reached across her body with her right hand and drew her sword from its sheath on the throne. She pointed the curved blade at Amlinn, then at Petra. "Choose now."

Jin held his breath.

35

SHATTERED VOWS

Petra stared at the sword in the Mother Queen's hand, the blade upon whose edge his life and Amlinn's were literally balanced. In his mind, he saw another chamber, another time, when he had just turned ten years old. Standing before his father and the other senior Priests, he had proudly repeated, one by one, the vows that made him a Priest-Apprentice of Vekrin.

He had sworn to die rather than break those vows. He had been certain that truth lay only with Vekrin and his Priests. But in scant weeks, all his certainties had been overthrown. Amlinn had taught him that Freefolk were not his enemies. Denthold had convinced him that Blue Fire could and should belong to all the people of Nevyana. And Jin—the Nightdweller they had aided, who had now saved their lives and knelt between them—Jin was proof the Nightdwellers were not mere savage beasts.

"Mother Highness," he said, the steadiness of his voice surprising him, "you ask me to betray my people."

"Is this *Liberator* a Gift of Vekrin?" the Mother Queen countered.

Petra shook his head. "No."

She looked at Amlinn. "Or Arrica?"

Amlinn shook her head much more violently. "No!"

"Your people have already attacked it. Some of your friends died in that attack." She looked at Petra again. "Your Priests will face this thing at every city. Can they stand against it?"

"I don't think so," Petra said.

"Then I am asking you to help your people as well as mine, am I not? In what way is that a betrayal?" She pointed the strange curved sword at his face. "Enough talk. Decide. Now!"

Petra looked at the Mother Queen, her nostrils flaring in her blunt, white-furred muzzle, her fangs bared, her eyes red-flecked obsidian pools beneath the silver crown. He looked at Jin, silver-furred, wounded, in pain. A hundred or more Nightdwellers waited all around him in the dim chamber. They were strange and deadly and had long been the enemies of his kind, but as Jin had proved, maybe they didn't have to be.

He could not let Denthold use the power of Blue Fire, the power he had convinced Petra could make the kingdom better, to destroy Jin's people. But to stop it, he would have to renounce the beliefs he had once known with all his soul to be eternal truths as solid as the Temple itself.

Temples can be overthrown, he thought, recalling the ruins in City Divpaxis. *And sometimes should be.*

His vows had ended with a solemn oath. "If I betray these sacred vows, may Vekrin burn me with Blue Fire, so that I may serve as both sacrifice and a warning."

Strike me down, Lord Vekrin, and I will believe in you again.

He squared his shoulders and looked Sayb in the eye. "Yes," he said. "I will help you."

❧ 36 ❧

"EVEN NIGHTDWELLERS"

For Amlinn, time froze when the Queen stood and drew her sword. All she could focus on was the glint of red torchlight on the razor-sharp edge and tip of the blade, poised to drink their blood.

But once Petra promised to aid the Nightdwellers, the Mother Queen turned to her.

Amlinn lifted her eyes from the glittering steel to Sayb's flinty furred face.

"And you, girl?" Sayb demanded. "The Freefolk have borne the brunt of the long war between us and the Daydwellers. Can you put that enmity aside?"

Amlinn bowed her head and closed her eyes. She thought of Sisspeth, the little rag doll Samarrind had given her on the night that Nightdwellers killed her parents. She thought of all the nights she had lain awake in her bed, clutching that doll, listening to Nightdwellers yowling outside the Fence.

But then she remembered the flashes of firelances aimed at attacking Freefolk, the thunder of *Liberator*'s giant weapon. Denthold and Axel might not intend to exterminate the

Freefolk as they did the Nightdwellers, but they would kill her family and friends with little compunction if they got in their way.

Amlinn raised her head and opened her eyes to meet the Queen's black gaze squarely. "Yes," she said. "I will help you."

The Mother Queen pulled her sword away and slid it back into its sheath. Then she looked around the Great Hall at the gathered Nightdwellers and shouted, "The Daydwellers' lives are spared!" A few angry mutters ran through the Great Hall in response, but she quelled them with an icy glare. "No one is to harm them, on pain of death." Her glance flicked back to Stin and Grul, who still stood behind Amlinn and Petra. "Take the Daydwellers to my chamber. Take Jin-Ra to the Healers." She raised her voice. "The rest of you, disperse. Warriors, you will be summoned when needed." Sayb turned, the white cape swirling around her sleek red body. She strode away into the gloom.

Stin pulled Amlinn upright. Shaky, her ankle still hurting, she found herself clinging to the furred, heavily muscled arm of the same Nightdweller who seconds before had been poised to slit her throat. He looked down at her, his eyes wide with curiosity. His furred face, so close to her own, half-convinced her that in reality, she lay in a broken heap at the base of the waterfall, and all that had happened since was nothing more than a fever dream.

But if it were a dream, she did not wake from it. After a short walk that felt long, their guards showed them into a much smaller chamber. Thick tapestries covered the walls, and short, red-cushioned couches surrounded a central fire whose smoke vanished through a hole in the ceiling. A fine metal screen surrounded the fire. Though maddeningly ill-lit, the room was clearly the domain of a prosperous and civilized woman, even if said woman went naked except for her own fur and had teeth and claws sufficient to rip out the throat of anyone who crossed her.

The guards pushed Amlinn and Petra down onto one of the couches near the fire, side by side. It was so narrow they could not sit without their shoulders and legs touching. Amlinn found it comforting. She reached for Petra's hand. He took hers and squeezed it. After a moment, Sayb emerged through an archway in the back wall and settled on an ornately carved wooden chair facing them. She had removed the white cape and the crown, which only emphasized her nakedness.

It made Amlinn uncomfortable. She didn't even want to know how Petra felt.

"I know you are both exhausted," the Mother Queen said. "But before I let you rest, Priest-Apprentice, I must hear from you everything you know about this *Liberator*. And Denthold."

Petra took a deep breath and began to talk. His voice sounded shaky and weak, but he gave a detailed account of what he had learned about the Mad Priest's plans. With every word, Amlinn's horror grew. Putting firelances into the hands of the peasants? Building more monstrosities like *Liberator*? Making Blue Fire freely available to all? Heresy! Blasphemy! Sacrilege to Vekrin and Arrica alike! And yet Petra had bought into it, at least until he had met the Night-dwellers.

She pulled her hand free. Petra shot her a surprised look.

The Mother Queen drew his attention back to her with the very question Amlinn wanted to ask. "You took vows to serve Vekrin. You broke them when you agreed to help us, but you had already broken them by agreeing to help Denthold. Why?"

Petra stared into the screened-in fire for a long moment. When at last he spoke, Amlinn strained to hear his quiet voice.

"Because he is right about many things, Mother Highness. Nevyana is dying, dwindling, and the Gods no longer care, if they ever did. Giving Blue Fire to everyone . . . it could reverse the decline, free us from the cities where disease has taken such a heavy toll."

"Everyone?" Sayb said. "Even Nightdwellers?"

Petra paused again. "Denthold wants to destroy the Nightdwellers," he said carefully.

"I am not asking you about Denthold's belief. I am asking you about your own."

Another pause. Then a long, shuddering breath. And then, "Even Nightdwellers," Petra said in a rush. "They, too, should have Blue Fire."

His words struck Amlinn like a slap. She twisted her body around to look at him. He met her gaze steadily, his pupils so large in the dim light that his eyes seemed all black.

Arm the Nightdwellers with Blue Fire? Let everyone in the kingdom have access to the Gifts of sunscales and firejars, of Fences and Curtains, of firelances and farspeakers?

Would that truly save Nevyana, or destroy it?

It would certainly destroy the way of life Freefolk had jealously guarded.

The thought frightened her. And yet ,Amlinn could not deny what Petra said. The cities' populations were dwindling and aging. And the plagues that had ravaged the cities had found the Freefolk, too. From a dozen Clans, the Freefolk had dwindled to three. Once they had lived proudly off the land, free wherever they went. Now they depended on the cities.

If nothing changes, the kingdom will die.

Yet she also well remembered one of the Wise Women's proverbs, taught to her long ago by Samarrind: *Be careful about praying to Arrica for change. Remember, things can always get worse.*

Abruptly, the Mother Queen stood. "Enough. You are exhausted. Sleep, and then we will talk again and make our plans." She strode from the room, the beaded curtain swirling and rattling as she as passed through it.

The guards took Amlinn and Petra through a bewildering maze of corridors to another chamber, much smaller than the Queen's antechamber, though here, too, thick tapestries softened the stone walls. Two beds stood on opposite sides of another heavily screened fire. A beaded curtain hung across an opening in the back wall. Beyond it, water gurgled.

One of the guards went away, and the other positioned himself outside the door. Amlinn guessed what lay in the chamber at the back and limped into it. Expecting to find little more than a hole in the floor to squat over, she instead found, by the dim illumination of a tiny red lamp over her head, a stone seat covered with a wooden oval to relieve the chill of the stone, the bowl beneath constantly flushed clean by a stream of water. On the opposite wall, more water trickled into a stone basin in which she could wash her hands. Amlinn emerged from the chamber feeling much more comfortable—and sleepier than ever.

She lay down on one of the beds while Petra made his own way into the back chamber. By the time he came out, she had almost dozed off—almost, but not quite. With her eyes closed, she sensed him cross, not to his own bed on the other side of the chamber, but to hers: sensed that he stood beside her bed looking down at her, breathing softly. She heard a whisper of cloth, and then a warm blanket was drawn up over her body, up to her shoulders.

Lips brushed her cheek, gentle as a butterfly wing.

She thought she should react somehow, maybe protest, maybe turn her lips toward that kiss, but the lethargy gripping her was too great.

So, instead, she slept.

❧ 37 ☙

COUNCIL OF WAR

Jin woke with a strangled cry from a terrifying dream of running through the forest while lightning shattered the trees all around him. He blinked up at blue draperies. *Where . . . ?*

A face loomed over him, and his eyes widened in confused astonishment. "Ser Mar?" he croaked. He tried to sit up, but the room swam around him, and he fell back again. For a moment, he thought he would be sick.

The old Scrollkeeper chuckled and patted him on the arm. "The same," he said.

"You're really here? But how—"

"I set out not two days after you left," Ser Mar said. "The more I thought about it, the more I realized I did not wish to remain wrapped in the stone cocoon of my chamber while momentous events were unfolding in our land." He laughed. "Governor Nix was all too willing to let me set out on my own. I suspect that, knowing a little of my unconventional views, he saw it as an excellent opportunity to be rid of me. I quite astonished the Mother Queen by showing up on her doorstep only a couple of nights after she'd dispatched a messenger to summon me. My only regret is that I will not be in Broken Tree Warren to see the look on Nix's face when that messenger arrives."

"But why would the Mother Queen—"

"That is the greatest wonder of all. It seems my heretical views are no longer so heretical. Sayb and her council suddenly find my views on the non-existence of the Gods—or at least their disinterest—compelling." He frowned. "Although I must have a word with my correspondent here. While I have appreciated his occasional letters informing me of events in the Great Warren, I suspect the flow of information has not been as one-way as I thought. Someone clearly told the Mother Queen about my unusual theories. Had events not conspired otherwise, the messenger sent to Broken Tree Warren might have carried a death sentence instead of a summons." The frown turned to a rather impish grin. "Strange though it may sound, I believe I owe Denthold my thanks."

Jin tried to sit up again, and this time succeeded. The coverlet fell away, and he looked down at his wounded side. A fresh bandage covered the wound. "Thanks? To Denthold?" He remembered his dream, the lightning shattering trees all around. He remembered the blinded Nightdwellers put to the sword in the brilliant light of the sunwagons. Anger surged through him. "Thanks?" he snarled.

Ser Mar's grin vanished, and he put a placating hand on Jin's arm. "I'm sorry, Jin. That was black humour at best."

Jin closed his eyes and let his anger drop away. It wasn't really directed at Ser Mar, anyway. "I'm sorry too, Master."

He opened his eyes again. "Now, please explain what you meant."

"Denthold's *Liberator* should be an abomination in the eyes of both Vekrin and Arrica, yet neither God nor Goddess has done anything about it," Ser Mar said. "This despite dire threats from Priests and Wise Women about the horrible fates visited on those who disobey divine decrees. The earth has not swallowed Denthold, lightning has not blasted his new sunwagons. If the Gods have not acted against this, then they will never act. And if they are incapable of acting, then how can they be Gods?" He smiled again. "Suddenly, old Ser Mar's crazy version of history makes sense."

"But if Vekrin and Arrica are not Gods . . ." Even though they were alone, Jin let his voice fall almost to a whisper. "Then what about Ell?"

"What indeed?" Ser Mar did not bother to lower his voice. "Our Mother Queen, it seems, has long been less than enamoured with our own class of God-botherers. She does not see a reduction in the power of the Scrollkeepers as a bad thing.

"In short, my boy, the time is ripe for a revolution in our thinking, and Denthold, the Mad Priest, made it possible. Except for the fact he would no doubt kill me on sight, I would like to shake his hand." Ser Mar heaved himself to his feet. "Can you walk? Or shall I get a wheeled chair?"

Jin swung his legs over the side of the bed. "I can walk."

"Good. Then come with me to the council chamber. Plans are afoot."

Jin suddenly realized he was starving. "I hope they involve food." Feeling only slightly unsteady, he followed Ser Mar out of the Rooms of Healing.

The last time Jin had been in the Mother Queen's council

chamber, with its starry ceiling and pale moon-lamp, he had delivered his news from City Divpaxis. He could not have imagined then that one day he would see Watchmaster Kar-Pur and the mightiest warriors of the Great Warren clustered with the Mother Queen herself around two young Day-dwellers in this, the very heart of the Nightdweller realm.

Maps covered the stone council table, and Petra was pointing out something on one of them to the Mother Queen. But someone was notably missing.

Jin turned to Ser Mar and whispered, "Where is Ser Hiv?"

Ser Mar chuckled. "He is no longer Senior Scrollkeeper of the Great Warren. He has retired."

"Retired? Then who has replaced him?"

Before Ser Mar could reply, the Mother Queen looked up and saw them. "Welcome, Senior Scrollkeeper," she said.

Oh, Jin thought.

"Welcome, Jin-Ra," the Mother Queen continued. "It is good to see you walking again."

"Thank you, Mother Highness," Jin said.

The Mother Queen indicated the maps. "You set all this in motion," she said. "And you were one of the few to survive the attack on *Liberator*." She gestured for him to join the group at the table. "Come. I have not yet heard your report of that disaster."

Jin went to her side. He cast his thoughts back to that night of terror and carnage. "They had no Fence," he said. "We thought they relied solely on the lights of the machine and on their sentries. We took out the lights easily and removed our goggles, but then, on all the wagons except the one stolen from the Freefolk, the sunscales themselves blazed with light. If I had not been looking away, I would have been blinded. Many others were." He touched his side. "And then their bows and firelances cut us down."

"I doubt you'll ever again find them without the protection of a Fence," Petra said.

Jin blinked, startled by how freely the Daydweller spoke—and how closely the Nightdwellers listened to him.

"Denthold certainly knows how to create one," Petra continued. "His mistake that night was not raising the Fence for protection. He relied on the sparkglobes, believing Nightdwellers knew nothing of bows and were not clever enough to shield their eyes from the light. Now he knows better. He is almost certainly raising the Fence every night. He would have raised it anyway before he reached Viandaxis. It is as good a protection against Priests and city guards as it is against you."

"Which brings me to the news I was about to share before Ser Mar's and Jin-Ra's arrival," said the Mother Queen. "Our scouts report that Denthold and Lord Axel have already reached Viandaxis, and they took it easily. However, the Viandaxis Priests had warning, perhaps from Freefolk. They took their secrets and fled along the King's Way with the duke and the city guards. Ordinarily, my warriors would harry them along the way, but not now, of course. Our scouts report that the gate was open for Denthold and Lord Axel. They installed Duke Felkor, who once ruled Divpaxis, as governor, and they have already begun the journey to Desmixis. They may well reach it tomorrow."

"The Priests will have farspoken their fellow Priests in every city," Petra said. "I believe Denthold and Axel will find all city gates open, every Temple deserted and emptied of its secrets, and every guardsman gone. They will be mustering at City Primaxis. Rather than fighting the forces of the kingdom piecemeal, when Denthold and Axel reach the end of the King's Way, they will face King Stobor's full army and every firelance the Priests can bring to bear." He looked pale. "It will be a bloodbath. On both sides."

"So," said the Mother Queen calmly, "best if we stop him first. How do we attack if they have the Fence?"

"You could attack during the day," Petra replied.

Sayb shook her head. "No. Our advantage still lies in the night, provided we can deprive them of light."

"Then we must stop the flow of Blue Fire," Petra said. "Without it, there's no Fence, no light, and no firelances."

The Mother Queen's eyes fixed on him. "How?"

Petra shook his head. "I don't know."

The Mother Queen turned her gaze to Amlinn. "Then, Amlinn, it falls to you. The sunscales and the firejars were the Gifts of Arrica. How do we disable them?"

❧ 38 ☙

THE CAVE OF SALT

Amlinn's blood and breath froze within her.

Sayb's gaze did not waver. Her eyes glowed in the dim light. "You vowed to help us. It is time for you to do so."

"I can't . . ." Amlinn choked out. "The Fence . . ."

"You must," Sayb growled, and her hand went to her dagger.

Suddenly, the ice in Amlinn's blood boiled away into hot anger. She heard herself screaming at the Mother Queen, vomiting furious words. "You killed my parents! I've spent my whole life listening to your kind howling outside the Fence, afraid you'll get in and kill Grandfather, or me, or my playmates! Only the Fence kept you out, and now you want me to give you its secrets?" Her throat closed on the last word. Sobs racked her. She put her head down, closed her eyes, and thought, bitterly, *And now she'll kill me.*

Amlinn felt Petra's touch on her shoulder. He seemed to be touching her more and more—reassuring, comforting touches. She liked it, but he could not save her from her own foolhardiness. She waited for the sharp kiss of the Mother Queen's knife.

But instead, she felt another gentle touch. Petra's hand tightened. She opened her eyes and blinked at long, furred fingers laid across her forearm. Her head jerked up. Sayb now stood beside her, her dark eyes level with Amlinn's. "I am sorry about your parents," the Mother Queen said softly. "Your people and mine have been at war for a long time. I, too, have lost people I love, to Freefolk and city guards. But now we have a chance to bring the killing to an end. Won't you help us seize it?"

Amlinn thought of all her nightmares of Nightdwellers, red-eyed, furred monsters, breaking through the Fence, killing her friends, killing Grandfather, killing her. Yet here she stood, in the very heart of the Nightdwellers' realm, with their Mother Queen placing a tender hand on her arm and offering sympathy and a way to move beyond fear forever.

But if she betrayed the secrets of Arrica to the Night-dwellers, would any of the Freefolk ever forgive her? Would Samarrind?

Would Grandfather?

She couldn't answer that question. But to her surprise, she found she could answer the one the Mother Queen had just posed.

"Yes," she said, or rather breathed, for she could hardly make a sound through her sob-choked throat. "Yes," she said again, louder. She swallowed a lump. "I can tell you how to disable the firejars."

Petra jerked his hand from her in surprise. She instantly missed his touch.

"Smash them," said one of the warriors whose name she did not know. "What more is there to it?"

But Amlinn shook her head. "The magic of their making protects them. You could throw one off a mountain, and it would survive. Nor can you mar their sigils. You simply cannot touch them."

"So, there's a sigil for disabling them?" Petra guessed.

"Yes," said Amlinn. "Temporarily. It lasts only until the next sunrise. Periodically, the firejars must be rejuvenated, their sigils redrawn. During those times, they must first be deactivated. Samarrind . . . the Wisest . . . showed it to me when she still thought I might become a Wise Woman. When I chose to dance instead, those lessons stopped, but I remember them."

"Can you teach it to me?" Petra said.

"It must be drawn once for each sunwagon," Amlinn warned. "And it is not drawn on the jars itself. Remember, you can't touch them. Instead, it must be drawn on the ground nearby."

"With what materials?" Petra said. "Charcoal? Chalk? Powdered glass?"

Amlinn looked around the table. So many eyes watching her, yet it was Petra's she noticed most, for his expression was strangely sad. *He knows how it feels to reveal the most sacred secrets of one's people.* She took a deep breath to steady her racing heart, then said a single word, "Salt."

Petra's expression changed to one of dismay. "Salt? Diamond dust would be easier to come by!"

"The Wise Women use salt given by Arrica herself," Amlinn went on. "It has been hoarded for centuries, every speck swept up again once it is used. But the magic is what it is. The sigil to disable the firejars must be drawn with salt."

Jin looked puzzled. "Salt?" he said. "Precious as diamond dust? But—"

The Mother Queen held up her hand. "Rather than tell them, Jin," she said, "why don't you show them? I think it will be instructive in a number of ways." To Amlinn's surprise, Sayb smiled.

Jin bowed. "Yes, Mother Highness."

"We will break for one hour. Then we will finalize our plans." The Mother Queen turned and walked away from the table, taking Watchmaster Kar-Pur by the arm as she did so. She spoke to him in a low voice as the others at the table dispersed.

For the first time since they had discovered him bleeding in the ravine, Amlinn found herself face to face with the young Nightdweller. Jin smiled at her without teeth. She'd already noticed that Nightdwellers seldom showed their teeth when they smiled, probably because their teeth were so alarming. "We have not actually spoken," he said. "But I have been watching you, following you, for a very long time."

Amlinn blinked. "What?" She resolutely kept her gaze on his face, as she tried to do with all of the Nightdwellers. She still hadn't gotten used to the fact that none of them wore clothes. Fur was fine as far as it went, but as far as she was concerned, it didn't go far enough. *At least the light is always dim,* she thought.

"From your first night outside City Primaxis," Jin said. "A Priest-Apprentice of Vekrin in the camp of the Freefolk was something I had never seen before. And when I told—" He turned. "Come. There is someone you must meet."

"What about the salt?" Petra said.

"It's not going anywhere," said Jin.

With Petra close behind her, Amlinn followed Jin to the Nightdweller whom Sayb had greeted as "Senior Scrollkeeper." He stood well back in the shadows, barely visible until they were very close to him. When at last she could see him clearly—or as clearly as she could see anything in the Nightdweller warren—her eyes widened. He was *old*. Far older than Grandfather, judging by the white fringe of fur around the bald spots on his head and belly, his round shoulders, and the cane upon which he leaned. But even in the dimness, his eyes sparkled, bright and alert.

"Amlinn of the Freefolk and Petra of the Priests of Vekrin, this is Ser Mar, my Master," Jin said formally.

"An honour to meet you both," said the old Nightdweller in a thin voice. "I feared I would live my whole life without ever speaking to a Daydweller. And now a follower of Arrica and a follower of Vekrin are here together in the Great Warren as allies! It is literally a dream come true."

Amlinn didn't know what to say to that.

"Ser Mar," Jin said, "was once the Scrollkeeper for Broken Tree Warren, my home."

"I heard the Mother Queen call you 'Scrollkeeper' when you came in," Amlinn said. "What is a Scrollkeeper?"

"Historian. Judge. Priest. Among other things," said Ser Mar. "But I have not been Scrollkeeper for Broken Tree for a long time. I developed heretical ideas."

"Heretical?" Petra questioned.

Ser Mar smiled. "For example, I once suggested that rather than killing Daydwellers on sight, we should try talking to them."

Amlinn surprised herself by laughing. She liked the old Nightdweller, though the idea she could like any Nightdweller still startled her.

"In fact," Ser Mar went on, "I went so far as to suggest that Daydwellers and Nightdwellers were once allies and could be again. This was not popular, and I was retired."

"And has spent the time since corrupting young minds," Jin said. "Well, one in particular."

Amlinn smiled at the affection in the young Nightdweller's voice.

"But the Mother Queen not only called you 'Scrollkeeper,' she called you 'Senior Scrollkeeper,'" Petra said. "Does that mean your ideas aren't heretical anymore?"

Ser Mar's smile faded. "It is obvious now, even to the Mother Queen, that Ell is not going to help her people. I doubt she ever has. Making us what we are, separating us from our fellow humans, sentencing us to live in the dark? Ell's 'Gift' is more like a curse."

Jin looked nervously around as though afraid they might be overheard. But Petra, his gaze fixed intently on the old Scrollkeeper, said, "And what of the Gifts of Vekrin and Arrica? Are they curses, too?"

"In a way," Ser Mar said. "Blue Fire has helped make life easier in this harsh land. But the way it was given, separating the followers of Arrica from the followers of Vekrin? That was a curse, leading only to strife and stagnation. Your own heretic, Denthold, is right about one thing. If Nevyana is to thrive, the barriers between Freefolk and the Citydwellers must be torn down, and Blue Fire in all its manifestations made available to all." He laughed. "But I am an even greater heretic than he, for I say that the barrier between Nightdwellers and Daydwellers must *also* fall."

Petra lowered his voice. "I have vowed to help the Nightdwellers, Ser Mar, and I will, but can you promise me that once your warriors have firelances, or even *Liberator* itself, they will truly make peace with the Daydwellers? Or will they turn those weapons against us?"

Ser Mar inclined his head. "You are a wise youth," he

murmured. "I am afraid I cannot give you the promise you seek. I cannot command the Mother Queen or her warriors, nor can I see into their hearts. All I can suggest is for you to be on guard." He glanced at the young Nightdweller. "You too, Jin. The risk is that all of this will do nothing to heal divisions, but simply provide new and more terrible weapons for war, war such as Nevyana has never seen."

"But not war such as humanity has never seen," Petra said.

Again, a glimmer of respect surfaced in Ser Mar's grizzled face. "They teach you the true history of the world, then, in the Temples?" He sighed. "No one in these warrens has wanted to hear it."

"What history?" Amlinn said, feeling lost.

"I will explain," Ser Mar said. He looked around. "But not here. We are the only ones remaining in this chamber, and a cold and drafty one it is, for all its beauty."

Amlinn thought it rather over-warm but said nothing.

"Come to my quarters, and I will tell you. And perhaps Petra can fill in gaps in my own knowledge."

"Can you fill in the gaps in my belly too?" Jin said. "I'm starving."

Ser Mar laughed. "I can."

Jin grinned, and this time, he did show his fangs. Amlinn shivered a little at the sight. "Thank you, Master." Jin looked at Petra and Amlinn. "But first, a side-trip, as the Mother Queen commanded."

"Ah," Ser Mar said. "That way is too hard for an old man. I will await you in my chambers."

"The chambers that used to be Ser Hiv's?" Jin said.

Ser Mar smiled. "The same."

He led the way out of the council chamber into the wide, high-ceilinged corridor, made of smooth, polished black stone. Then he turned right, while Jin, Amlinn, and Petra turned left. After a hundred yards or so, they turned left again down a side corridor still comfortably wide and high but not so smooth. After about ten minutes, they stopped at a dark opening. Jin took a dimly glowing torch of greenly luminescent moss from a sconce by that entrance and led them into a narrow, twisting tunnel. Water streaked the walls and puddled on the floor, deep enough at one point for them to splash through. The ceiling dipped lower and lower until they had to stoop to save their skulls. For the first time, Amlinn really sensed the weight of stone and earth above their heads. She found it far too easy to imagine the tunnel collapsing, burying them alive. She also wondered how far they would have to walk. Her ankle, though much improved, still pained her with every step.

Suddenly, the walls and ceiling around them receded. Jin raised his mossy "torch," and in its strange light, an enormous chamber seemed to spring into being around them. Giant crystals picked up the dim light of the glowing moss and reflected it back in flecks of green.

Amlinn gasped. "It's beautiful."

"It's more than that!" Petra sounded awed. He knelt and picked up a tiny sparkling crystal from the floor. He touched it to his tongue. "It's salt," he said wonderingly. "This whole cavern is made of salt!"

Amlinn stared around, open-mouthed. "But—Blessed Arrica—you could buy all of Primaxis with this much salt!"

Jin smiled without fangs. "And this is only one chamber of it. There are others. We have little use for it except to flavour and preserve food. Ser Mar claims it was left behind when some ancient ocean dried away to nothing, but I do not see how that can be possible."

"Unbelievable." Petra stared around the cavern. "What other wonders do you Nightdwellers have tucked away, Jin?"

‍ ❦ 39 ❦

A CURSE FOR THE GODDESS . . .

Seeing Amlinn's and Petra's wide-eyed faces in the salt cave, Jin realized for the first time that things he took for granted were wonders to Daydwellers, just as he was sure many things they took for granted in the sunlit world would be wonders to him.

"Ser Mar tells me we have many things the Daydwellers value more than we do," Jin said. "Gold. Silver. Gems. Copper and iron . . ." He thought of something else Ser Mar had told him, and a sudden surge of suspicion hardened his voice. "Things the Daydwellers would seize by force if they could."

Petra nodded. "They would," he said. "Prince Axel for one and for certain." He stood up from where he had knelt to taste the salt. "But if we can bring peace between Nightdwellers and Daydwellers, these riches will benefit all of Nevyana."

"Ser Mar says Nevyana could thrive beyond anyone's dreams if only all three peoples shared their knowledge," Jin said. He thought of all the nights Ser Mar had murmured heresy to him in his remote chamber of the Broken Tree Warren. Now the Mother Queen had elevated him to Senior Scrollkeeper of the Great Warren.

The thought emboldened him. "The Gifts of the Gods should belong to everyone. The Gods are gone. They probably weren't Gods, to begin with. We don't need to concern ourselves with their wishes any longer." And then, suddenly and to his own surprise, driven by everything that had happened and was about to happen, he shouted, "You hear that, Ell?" His voice echoed around the giant chamber of salt. "You cut us off from daylight and made us live in the earth like animals, but you can't keep us here forever! Do you hear my blasphemy, Ell? If you're really a Goddess, strike me down now!"

His voice echoed away into silence. Ell did not strike him down. Ell did not respond in any way.

Jin's heart pounded. He had terrified himself with that shout, but proved something, too. Whatever she might have been when she made the Nightdwellers what they were, Ell no longer listened to them. She no longer cared what they thought, if she ever had.

His fear turned to fury, and at the top of his lungs, he bellowed, "Then to hell with you! You hear me, 'goddess'? To hell with you!"

40

...AND FOR THE GOD

Petra's heart thudded in his ears and drowned out the fading echoes of Jin's defiant shout. Everything Petra had struggled with since he saw the Heretic and *Liberator*, untouched by Godly retribution, poured into his head, and then he, too, found himself screaming. "You're a fraud, Vekrin! A trickster, a liar! Your Godstones should have been gifts to all humanity, not just your own blind followers. Strike me down now if you're listening! Otherwise, to hell with you too!"

The cavern of salt swallowed his shout. Nothing else happened.

Petra took a shaky breath and turned to Jin. He felt light-headed, free in a way he hadn't felt since . . . since before he'd taken his vows as Priest-Apprentice. "Forget the Gods," he snarled. "They've certainly forgotten us. Let's go figure out how to stop this war before it begins."

He glanced at Amlinn. She stood stock-still, staring into the darkness, her face a pale blotch in the dim light. "Yes," she said. "Let's get out of here."

Moss-torch in hand, Jin led them back into the tunnel.

41

COMFORT AMID CONFUSION

The boys' angry screams at their deities echoed in Amlinn's mind as she followed Petra and Jin back up the tunnel. Her hands shook. Her limbs felt weak. Even her insides trembled, filled with some emotion she had no name for. Shame? Fear? Longing?

She had already betrayed Arrica by sharing the secret of disabling firejars with Petra and the Mother Queen, but to deny the Goddess even existed? To openly shout her defiance, curse Arrica, dare her to act?

Samarrind was wrong about the Nightdwellers. Amlinn studied Jin's broad furred back in front of her as they walked. Samarrind had told Amlinn they were savage, ignorant, beast-like monsters that drank blood and devoured children. None of it was true. But that didn't mean everything Samarrind had taught her was wrong. It didn't mean that Arrica had lied, or died, or left Nevyana forever and no longer cared what happened to her followers. It only meant the Wise Women were human.

Amlinn knew in her heart she could never repudiate

Arrica as Jin and Petra had repudiated Ell and Vekrin. She could not. Not without also repudiating all her friends, her dead parents, Grandfather, the children she'd grown up with, and Samarrind, who had been like a mother to her. *But if the Freefolk found out what secrets I've already shared, I could lose them anyway.*

So, while Petra and Jin strode away from the chamber of salt with new purpose, Amlinn hung back. Indecision and anguish dogged her feet far more than the still-lingering ache in her tightly bound ankle. She stared at the back of Petra's head. He confused her, frustrated her, and yet attracted her. She knew he wanted to be more than just a friend, and many days she felt the same.

But then he would do something she couldn't understand.

His apparent decision to help Denthold had infuriated her so much that she'd believed she could never respect or befriend him again—and then he'd come to her rescue when the runaway horse carried her wagon off. He'd helped her in the ravine with tenderness and consideration. He clearly worried for her and about her.

In the warren, they had grown closer once more. They shared a chamber, after all. She recalled their first night there, when he had tucked her in as she drifted off to sleep. He often took her hand. She wondered if very soon now, she might let him kiss her. But after his outburst in the cavern cursing Vekrin, daring him to strike him down . . . she shook her head. All of a sudden, she wondered if she really knew Petra at all.

The three of them joined Ser Mar in the Senior Scroll-keeper's chamber, hung with gold cloth and furnished with beautifully carved red-cushioned chairs and couches, though it was all, to Amlinn's eyes, sadly under-lit, of course. Which was just as well, when Jin tore into a hunk of bloody meat with his fangs. Amlinn gulped and averted her eyes.

Ser Mar told a fantastic version of history. The Scroll-keeper claimed that once the three Gods who survived the War of the Twelve had bestowed gifts on their followers in the new land of Nevyana, they abandoned the world forever. "Never to be heard from again," he said. He paused, and then repeated with more emphasis, *"Never to be heard from again. There has not been a single substantiated instance of any of the Gods acting directly in the world since the Godstones were planted, the King's Way laid, the sunscales created, and the Nightdwellers changed. The Priests of Vekrin were left with their holy book of instructions, the Wise Women of Arrica with the knowledge they hand down from generation to generation, the Nightdwellers with the First Scrolls, and all of us were left on our own."*

"But . . ." Amlinn saw the other three looking at her expectantly and realized she had spoken aloud. She tried to marshal her thoughts. "But Samarrind, the Wisest, says that Arrica is with us every moment, that she watches over us in the wilderness . . ."

"Watches over you to protect you from *us*," Ser Mar pointed out. "As we are taught by our Scrollkeepers that Ell watches over us to protect us from *you*. Yet, I can tell you that there is no record in our scrolls of any attack by our people on yours or yours on ours being turned back by supernatural means. Have *you* ever heard of such a miracle?"

She wished she could have said yes, but instead, an old familiar thought ran through her mind. *There was no miracle the night my parents died. If Arrica watches over me, why am I an orphan?*

She had once asked Samarrind that very question. Samarrind's expression had darkened and her voice had turned icy. "Arrica's ways are not our ways and to question her is to open the Fence of your soul to darkness," the Wisest had said severely. "Take care, lest you find yourself cast out of the camp."

It had not been a satisfactory answer then, and it was even less satisfactory now, as Amlinn sat in the Great Warren with Nightdwellers. Confused and troubled, she said nothing.

"For our part," Ser Mar said, "every raiding party goes forth with the blessings of Ell rained down upon the warriors' heads by the Scrollkeepers. And yet, our warriors suffer hardship and failure and death at exactly the same rate as you would expect were no such blessings provided." His voice hardened. "If Ell protects her people, then why did so many die in the attack on *Liberator*?"

"Vekrin has no more interest in the welfare of his people or any other," Petra said, "or *Liberator* could never have been built."

Ser Mar nodded. Then he scratched under his chin. "And now, at last, my heretical thoughts no longer seem so heretical to the Mother Queen and many others. Oh, Vekrin, Arrica and Ell certainly existed, and did indeed give Gifts to their respective followers, or we would not look as we do." He reached up and tugged on one pointed ear, making Amlinn smile. "There's no question they established humans in this new, untouched land. But then they went away, and after several centuries, it seems unlikely they will return."

"But they might," Amlinn protested. "The Wisest says Arrica will return someday, could return at any moment.

That's why we have to keep faith, keep our secrets and traditions—"

"I cannot argue that point," Ser Mar said, surprising Amlinn. "The fact the Gods have not been heard from for five hundred years does not prove they will not return tomorrow. But it seems a thin thread on which to hang the living of your life, and little reason to accept death, suffering, and the slow decline of our civilization."

His words felt like a dagger piercing Amlinn's heart. Had Samarrind lied to her? Samarrind, the woman who had taught her to sing and weave and sew, taught her about the ways of animals and the ways of men and women; Samarrind, who was like a mother to her?

She wanted to defend the Wisest. But she had no words with which to do that, so she said nothing.

Ser Mar heaved himself to his feet, leaning on his cane. "The hour is up," he said. "We must return to the council chamber." He gave Jin an amused look. "Unless you need to devour another haunch or two."

Jin wiped his bloodstained mouth with a napkin and set it aside. "No, I think I can manage," he said. He took a long draft of water from a pewter cup, then stood. "I feel much stronger."

The three of them returned to the chamber with the starry ceiling and the moon-lamp. They were the last to arrive. The Mother Queen gestured them to the table. "Watchmaster Kar-Pur and I have finalized our plans," she said without preamble. She nodded to the big black-furred warrior.

"We depart in the morning," Kar-Pur said to the gathering. "While our main force tracks Denthold's and Axel's army, scouts will attempt to discover the location and movements of the Freefolk. We will shadow Denthold and Axel until the Mother Queen deems the time right for the attack. With the knowledge Amlinn has provided," he nodded in Amlin's direction, "we will disable the firejars. Without Blue Fire for their lights and firelances, they cannot stand against us."

Amlinn couldn't fault any of that. *Liberator* had to be stopped. But she still felt as if she carried a lump of lead inside her that grew heavier every time she thought of Arrica and Samarrind and Grandfather, of the Freefolk life she had known.

In the quarters she shared with Petra, she sat on her bed while he went into the water chamber.

When he emerged, he sat next to her. "What's wrong?" he asked. His gentle voice broke the dam holding back her tears, and she wept, sobs racking her body. Petra put his arms around her and pulled her close, and she pushed her head tight to his chest, his heart a comforting drumbeat in her ear.

At last, she gained control of herself. She straightened, wiping the tears from her face. "I'm . . . sorry," she said. "I don't . . ."

"Don't apologize." Petra gave her a crooked smile. "None of this is easy. For any of us."

She chewed her lip a moment, studying his face. "Petra," she said at last, "what you did back in the cave—rejecting Vekrin, cursing him to his face, daring him to strike you down—did you really mean that? Your father is First Keeper of Primaxis. You're a Priest-Apprentice of Vekrin. Everything you were taught—"

"Was a lie."

"Not all of it, surely."

"Most of it." Petra leaned closer, gaze and voice intense. "If Vekrin were a God and capable of action, he would have acted by now. The fact he has not . . . we're on our own, Amlinn. There are no Gods, not anymore. At least not ones who care about what's happening here."

Amlinn looked at her hands, twisted together on her lap. "I don't know what to think," she whispered.

"Then think this." Petra reached out and took those hands, clasping them in his own. He leaned in close.

Her breath caught in her throat at his nearness.

"If there are no Gods," he murmured, "then there is no one to offend when a Freefolk girl and a Priest-Apprentice of Vekrin . . ."

He kissed her.

She held back for a moment, but his lips were warm, and she needed warmth, needed love, needed something to hold onto as the world she had always known crumbled around her. Petra was there, and he loved her. The Gods might be a lie, but that was the truth.

Her arms went around him and his arms around her, and as she melted into the kiss, into him, her doubts and fears and worries melted away as well, maybe not forever, but for now.

And for now, that was enough.

42

THROUGH THE FENCE

Three weeks of exhausting travel later, Petra lay on his stomach atop the slope of a deep gully far to the south of the Great Warren, Amlinn on his left and Jin on his right, peering through a screen of bushes at the camp of Lord Axel's army.

Liberator had completed half its journey from Divpaxis to Primaxis. Nightdweller scouts reported that at each city, Lord Axel's firelancers poured through the streets and quickly seized control of the Temple, a Temple that in every city already stood open and empty. The Priests had taken their own firelances and secrets south toward City Primaxis. As fast as Axel's men marched, the farspoken messages of Vekrin moved faster.

Battle, it seemed, would begin at the very end of the road, before the Great Gate of Primaxis, just as Petra had predicted.

The Nightdwellers had also found the Freefolk. All the clans were joined together in one giant camp about a day's journey away at the Field of Arrica, the gathering place just south of the giant wooden bridge Petra remembered crossing on the journey north with Clan Therra. Whether the Freefolk were planning their own attack or preparing a last-ditch defence should Lord Axel march against them, the Nightdwellers did not know.

Nor, it seemed, did Amlinn. She'd only shrugged when Sayb questioned her. "Ask my grandfather," she replied. "He did not discuss such matters with me even before I was captured. I have no insight into his thoughts now."

Almost every night along the way, the Nightdwellers led by Kar-Pur from the Great Warren had been joined by warriors from other warrens. Now more than two hundred Nightdwellers waited for the Daydwellers' Fence and lights to fail. Tonight, though, only Jin, Amlinn, and Petra had come to the Daydweller camp. The rest of Kar-Pur's force was encamped not far away in a cavern. It was one of the large dayshelters Ell had provided to the Nightdwellers along the length of the King's Way, to facilitate their regular patrols of the King's Way—something they did even when an army wasn't marching south along it.

Petra gave Amlinn a sideways glance. He should have been happier than he'd ever been. That night after he and Jin had shouted their defiance to the Gods, he'd finally done what he'd longed to do for weeks and kissed her. She'd returned the kiss enthusiastically. There had been a great deal more kissing since. And yet, though they were now physically more intimate, Amlinn seemed more spiritually distant than ever. He knew she still wasn't prepared to renounce the Gods as he and Jin had done. He hoped her withdrawal reflected only her own disquiet and wasn't a sign that she regretted her vow to help the Nightdwellers—especially considering what Petra was about to attempt with the help of Freefolk secrets she had shared.

He touched the heavy pouch filled with salt on his belt—enough salt to purchase a large house in City Primaxis—just to reassure himself it was still there. Then he turned his attention back to the Daydweller camp.

The four sparkglobes on *Liberator* blazed so brightly that even Petra could barely look at them. Like the other Night-dwellers, Jin wore his smoked-glass lenses. But the camp was no longer protected only by light. All around it, the air shimmered blue: a Freefolk Fence. Inside that glimmering barrier, armed guards patrolled, alert eyes turned always toward the forest but sliding right over Petra and the others where they lay in the shadowed grass.

Petra rolled over on his back and slid down into the gully, which was deep enough to hide him from the guards. Amlinn and Jin joined him.

Jin pushed the goggles up onto his furred forehead. "Will they really let you in?" he asked. "Will Denthold believe you?"

"Well, he won't have me killed outright," Petra said, hoping that was true. "Beyond that, I don't know. I will do what I can. Keep following the camp. It may not be tomorrow night, but eventually, the lights will go out. Be ready."

"We will," Jin said.

Petra took a deep breath. "I'm not looking forward to this next bit." He scrambled to his feet and faced Jin. "All right," he said. "Do it." He looked down at himself. In the darkness, he couldn't clearly see his shirt and vest and trousers, but he knew they were filthy, travel-stained, ragged. He had rolled in dirt and mud and brambles to make sure of it.

Petra looked up again just in time to catch the flash of

Jin's dagger. It slashed through the stained sleeve of his shirt and into the flesh of his shoulder. He gasped at the pain. Warm blood welled up, soaking the shirt. Then Jin's fist crashed into the side of his face, knocking him to the ground. He sat up, groaning. His head pounded, and he could feel his eye swelling shut. "I think you enjoyed that," he muttered.

"You aren't seriously hurt," Jin said. "But you are also not hurt in a way you could easily do to yourself." He paused. "And I did *not* enjoy it." He held out his hand and pulled Petra back to his feet.

The cut in his shoulder flamed. "Maybe not," he said. "But I'm still pretty sure it hurt me more than it hurt you."

Amlinn stared at him wide-eyed over the hand covering her mouth. She lowered it to say, "Are you going to be all right?"

"He is not seriously hurt," Jin repeated, sounding cross.

Amlinn stepped toward Petra and gingerly kissed him on the lips. "Good luck," she murmured.

"Thanks," Petra said. He licked his lips. "I'm going to miss that for the next few days."

Jin snorted. "Young mated pairs are all alike. They only ever think about one thing."

"We're not . . . we haven't . . . I mean . . ." Amlinn spluttered.

Petra was glad it was too dark for Amlinn to see how red his face had become. *Although Jin can probably see it.* He forced a laugh. It made his jaw hurt. "Be careful, Amlinn. Jin. Don't get yourselves killed." He took a deep breath. That hurt too. "Here goes."

Petra scrambled out of the gully. Clutching the shallow wound in his left shoulder with his right hand, he pushed through the screen of bushes and ran stumbling toward the Fence. "Let me in! Let me in!" he shouted.

Half a dozen shadowy figures rushed to the Fence, silhouettes against *Liberator*'s glare. "It's the Priest-Apprentice, Denthold's favourite!" someone shouted. "Open the Fence!"

A gap appeared in the blue shimmer. Petra staggered through it and collapsed on the ground. It wasn't entirely an act. He felt lightheaded and wondered just how much blood he was losing from Jin's "you aren't seriously hurt" dagger-slash.

A grey-haired man he recognized as one of Denthold's Healers knelt over him. The Healer bandaged his wound with supplies from the satchel he carried and took Petra's chin, turning his head this way and that. "A black eye. No serious damage done." The Healer stood. "Take him to Denthold. I will attend to him further once they have spoken."

Soldiers hauled him to his feet, one on either side. They hurried him through the rows of tents and campfires toward Denthold's personal wagon. One of them mounted the steps and knocked on the door. It opened a crack. Voices murmured. The soldier returned, helped Petra up the steps, and pushed the door open to usher him inside.

Denthold sat at the fold-down table in the middle of the wagon wearing a Priest-blue nightrobe. As the soldier closed the door, Petra swayed. He grabbed the table for support and then half-sat, half-collapsed onto the bench across from Denthold.

"This is most unexpected," Denthold said. His voice held no warmth. "You vanished on the day the Freefolk attacked, more than three weeks ago. I told Lord Axel you were kidnapped by them, but I confess I thought it more likely you took your chance to escape and rejoin them. Yet here you are, far from the Freefolk camp. How did you escape them—if you did—and how did you survive the night?"

"Escaping the Freefolk wasn't hard," Petra said. He still felt lightheaded, but he knew he had to keep his wits about him. "With all the clans mixed together, they're not as well-organized as usual. As for the Nightdwellers . . ." He put his hand, still sticky with drying blood, to his bruised face. "That was how I got this. I fought one not far from here."

"And survived?" Denthold said skeptically.

"It was a young one. Smaller and weaker than me. I surprised it just as it came out of a hole in the ground. We scuffled. It cut me with a knife, but when I knocked the knife away, it scuttled back down into its hole. I ran before it came back with help."

Denthold studied him. "Well, you certainly didn't do that to yourself," he said at last. "But I still have questions. How did you know we were here? Did the Freefolk tell you?"

Petra shook his head. "I wasn't looking for you. I was trying to reach City Pentaxis. I saw sparkglobe light reflecting off the clouds. I didn't know I'd found you instead of a Freefolk clan until I came out of the forest."

Denthold looked at him through narrowed eyes. He clearly wasn't convinced, but Petra doubted he would suspect the truth, that Petra was working with Nightdwellers. More likely, he thought Petra was spying for the Freefolk. Finally, Denthold nodded and leaned back, placing his hands flat on the table in front of him. "So. You have come back to us. What do you know about the status of our campaign?"

"Only what the Freefolk know. That you have taken city after city. That the city guards and Priests flee at your approach. That they have not offered battle."

Denthold snorted. "Not likely, not while we have

Liberator. King Stobor and your father aren't fools. They are consolidating their forces, hoping to field a force against us at City Primaxis that is great enough to overcome even *Liberator*. They will give battle there—they have no choice—but they will be defeated. And then the world will change forever." He folded his arms. "Enough talk. You need to rest and heal." He glanced at the soldier waiting just inside the door. "Take him to his old wagon." He returned his gaze to Petra. "Sleep, and we will talk again in the morning. Tomorrow we pass City Pentaxis, which stands open to us like all the others."

"What about the people?" Petra said as the soldier stepped forward. "Don't they fear the city being pillaged?"

"City Viandaxis feared it," Denthold said. "But we pillage nothing. We leave the city unharmed but free of Priests. My own men seize the Temple and the Godstone. The Priests disable it before leaving, of course. They don't know I can easily activate it again."

"City Primaxis will fight to the last man to keep you from their Godstone," Petra said. "They will believe they have kept the knowledge of its use secret from you."

Denthold shrugged. "Let them fight. Let them die. The fewer Priests of Vekrin remaining after all this is over, the more solid the foundation of the new world."

Petra heard the unspoken threat, and his blood ran cold.

Father.

Denthold's casual remark erased the last of his lingering doubts. Petra no longer cared about Vekrin, but he did care for the old Priests who had taught him; for Cort, his best friend; and yes, even for his father, cold and distant though he had always been. None of them deserved to die simply because their continued existence might be inconvenient to the new rulers of Nevyana.

The soldier gripped his shoulder. Petra stood. The soldier led him out of Denthold's wagon and back into the cool night air.

The light of *Liberator* made the camp so bright they needed no lantern or lightwand to weave between wagons to the one he had lived in before the Freefolk attack. It was dark inside the wagon, of course, but the soldier lit a candle before taking his leave and closing the door behind him. By the flickering yellow light, Petra struggled out of his bloodstained shirt. He blew out the candle and eased himself down on the cot, groaning. His wounded shoulder burned and his left eye, swollen almost shut, throbbed. Sleep seemed impossible.

A few minutes later, the door opened again. Startled, Petra sat up and cried out as his wound protested. Clutching the bandage, he blinked with his good eye at the dark figure in the doorway. A white halo of hair surrounded its head. It was the old Healer who had treated him after he'd passed through the Fence.

The Healer entered the wagon, rocking it under his weight. He placed a metal box on the table and touched it, and Petra winced as it suddenly emitted bright light. *A portable sparkglobe!* he realized in wonder. The Priests had never conceived of such a thing.

The Healer closed the door behind him and turned to Petra. "Hurting?" he said.

Petra nodded.

"I'm not surprised. Lie down."

Petra complied. The Healer leaned over the cot. From his satchel, he took a damp-looking lump of cheesecloth. "A poultice for your eye, which I prepared while you were speaking to Denthold," he said. He applied it to Petra's face and tied it in place with a strip of cloth around his head. Petra sighed in relief. Next, the Healer removed the bandage from Petra's shoulder wound. He reached into his satchel again, this time pulling out a small leather pouch. He opened it and sprinkled its powdery yellow contents onto the cut.

Petra yelped. The poultice had soothed his pain, but this stuff burned like fire.

"To prevent putrefaction," the Healer said. "Now, I must do some sewing."

"Sewing?" Petra asked weakly.

"The bandage was temporary. The wound must be stitched closed. Drink this." He gave Petra a small vial of milky-white liquid. Petra drank the sweet-tasting fluid and grimaced at its bitter aftertaste.

Then suddenly, he yawned. Already, lethargy seeped into his limbs.

"Sleep," the Healer said.

Obediently, Petra closed his eyes.

He didn't open them again until morning.

43

A PARTING OF THE WAYS

Jin did not enjoy hurting Petra. Petra had saved Jin's life and agreed to help the Nightdwellers. On the other hand, the Priest-Apprentice had helped Denthold, so perhaps Jin's knife dug a little deeper and his fist hit a little harder than was strictly necessary to produce convincing wounds.

Lying side by side with Amlinn back at the top of the gully, Jin watched Petra run toward the Fence, saw him escorted through, saw him hustled deeper into the camp to a large wagon.

"I hope he'll be all right," Amlinn murmured.

Jin glanced at her. "Are you truly not a mated pair?" he asked.

Amlinn shot him a look. "We call it being married," she said. "There's a ceremony before we're supposed to . . . and we haven't . . . I mean, we're not . . ." Her voice trailed off again.

Enough light came from *Liberator* for Jin to see, even through the smoked-glass goggles, that her face had reddened. He'd now spent enough time around the Day-dwellers to understand that such a reaction, betrayed by their fur-free faces, meant strong emotion. Was it anger? Embarrassment? He couldn't understand either response to such a straightforward question.

"A ceremony? Why should there be a ceremony?" he asked, puzzled. "You tell each other you want to be mated, and you are mated."

"Marriage is supposed to be for life," Amlinn said.

"So is becoming a mated pair," Jin said.

"But what if it doesn't work out?"

Jin shrugged. "Then you stop being a mated pair. What happens if a marriage does not work out? Do you have to have another ceremony?"

Amlinn sighed. "Something like that."

"Daydwellers are strange," Jin said.

"Nightdwellers are stranger. At least we wear clothes." She turned her attention back toward the camp.

"Only because you can't grow fur."

Amlinn started to reply, but then her eyes widened. "Petra!"

Jin followed her gaze. The Priest-Apprentice had emerged from the large wagon to which he had been escorted. Accompanied by a guard, he crossed the camp to a smaller wagon. Both he and the guard went inside. Candlelight flickered behind the wagon's tiny windows, and then the soldier emerged again, stationing himself at the wagon door.

The candlelight went out, but a moment later, someone else approached the wagon—the grey-haired man who had treated Petra's wound when he'd first entered the camp. He went inside, and light far brighter than candlelight shone through the wagon windows. Amlinn gasped. "That's from a sparkglobe! But inside a wagon? How?"

Jin, of course, had no answer.

Several minutes passed before the light went out. The door opened. The white-haired man appeared again, closed the door behind him, stepped down from the wagon, and vanished deeper into the camp somewhere on the far side of *Liberator*.

"That's it," Jin said. "Petra must be asleep. We should report back." He put a hand on Amlinn's arm, but she shrugged free.

"Just a few more minutes."

Jin hesitated, then sighed and settled back into position. *Not a mated pair?* he thought. *Not yet, maybe.*

He stared back at the camp. Now only guards patrolling the Fence moved among the wagons. After perhaps ten more minutes, he was about to insist Amlinn come with him when she surprised him by rolling over and sliding down into the gully. Jin hurriedly followed.

At the bottom, he took off his goggles and led the way back to the Nightdweller camp. He could see clearly, but Amlinn, following close behind, stumbled every now and then.

The Freefolk girl worried him. She had clearly not lied about her willingness to help—the Mother Queen would have known and slain her on the spot had she done so—but she certainly did not seem to have much enthusiasm for what they were trying to do.

But then, he could not really imagine how recent events had affected her. He did not think she could any better imagine how they had affected him. "Daydwellers are strange," he'd said, and, "Nightdwellers are stranger," she'd responded, and that pretty much seemed to sum it up. For all that they were allies now, until recently, their worlds had been completely separated by the great divide of sunrise.

Which now drew near. Even though they had left the bright-lit Daydweller camp behind, darkness had lessened, and the air smelled different. He wondered if Amlinn could sense the day's arrival as he did.

As they approached the watchstone marking the dayshelter entrance, a heavyset brown-furred Nightdweller rose behind it. "Jin-Ra," he said. "Freefolk girl."

"Her name is Amlinn, Ral-Pur," Jin said. "As you well know."

Ral-Pur only grunted. "Watchmaster Kar-Pur awaits your report in the southern chamber."

Jin nodded. He passed Ral-Pur with Amlinn in tow and pushed through a screen of hanging vines into the tunnel beyond. As he had explained to Amlinn and Petra when they first arrived at the dayshelter, it was one of two entrances to this particular cavern. The other was a shaft in a back corner, carved with hand- and foot-holds, that led into a small natural cavern in the hill above. That "back door," also hidden by a watch sigil, provided an emergency escape route should Daydwellers somehow find the front entrance.

After about twenty feet, the entrance tunnel opened out into a large, circular chamber with a high ceiling. Nightdwellers moved through the green glowmoss light, spreading out bedrolls in preparation for the day's sleep.

Jin turned to Amlinn. "I have to report to Watchmaster Kar-Pur," he said. "You should go to bed." He put a hand on her shoulder. "Try not to worry about Petra. They have clearly accepted him, or they would not have given him a wagon and sent a Healer to tend his wounds. Perhaps this very night he will bring down the Fence, and we can end this."

Amlinn's eyes glinted strangely bright, as though she had been weeping, but all she said was, "Good morning, Jin." Then she turned away from him and picked her way along the wall of the cavern toward the northeast corner.

Jin turned the other way, circling the cavern to a smaller chamber that opened off its southern end. There he found Watchmaster Kar-Pur and two of his lieutenants studying a map of the King's Way. Kar-Pur turned as Jin entered. "Success?"

Jin nodded. "They let Petra in and treated his wounds. He's guarded, but he anticipated he would be. He will act as soon as he can."

"Then we travel by day," Kar-Pur said to his lieutenants. "We will move out at noon. Spread the word. We must be in position by midnight each night so that we are prepared to attack the moment the Fence falls." He looked back at Jin. "Good work, Jin-Ra. You're dismissed. Get some sleep."

"Yes, Watchmaster," Jin said. He turned away quickly to cover the huge yawn that seized him. It wouldn't do to yawn in the face of the Mother Queen's supreme commander. Back in the main part of the cave, he found his bedroll where he had left it spread out, and he slept almost at once.

Rough hands shook him awake from a dark dream of the first failed attack on *Liberator*. He cried out and pushed the hands away, then opened his eyes to see Watchmaster Kar-Pur's black-furred face glaring down at him.

"Get up," Kar-Pur snarled. "It's mid-day, and the Freefolk girl is gone."

❧ 44 ❧

HOMECOMING

Amlinn watched Jin wound Petra, and hated it. She watched Petra make his way into the camp, and hated that, too. No, they weren't a "mated pair" but maybe, just maybe, they would be one day.

If they survived.

If their world survived.

And the biggest "if" of all: if Petra's love for her survived what she intended to do next.

She lingered with Jin in the grass atop the gully long after the Healer left Petra, reluctant to leave, terrified that her glimpse of Petra disappearing into the wagon had been the last time she would ever see him. But she couldn't stay there all night, so after a few minutes, she tore herself away, rolling over and sliding down the slope and out of sight of the camp. *Be safe, Petra*, she thought.

Jin slid down to join her, took off his goggles, and started down the gully toward the cavern where the Nightdwellers camped. She glanced back once. From the bottom of the gully, all she could see of the Daydweller camp was the glow of *Liberator*'s lights above the gully slope.

Arrica, if you're there, please keep him safe.

Amlinn entered the dayshelter with Jin, said her "Good morning," and picked her way to her carefully selected sleeping place. No Nightdweller seemed to want to sleep too close to her, and she'd taken advantage of that aversion. Tucked away in an indentation in the northeast corner of the cavern, her chosen spot had two advantages: it hid her from sight, and it was just around the corner from the shaft Jin had called the "back door."

The day guard who made regular rounds of the chamber came by every twenty minutes or so, thrusting his glowmoss torch into the shaft, quickly glancing in, and then moving on. Amlinn waited until he passed and then stood up. She stuffed her pack and a spare blanket inside her open bedroll to give the appearance she still slept, then slipped around the corner and climbed the shaft.

She emerged through a trapdoor into a tiny hillside cave, eased the door closed behind her, and gaped in astonishment as it simply . . . vanished. It was the first time she'd witnessed the magic of the Nightdweller watch sigil so directly. No wonder their lairs remained hidden.

She had no intention of finding this one again and wanted to get away from it as fast as possible. She dashed out of the cave and into the forest. Let Petra and Jin shout defiance at their God and Goddess and throw aside their oaths. She wasn't ready to give up on Arrica so easily. She had to talk to Grandfather and Samarrind. She owed them that much, at least.

She set off to the southeast. That course would take her

to the gorge down which flowed the tributary of the Great River. She had only to follow it upstream to find the bridge leading to the Field of Arrica and the gathered Freefolk.

It seemed a simple enough task, and indeed it was simple, except the stream lay farther south than she expected. She didn't find it until early afternoon, when it emerged into sunlight on the edge of a deep ravine, white water tumbling westward far below. Relieved but worried about how much farther she might have to travel, she turned upstream, travelling east along the heavily wooded northern rim of the canyon.

She rested only once, to stuff herself with berries from a laden bush. The Freefolk cooks made excellent pies from the same kind of berries, but these were unripe and tasted sour in her mouth. Still, she needed food, and she thought they were better than nothing—until her stomach began to growl and then cramp. The pain sometimes brought her to a stop, doubled over, panting, waiting for it to pass. And all the while, her shadow lengthened before her. The bridge and the Freefolk remained out of sight. There were other Night-dwellers in the woods than those she had left in the dayshelter. Scouts were keeping watch on the Freefolk. If she were still in the forest when night fell, they would surely find her.

I'm under the Mother Queen's protection, she thought. And no word could have yet reached the scouts out here about her betrayal.

Could it?

She really needed to find that bridge.

As the sun touched the distant blue line of the western mountains, she finally saw massive wooden beams spanning the chasm, an alarming distance away.

She remembered asking Grandfather why the Nightdwellers had never destroyed the bridge. He had told her they were too stupid to think of it. Knowing what she knew now, she suspected the real answer was that they found the bridge as useful as the Freefolk did.

Smoke, orange in the setting sun, drifted above the trees on the far side of the river. Amlinn glanced west. The saw-toothed peaks of the mountains had already taken a good-sized bite out of the sun's orb. She looked back to the bridge. She needed to reach it before dark.

It would be close.

Her stomach cramped again, and she doubled over, gasping. When at last she straightened, the sun had sunk noticeably lower. She broke into a run. She had to stop twice more, bent over with pain. Each time, she lost more precious seconds, more precious light.

The sun vanished. Twilight slipped inexorably into night. The fires of the Freefolk camp twinkled across the gorge, and the Fence glimmered blue through the trees, but the safe haven they promised might as well have been a hundred miles away. She was still fifty yards from the bridge, stumbling, gasping, clutching her stomach.

A dark shape leaped from the bushes and slammed her to the ground, driving the breath from her body. She gaped up soundlessly and helplessly at a furred, snarling face. The Nightdweller's eyes flickered red, reflecting the Freefolk fires. So did the edge of his long dagger. Amlinn waited helplessly for the blade's bite, but it never came.

"I know you," the Nightdweller said in surprise, lowering his weapon. "From the Great Warren. You went with those sent to attack the monster machine." The knife lifted again as his eyes narrowed in suspicion. "Why are you here?"

"To find out what my people . . . the Freefolk . . . are planning," Amlinn choked out, barely able to pull in enough air to speak. Her stomach cramped again, and she winced. "They may . . . be planning to attack . . . too. We could help . . . each other."

"Help the Freefolk?" The Nightdwellers sounded astonished, then suspicious. "The Mother Queen sent you on this mission?"

Amlinn hesitated. The Mother Queen could detect falsehoods. But could this ordinary Nightdweller? Probably, if she took too long to answer. "Yes," she lied firmly, her breath coming more easily at last. "I hoped to be in the Freefolk camp before dark. I'm sorry to have caused you concern."

The Nightdweller stared at her a moment, then stood, sheathing his knife. "I'm sorry to have attacked," he said. "But Daydwellers all look alike to me. I did not recognize you at first." He nodded at the Freefolk camp. "I have never seen so many of the Freefolk in one place. There are more than I dreamed existed. If they can indeed be changed from enemies to allies . . ." He shook his head. "Strange times, Daydweller. An alliance between the people of Arrica and Ell? It is like something out of an ancient tale. I would never have dreamed it possible."

"Nor I," Amlinn said truthfully. "May I go?"

"Go," the Nightdweller said. "I will send word to the Mother Queen that you have safely arrived."

Amlinn didn't let her expression betray it, but she was very glad she would not be anywhere near when the Mother Queen received that message.

Free from fear of Nightdwellers—at least for the moment —Amlinn walked the rest of the way to the bridge. Her heart slowed, and her breathing eased before she set foot on the wooden span. Even the stomach cramps subsided now that she was no longer running. Her footsteps over the planks echoed off the walls of the gorge. "Hello, the camp!" she shouted when she was halfway across. The last thing she wanted to do was alarm some guard with an itchy finger on a crossbow trigger. "Let me in!"

She could not see beyond the torches lighting the bridge, but she heard muffled voices, a sharp shout, the sound of men running, and footsteps pounding toward her across the planks.

An instant later, her grandfather flung his arms around her, hugging her so tightly she could hardly breathe. "Amlinn, my precious Amlinn!" he cried. "I thought you were dead!"

Tears flooded Amlinn's eyes, and she hugged back as hard as she could. "I thought you were too, Grandfather!"

Men surrounded them. "We must get back inside the camp," a voice shouted. "There are Nightdwellers about. It's not safe."

Yes, it is, Amlinn wanted to say, but she couldn't. Not yet. Not here.

Grandfather gripped her hand, his touch flooding her with memories of all the other times she had held his hand as a little girl—walking through snowy forests, splashing across creeks, going to her lessons with Samarrind.

Samarrind, who would reject everything she had to say as rankest heresy.

She squeezed Grandfather's hand even tighter. She remembered those long-gone days when she had been certain nothing could ever go so wrong that he couldn't put it right, but she couldn't re-summon her childish faith. This time, if things were to go right, she would have to make it happen herself.

They reached the end of the bridge and entered the camp of the Freefolk. For the first time in weeks, Amlinn was home in familiar surroundings, surrounded by people she had known all her life

Strangely, she had never felt more alone.

45

A MOMENT OF DOUBT

Petra woke to the swaying and creaking of his wagon. Bright sunlight streamed through the high, narrow window above his bunk. Clearly, the army of Axel and Denthold had resumed its journey south.

He undid the strip of cloth holding the poultice to his eye and was pleased to find that the swelling in his face had gone down. Though his shoulder ached when he lifted his arm, only a small spot of blood marked the dressing.

He found some of his old clothes in the drawers beneath his bed, and with some difficulty, stripped off his dirty, tattered trousers in favour of a fresh pair, along with a clean white shirt. Someone had put crusty bread, soft blue cheese, and two apples on the table, and a particularly welcome flask of cold water. He made short work of it all and then clambered out through the door at the end of the wagon onto the seat next to the driver, who wore the black-crossed red surcoat of Lord Axel's men.

"When do we reach City Pentaxis?" Petra asked.

The soldier shrugged.

Not one for small talk, Petra thought. *Or, more likely, under orders not to tell me anything.* He stared ahead at the sunwagons gleaming glassily in the bright sunshine, reminding himself of where their doors were, reminding himself of what they would look like inside, with firejars racked on either side of a central aisle. Despite the sun, he felt cold imagining what successfully disabling the firejars would mean: sparkglobes fading out, the Fence vanishing, arrows singing through the darkness, furred, fanged Nightdweller warriors swarming the camp. In his mind's eye, he saw soldiers trying to fight by firelight, hampered by shadows and confusion and cut down as they emerged half-dressed from their tents, dying in blood and mud all around the impotent bulk of *Liberator*, firelances reduced to nothing more than clumsy clubs.

His stomach churned. *I'm siding with the Nightdwellers against my own kind!* But he pushed back violently against his own shame. *No! The Nightdwellers are my kind. So are the Freefolk. We're all the same kind. We've just been separated by the so-called Gods.*

Liberator had to be stopped, or Axel's men would soon be slaughtering men in City Primaxis. Guards he'd seen on the streets all his life. Priests he'd grown up with.

And my father.

That simple, ice-cold fact drove all his doubt away.

One way or another, there would be bloodshed. Petra hadn't started it, and he couldn't stop it. All he could do was try to ensure that something better emerged from it. He pushed away the grim visions. Tonight, he would let in the Nightdwellers.

He turned and crawled back into the swaying wagon. In

the dim light, he pulled off his left boot, and with his knife, cut away its tongue. Then he pulled out the laces.

When the time came, he would need a diversion, and he knew just how to create one.

46

NIGHT MARCH

With the rest of the Nightdweller force, Jin strode grimly through the night in pursuit of the army of Denthold and Axel. There could no longer be any doubt. Amlinn had betrayed them and her promise to the Mother Queen. Confirmation had come two hours after sunset as they approached the hidden entrance to the dank tunnel the Nightdwellers had dug beneath the same gorge that the Freefolk bridge spanned much farther upstream. A scout intercepted them with a message: Amlinn had successfully rejoined the clans at the Field of Arrica "on her mission from the Mother Queen."

By now, she's told her grandfather everything, Jin thought savagely. *She knows where the Great Warren lies. She knows where some of the dayshelters are. The watch sigils hide them, but not perfectly. With effort, they can be found.*

But what concerned Jin even more was the possibility— the likelihood—that Amlinn had betrayed her promise to the Mother Queen even before she left them, lying about the power of the salt-sigil she had shown to Petra to shut off the firejars.

If Petra even has any intention of using it.

Jin growled, earning a startled look from the warrior at his right. Jin had trusted Amlinn, and she had betrayed them. Had he been just as wrong to trust Petra? They were both Daydwellers, and Daydwellers had always been Nightdweller enemies.

No! They helped me when they found me wounded. And the Mother Queen would have known if either of them had lied to her.

But then, an even darker thought joined the throng of doubts perched like crows on the branches of his heart. The Mother Queen knew when a Nightdweller lied to her. But a Daydweller? Daydwellers had no honour. What if they could lie and make it seem like the truth, even to the Mother Queen?

He growled again and slapped a branch out of his path with more force than necessary.

Half an hour later, the column halted. Jin sank, groaning, to the ground. Every muscle in his body ached after the endless days of marching. He massaged his feet and waited to hear why they had stopped.

The answer came soon enough. Watchmaster Kar-Pur called for all the warriors to assemble near him. "Our scouts have spotted the army we pursue not far from here, a short distance south of City Pentaxis. Like the other cities, Pentaxis offered no resistance, but taking it slowed their advance. We have even more time than we'd hoped to position ourselves and wait for Petra to act."

If he acts, Jin thought. From the muttered comments he heard around him, others had the same doubts.

They marched on. Long before they reached the camp,

they saw a glow in the sky from *Liberator*'s brilliant lights. Kar-Pur ordered his warriors into position on both sides of the King's Way. The order to attack, when and if it came, would be communicated through the watchbelts.

Crouched in the forest with his cocked and loaded crossbow at the ready, Jin peered at the brightly lit camp through his smoked-glass goggles. Soldiers patrolled the Fence as they had the night before.

Well, Petra? Will you betray us, too?

47

HORSES AND SALT

To allow the Nightdwellers time to get into position, Petra's attempt to disable the firejars was scheduled for three hours past midnight, roughly three hours before daybreak. Afraid of oversleeping, Petra decided not to sleep at all. He sat in the dark as the night dragged on, reviewing everything that could go wrong with the Nightdwellers' plan.

At last, he heard the exchange of passwords that marked the second changing of the guard. It was time. He slipped on his jacket and boots, the left one feeling rather floppy and loose with the tongue and half the laces gone. He hung the bag of salt on his belt, opened his door a crack, and peered out into the night.

The camp blazed with bright white light, but that light created black shadows that pooled like ink near *Liberator* itself and on the sides of the sunwagons facing away from *Liberator*.

Petra's guard sat on the wagon steps, right elbow on knee, chin on fist, dozing, or possibly just bored out of his skull. The plank Petra had pulled from the wagon floor made a crunching thud against that skull as he swung it with all his might. The guard crumpled. Petra jumped down from the wagon and pulled the man into the shadow beneath his wagon. Just to be safe, he gagged the guard with the strip of cloth the Healer had used to tie the poultice to his eye, and he tied the man's hands behind his back with the laces from his own boots.

Hidden in darkness, Petra peered out at the camp and watched the movements of the firelance-carrying guards. Though they were rarely out of sight, they rarely looked inward, either. By order of the king, no trees were permitted within a hundred-yard-wide strip on either side of the King's Way. *Liberator*'s light turned the long grass growing in that cleared strip to a bright, daytime green and cast the trunks of distant trees into sharp relief. Looking for any movement out there, any flicker of red eyes, the guards had little attention to spare for movement behind them.

Petra took a deep, shaky breath and then scrambled up from the damp grass. He slipped, quick as Blue Fire, to the shadow beneath the next wagon, and from there to the next, and from there to the sunwagons, until he was close to *Liberator*.

Catching his breath, he fingered the bag of salt. Amlinn had said the sigil would disable all the firejars within a radius of about six wagons' lengths. From where he was now, that would encompass all the sunwagons in the caravan and *Liberator*. But he needed time to draw the sigil, and the longer it took, the more likely either he—or the unconscious guard beneath his wagon—would be discovered.

Which was why he needed a diversion.

From the safety of the sunwagon's shadow, he had a clear view of the corral, where horses grazed or dozed behind taut-stretched ropes. Though the animals perceived the ropes as a barrier, they could easily push through them if they wanted to.

Petra intended to make them want to.

When no guards were looking his way, he stood and pulled from his belt the slingshot he had made from the tongue and laces of his boot. He fit a stone into the leather pocket, whirled the slingshot over his head, and let fly toward the horses. Then he crouched down into the shadows once more.

A solid smack sounded as stone hit flesh. A horse screamed and reared. Another horse whinnied. The disquiet spread through the herd like ripples in a pool. Horses began to trot and then gallop, a mass of horseflesh swirling around the corral in terror.

Then the rope gave way, and they plunged into the camp.

Guards shouted. Half-dressed men stumbled out of their tents. One horse tripped over a tent rope and crashed to the ground, pulling two tents down with it. It lay on its back, legs flailing madly in the welter of canvas. Men shouted and cursed, hooves thundered, soldiers and horses dashed hither and yon.

Unnoticed, Petra pulled his knife from his belt, reached down, and scraped the sigil Amlinn had shown him into the damp earth. A horse squealed, and Petra jerked his head in that direction to see it fall twitching across the Fence line, Blue Fire arcing around it like lightning. Black smoke erupted from its body. A stench of burned meat and hair drifted over the camp. Petra's stomach turned. He hadn't wanted that to happen.

But he couldn't worry about it. He pushed his blade back into its sheath. Then he opened the pouch of salt and began pouring the precious crystals into the complex emblem, aware as he did so that the hullabaloo was quieting.

Suddenly he heard voices, coming closer.

". . . something spooked them . . ."

". . . came from over there by the sunwagons . . ."

Then an angry shout. "Hey, you!"

Almost done. Petra kept pouring salt, now tracing the outer circle of the magical emblem. Footsteps raced toward him. He didn't look up. *Almost done . . .*

A hand grabbed his arm and jerked him away from the sigil, just as the final grains of salt poured into place. He cried out as pain stabbed his wounded shoulder—but in the same instant, the sigil flashed blue, and the lights went out.

48

THE ATTACK

A squealing horse brought Jin to alertness from a near-doze, even before the watchbelt silently urged him to prepare to attack. With his fellow warriors, he crept to the very edge of the forest. All the camp's horses were in motion, running around and around their rope corral. Suddenly they burst into the camp itself. Men shouted and ran after them. Tents collapsed. But the Fence still burned steadily. One horse charged into it and screamed and thrashed and died, smoke rising from its still-twitching body.

Petra had said he would have to create a diversion before he could approach the sunwagons. Surely this was it. Yet the lights continued to burn, and the Daydwellers quickly brought the horses under control.

Maybe it had nothing to do with Petra at all. Maybe something else spooked the horses.

Then new shouts broke out in the middle of the camp. A half-dozen men ran toward one of the sunwagons and disappeared behind it, but almost the instant they did so, the blinding radiance of the sparkglobes vanished.

So did the blue, shimmering Fence.

Jin yanked the goggles from his eyes, raised his crossbow, and took aim at a guard in Denthold green who stared uselessly out into what to him must have been impenetrable darkness. The watchbelt prompted Jin to fire in unison with Nightdwellers up and down the lines on both sides of the King's Way. His bolt slammed into the guard's left eye. The man fell backward in a spray of blood. All around the camp, Daydwellers dropped like stones, struck down so swiftly few even cried out.

Charge! came a new silent command through the watchbelt. Jin scrambled to his feet, drew his sword, and in concert with every other warrior in the Nightdweller army, ran toward the Daydweller camp. The watchbelt's magic revealed seven Daydwellers behind the sunwagon he had seen earlier. Even as he ran, five of those Daydwellers dispersed to defend the camp. The other two were no longer behind the wagon. They were inside it.

Through the watchbelt, he sensed dozens of Daydwellers dying at the hands of his fellow warriors, the sparks of their lives snuffed out and vanishing from his senses. But the two in the sunwagon burned steady. He slowed as he approached the vehicle, creeping silently and cautiously to its far side. Mingled salt and dirt and a few scratches in the earth were all that remained of the intricate sigil that had disabled the fire-jars. The sunwagon's door hung loosely in its frame, wooden splinters scattered across the ground beneath it.

From the other side of that door came voices.

49

SURRENDER

As men screamed and steel clashed, the soldier who had seized Petra swept his foot through the sigil. Its fading blue glow vanished, but it had done its work, just as Amlinn had promised.

"Keep him here, Grido," another man ordered the soldier. Then he and the others drew their swords and ran off into the camp.

"Damn you," snarled Grido, one of Denthold's men, Petra knew from the colour of his uniform.

Grido twisted Petra's left arm behind him and then wrapped his free arm so tightly around Petra's neck that Petra could hardly breathe. Petra scrabbled uselessly at Grido's arm, but it was as solid and immovable as cast iron.

Grido dragged Petra toward the closest sunwagon. He released Petra's arm but kept his choke-grip around Petra's neck, only shifting it enough so that he could turn and kick in the sunwagon's locked door. The frame splintered, and Grido pulled Petra into the pitch-black interior. He slammed the door shut behind them. It hung askew in the broken frame.

Outside, the unearthly howls of Nightdwellers mingled with the hoarse shouts of terrified men and the renewed neighing and squealing of frightened horses.

"You little bastard!" Breathing in ragged gasps, Grido tightened his grip. Roaring filled Petra's ears, but he heard a dagger slide from its sheath. "I'll rip your guts out!"

Consciousness fading, Petra waited for the killing thrust —but the broken door swung wide. A Nightdweller stood silhouetted against the faint red glow of distant firelight.

"I have your spy," Grido shouted, voice tight with fear. "Stay where you are, or I'll kill him!"

"Petra?"

Petra recognized the voice instantly as Jin's.

"Are you all right?"

Petra could manage only a strangled grunt.

"Did you hear what I said?" Grido yelled. "I'm warning you—"

"The camp has been taken," Jin said. "Can't you hear?" And indeed, the clash of sword on sword had all but ceased, though shouts and yowls continued. "Your fellows are surrendering. Do the same, and no harm will come to you."

"Trust a Nightdweller? I'd be cutting my own throat."

"But you have no choice," said Jin. "We have your camp. We have your firelances, your precious *Liberator*, your sunwagons and firejars and Fence. Your commanders are dead or captured. Surrender Petra and live."

The iron arm across Petra's throat slackened for just a moment, as though Grido considered giving in. But then Grido's arm tightened again, and he screamed, "Die, trai—"

The word ended in a horrible, gurgling sound. Hot liquid

poured down the side of Petra's neck and onto his shoulder and chest. Grido's arm fell away, and Petra jerked free, grabbing a post of the firejars' shelves for support. He turned back to see Grido's dark form slipping to the floor. Blood, black in the dim red light, pooled on the sunwagon's floor.

The same blood covered Petra's neck and shoulder. As Jin bent down to retrieve his knife from Grido's throat, Petra swung his head away, dropped to all fours, and vomited up what little he had eaten at supper. He stayed on his hands and knees for a few moments after his retching ceased, then swallowed hard and lurched to his feet. He pushed past Jin into the cool night air, falling to his knees yet again in the remains of the salt-sigil. He gulped air, waiting for his stomach to settle. The wound in his shoulder burned, and his bruised neck, sticky with Grido's blood, ached.

Jin crouched beside him. "It's over," he said. "We have taken the camp."

Petra knew he should be grateful to the Nightdweller for saving his life, but all he could think of was the dead soldier in the wagon. "How many have you killed?" he gasped out.

"Besides the one who was about to drive a knife into your back? Only one."

"I mean, all of you."

Jin snapped to his feet. "How should I know?" He sounded angry. "Only as many as we had to. Not as many as deserved it." He drew a deep breath. When he spoke again, his voice was calmer. "Come on. We'll find out."

Feeling numb, Petra staggered behind him toward the dark bulk of *Liberator*. "Is Amlinn with you?" he asked.

"No," Jin said shortly.

They passed other bodies, though not as many as Petra had feared. The surviving Daydwellers—Petra estimated some two hundred men and a few frightened serving girls from the cookwagons—had been gathered into an open space in front of *Liberator*, sullen and silent silhouettes in the flickering light of the dying campfires. Some clutched wounds. Many were half-naked, having rushed from their beds when the horses stampeded. A stench of sweat and blood and voided bowels hung over the camp.

Watchmaster Kar-Pur turned as Jin and Petra approached. "Good work, Petra," he said. Then he turned back to the Daydwellers. "Denthold," he shouted. "Lord Axel. Your army is defeated. Stand forth and surrender."

A shocked mutter ran through the gathered men at his words.

They still thought the Nightdwellers were savage beasts, even after the last attack, Petra thought.

Silence settled across the gathered men for a moment, broken only by the lonely cry of a night bird far overhead. Then Denthold pushed his way through the soldiers. He wore trousers and a shirt, but his feet were bare. A moment later, Lord Axel joined him. He wore only his drawers, and his body, wet with sweat, gleamed red in the fading twilight. But he held himself as proudly as ever. He gave Petra a contemptuous look, then turned toward Denthold. "So, your apprentice is the traitor. I thought his arrival last night was a little too convenient. I'll hold you responsible for this, you—"

"You are hardly in a position to hold anyone responsible for anything," Kar-Pur said coldly. "Be quiet."

Axel jerked as though stung. His jaw and fists clenched, but he obeyed.

"You and your men will be led to caves not far from here," Kar-Pur continued. "Tell your followers that any attempt to escape will be met with instant death. Remember, we can see, and you cannot."

"Caves?" Denthold said. "Or a slaughterhouse?"

"We have no intention of slaughtering you unless we have to," Kar-Pur said. "You will not be harmed. We have much to discuss with you."

Denthold glanced at Axel, whose lips were pressed tightly together. Axel nodded sharply, once. Denthold inclined his head in Kar-Pur's direction, then turned and shouted to the men. "Go peacefully with the Nightdwellers, and you won't be harmed. They have given their word."

There were mutters and one sharp bark of disbelieving laughter, but Denthold ignored it. "That is all I can do," he said to Kar-Pur.

"That is all I can ask," said Kar-Pur. He nodded to his lieutenants. "Get them moving."

Petra watched Daydwellers move from the campsite into the dark forest under the guard of the Nightdwellers. Other Nightdwellers began harnessing horses to the wagons. They would be hidden in the forest, leaving behind no trace of the camp. It was unlikely any travellers would come along the King's Way. Everyone north of this spot would be breathing sighs of relief that their cities had not been sacked, and everyone south would know an army was heading their way. But the Nightdwellers did not want news of their attack to get to Primaxis, so secrecy was to be maintained as much as possible.

The enormity of what had just happened suddenly struck home. Unbelievably, the Nightdwellers had succeeded. They had seized the firelances, the sunscales, the firejars, and *Liberator*. They had their own Gifts of Ell *and* the Gifts of Arrica and Vekrin. They could negotiate with both Freefolk and the king from a position of strength, prevent further bloodshed, and ensure that from this day forward, all the people of Nevyana would share all the Gifts of the Gods equally.

A brave new age, and I had a hand in bringing it about, Petra thought.

He willed himself to feel some sense of triumph, of having done a great deed, but as Nightdwellers began hauling the bodies of soldiers and a few of their own into the woods for burial, he found nothing in his heart but grief, doubt, and foreboding.

From behind the sunwagon where Jin had found Petra, two Nightdwellers appeared, dragging the corpse of Grido.

Grido's blood still covered Petra, sticky in the folds of his neck as he turned to watch.

What have I done? What have I really done?

And then a new thought came to roost, like a black crow on a barren tree limb. *And where is Amlinn?*

❧ 50 ☙

HERESY

As Amlinn stumbled through the Freefolk camp, her grandfather supported her with an arm around her waist. She felt countless eyes on her. She knew the Freefolk wanted to hear her tale, knew Grandfather wanted to hear it, but she couldn't tell it. Not yet.

"The clan leaders will want—" Grandfather began.

Amlinn shook her head so hard that he didn't finish the sentence. "Please, Grandfather," she whispered. "Not tonight. I'm exhausted."

"Of course," Grandfather said at once. "Tomorrow will be soon enough."

Amlinn almost sobbed with relief. She'd never felt more tired, a deep weariness born of her long day's journey on foot, so many recent nights spent awake, and days spent in fitful sleep. But more than that, she felt shaken and uncertain and fragile, flooded with conflicting emotions as the familiar scents and sites of a Freefolk camp surrounded her once more.

Grandfather led her to their wagon and opened the door

for her. She climbed inside. As he closed the door behind her, she heard him saying to someone, firmly, "She will speak to the Grand Council in the morning. Not before . . ." His voice trailed off as he moved away from the wagon.

She opened the drawers beneath her bed and found one of her flannel nightgowns. She stripped off her travel-stained clothing, pulled the nightgown on over her head, and then settled into the same bed in which she had spent every night of her childhood.

Her little rag doll, Sisspeth, still rested on her pillow. She hugged it to her breast and wished with all her heart that she was a little girl again.

She slept almost at once, but not well, tossing and turning in the grip of fitful dreams full of angry Night-dwellers, flashing firelances, and worst of all, Petra. He looked at her sorrowfully and said in a mournful voice, "Why have you betrayed us?"

She woke to a sharp rap on the wagon door. Daylight streamed through the windows. The angle suggested that it had to be almost mid-day. She got up and padded barefoot to the door, opening it to see a strange young Freefolk man, presumably from one of the other clans. He glanced at her in her nightgown, quickly looked away, and said, "Beg pardon, miss, but the Grand Council of the clans is meeting, and Clan Leader Dainann asked me to bring you to them."

I can't put it off any longer, Amlinn thought. "Just a minute," she said. She closed the door and dressed in fresh clothes—trousers of supple brown deerskin, a yellow blouse, a brown leather vest. She found her spare knife and hung it from her belt. She pulled on thick grey socks and her boots and then opened the door again. Her stomach growled, but food would have to wait. "What's your name?" she said as she stepped down from the wagon and closed the door behind her.

"Trillan, miss."

"Lead on, Trillan. And call me Amlinn."

"Yes, miss . . . Amlinn."

They made their way through the camp toward the Grand Council tent. Constructed of dark-green canvas, it was smaller than the plain white council tent of Clan Therra—but then, the council tent only had to hold three clan leaders and the Wisest, not ten wagonmasters. As they approached it, Amlinn heard hooves drumming on wood. She turned to see a horseman galloping across the bridge. He reined to a halt and jumped down, then darted across their path as he ran for the council tent, unimpeded by the guards ringing it. Certain she knew what news he brought, Amlinn left Trillan behind and ran after the new arrival. Other Freefolk hurried toward the tent from every part of the camp. The guards let her past but spread their arms to stop anyone else from getting closer.

"What's happening?" someone shouted.

"What news?" cried someone else.

Others muttered angrily, voices too low for Amlinn to make them out.

She reached the tent, flung open the flap, and entered.

"The Heretic and Lord Axel have vanished," the horseman said breathlessly. He wiped his brow with the back of his right hand, in which he also held his broad-brimmed brown hat. "The soldiers, the wagons, that monstrous machine . . . gone."

Grandfather sat with Clan Leader Shinnian of Clan Pirra and Clan Leader Ferrdri of Clan Fell at the Grand Council table. Like Clan Therra's council table, it was constructed from pieces brought to the meeting by the council members.

One piece came from each of the clan leaders and one from the Wisest, Samarrind. She sat a little back from the table, her face shadowed by the hood of her yellow robe.

"That's impossible," said Shinnian, the imposingly tall, imposingly broad-shouldered woman who led Clan Pirra. "You can't 'vanish' that many men and wagons. And they were in Pentaxis just yesterday."

"I rode the King's Way for miles south of Pentaxis," the messenger insisted. "The camp is gone."

"There must be tracks," said Ferrdri. Half the size of Shinnian in every dimension, he was no less imposing, his voice a booming growl at odds with his diminutive size. "You looked for tracks?"

"Of course, I looked," the messenger snapped. Like other lone riders who dared the night on their own, he was not easily intimidated, even by clan leaders. "I found some confused marks on the east side of the King's Way. But they were unclear and led nowhere."

"Nightdwellers," said Amlinn's grandfather.

But the messenger shook his head. "Impossible," he said. "They would have slaughtered everyone and left them where they lay. They have no use for wagons. They have no use for the Heretic's monstrous machine. They'd have no clue—"

I'll never get a better opening than that. Amlinn stepped to the edge of the table. "You're wrong," she said.

Her grandfather blinked at her. "Amlinn? I know I said we wanted to see you, but please let us first deal with—"

"Clan leaders. Wisest," Amlinn said, raising her voice to be heard above Grandfather's. "How do you think I came here last night?"

"You escaped the Heretic," Grandfather growled, clearly irritated by her interruption. "Amlinn, you—"

"I escaped the Heretic days ago, when you attacked his caravan. I did not escape him yesterday. I was not travelling with the Heretic as he came south." She paused, looking from one puzzled face to the next. "The truth is that I have been travelling with Nightdwellers."

Grandfather gaped at her. "What?"

"Impossible!" said Shinnian.

Ferrdri's eyes narrowed.

The messenger looked nervously from one clan leader to the next, twisting the brim of his hat. Samarrind rose, throwing back the hood of her robe. She said to the messenger, "Dismissed," and he fled from the tent as though Nightdwellers were after him personally.

Then Samarrind turned to Amlinn. Her eyes blazed in the lantern light. "You lie, daughter." Her voice held none of the warmth that usually coloured it when she spoke to Amlinn.

Amlinn felt as though she'd been slapped. "Have I ever lied to you before, Wisest?" she snapped.

Samarrind's lips tightened.

Amlinn switched her gaze back to the Clan leaders. "Everything we have been taught about the Nightdwellers is wrong. They are not mindless beasts. The Goddess Ell changed them, but they are as human as you and I. The long war between us can be ended forever if we join with them against Lord Axel and the Mad Priest."

Samarrind slammed her hands palm-down on the table. "Heresy!" she shouted. "Retract your words, daughter, or I will have you put outside the Fence!"

It was the worst punishment the Freefolk had, tantamount to a death sentence if it were carried out in the wilderness. At least it always had been and still might be, even for Amlinn, if the Mother Queen had learned of her apparent betrayal.

Grandfather rose, face purpling with rage. "You'll do no such thing!" he roared. "Have you gone mad?"

Samarrind's face paled, but angry spots of red flared on each cheek. "I am the Wisest and—"

"That's my granddaughter you're—"

"Aren't you listening?" Amlinn shouted. "I have *already* been living outside the Fence!"

They turned to stare at her, as did the other two clan leaders. Amlinn lowered her voice. "I spoke—spoke, you hear me?—to a Nightdweller across the bridge last night. He allowed me to come to you. I have lived with the Night-dwellers for the past two weeks. I have met their Mother Queen. I have befriended a Nightdweller boy." *Though I wanted to kill him on sight, and he probably wants to kill me, now.* "They have been our enemies. The fault is ours as well as theirs. But we need not be enemies any longer! Do you hear me? None of us need live in fear of the night!"

"Amlinn," Grandfather snapped, "listen to yourself! You sound like a lunatic! The Nightdwellers killed your parents and my daughter! How can you forgive them? How can *I* forgive them?"

Amlinn clenched her trembling hands into fists. "Have you not killed Nightdwellers, Grandfather? You have spoken of it to me with pride. But if Nightdwellers are human—and they are, I swear it—then you, too, have killed someone's son, someone's daughter, someone's father, someone's mother, someone's brother or sister. Just because they have killed some of us, and we have killed some of them, must the killing go on forever? If we have a chance to stop it, shouldn't we take it?"

Grandfather's face, so red a moment before, paled, and he sat down heavily, as though his legs would no longer bear his weight. "Amlinn—"

Samarrind remained standing, face hard, white, and cold as carved ice. "I have heard enough! Though it tears my heart to do so, I banish you, Amlinn, daughter of Therran, granddaughter of Dainann. You are no longer of the Freefolk. You will leave this camp to face your fate in the forests of the night. We reject you and your heretical poison. We spit you out that we might—"

"You reject me?" Fury at the woman she had once thought of as a mother roared up in Amlinn like fire. She suddenly understood why Jin and Petra had screamed defiance at their Gods in the cavern of salt. "I reject *you*. Everything you taught me was a lie! We've fought and killed the Nightdwellers, and they've fought and killed us, for centuries, for nothing! Vekrin, Ell, Arrica—they weren't Gods! They were nothing but spoiled children, toying with humans as though we were rag dolls. And now they're gone, but their games continue, only they've turned nasty and deadly. It's time to stop playing their games. It's time to build a world without the 'Gods,' a world far better than the one they intended for us. This is our chance! If we join with the Nightdwellers, we can be—"

"Friends? Allies? Family?" Shinnian spat the words. "These are Nightdwellers you're talking about!"

Grandfather sat and clenched the arms of his chair with gnarled hands, looking stricken and pale and suddenly very old. Amlinn's heart went out to him. *I didn't want to hurt you, Grandfather!*

He took a deep, shuddering breath. "Amlinn is my granddaughter. She deserves a chance to prove that what she says is true."

"It *cannot* be true!" Rage so thickened Samarrind's voice that Amlinn hardly recognized it. "And she deserves nothing. I am the Wisest, and I have banished her!"

The colour flooded back into Grandfather's face. He rose suddenly. "But I have not!" he roared with a vigour that belied his apparent weakness of a moment before.

Startled, Samarrind stepped back.

"Are you so certain you have the truth? Because by your 'truth,' no sunscales could ever have been stolen from us. Arrica should have struck the thief dead on the spot. And yet, sunscales were stolen. By your truth, Arrica would surely have given us victory when we attacked Axel's army, but the attack failed, Freefolk died, and the Mad Priest's monstrous machine rolled on undeterred, *powered by Arrica's sunscales*. If your 'truth' is so certain, Wisest, where is Arrica?"

His question hung in the air.

Amlinn found it hard to breathe. For her to dare heresy was one thing, but for a clan leader . . .

The red spots in Samarrind's cheeks flamed. She seemed to be having trouble breathing. "You . . . you cannot . . ." She thrust out an accusing finger, pointing it at Dainann's heart. "This cannot be borne!" she screeched. "I banish you! You—"

"I think not," Ferrdri growled.

Samarrind whipped her head around to stare at him.

"Piety is all very well," said the leader of Clan Fell, "but it is no substitute for clear thinking and dispassionate planning. This child has made an extraordinary claim. Ordinarily, I would dismiss it out of hand, yet here she stands, unharmed, after traversing the wilderness without protection for days. Clearly, the Nightdwellers have not harmed her.

Clearly, that means the Nightdwellers are not what we have thought them to be. She says she knows their true nature. An eyewitness always beats hearsay, and frankly, Wisest, everything the Wise Women have ever told us about Arrica is hearsay, for Arrica herself has never made an appearance. Not even after recent events, as Dainann has rightly pointed out, events which, by your teachings, she should never have allowed.

"So, I say we listen to Amlinn. I say we give her the opportunity to prove the truth of her tale. And then we will decide what we, as leaders of the Freefolk, will urge our clans to do, without regard to Arrica's supposed wishes."

Samarrind's mouth opened, then closed again. She stared at Ferrdri. Her lips compressed. She turned toward Shinnian. "And you, Shinnian?" she said. "Do you agree with this mad proposal?"

Shinnian looked from Ferrdri's calm face to Grandfather's stormy one. Then she dropped her eyes and, to Amlinn's surprise, muttered, "I do."

"As do I," Grandfather growled, his own voice still dark with anger.

Samarrind drew up her hood and strode from the tent.

Amlinn and Grandfather exhaled sharply at the same moment. Grandfather's mouth twitched as he caught Amlinn's eye, then he pointed to the chair that had been Samarrind's. "Granddaughter?"

Amlinn gratefully sank into the chair before her shaking knees could collapse. Grandfather resumed his seat. "Now," he said. "Begin at the beginning and leave nothing out. What has happened to you since you were taken from us?"

Amlinn took another deep breath and launched into her tale.

THE TRUTH REVEALED

With its firejars deactivated, *Liberator* was nothing but a giant wagon, and worse, a wagon that could not be drawn by horses since it had no tongue. Petra joined several Nightdwellers, including Jin, to push it along a narrow track deep into the trees. Behind them, others worked feverishly to erase every trace of the battle.

"They can't possibly hide everything," Petra panted as he pushed.

"They don't have to," Jin gasped out. "They're placing a watch sigil."

Petra didn't have enough breath to ask Jin exactly how that would help until they had finished pushing *Liberator* into its hiding place.

As they rested, Jin explained. "A skilled tracker might be able to tell where they were camped last night, but that's about it," he said. "The watch sigil will keep him from following the tracks into the woods or even seeing them as anything more than confused marks. It will appear as though the whole army disappeared into thin air."

"Even though all the wagons are here?" Petra looked around at the wagons tucked in among the trees. "They aren't even half a mile from the campsite."

"Exactly."

"A useful Gift," Petra admitted. He rubbed his aching, wounded shoulder. So many had died in the night's attack. He had washed his shirt over and over, but a pink stain remained from the blood of Grido, the soldier Jin had killed in the sunwagon to save Petra.

A little way off, he could see the captured Daydwellers surrounded by Nightdweller guards. The grey-haired Healer had survived the attack and was allowed to retrieve his supplies. He moved among the prisoners, tending the wounded. At least three wounded had since died, their bodies joining the other slain Daydwellers in a mass grave, also not far away through the trees.

But how many would have died had Petra not helped the Nightdwellers? Denthold had said he would willingly turn his firelances against the Priests and had promised to eradicate the Nightdwellers entirely. Yet, Petra still felt responsible for every Daydweller death.

And he still didn't know where Amlinn was. Jin would only say she had not accompanied them to attack the camp. "I'm not sure where she is right now."

He's hiding something.

They waited near the wagons until the Nightdwellers erasing signs of the camp joined them. Then Watchmaster Kar-Pur led all of them deeper into the forest—Nightdwellers and Daydwellers alike.

From the very beginning, the Mother Queen and her warriors had insisted that the attack should take place either just north or just south of City Pentaxis. Long after sunrise,

Petra understood why. They came to a hillside that looked like every other hillside—until suddenly, it did not. Kar-Pur strode past a large boulder to what Petra thought was a bush. He reached into the bush, and Petra saw that it wasn't a bush at all, but an iron gate set in the hillside. One instant, it wasn't there, the next, it was. He glanced at the boulder.

A watchstone.

Kar-Pur unlocked the gate and swung it inward, and one by one, they all entered the tunnel it guarded. Petra and Jin brought up the rear. When at last they reached the end of the tunnel, perhaps a hundred feet in length and lit by the glowing moss the Nightdwellers favoured, Petra found himself on the edge of a vast cavern. It was similar in size to the one in the Great Warren where he and Amlinn had been presented to the Mother Queen, but very different in design. Instead of a throne, the centre of this chamber held a huge pit that looked like a pool of ink in the uncertain light flickering from a handful of screened fires around the chamber's edges. Off to the left, Nightdwellers stacked crates and sacks in a gloomy side chamber.

"What is this place?" Petra asked Jin.

"Blood Oath Warren," Jin said. "There are twelve like it, one near each city. They were built in the very early years of the battles between Nightdwellers and Daydwellers, before the walls rose to protect cities and villages from Nightdweller raids. They served as bases for the raiding parties. Warriors still take shelter in them sometimes while on duty patrolling the King's Way."

"And that pit?"

"For horses, originally," Jin said. "But now . . ."

But now, with much shouting and prodding, the surviving Daydwellers—including Axel and Denthold—were forced into the pit down a long ramp. Once they were all inside, an iron gate like the one at the entrance to the warren slammed shut at the bottom of the ramp. Nightdweller guards positioned themselves around the lip of walls that were too high and smooth to climb.

A watchcaptain called for Jin to help shift stores. While he moved bags of meal and lentils, Petra circled the cave and peered into side chambers in search of Amlinn, finally ending up where he'd begun, right by the entrance. *Where is she?* He looked across the chamber to where Jin laboured. *Jin knows. It's time I made him tell me.*

But he'd taken only two steps in Jin's direction when a commotion arose behind him. He turned. Three Nightdwellers emerged from the entrance tunnel, two large males, and—

"Mother Highness?" Petra said, astonished. "What are you doing here?" There had been no hint in any of the planning sessions he'd been involved in that she might join Kar-Pur's warriors in person.

"Not that it is for you to question me," Sayb said sharply, "but where else should I be? We near the end of this game, and as one of the players, I must be at the table." Then something like a smile flicked across her furred face, and she startled him by bowing her head slightly. "My thanks and congratulations, Priest-Apprentice. You kept your promise. You have saved my people."

Petra remembered Grido's blood pouring over him in the sunwagon, and revulsion roiled his stomach. "Don't thank me," he snapped, too tired, too confused, to weigh his words. "And don't call me Priest-Apprentice. I'm not. Not anymore. I saved your people, but I betrayed mine. In their eyes, I am the worst sort of traitor."

The Mother Queen cocked her head to one side. "Betrayed your people? Surely Denthold is no more a friend of the Priests of Vekrin than he is the People of Ell." Her voice softened. "Or do you mean Daydwellers in general?"

Petra looked down. "I believe that Ser Mar speaks the truth, that we are all the same people, that the evil whims of the Gods are all that have separated us through the centuries. But I still feel like I betrayed my kind." Sudden grief gripped his throat, almost choking him. "All those men . . . so many dead . . . I don't know what to think anymore."

"It is hard to overcome a lifetime of teaching," the Mother Queen said. "It will be even harder for other Daydwellers, who have not seen the Great Warren or spoken to us as you have."

Petra lifted his head again, meeting her eyes. "I'll do my best to convince them, Mother Highness. But if they find out what I did, I do not think anyone will listen to me or forgive me." He swallowed hard again. "Especially not my father."

"It does not matter," the Mother Queen said. "I neither need nor expect you to convince them."

Petra frowned. "But with *Liberator* hidden away, Lord Axel's army captured, the Heretic a prisoner . . . surely the next step is to send envoys to King Stobor and my father in City Primaxis. We want to arrange negotiations between—"

"There will be no negotiations. Stobor and the Priests will surrender all power to me, and I will become Queen of Nevyana."

Petra's mouth dropped open. "What?"

"I will rule this land," Sayb said. "From Primaxis to Divpaxis, all will bow to me. And thus, at long last, we will have peace."

Roaring filled Petra's head. "You lied to me! You used me!

To give you *Liberator!*" His legs gave way, and he dropped to the floor. "All those deaths—"

"You played your role well," the Mother Queen said, her voice as cold and hard as the stone beneath his knees. "Now that we have *Liberator*, King Stobor will surrender power to me or one by one his cities will burn, until all of Nevyana calls me queen." She glanced at the warriors accompanying her. "Put him with the other Daydwellers. He has served his purpose."

The big Nightdwellers stepped forward. Strong hands seized Petra's arms, hauled him to his feet, and dragged him away.

Ahead, the black pit at the centre of the cavern loomed like a doorway to hell.

52

WOUNDED

Jin pushed the last barrel into position in the store chamber and then straightened his aching back. He turned toward the main cavern, intending to rejoin Petra.

Two of the Mother Queen's personal guards were dragging a Daydweller toward the central pit. A straggler?

No. Petra!

Behind Petra stalked the Mother Queen herself. Jin rushed into the cavern and ran to the edge of the old horse-pit, now a mass prison. Most of the soldiers had stretched out on the ground to sleep, but a few stood in small groups, talking in low voices, stealing glances at the guards above. A half-dozen serving girls huddled together in a corner. They looked as frightened of the men in the pit as they were of the Nightdwellers looking down from above. Denthold and Prince Axel stood by themselves at the end of the pit farthest from the ramp, talking.

The warriors dragged Petra down the ramp to the iron gate. It squealed in protest as they opened it. They shoved

Petra through and closed it again. He tripped and fell on all fours, then scrambled up and spun back to face the gate, grabbing its bars with both hands and glaring at the warriors, who remained just the other side. At the top of the ramp, Sayb stood watching.

"It's the traitor!" someone shouted in the pit.

Jin's heart lurched. He stared down, seeing heads turning toward Petra, who twisted around and pressed his back against the gate.

"He let them in," shouted someone else.

"He betrayed us!"

The scattered groups of men moved toward the gate, coalescing into a mob. Axel and Denthold watched from the far end but made no move to intervene. Petra stood silently, face pale, watching the approaching soldiers.

Jin glared in Sayb's direction. His fists clenched, claws digging into his palms. *She knew this would happen, but she put him down there anyway!*

Six warriors joined Sayb at the top of the ramp. They drew their swords.

And then, down in the pit an angry voice screamed, "Get him!"

The mob surged forward. Petra vanished into a melee of punching, kicking men. Bile rose in Jin's throat. He stepped toward Sayb.

The warriors who had closed the gate on Petra swung it open again. The warriors waiting at the top of the ramp charged. Claws slashed. The flats of swords slapped against skin. Hilts thudded on skulls. The Daydwellers surrounding Petra fell back, and the same warriors who had dragged him into the pit picked up his limp body and dragged him out of it again. The other warriors retreated through the gate. It clanged shut.

While the Daydwellers in the pit hurled obscenities after him, Petra was carried off to one of the side chambers.

Jin sucked in air and realized he'd been holding his breath. Then he followed.

The side chamber held only a pile of straw with one blanket on it and another folded at its foot. A bowl of glow-moss dangled from the ceiling on a chain. The warriors dumped Petra on the bed without ceremony, then retreated, brushing past Jin. With a groan, Petra turned onto his side. He folded himself into a tight ball, his breath coming in short, moaning gasps. Blood from his nose soaked into the blankets. More blood flowed down his cheek and neck from a cut just above his ear. The black eye he still sported from Jin's blow had swollen shut again. The stitches in the cut Jin had inflicted on his shoulder had given way, and fresh blood also stained his shirt. Jin took a step forward, wanting to help but afraid to touch. He was pushed aside from behind.

"Out of the way, youngster," said a gruff voice. With relief, Jin recognized Lir-Pur, the Mother Queen's own Healer. The old man knelt beside Petra and placed a leather pouch on the floor. "Roll onto your back and let me see what's what, boy."

Groaning, Petra did so.

Jin took a step forward. "What can I do?"

"Leave me alone to work. Return to your duties," Lir-Pur said without looking at Jin.

Jin hesitated, then swore, turned, and stalked back into the cavern—not to his duties, but in search of the Mother Queen.

He found Sayb in another of the side chambers. She stood

on one side of a table jury-rigged from a couple of planks stretched across two ale barrels, looking down at a map. Watchmaster Kar-Pur and other of her advisers from the Great Warren clustered around her. Jin stalked up to the table, shouldered his way between two startled warriors, and slammed his open palms down on the table. "I would speak to you, Mother Highness!"

Watchmaster Kar-Pur whipped out his sword and aimed it at Jin across the table, the point inches from his throat. "You forget yourself, Jin-Ra!"

The Mother Queen reached up and pushed the blade aside. As Kar-Pur reluctantly returned it to his sheath, she said, "I do not recall inviting you to this council, youth. Why have you interrupted us?"

"You know why, Mother Highness." The term of respect spewed from his mouth like an insult. Nightdwellers had been staked on the King's Way in the sunlight for less, but Jin didn't care. "You have made a mockery of honour with your betrayal of Petra. He believed your fine words about the three peoples of Nevyana working together."

Kar-Pur snarled, baring his fangs, but the Mother Queen raised a hand, quieting him. Her eyes remained locked on Jin's as he raged on.

"He betrayed everything he was raised to believe to help us—his enemies—in the hope that enmity might end. He and he alone gave us victory over Axel's army. And for his reward, you reneged on all your fine words and promises and threw him into a pit to be beaten!" Jin's voice rose to a shout, the pure fire of fury burning inside him, leaving no room for fear. "And so, you prove that the Daydwellers have been right all along. Nightdwellers are sub-human beasts. The world would be better off if we were exterminated!"

Every sword in the room whispered from its sheath. Fangs and steel gleamed all around him. "Let me kill him for you, Mother Highness!" howled the man to Jin's right, whose name he did not know. "Let me honour you!"

"If I want him killed, I will kill him myself." Sayb's voice remained calm and very, very cold. "Put away your weapons. Jin-Ra's concern for honour does him credit, however intemperate his words."

The warriors reluctantly sheathed their swords, but their fangs remained bared. Kar-Pur flexed his right hand, claws gleaming red as though already drenched in Jin's blood.

Jin didn't care. "It is your actions that are 'intemperate,' Mother Highness. Why have you treated Petra with such disdain?"

"Petra is a Priest-Apprentice of Vekrin," said the Mother Queen, and for the first time, let a hint of heat into her voice. "Whatever he or has not done, his kind has done more than enough for us to kill them all on sight. Simply allowing him to live has been more mercy than he had any right to expect."

"If mercy explains why he lives, what explains your lies?" Jin shot back.

"I did not lie," the Mother Queen responded, every word separate and distinct, like rocks dropped one by one into a deep, cold pool. "I told him the peoples of Nevyana must be united. That is true. I told him that if Denthold and Axel captured the throne and built more weapons like *Liberator*, unity could never be achieved, because they would use those weapons to hunt down and exterminate our people. That is also true.

"I told him no lies. I simply omitted telling him that I believe the only way the people of Nevyana can be united is under my rule." Her eyes narrowed. "I do not lie. I did not lie. And I have shown you as great a mercy as I have shown Petra by allowing you to make that claim. Do not make it again."

Jin thought back to everything the Mother Queen had said in Petra's presence. Not once had she promised not to seize *Liberator* for herself. She had only emphasized that Denthold and Axel could not be permitted to use it.

How could he have been so blind? "You may not have lied, but you did not tell him everything."

"I do not tell anyone everything. I would be a poor ruler if I did."

"But why throw him into the pit? You knew they would beat him. They would have killed him, given a few more minutes."

"But I did not give them those minutes." The Mother Queen shrugged. "He will be in pain for a day or two, but I doubt he suffered any permanent harm."

"So, why do it? He risked his life to open Axel's camp to you! Why reward him in this way?"

"For instruction. Because I suspected that once he knew the full extent of my plans, he would be tempted to return to his own people. I have demonstrated to him that that is impossible. They will not have him. He has thrown in his lot with us, and there can be no turning back."

Jin glared at her. She stared back, eyes as cold and black as obsidian pebbles. His heart still pounded with rage, and his clenched fists trembled with fury he had to control, or he would die. Sayb had already given him unheard-of leeway. She would give him no more.

She held his gaze for five long seconds, and then looked down at the map again as though he no longer held any interest. "You are dismissed."

For one more moment, he held his place. Then he expelled his breath in an explosive rush, spun on his heels, and left the Mother Queen's presence.

Still shaking with unspent fury, he strode back to Petra's chamber. Lir-Pur had left, and Petra lay on his back, breathing more easily, though only through his mouth. Lir-Pur had undressed him, so he lay as unclothed as Jin, but pink and almost hairless. An ugly splint and bandage covered his nose. A bandage also wound about his head, and a salve glistened around his blackened, swollen eye. Bandages wrapped his ribcage, bruises purpled his belly and thighs, and another bandage, spotted with blood, bound his right calf. A fresh bandage also covered the wound Jin had inflicted on him before he infiltrated the camp. Jin thought him asleep, but Petra's head turned. "Jin?" he croaked.

"Yes." Jin crossed the chamber and knelt by the low cot. "How are you? What did the Healer say?"

"I'll live. No permanent damage." Petra tried to take a deep breath and winced. "Broken nose. Cuts and bruises. Cracked ribs." He shivered. "I'm cold. I don't have fur like you. Is there a blanket?"

Jim unfolded the one at the foot of the straw pile and spread it over Petra's naked body.

Petra sighed in relief. "Two more minutes and they would have killed me."

"The Mother Queen planned it carefully," Jin said bitterly.

"She planned everything carefully," Petra said. He shifted position and winced.

"I am sorry, Petra." That seemed inadequate, but it was all Jin had to offer. "I swear I did not know Sayb's intent. Like you, I thought we would capture or destroy *Liberator*, then approach King Stobor and negotiate a peace. I did not know the Mother Queen intended to seize power for herself alone. I swear it!"

"I believe you," Petra said wearily. "I was a fool." He shook his head. "A fool. A traitor. A heretic. A murderer. What further dishonour can I heap upon myself? The Mother Queen should not have had me pulled from the pit. She should have let them kill me. What is my life worth now?" His voice dropped to a whisper. "And when my father finds out I dishonoured him, myself, my dead mother . . ." His lower lip trembled. He clamped his jaw against it. "And where is Amlinn?" he said plaintively. "Why hasn't she come to see me?"

Jin didn't want to tell Petra what he knew. But Petra had been lied to enough. "She left us," he said. "The morning after you entered the camp. She went to the Freefolk."

Petra's good eye widened. "What? Why?"

"I don't know," Jin said. "I thought of it as betrayal, but now I think maybe she had the right of it. The Freefolk need to know what's happening. Maybe they can do something. Maybe they can stop Sayb's grab for power."

"Or maybe more people will die," Petra muttered. He closed his eyes. "At least she's safe." His breathing slowed as he slipped into sleep.

Is she? Jin wondered as he made his way to his own bed. *Is anyone?*

Jin lay unsleeping for a long time, wishing someone would comfort him, but no Healer had a salve for wounds of the spirit.

53

THE GRAND COUNCIL'S
DECISION

Having told the clan leaders everything she knew and answered their many questions, Amlinn was summarily dismissed. She blinked in the sunlight outside the council tent, staring uneasily at Samarrind's wagon, not far away. Its door remained shut and its windows shuttered. She could not tell if the Wisest was inside.

The crowds that had gathered when the horseman arrived had dispersed, but clusters of Freefolk remained nearby, and they turned to stare at her. She turned away, passed through the gauntlet of guards around the tent, and headed for a hill at the edge of camp. She climbed to a rock shelf near the top of the slope and wiled away the rest of the day in solitude, watching the camp, descending only to get bread and cheese and a couple of sausages from the cookwagons at lunchtime. No one emerged from the Grand Council tent until evening. When Grandfather finally did come out, accompanied by Trillan, her escort from that morning, Amlinn hurried down the slope to join him.

"Hello, Amlinn," Trillan said as she ran up.

"Hi," she said, then, to Grandfather, "Any decision?"

"No," Grandfather said. In the slanting rays of the setting sun, his face looked ten years older than it had before the night the thief stole their sunscale, scant weeks ago. At least his wry smile seemed unchanged. "We sent out more scouts. We're awaiting their reports. And that's all I will say. Come and eat with me."

They talked of inconsequential things at dinner before returning to their wagon. In the morning, when Amlinn woke, Grandfather had already gone. She took her breakfast up onto the same shelf of rock where she had spent most of the previous day and settled in again.

Two scouts returned near midday, galloping across the bridge within minutes of each other. They dismounted and hurried into the Grand Council tent. About half an hour later, they emerged together.

An hour after that, Trillan pushed through the tent flap, crossed to Samarrind's wagon, and knocked. The Wisest opened the door, listened to him stone-faced, then stalked to the council tent. She did not stay long, emerging minutes later to stride back to the circled wagons of the Wise Women. She knocked on each door in turn. Like a flock of yellow birds, the Wise Women gathered within the circle of the wagons. Amlinn could see Samarrind talking to them, her hands chopping the air in angry gestures. Amlinn's heart sank. Clearly, the Wisest remained at odds with the clan leaders.

The gathering of the Wise Women lasted half an hour. Then they dispersed again, yellow-robed women moving out among all the wagons of the camp, talking to Freefolk. Samarrind returned to her own wagon and closed the door.

And still, the day ground by with no sign of a decision from the Grand Council.

Late in the afternoon, Amlinn lay on her back with her hands beneath her head, watching the clouds drifting over the blue sky, feeling bored, anxious, and helpless. She felt certain the clan leaders had accepted her tale. How could they not, when she had obviously travelled alone through the night to reach them?

So why didn't they act?

A gentle breeze brushed her face, reminding her of the touch of Petra's lips on hers. She hoped desperately he was all right, hoped even more desperately he would still love her when they met again. *If* they met again. Would he think she had betrayed him? Had she broken something precious, just as she gained possession of it? The thought made her sit up and hug her knees to her chest. She blinked away tears. As her vision cleared, she saw Trillan emerge from the tent and look around. Seeing her on the hill, he waved and started in her direction.

"I'm coming," she called, and headed down the slope to meet him.

He waited where he was. "The clan leaders have summoned you, Amlinn," he said as she reached him.

Her mouth went dry. "Lead the way."

The three clan leaders sat in their usual places. Samarrind's chair remained empty.

"Amlinn," Grandfather said as she entered. "Remember when I used to tell you that you would do great things?" He gave her a small smile. "I had no idea."

Amlinn managed to smile back, but her heart fluttered.

Grandfather's smile faded, and he nodded to the grim-faced Shinnian and Ferrdri. "We have made a decision. It is a unanimous decision, but for the first time in the history of the Freefolk, the clan leaders are acting without the blessing of the Wisest. What this means in terms of our people supporting our decision, we will soon find out." He looked down at his gnarled hands resting on the tabletop, took a deep breath, and then lifted his eyes to Amlinn once more. "You saw our scouts return?"

Amlinn nodded.

"They report that *Liberator*, the sunwagons, and all the other wagons of Denthold and Axel's army have reappeared on the King's Way, but now they and the firelances that were carried by Denthold and Axel's men are controlled by Nightdwellers." He shook his head as if he still couldn't believe what he had been told. "Nightdwellers, furthermore, who have no fear of the day." His voice hardened. "They also report that the Nightdwellers are journeying south along the King's Way."

"Did . . . did anyone see Petra?" Amlinn said.

"Yes," Grandfather said.

Amlinn's heart leaped. *He's alive!*

"He is driving *Liberator*."

Her relief turned to horror. "What? Why?"

"We do not know," Grandfather said. "We do not know if he does so willingly or if he is being coerced. Nor do we know the Nightdwellers' intentions. And if they continue down the King's Way to City Primaxis armed with weapons originally intended to overthrow the king, we may not discover their intentions until they arrive at the Great Gate. We," he indicated the other two clan leaders, "think we should be there first.

"We will therefore approach the city cautiously, using the secret ways of the Freefolk. We can move faster than the

Nightdwellers can, at least while they are burdened with that slow-moving monstrosity. We will consult with King Stobor and First Keeper Pelidor. Then we will wait, prepared to talk to the Nightdwellers if they will let us, but also prepared for war. We will assess the situation carefully and then act in the best interests of the Clans.

"The Wisest, as I said, does not support this action," Dainann continued heavily. "She says we are the people of Arrica, and we should have nothing to do with Heretic, Prince, king, or, especially, Nightdwellers. She calls you a liar, Amlinn," and in his voice, she heard an echo of her own pain at hearing that insult coming from the lips of one she loved so deeply. "A liar and a heretic. She can do naught else, for all you say about the Nightdwellers is contradicted by the Wise Women's teachings.

"But we clan leaders do not call you a liar. Believing you, we must act on the information you have provided." He glanced at Samarrind's empty chair. "I do not know how the Wise Women will react. If they denounce us as I suspect they will, some of our people may refuse to accompany us to City Primaxis. Our forces may be greatly diminished when at last we stand before the walls of the city.

"But we will stand. We will listen. And if we must, we will fight." He pulled Samarrind's chair out from the table and indicated it with a wave of his left hand. "Sit, Amlinn. Before we announce our decision to the people, we have more questions about what you have seen and heard."

With her heart full of a strange mix of elation, fear, doubt, sorrow, and excitement, Amlinn sat in the seat of the Wisest once more. Samarrind had once hoped Amlinn would join the ranks of the Wise. Now, ironically, she had taken Samarrind's place in the councils of the Freefolk.

Even stranger, though, she felt as if she had taken Arrica's place.

The blasphemous thought did not cause clouds to block out the sun or draw fire from heaven to consume them all. The sun beat down on the walls of the tent, untroubled.

Amlinn put the Goddess out of her mind.

The Goddess, after all, had obviously put the Freefolk out of hers.

54

"HERE'S WHAT I THINK WE SHOULD DO . . ."

Petra lay in pain through the long day, drifting in and out of troubled sleep. Late in the afternoon, he became aware of more activity outside his chamber. Voices. The clink of weapons. The smell of roasting meat drifted in, making his mouth water. Groaning, he sat up, tossed aside his blanket, and made his way to the curtained opening. Naked, which hardly seemed to matter in the world of the Nightdwellers, he swept open the curtain. A black-furred guard instantly turned toward him, growling. Petra ignored him and peered into the dimness. All the Nightdwellers seemed to be awake, stowing bedrolls into packs, buckling on weapons. And weren't there more of them than there had been?

The guard growled again and stepped toward him. Petra turned away and let the curtain fall closed. Even without the guard's encouragement, he would have returned to his bed. His head ached, his side ached, his limbs ached. It would be easier to list the parts that *didn't* ache. He sank back down onto his blanket with a groan.

Then someone else flung open the curtain—not the guard

as Petra expected, but Jin. He entered, dropping the curtain back into place. "Another hundred warriors just arrived from my old warren, Broken Tree. Including my old watchpack. By the time we reach City Primaxis, many more will have joined us." He tapped the goggles hung around his neck. "The Mother Queen is in a hurry. We will travel night and day to arrive in five days instead of ten. And then this will all end, one way or another."

"The Mother Queen will take the city by force," Petra said bitterly. "Just like Axel would have."

"If need be." Jin shook his head. "I came within an inch of being gutted, telling her to her face that she has betrayed your trust." He sighed. "But the truth is, she never lied to you. We just heard what we wanted to hear."

Petra could not see Jin's face well but heard the sorrow in his voice.

"I did not want this," Jin continued. "Nor did Ser Mar. We wanted peace, not war. Cooperation among the three people, not a Nightdweller monarchy. But with *Liberator*, sunwagons, Fence, and firelances in Sayb's hands, and the largest force of Nightdwellers ever assembled to wield them, I do not think even City Primaxis can stand against her. And if it tries, the bloodshed . . ."

Petra thought of the fat and lazy city guards making their slow, friendly circuits through the streets of City Primaxis, chatting with shopkeepers, rarely called to do so much as chase down a pickpocket. Most had a kind word for Petra or any other Priest-Apprentice they saw on the streets. A few were officious and a little too full of themselves, but even they did not deserve to die in blasts of Blue Fire.

The Priests of Vekrin would have their own firelances, of course. But each Temple had only a handful, and even if the

Priests fleeing south added theirs, Petra did not believe they could be used in Primaxis. The sigils that drew fire from the Godstones differed slightly from city to city, so that each firelance could only be used in the city where it was built. The Temple could be held indefinitely against assault, but it was not self-sufficient in food or water. Soon enough, the Priests inside would be forced to surrender or die, though not without first disabling the Godstone.

And then?

Then the Nightdwellers would have the city, but Blue Fire would be silenced. Denthold might be able to reactivate a disabled Godstone, but the Nightdwellers could not. Lights would fail. Water would cease to flow. When winter came, the Hearths would give no heat.

The sunscales and firejars could not meet the need for Blue Fire. And how long could the Nightdwellers rely even on those? The firejars were easily disabled, as he had proved. The sunscales were fragile and easily sabotaged, and though more could be made, who would make them? The Freefolk knew how, Denthold knew how, but the Nightdwellers?

Civilization in Nevyana would degenerate, everyday life becoming more and more primitive. Instead of spreading the knowledge and benefits of Blue Fire among all the citizens as Denthold had planned, the Nightdwellers would take it away entirely.

Unless . . .

Petra looked into Jin's silver-furred face. He liked the Nightdweller boy. Improbably—impossibly, he would have said at one time—they had become friends. And Jin had had nothing to do with the Mother Queen's treachery. Quite the opposite. He had risked his life to speak out against it.

Or so he said. Could Petra really trust him?

What does it matter? On my own, I'm helpless. Together, maybe we can do something. And even if Jin proves false, what else do I have to lose?

Shouts sounded outside the chamber from watchcaptains rallying their men to move out. Soon they would come for Petra and Jin.

"Jin," Petra said quietly. "Come closer, so we can't be overheard."

Jin froze for a moment. Then, with a nervous glance at the curtain, he sat beside Petra on the bed. "What?"

Petra drew as deep a breath as he could against the pain in his side. "Here's what I think we should do . . ."

55

THE FREEFOLK DIVIDED

The clan leaders' proclamation of their decision, shortly after nightfall, proved as divisive as Grandfather had feared. The three clans had arranged their wagons to leave a large open space for music, dance, storytelling, and socializing. The same wooden stage on which Amlinn had danced the night the sunscale was stolen had been erected for the performers, and it was from that platform that Grandfather, Shinnian, and Ferrdri made their announcements. Grandfather spoke first and then the other two, grim-faced, expressed their support.

Amlinn kept to herself on a bench in the shadows, watching as the crowd erupted into arguing clumps of men and women. The clan leaders allowed the commotion to continue for a few minutes. Then they signalled the guards ranging around the platform, who banged their spears on the floor of the stage. The hollow booming cut through the noise and silenced the crowd.

"We are aware that many of you may oppose this decision," Grandfather said. "As do the Wise Women. That alone must give some of you pause." He opened his arms, the gesture encompassing the whole camp. "We are the Freefolk, so there will be no coercion. Those who wish to come with us, gather to the north. Those who do not may remain here or travel where you will. For the moment, based on what Amlinn has told us, we do not believe we need to fear the Nightdwellers."

That caused another uproar, and again, the guards' spears beat the uproar to silence.

"And to prove it," Grandfather continued, "those who travel with us to City Primaxis travel without the Fence."

No outcry followed that astonishing announcement, only stunned silence.

"That is our signal to the Nightdwellers that we want peace, that we believe they want peace, as their Mother Queen told Amlinn. We will still post guards and light our camps well, but the Fence remains here, surrounding the Field of Arrica for those who remain behind."

Grandfather nodded to the west, where the last glow of the sun was quickly fading. "You have this night to discuss it. We will be in the council tent to answer any questions we can. At first light, we gather. By the second hour of the morning, we depart." He turned and rejoined the clan leaders. The guards moved to surround them as they stepped down from the stage and walked back toward the Grand Council tent.

This time, the uproar did not end. Men and women argued. In two places, fistfights erupted, onlookers pulling apart bloody-nosed combatants. Children watched wide-eyed or burst into tears, comforted by mothers who looked to be in need of comfort themselves. Throughout the night, lanterns and campfires burned brighter and longer than usual, and a constant stream of people went into the council tent to talk to the clan leaders, or to the wagons of the Wise Women.

Many people sought out Amlinn, too. She answered their questions as best she could. Most were friendly, but well after midnight, as she made her way to her wagon in exhaustion, a man she'd never seen before stepped out from the dark shadows beneath a tree. Two boys followed him, one almost full-grown, the other no more than thirteen.

"This is your fault," the man growled. "Your lies are tearing apart the Freefolk. You would hand us over the monsters of the night!"

Amlinn froze, suddenly conscious of how alone she was. "I told no lies. I told what I saw. The clan leaders decided—"

The man took another step toward her, hefting something in his hand, and she realized he carried a club, the spoke of a wagon wheel.

Amlinn's heart pounded.

The boys shuffled forward, holding similar weapons.

"And we have decided what to do with *you*. Boys—"

"Hold," growled a voice from behind Amlinn. Her heart jumped in her chest like a frightened deer. She turned to see Trillan holding a naked sword in his right hand. "I know you, Jonnkar," Trillan said. "And your sons. And if you do not put down that weapon, I will kill you where you stand."

"You would take her side?" Jonnkar snarled. "You would stand with the Nightdwellers?"

"I stand with the clan leaders. Now go back to your wagon!"

"Father," the smaller of the boys pleaded. "Please, don't—"

"Shut up," said Jonnkar. His eyes, wide and white, convinced Amlinn he would risk attacking her anyway, but he flung the club aside. He turned to the boys. "Let the bitch lead them all to their deaths, and may Ell feast on their bones! We'll stay with the true followers of Arrica." He strode away.

The boys stared at Amlinn and Trillan for a moment, then exchanged quick glances before tossing aside their own weapons and scurrying after their departing father.

Amlinn let out a breath she hadn't realized she'd been holding. "Lucky you came by," she said to Trillan.

"Luck had nothing to do with it," he said. "I've been watching you all evening. Your grandfather feared something like this might happen. Some people react to an unwelcome message by punishing the messenger." Trillan took a quick look around and did not sheathe his sword. "I'll see you to your wagon."

Shaken, Amlinn walked on. How could the people of Nevyana put aside their differences and work together if Freefolk themselves were willing to kill each other to stop that vision from coming true?

She had no answer, and none presented itself in the tossing, turning hours she spent in her bed that long, troubled night.

56

THE NIGHTDWELLERS MARCH SOUTH

Something hot and soft squished beneath Jin's foot, and he looked down to see that he had just stepped in a fresh pile of horse manure. He hoped it wasn't a metaphor for the decision he had made to help Petra in his mad scheme.

Mad? he thought. *Try traitorous.* After all, he intended nothing less than the complete betrayal of the Mother Queen.

Jin scraped off the manure as best he could on the King's Way's smooth surface and marched on, his pack pulling at his shoulders. It contained food and water that he would consume as he walked, gradually lightening the load a bit; his bedroll, which it seemed so unlikely he would get to use that he might as well have left it behind entirely; and bolts for his crossbow, which he hoped he would not have to fire. Other than his crossbow, he carried only his sword and dagger as armament. He had not been offered one of the precious fire-lances, though whether that was because he was not trusted after his outburst before the Mother Queen or because of his youth, he didn't know.

Trudging along with his fellow Nightdwellers behind *Liberator* and all the other wagons and their horses, he stepped around another steaming pile. He couldn't see the Mother Queen's wagon, but he knew she was there, leading the column along the King's Way. Her destination—City Primaxis. Her goal—nothing less than the complete capitulation of King Stobor and the Priests.

Why not *betray her?* he thought. The Mother Queen had betrayed his trust and Petra's. Petra had betrayed his people for the good of all. Amlinn had betrayed everyone. There were betrayals everywhere he looked.

Now it's my turn.

They'd been on the road for hours already. Leaving Blood Oath Warren shortly after nightfall, they had marched to where *Liberator* and the other wagons were hidden. *Liberator*'s sunscales had refilled its firejars during the day, and the sunwagons had likewise recharged. It took the first part of the night to harness the horses and to push *Liberator* back onto the King's Way. Petra, bruised and bandaged though he was, now sat in the cockpit of *Liberator*, guarded by two grim-faced warriors. He alone knew how to drive the giant wagon, though he would be teaching a Nightdweller as they travelled.

Other than Petra, only eight Daydwellers accompanied the Nightdwellers. Two of them, Denthold and Lord Axel, were chained in the back of one of the wagons. The remaining six were the serving girls, whom the Mother Queen had ordered released from the pit. They would continue their cooking and serving duties for the Nightdwellers. They seemed grateful.

Shortly after midnight, they finally began the march south. Though they would use the King's Way to cover most of the distance, they would leave it to circle around Ceturxis, Trexis, and Otraxis, the remaining cities between them and Primaxis.

"Let them wonder what happened to Denthold and Axel's army," Watchmaster Kar-Pur had said when Jin asked him about that decision as they harnessed horses to the sunwagons. "Let their Priests and city guards remain, rather than swelling the ranks of the king's forces. The Mother Queen's only concerns are City Primaxis, the Great Temple, and the king."

"What about the Freefolk?" Jin dared to ask. "If Amlinn has warned them—"

"Let them do what they will." Kar-Pur frowned at two Nightdwellers struggling to get a recalcitrant gelding into its traces. "They have no weapons to match our firelances. Let them cower behind their Fence."

But will *they cower behind their Fence?* Jin wondered.

Kar-Pur stalked toward the struggling Nightdwellers and raised his voice to a roar. "No, you fur-for-brains fools!"

One warrior dropped the reins and just managed to snatch them up again before the horse galloped free.

Now Jin marched southward as just one more foot soldier in the Nightdweller brigade. As dawn approached, they halted. "Goggles!" came the order, passed down the line from somewhere up ahead.

Unlike the warriors who had come from the Great Warren and other warrens farther north, the warriors from Broken Tree had never seen the dawn. Ket, Rith, and Rath, Jin's old watchpack mates, stood not far ahead of him in the column, fumbling with the smoked-glass lenses, their hands trembling as the sky brightened.

Then Mother Queen Sayb herself walked back toward her foot soldiers along the column's length. She had not yet donned her goggles, despite the waxing intensity of light. She came alone, unaccompanied by her bodyguards. The wagon drivers, foot soldiers, and mounted men from Silver Warren broke ranks to gather around her, towering over her slim, red-furred body. Jin joined the back of the crowd.

"I have already done this," Sayb said. She looked from man to man, catching their eyes. "And I was unharmed. My warriors have done this. They were unharmed. And now you will do this, and you will be unharmed."

She donned her own goggles, and all around her, the men did the same. "With these," she said, once more turning a slow circle, "we are free from Ell's Gift-curse. From this time onward, we are no longer creatures of the night. From now on, we rule both day and night, and soon we will rule all of Nevyana!"

Some of the warriors still looked unconvinced, but Jin saw Ket, among others, straighten his back and look about with new confidence—or at least new bravado.

The Mother Queen stepped eastward, the ranks parting before her like water before a boat's prow. At the edge of the King's Way, she pointed toward the peaks of the Sunrise Mountains, sharp black silhouettes against the brilliant sky. She waited . . . and waited . . . and then shouted, "Behold the sun!"

As if at her command, an eye-searing edge of light appeared above a jagged ridge of rock.

Jin remembered his fear on the day he had dared to wait

outside for sunrise with Ket. Even though he had seen the sunrise several times since then, he still shivered a little as the bright sunlight touched his fur. He shivered, but then relaxed as the sun's warmth flowed into him, pleasant and invigorating. It felt like something Jin should have been feeling every day of his life. It certainly did not feel like the Nightdweller-burning "Curse of Arrica" that some Scrollkeepers called it.

Betrayal of another kind, Jin thought, looking around. Thanks to the goggles, he saw clearly and painlessly, as if it were night, that the other Nightdwellers were likewise relaxing and welcoming the kiss of the sun.

Betrayal by the Scrollkeepers.

No. Put the blame where it belonged. Not on those who kept the scrolls, but on the author of the scrolls, Ell, the "Goddess" who had changed the Nightdwellers, lied to them, and kept them literally in the dark.

Any lingering doubts Jin had about his own planned act of betrayal vanished. Ell did not command his respect or obedience. Nor did the Mother Queen. His responsibility was to himself and to all the people of Nevyana, Nightdweller and Daydweller alike, without regard to the petty divisions created by the so-called Gods.

He would carry out Petra's plan and let the dice fall where they may.

THE BREAKING OF THE CLANS

In the morning, those of the Freefolk travelling to City Primaxis gathered at the edge of the camp. Those staying with the Wise Women remained near the sunwagons.

More Freefolk chose to stay behind than to accompany the clan leaders, but even so, Amlinn counted about fifty wagons and perhaps two hundred men and a few women. Mothers and children remained behind, of course, even if their husbands and fathers supported the clan leaders. There were only about twelve hundred Freefolk in all three Clans combined, of which only about a third were men of fighting age. The clan leaders mustered about half of the total available force.

As she climbed up to her accustomed place on Grandfather's wagon at the head of the long caravan, ten yellow-robed Wise Women walked the length of the line from the rear, Samarrind at the head. They stopped and took a hard look at each wagon in turn. The drivers who saw them instantly found somewhere else to look or something urgent to do. The Wise Women never came closer than thirty yards and spoke to no one.

When at last they reached Grandfather's wagon, Samarrind stared straight at Amlinn, her face set in an expression of grim disapproval.

Like the others, Amlinn looked elsewhere—back down the line of wagons.

On the other side of the wagons, the clan leaders paced in the opposite direction to the Wise Women, from front to rear, discussing the order of procession and other matters with the drivers. Once they had spoken to everyone, Shinnian and Ferrdri returned to their own wagons. Grandfather walked back to the front of the line and climbed up beside Amlinn. He turned his head away from Amlinn to glance at Samarrind. Samarrind looked even grimmer than before.

Grandfather turned forward again, his jaw set. He took up the reins and flicked them. Their wagon began to roll. The others followed. Amlinn twisted around in her seat to watch each driver pass the Wise Women's cold, implacable glares. When the last wagon had rolled past them, the Wise Women turned their backs on the departing Clan members and disappeared back in the direction of the camp.

Amlinn twisted forward again. Though the road was smooth, she gripped the edge of the seat, suddenly so shaken she feared she would fall from the wagon. From this day forward, the Freefolk would be divided between those who had followed the clan leaders and those who had held tight to their faith in Arrica.

The unity of the Freefolk had been shattered, and she was the one who had shattered it.

She still thought she had done the right thing.

So why did she feel like throwing up?

58

DRIVING LIBERATOR

P etra eased back on the throttle of *Liberator* and pulled the brake lever as the Mother Queen's wagon rounded a shoulder of grey stone ahead of him. The Nightdweller to his right was both his guard and his pupil, and he watched intently through his smoked-glass goggles as Petra turned the wheel. *Liberator* rounded the stone corner too, and then Petra had to open the throttle again, allowing more Blue Fire to flow from the sunscales to the motivators so *Liberator* could climb the slight hill on the far side without anyone having to push.

He'd become adept at driving the giant wagon as the Nightdweller army marched south, had even come to enjoy it once his wounds had healed enough that he wasn't in constant pain. How could you not enjoy controlling something so large and powerful? But all the time, he wondered if he were driving to his death. His "plan" was nothing more than a faint, desperate hope that open war could still be prevented. He and Jin could probably put it into practice, but he wasn't at all sure that either of them could survive.

Well, he thought, if the Mother Queen takes City Primaxis by force, my father and friends are likely to be among the dead. At least I'll have company in the afterlife.

If there was an afterlife. Had Vekrin lied about that, too?

Liberator crested the hill and began to gather speed down the other side. Once again, Petra had to reduce power and apply the brake.

Despite the Mother Queen's betrayal, he did not regret his decision to help the Nightdwellers. Jin had become his friend, and he blamed neither him nor his mentor, Ser Mar, for Sayb's actions. He supposed he could not even really blame Sayb. She did her duty as she saw it, as his father did his, as Samarrind and Amlinn's grandfather did theirs—all trying to do what they thought best for their respective people.

But Petra had broken his vows to Vekrin. He no longer bore loyalty to King Stobor or his father. Jin had renounced Ell and seemed to feel he no longer owed allegiance to the Mother Queen. No longer were they Daydweller and Nightdweller, kept apart by their respective Gods. Now he and Jin were just people of Nevyana wanting something better for everyone. Peace instead of warfare, friendship instead of enmity, prosperity instead of slow decline.

He and Jin.

And Amlinn?

The thought of the Freefolk girl made his hands jerk on the wheel, throwing the Nightdweller on his left against the edge of the cockpit and the one on his right against him. Both growled. "Sorry," Petra muttered, and steadied the controls.

On the night Petra entered Axel's camp, Amlinn had said goodbye to him with no indication she intended to abandon him and Jin. She'd kissed him. He remembered other kisses and embraces and had to blink away hot tears, though whether of grief or anger, he couldn't say. Had she really chosen loyalty to her people and the "Goddess" Arrica over the new world they had hoped to bring about together?

More to the point, had she chosen loyalty to her people and Arrica over loyalty to him? To the love they had been building?

It looked that way.

It *felt* that way.

It felt like betrayal.

Which left just him and Jin against possibly everyone. Would anyone share their vision? Among the Nightdwellers, Ser Mar did, but how many others? Among the ordinary denizens of the cities and villages who wanted only to live their lives in peace, there must be many who would support them if given the chance. Perhaps even King Stobor, whose own responsibility, after all, was to ordinary citizens, not to the Priests. He might indeed resent the Priests' power.

A lot of "mights," Petra thought. He shivered in a sudden cool breeze and looked up to see a dark cloud blocking the sun. A few drops of rain spattered on his head, and he hunched his shoulders against it.

If his plan failed, if he and Jin died, who would offer a different vision? The Mother Queen would seize City Primaxis with Blue Fire and bloodshed. How could trust between Nightdweller and Daydweller ever take hold after that?

Civil war would follow. Though Nightdwellers had the largest stock of firelances at the moment, Priests throughout the land knew how to make them. Those Priests could surely find allies among the Freefolk who would be willing to provide sunscales and firejars to charge them. If Denthold had figured out how to modify the sigils to let firelances draw from firejars, others could do the same, once they knew it was possible.

And unbeknownst to the Mother Queen, Denthold had sabotaged the firelances he provided Axel, the ones now carried by Nightdwellers. They would not work for long, and when they died, so would many, many Nightdwellers.

Jin and I can't fail. We've got to succeed. We've got to survive.

The rain strengthened. Petra could not leave the controls to rig the canvas canopy over the cockpit, and neither of the Nightdwellers showed any inclination to do so.

I might not even survive this trip, Petra thought morosely. Cold, wet, still bruised and aching, he shifted his weight on the hard wooden seat, resettled his grip on the wheel, and drove *Liberator* on down the King's Way, ever closer to City Primaxis.

59

A CONVERSATION WITH THE HERETIC

As the sun set on the Nightdwellers' first day of travel, Watchmaster Kar-Pur called a brief halt to allow the warriors to remove and stow their goggles and rest.

Jin strolled along the length of the caravan as far as *Liberator*, though he stopped to the rear of it. He didn't think it would be safe to come anywhere near Petra. Turning back, he threaded his way among the wagons, whose drivers were checking their horses' hooves or giving them food and water.

As he approached the one where Denthold and Axel were imprisoned, he slowed to assess the situation. As he had hoped, both men were outside. Better than he had hoped, they weren't together. Accompanied by two guards, Axel stood at the side of the King's Way relieving himself. Denthold paced awkwardly back and forth, his ankles loosely shackled together, the shackles chained to a wagon wheel.

Jin circled the wagon, one of the larger storewagons, with a wooden rather than a canvas roof, keeping its bulk between himself and the guards watching Axel. He peered around the corner. Denthold had his back to him. "Don't turn around, Denthold," Jin whispered. "I don't want the guards to know I'm talking to you."

Denthold stiffened. Then he eased himself down to the ground, his back to the wheel to which he was chained. He stared off into the darkening woods. "Who are you?" he whispered back.

"My name is Jin-Ra."

"Your name means nothing to me."

"You need to know it all the same. As you need to know that I am a friend of Petra's."

Denthold stiffened. "If you are friends with that filthy traitor, you're no friend of mine. After the kindness I showed him . . . I should have had him drawn and quartered the day he appeared in my city with that Freefolk brat!"

Axel's guards still had their backs to the wagon. Jin stuck his head out a little farther and growled, "That traitor listened to everything you said and understood better than you what it meant. You've been using Lord Axel. You want to spread the knowledge of Blue Fire to all the people of Nevyana. You seek to shatter the power of Priests and Wise Women and allow us to move out of this disease-plagued narrow valley into the wider world beyond. Am I right?"

Denthold's head jerked toward him, though just a fraction of an inch before he caught himself. "A remarkably accurate and concise summation."

"Especially since it comes from someone you considered a beast to be exterminated without mercy."

Denthold's jaw tightened.

"Do I sound like a savage to you, Heretic?"

"No," Denthold said through clenched teeth.

"Do any of the Nightdwellers you have seen look like ignorant beasts?"

"No."

"Then you understand the fatal flaw in your scheme. You wanted to give Blue Fire to all the people of Nevyana. But you did not count the Nightdwellers as people."

Axel now seemed to be doing some kind of stretching exercises, to the accompaniment of taunts and scornful laughter from his watching guards.

"You convinced Petra to support you," Jin continued. "But then he encountered Nightdwellers and learned that we are as human as you, that what he had been taught was a lie, and what you intended would be genocide."

"And so, he handed *Liberator* over to the Nightdwellers?" Denthold demanded. "So Daydwellers can be slaves of Ell instead of Vekrin and Arrica? How is that better? I want people to be free to make their own decisions, choose their own leaders, use the Gifts of the so-called Gods to better their lives. You're just exchanging one tyranny for another."

"You're wrong," Jin said. "Petra and I have also been betrayed. By the Mother Queen."

Axel stretched prodigiously one more time, reaching toward the sky. In a moment, he'd be returning to the wagon.

Jin lowered his voice further. "We are going to try to do something about it."

"What do I care?" Denthold said. He grabbed the chain attached to his ankle, held it up, and shook it. "I'm a prisoner."

"You won't be when the time comes," Jin whispered. Then he pulled his head back and slipped off between the wagons before the guards could see him.

As he took his place again in the reformed ranks, he saw Axel and Denthold being loaded once more aboard their prison wagon. Just before he disappeared, Denthold's searching eyes found Jin. He stared for one long second before the guards forced him back into his wagon.

60

THE KING AND THE FIRST
KEEPER

The Freefolk rolled into their traditional campground not far from the walls of Primaxis in the grey light of early morning. Thick mist swirled around them. Amlinn strained her eyes in the city's direction from atop Grandfather's wagon. She could barely make out its black bulk and the tiny east gate through which she had chased the sunscale thief on the rainy night when all this had begun.

"Any sign of *Liberator*?" Grandfather said. "Or Night-dwellers?"

"No," Amlinn said. "But there could be an entire army camped in front of the Great Gate, and I couldn't see it from here in this blasted fog."

Distant shouts, indistinct but urgent, rang out from the city wall. "The city guards have apparently seen us," Grandfather said. "We'd better make camp. We'll have visitors soon. See to the horses."

Amlinn nodded. The familiar routine of unharnessing, grooming, feeding, watering, and then corralling the horses could not entirely keep her from worrying about what the mist might hide, but it helped. As the camp took shape, Grandfather, Shinnian, and Ferrdri walked together among the wagons and stopped to chat with their respective clan members. But always, like Amlinn and everyone else, they kept an eye on the city.

About an hour after they had arrived, trumpets rang out, the sound tinny with distance. Back in her seat on the wagon, Amlinn watched open-mouthed as the east gate opened and a dozen guards marched out in single file. Clad in red surcoats over silver chainmail, each guard carried a spear and wore a spiked helmet. Each spear and spike bore a bright red ribbon that was no doubt meant to flutter bravely in the breeze, but this morning hung lankly, like sodden hair.

The troupe faced each other in two rows of six, a silver-and-scarlet corridor of armoured men. Through it strode a stout man dressed like the guards but with a gold circlet on his head and a red cape lined with fur on his shoulders. A tall, gaunt man in the blue robes of a Priest followed, his short-cut, dark-brown hair shot with silver at the temples.

The man crowned with gold had to be none other than King Stobor himself. And that almost certainly meant that the Priest accompanying him was Pelidor, First Keeper of the Temple of Vekrin in City Primaxis.

Petra's father.

Work in the campground ground to a halt as person after person turned to watch the guards escort their charges along the well-worn path from the city to the *de facto* border between city and Freefolk. At the point where, in happier times, greeters would welcome Citydwellers to the Freefolk camp and the entertainment it offered, the clan leaders met the king and the First Keeper.

Amlinn had not been invited to be part of that meeting,

but she jumped down from the wagon as the delegation approached. With a little quick footwork, she positioned herself close behind the three clan leaders. Grandfather glanced over his shoulder at her but said nothing. Emboldened, she moved a little closer and gazed at King Stobor with interest. She had never seen him before. He had tired green eyes and a red beard concealing a rather weak chin. Not that a weak chin meant a weak man, of course, but appearance mattered in a king, and no doubt that was the reason for the beard, an unusual affectation among Citydwellers. Amlinn could not deny that his fraternal twin, Axel, looked kinglier.

The king cleared his throat. "City Primaxis welcomes the Freefolk," he said formally. "As it always has. And I, Stobor, by the grace of Vekrin, King of Nevyana, Duke of Primaxis, and Protector of the Twelve Cities, welcome you as well."

"The Freefolk are pleased by the welcome," said Grandfather. "And honoured that the king himself and the First Keeper of the Temple of Vekrin," he nodded to Petra's father, "have come to extend it. I do not believe this has ever happened before."

"These are unusual times," said the king. "As I am sure you are aware."

"They are," said Shinnian. "Nor, I think, will 'usual times' ever return."

"They will." First Keeper Pelidor voice rumbled like distant thunder. "The will of Vekrin will not be thwarted by the Heretic and an upstart prince—"

"Denthold?" said Grandfather. "Axel? Is it still they who most concern you?"

The king frowned. "Who else?"

"The force led by Denthold and Prince Axel was overpowered en route to City Primaxis," said Grandfather.

"Overpowered?" The king looked blank. "By whom?" His eyes widened. "Freefolk?"

"No," said Shinnian. "By Nightdwellers."

Pelidor laughed scornfully. "Nightdwellers! Those animals? Impossible! Denthold has the Freefolk Fence, Axel has firelances. They would have—"

"Denthold trusted too much in the Fence and in light and in the power of his monstrous *Liberator*," Grandfather said. "And too much in the false stereotype we have all clung to of Nightdwellers as ignorant savages. Someone within Denthold's camp sabotaged his firejars, cutting off *Liberator* and firelances alike from Blue Fire. The Nightdwellers overran the camp."

The king let out a huge gust of relieved breath that fluttered his moustache. "Then we are saved! They'll loot the bodies and fade back into the forest. I never thought I'd be grateful to Nightdwellers—"

"Don't be grateful," growled Ferrdri. "Be afraid. They did not destroy what they stole. They took all for their own —*Liberator*, sunwagons, firejars, Fence, and firelances. Now it is they, not Denthold and Axel, who are rolling down the King's Way toward City Primaxis."

"Impossible!" Petra's father exploded. "Nightdwellers could no more use a firelance than a dog could drive a wagon!"

That was too much for Amlinn. "That's what Denthold thought!" she said. She stepped forward and around Grandfather. He looked down at her, but rather than reprimand her as she expected, he gave her the slightest of slight smiles. She shot a look at Ferrdri, who raised an eyebrow but likewise said nothing. Shinnian's face clouded into a frown, but she pressed her lips together, folded her arms, and held her tongue.

Emboldened, Amlinn turned back to the king and First Keeper. "Denthold thought the Nightdwellers were animals because that is what the Priests of Vekrin and the Wise Women of Arrica teach. But they are *not* animals. They're as human as we are, changed by Ell to live in the dark, but people like us. They—"

"Who is this girl?" Pelidor bellowed, his face cycling from red to purple. "How dare she speak to us like this?"

Amlinn drew herself up and said, clearly and coldly, "I am Amlinn of the Freefolk. It was I who saw Denthold's man steal a sunscale and slip through the Fence of the Temple. It was I who saw your son, Petra, stunned by a stolen firelance—"

The First Keeper's eyes widened.

"It was I who was taken captive with him by Denthold and held in City Divpaxis. When my people attacked Axel's force south of the city, Petra and I escaped, only to be captured by Nightdwellers, and that was when I learned the truth about them. Yes, the Nightdwellers know how to use firelances and Fence, sunwagons and firejars, and Denthold's *Liberator*. They are coming here. They intend to force change on Nevyana whether we want it or not."

Pelidor's face had darkened into a credible impression of a thundercloud. Anger boiled up inside Amlinn, anger, and a fierce desire to penetrate his Vekrin-worshipping armour. "And it was your son, Petra, who used the secret Freefolk sigil I taught him to disable Denthold's defences and allow the Nightdwellers to defeat him!"

In an instant, Pelidor's face went from purple to pale. His mouth fell open.

The king looked from his First Keeper to Amlinn. His brows drew together into a frown. He opened his mouth to speak—

A long, wailing blast blared from the walls of the city. A young boy wearing the king's livery charged through the East Gate and dashed toward the king. Stobor and Pelidor turned as he reached them. "Your Majesty," the boy gasped out, "It's the . . . the thing . . . um, *Liberator*. It's coming down the King's Way with an army behind it. An army of Night-dwellers!" He sucked more air in and shouted, his voice high with terror, "In the daylight!"

Amlinn's mouth went dry. *It's beginning.*

But how will it end?

❦ 61 ❦

PRIMAXIS

As the long journey to City Primaxis ground on, Petra felt trapped in a nightmare. During short stops, he would stumble to whatever latrine had been scraped in the woods and then stagger back to *Liberator*'s cockpit, where bread and meat and water would await him. He'd eat and then fall asleep where he sat until his Nightdweller guards, who accompanied him everywhere—even to the latrine— nudged him awake again. Though one of them was supposed to be his pupil, learning to operate *Liberator*, he made no move to relieve Petra of his driving duties. Petra suspected the guard would only do so if Petra dropped dead or began raving and drooling, which at times seemed the most likely outcome.

By the time the sky lightened on the mist-shrouded morning of the sixth day, Petra felt as if he had been trapped between the taciturn warriors and driving *Liberator* for his entire life. The Mother Queen's wagon rolled to a stop ahead of him, so he shut off the throttle and braked. Then he sat there, eyes closed, hoping desperately for a rest break, perhaps even a chance to snatch an hour or two of sleep.

The guard to his left moved behind him, and a much smaller Nightdweller slipped in next to him on the bench, jerking him out of a doze with the warmth of her furred body beside him in the chill pre-dawn air. "Mo-Mother Highness?" he stammered. "What . . .?"

"*Liberator* will now lead the army, and therefore I will ride here the rest of the way," she said. Ahead of them, the wagon in which she had ridden until now turned sharply left and disappeared to the rear. "Drive," the Mother Queen ordered.

Blinking fatigue-blurred eyes, Petra opened the throttle, released the brake, and rolled on down the King's Way.

Dawn came, still mist-shrouded. The Nightdwellers donned their smoked-glass goggles. Through the fog, Petra saw only the endless white pavement of the King's Way appearing from the grey wall ahead and rolling out of sight beneath *Liberator*'s wheels. The mist began to lift and then, as if from nowhere, the walls of City Primaxis materialized out of the fog. The King's Way led straight to the closed Great Gate, the golden twelve-pointed crown of the king glinting dully on its thick timbers in the uncertain light. Some distance to the right, the river entered the city through a low arch barred by a great, rusty portcullis.

From atop the walls, a horn wailed. It paused, as though the wielder had stopped to draw breath, and then wailed again and again, over and over.

The Mother Queen raised her hand. "Halt," she commanded.

Petra killed the throttle and braked. *Liberator* rolled to a halt.

"They've seen us," Sayb said. "We will give them time to

think about what our arrival means. In half an hour, we will move closer to the Great Gate but stop out of range of both bow and firelance. We will see who, if anyone, they send out to meet us. And then we will make our demands." She glanced at Petra. "You have done well."

Petra clenched the wheel so tightly his knuckles whitened. The Mother Queen glanced down and smiled. Then she stood and left the cockpit by climbing down the ladder at the back of the compartment. Petra released the wheel and twisted around to look at the guard behind him. "Can I stretch?"

The Nightdweller grimaced but jerked a nod. Grateful for even a short reprieve, Petra also climbed wearily down from *Liberator* and stretched his aching limbs. He longed to fling himself into the grass by the King's Way and sleep, but he dared not. He had to remain awake and keep what few wits remained in his sleep-deprived head, ready to seize the moment when—if—it came.

The exact timing of that moment was up to Jin. Petra could only wait and hope Jin had not changed his mind about the whole mad scheme.

If Jin did not act, Petra believed nothing could save the city and eventually all of Nevyana from a maelstrom of blood and fire. On the other hand, if Jin did act, the two of them might well suffer a similar fate.

Which will it be?

Petra strode back and forth on the King's Way, clapping his shoulders to ward off the chill of the morning mist, and waited to find out.

✿ 62 ✿

LIBERATOR LIBERATED

Jin waited in the ranks: waited and watched. The time to act would not come, if it came at all, until the Night-dweller army moved closer to the Great Gate, and the Mother Queen left to meet with whatever delegation the city sent forth. With all possibilities balanced on a knife's edge, that would be the moment when a sudden shove in one direction or another could change everything.

The warning horn stopped bleating at last. Distant shouting followed. Jin saw no movement atop the city walls, but between his goggles and the thick mist, he suspected a whole army could run laps around the city without him spotting it.

Half an hour after they first stopped, Jin watched Petra climb wearily back to the controls of *Liberator*, his guards following. The Mother Queen remained on the ground. She ordered the army forward again, and they proceeded another quarter mile, halting about three hundred yards from the walls, just beyond effective bowshot range, and far beyond the range of any ordinary firelance.

The walls, however, were well within *Liberator*'s range.

Watchcaptains shouted orders, and the Nightdweller foot soldiers formed four rows. Meanwhile, the smaller wagons were arrayed around *Liberator*, which squatted at their head like an enormous toad, its giant weapon aimed at the Great Gate. The sunwagons and, at the very rear, the wagon carrying Axel and Denthold were tucked in behind it. The horses were taken from the traces and moved to a hastily constructed rope corral in the woods to the west of the King's Way.

When all was sorted, the Mother Queen stood in front of her troops and nodded to a mounted warrior. He saluted and spurred his horse, galloping to within a dozen yards of the Great Gate.

"The Mother Queen of the Nightdwellers greets Stobor, King of Nevyana, and Pelidor, First Keeper of Temple Primaxis, and asks that they come forth to parley!" The warrior's voice rang clearly across the intervening distance in the still morning air. Without waiting for an answer, he turned and galloped back to the Nightdweller lines.

A long moment's silence—Jin counted a hundred heartbeats—and then the Great Gate opened just enough to let a single rider through. Dressed in silver chainmail, his red surcoat emblazoned with the king's golden crown, a scarlet ribbon fluttering from his spiked helmet and another from his lance, he trotted his horse to a point halfway between the Gate and *Liberator*. He reined to a halt and shouted, "King Stobor, by the Grace of Vekrin, King of Nevyana, Duke of City Primaxis, and Protector of the Twelve Cities, and Pelidor, First Keeper of the First Temple of the Great God Vekrin, graciously accede to your request. Will you come forth under a flag of truce?"

"Not alone," Watchmaster Kar-Pur said sharply to Sayb.

She gave the barest of nods to him, then called back, "We will come forth. With two guards. No more for us, and no more for you."

"That is acceptable," shouted Stobor's herald. He wheeled his black horse around smartly and trotted back toward the Great Gate, which opened briefly again to admit him.

Kar-Pur pointed to two of the Mother Queen's mounted bodyguards, who hefted their firelances, loosened their swords in their sheaths, and settled themselves more firmly in their saddles. Their heavy goggles gave them an insect-like look. Between that and the erect fur on their heads and the backs of their necks, they appeared fearsome and strange even to Jin. How the Daydwellers would react to them, he could not imagine.

He could be no more certain how the Daydwellers and the Nightdwellers would react to what he and Petra hoped to do. But the time had come to find out.

As the Mother Queen waited for the king and First Keeper to emerge, Jin slipped out from the ranks of watching Nightdwellers and back to where Denthold and Axel were imprisoned, at the very back of the group of wagons. To Jin's surprise, their guard was none other than Ket, his old watch-master from Broken Tree Warren.

Ket looked up as Jin approached. "Jin-Ra," he said, showing his fangs in a toothy, and therefore not particularly friendly, smile.

"Ket-Ra," Jin said.

Ket jerked his head in the direction of the city. "What's going on? I can't see or hear a thing back here."

"You're about to find out," Jin said. "The watchcaptain

wants you in the front line." He nodded at the wagon. "I'm to take your place here."

Ket grinned again, this time without teeth. "And welcome to it!" He jerked a thumb at the wagon. "They haven't made a sound all morning. I think they're asleep." He hurried toward the front of the lines.

Jin only had minutes before his deception was discovered. That lie had been the first cast of the dice. Now he had to play the game to its conclusion.

He slid aside the bolt and pulled open the wagon's back door. White eyes stared at him as the prisoners rose up on their elbows. Wearing his dark goggles, he found it hard to see them in the gloom. "It's time," he said to Denthold. "We are at the Great Gate."

Axel jerked upright. "Of City Primaxis? My brother—"

"Is about to meet with the Mother Queen," said Jin. "Along with the First Keeper of the Temple." He stepped aside. "Would you like to join them?"

Axel surged forward. Pushing past Jin, he jumped out of the wagon and dashed away—not toward the city, but off the King's Way and straight into the woods.

"I guess not," Jin said to no one in particular as he watched Axel run.

Denthold climbed out more slowly. "Stobor would kill him on sight," he said, nodding after Axel. "The king might do the same to me. If he doesn't, Pelidor will try to talk him into it." He cocked his head to one side. "Why should I do what you want me to do? Why shouldn't I follow Axel?"

Snarling, teeth bared, Jin shoved Denthold back against the wagon so hard the Heretic's head thudded against the wood. He pinned the Daydweller there with his left arm across his chest. With razor-sharp claws extended, Jin held his hand inches from Denthold's suddenly wide eyes. "You set all this in motion. And though I would gladly rip out your eyeballs here and now and jam them down your own throat as revenge for my friends who died trying to stop that monstrosity of yours, I find that I have joined your cause, or Petra's version of it, anyway." He shoved Denthold hard again and was rewarded with another satisfying thud of bone against wood. "You *will* help us try to achieve your dream—or die with it and us." He released the pressure on Denthold's chest and pointed toward the city. "Well?"

Denthold rubbed his chest, then the back of his head. He looked at Jin thoughtfully and then nodded once.

"You're my prisoner," Jin said. Then he took Denthold's arm and started back toward the ranks of Nightdwellers.

Jin saw Ket, wearing a puzzled look, talking to a watch-captain. He gave him a wide berth and led Denthold to the left end of the line while staying well back of the ranks. Not a single Nightdweller looked his way. All their attention was on the King's Way between the Nightdweller force and the Great Gate, where the Mother Queen and her two guards had just met the delegation from the city.

Jin craned his neck to see. He found the king disappointing. Rather short, rather stout, and with an untidy beard, he looked nothing like his fraternal twin, Axel. The other man, in priestly blue, had to be First Keeper Pelidor. Jin wondered how seeing his father made Petra feel.

He wondered what it would feel like to have a father.

Like the Mother Queen's bodyguards, the two red-clad soldiers accompanying the king and First Keeper remained on horseback, but the king and the First Keeper dismounted. They handed their reins to their guards and faced the horse-less Mother Queen on foot.

Whatever King Stobor and First Keeper Pelidor thought was about to happen, Jin knew the Mother Queen was not there to negotiate. She would issue a simple demand: surrender the city, or see it fall to the power of Denthold's *Liberator* and the firelances of the Nightdwellers.

It's time. Jin grabbed Denthold's arm and, half-dragging him, plunged into the ranks of the Nightdwellers from behind. Annoyed faces and bared fangs turned his way. "The Mother Queen ordered me to bring Denthold to her," Jin panted, as if he'd been running. "He resisted. I'm late. He needs to be escorted out to her—"

Ket glanced Jin's way, and his eyes widened. He started pushing through the ranks toward him.

Jin had chosen his spot carefully, recognizing in the front rank a leading watchcaptain and a silver-furred warrior who was one of the Mother Queen's bodyguards. The warrior frowned at Jin, then grabbed Denthold's arm. "I'll take him," he growled, and strode toward the parlay.

Jin slipped back behind the ranked warriors again and ran for *Liberator* as fast as his feet could carry him.

"Jin!" Ket shouted after him. "What's going on?"

Jin ignored him.

Ten feet overhead, Petra's guards watched the events unfolding before the Great Gate, their gaze directed far over Jin's head. At a dead run, Jin leaped straight from the ground into *Liberator*'s cockpit. He slammed into the warrior on Petra's left, who slammed into Petra, who used the momentum to shove the startled warrior on his right completely out of the cockpit. The warrior thudded to the ground with a cry of pain

Jin grappled with the other warrior. Though he was bigger than Jin, Jin had the element of surprise. Jin twisted and heaved, and with a sharp, sickening crack and a spray of blood, that warrior, too, crashed to the ground, screaming and clutching at his thigh, where white bone protruded.

The other warrior struggled back to his feet. His face contorted with pain and rage, he leaped up and grabbed the edge of the cockpit. Petra smashed his fists down on the warrior's fingers, and the Nightdweller fell again with a hoarse cry. Then Petra seized the wheel with his right hand, and with his left, shoved the throttle forward as far as it would go. The wagon surged into motion. Something thumped under its rear wheels, and Jin looked back to see the warrior who had just fallen writhing on the ground, clutching his leg.

"I see Denthold," Petra shouted to Jin. "Where's Axel?"

"Ran away," Jin said. "Coward."

They had no more time for conversation. Petra drove *Liberator* straight through the wagons arranged in front of it and shoved them aside with a splintering crunch. Foot soldiers shouted and scattered.

Off to the left, Jin caught a glimpse of Ket staring up at him as they accelerated into the open ground in front of the Great Gate. Faster than a man could run, they hurtled toward the Mother Queen, Denthold, who had just arrived in the company of his guard, King Stobor—and Pelidor, First Keeper of Temple Primaxis.

Petra's father.

THE FALL OF THE GREAT GATE

Father! Petra's heart leaped in a complex surge of joy, fear, guilt, and regret. But none of that would stop him.

He killed the throttle, pulled back on the brake lever, and twisted the wheel. *Liberator*'s iron-clad wheels screeched on the King's Way's smooth stone as the massive wagon jerked sideways and skidded to a halt, its left side facing the city. Petra reached to his right and spun the small wheels that aimed the giant firelance.

Then he pulled the trigger lever.

Furnace-like heat washed over Petra, and light as bright as the sun stabbed his eyes. Jin cried out and flung up an arm. Sayb and her two bodyguards twisted away, throwing their hands over their goggled faces.

The Great Gate ignited in a gout of orange flame and black smoke as massive timbers burned and splintered. The deafening thunderclap of Blue Fire and the ear-shattering explosion of the Gate drove humans and Nightdwellers alike to their knees. Flinders of wood and twisted pieces of black iron hurtled outward and skyward, then fell like deadly hail.

A jagged chunk of metal slammed into the floor of the driver's compartment behind Petra and Jin and stuck there, quivering. Nightdwellers cried out in pain.

Petra knew there must have been casualties inside the walls, but he couldn't think about that. The important thing was that the Great Gate now slumped in smoking, impassable ruin. No reinforcements would pour out of the city from that direction.

Petra spun the aiming wheels again to swing the firelance right and down so that it pointed directly at King Stobor, the Mother Queen, Denthold . . . and his father. The Night-dweller and Daydweller soldiers tried to calm their terrified horses.

The First Keeper's gaze met Petra's. His face went white and slack. Petra's heart ached at the sight. He hadn't seen his father for weeks. The Priests must surely have thought him dead. For his father to see him now, just after he had destroyed the Great Gate, possibly slain men on the other side, friends of his father, friends of his . . .

But then anger boiled up inside him. His father had ignored him, belittled him, made it clear he thought Petra would amount to nothing. And now Petra had reappeared, not just at the centre of events, but in *control* of events.

He stood up in the cockpit, keeping his hand on the trigger lever. Ears still ringing from the blast, he shouted, "This ends now! There will be no war!"

The goggles shielding the Mother Queen's eyes glinted in the mist-dimmed sunlight as she faced him. "So, you would kill us all, Priest-Apprentice?" she called scornfully. She pointed at King Stobor and First Keeper Pelidor. "Your monarch and your father included?"

"To keep you from taking City Primaxis and plunging

Nevyana into a bloody civil war, yes!" But his hand trembled on the trigger lever as he said it.

His father's face, snow-pale an instant before, now flushed with fury. "Petra!" he shouted, his deep, booming voice echoing from the city walls. "You are a Priest-Apprentice of Vekrin and my son! Have you forgotten your vows?"

Petra's hand still trembled. He pulled it from the lever and clenched it into a fist. "No, Father! I have not forgotten them." The bitterness and defiance that had flooded him in the cave of salt now filled his voice with fire. "I have rejected them! I have broken them! Over and over again. They hold no power over me now. Nor does Vekrin!"

"Petra!" his father bellowed, but Petra shouted even louder, hoping they would hear him even on the City walls.

"If Vekrin still lives, he cares nothing for us! We have been fools, obeying the commands of a monster who used us as playthings and then abandoned us as a child abandons a broken toy!"

Pelidor's eyes blazed, and he opened his mouth to shout something else, but the Mother Queen cut him off. "Jin-Ra!" she called. If the First Keeper's voice had blazed like Blue Fire, hers was cold as a frozen river. "Would you, too, betray your vows? Not to Ell, but to your people? To me?"

Jin did not hesitate, though his voice shook. "I would. I have. And I will again." He leaped up onto the driver's bench. "We are one people, not three!" he shouted, not just to the Mother Queen, but to all the Nightdwellers behind them, their neatly ordered ranks of a few moments before now a confused muddle. "We were torn apart by the so-called Gods. But the Gods are gone, and they're not coming back. There is no need for fighting. We can share the land in peace. We can share Blue Fire in peace. And together, we can make Nevyana greater than it has ever been!"

He stopped. The echo of his voice died away. The king, the First Keeper, and the Mother Queen all stared at the two boys in *Liberator's* cockpit. Warriors fingered their weapons but dared not move forward. Daylight glinted off the helmets of the bowmen on the city wall, but *Liberator* remained at the very edge of their range, and their own leaders stood between them and the giant vehicle.

Stalemate, Petra thought. His throat was dry. He unclenched his fist; his hand still trembled. He gripped the trigger lever again. *What happens next?*

❦ 64 ❦

AMLINN'S CHARGE

As the king and First Keeper and their escort hurried back to the east gate in response to the young messenger's frightened announcement, Grandfather climbed up onto the seat of the nearest wagon and turned to address all the gathered Freefolk. "This day will decide the future of Nevyana," he shouted. "It will determine whether we continue to fear and fight the Nightdwellers, whether we continue to trade with the cities, whether we are free to roam the countryside as we always have."

Amlinn looked past him to the city. She could not see the approaching Nightdweller army, rolling down the King's Way toward the Great Gate in the north wall. She could not have seen it even if the day had been less misty.

Which meant the Nightdwellers couldn't see the Freefolk, either.

Do they even know we're here?

Hard on the heels of that question came the one to which she really wanted the answer.

Is Petra with them?

"See to your weapons," Grandfather ordered. "I pray to Arrica—" He stopped abruptly.

Amlinn thought she knew his reason. Why pray to Arrica when clearly, she would not act, even if she heard?

Grandfather took a deep breath before continuing. "I hope that there will be no fighting. But hope alone is not enough to ensure peace. Sometimes it must be earned through battle. Mount up!"

The assembled men and handful of women, already armed and armoured in preparation for whatever the day would bring, ran to their horses.

Amlinn knew Grandfather expected her to stay with the wagons. But she couldn't. All this had been set in motion the night she pursued the thief who had stolen their sunscale into City Primaxis. She would see the end of it, whatever that end might be.

Even more than that, she needed to know how Petra and Jin fared.

Taking no weapon but her ever-present dagger, she hurried through the camp to the rope corral, where a few horses remained. She led a bay mare behind a storewagon, mounted it bareback out of sight of gathering Freefolk fighters, and rode into the still mist-shrouded forest.

She circled the city until she could see the Great Gate through a screen of bushes. Nightdweller warriors stood in ranks before it with *Liberator* a looming hulk surrounded by smaller wagons. She strained her eyes to see who was in the cockpit. All she could make out was the black bulk of a Nightdweller.

There were not so very many more warriors, despite the additions from other warrens, since Amlinn had last seen the force, but fifty of them carried Axel's firelances. Unclothed even when facing battle, furred, fanged, and wearing large, glinting goggles, they looked fearsome indeed.

The Great Gate creaked open, and a lone rider emerged shouting, but Amlinn was too far away to understand his words. Frustrated, she urged her horse a little closer to the edge of the forest, trusting the mist and everyone's focus on the city to keep her unobserved.

The rider wheeled and rode back to the gate.

After a few minutes, the gate again opened a crack. King Stobor, the First Keeper, and their guards emerged. The Mother Queen and two of her bodyguards went to meet them.

Amlinn glanced east. Where was Grandfather? Why hadn't the Freefolk made their appearance?

He's waiting, she thought. *Waiting until the right moment.*

Shouting from the Nightdwellers' ranks drew her attention. Two new figures emerged from the rows of warriors—a Nightdweller dragging a Daydweller.

Denthold!

More cries. Amlinn's gaze snapped back to *Liberator.* There was scuffling in the cockpit. Two warriors fell from it, leaving behind a silver-furred Nightdweller and a young Daydweller.

She gasped in mingled relief and startlement. Jin—and Petra!

Liberator jerked into motion, rolling forward, shoving aside lesser wagons. Wood splintered. Nightdwellers flung themselves from *Liberator*'s path. It skidded to a halt in the open, turning as it did so. The giant firelance swung toward the Great Gate.

Lightning flashed. Thunder split the air. Her horse reared.

She flung her arms around its neck to keep from being thrown and gentled it back to trembling stillness. Only then did she look up to see what *Liberator*'s firelance had wrought.

The Great Gate of City Primaxis lay in smoking ruins, licked by flame. She heard more unintelligible shouting. Petra's voice . . . a man's voice . . . the Mother Queen's . . . Jin's.

And then a different kind of thunder rumbled to her left, and she turned to see Freefolk galloping around the corner of the city wall at last, swords out. The three clan leaders—Grandfather, Shinnian, and Ferrdri—rode side by side in the vanguard.

Shouts of defiance rang from the Nightdwellers. Swords whipped from scabbards. Firelances and crossbows lifted.

"No!" Amlinn screamed. She dug her heels into the mare's flanks and galloped into the open, angling to get in front of the onrushing Freefolk before they were within range of the firelances. Grandfather saw her and reined his horse to a rearing stop, shouting, "Halt!"

Shinnian and Ferrdri followed suit and the Freefolk charge came to a stumbling, disorganized stop, just as *Liberator* hurled lightning once more.

Blue Fire tore open the ground not fifty feet in front of Amlinn's galloping horse. Terrified, it shied left. Amlinn hurtled from its back. She tried to roll as she had been taught, but the impact drove the breath from her lungs. At the same moment, she heard a sickening crack, and agony flared in her left wrist. She tumbled over and over, finally coming to rest at the very edge of the smoking, blackened gouge in the earth.

The other Freefolk fought to control their own mounts.

Some bolted, galloping with their helpless riders back toward the camp or the woods. The Nightdwellers held their positions, bows and firelances raised.

Amlinn struggled for breath. She couldn't speak, and spots danced in her vision.

As if from a great distance, she heard Petra's voice ring out. "Your Majesty, Mother Highness, Clan Leader Dainann, Father . . ." Petra sounded young and frightened, but determined. "Don't do this. A war will drown Nevyana in blood. Negotiate, instead. We have so much to offer each other . . ."

"We outnumber the Nightdwellers," Amlinn heard Shinnian shout to Grandfather. "If we rush them . . . even with that toy, he can't stop us all . . ."

Amlinn still did not have a full measure of breath, but she hauled herself to her knees and then to her feet. Pain flared in her side. *Cracked ribs.* She held her broken left wrist against her body as she stood. "You will have to ride over me," she gasped out. "Grandfather, please. Stop this war before it begins."

Grandfather stared at her, face pale. She had always thought of him as her rock, her safe haven against anything the world might throw at her. But now, he looked shaken.

Uncertain.

Lost.

The Mother Queen's voice rang out behind her. "My warriors have many firelances, Petra. You have only one. We will seize *Liberator* and take the city as I intended. Daydwellers have ruled Nevyana long enough. It is the Nightdwellers' turn."

"And what kind of Kingdom will it be?" cried a new voice.

Jin! Amlinn turned painfully to see the young Nightdweller leap from *Liberator*'s cockpit onto the ground and stride toward the Mother Queen and the others.

Cradling her broken wrist against her aching side, she waited to hear what he would say.

65

JIN CONFRONTS HIS QUEEN

Jin's heart pounded. His fur bristled. His muscles trembled, ready for battle. He kept his gaze locked on the Mother Queen's face, though he could not see her eyes behind the blank glare of her goggles. "Mother Highness, the rulers of the Nightdwellers have never been tyrants," he called as he approached her. "You and your ancestors have ruled us with wisdom and humility. You do not live in luxury while your people go hungry. No one could ever accuse you of putting your own glory ahead of the good of your people."

He stopped ten feet from her.

She stood unmoving, as though carved from stone. One of her bodyguard's horses blew and stamped its foot, still unsettled by the firing of *Liberator*.

"So why do you seek to become a tyrant now?" Jin continued quietly. "If you seize the throne, your kingdom will be based on terror, with Daydwellers as your frightened subjects until they turn against you and us. You're sworn to protect the Nightdwellers. If you fight here today and win, you will ensure our destruction."

He stopped, argument made, and held himself ready to do whatever might be required next.

The Mother Queen still did not move. The moment of silence stretched on and on, a tense, frozen silence, like the silence between two wild animals facing each other with bristling fur and stiff legs.

At last, she stirred. He thought she was about to speak. Had he convinced her?

He didn't find out. From the north came the sound of pounding hooves, and a many-throated cry, "For Axel and Nevyana!"

Jin and everyone else spun to see a hundred Daydwellers, lances lowered, charging the Nightdweller lines from the rear.

66

LORD AXEL RETURNS

Petra barely registered the lone rider galloping out in front of the Freefolk as he swung the firelance in that direction and fired a warning shot. As the blast seared the air and ripped the ground open, he saw the horse shy and its rider tumble to the very edge of the smoking scar left by the Blue Fire. It wasn't until she hauled herself to her feet that he recognized Amlinn.

Oh, Vekrin! he cried silently, even though he no longer believed in the God. *I might have killed her!*

Yet, for a moment, he could give her no more thought. He turned back to the leaders and made his plea for peace, then jerked his head around in astonishment as Jin, who had been standing on the bench beside him, leaped from *Liberator* and strode across the ground to make his own appeal. Watching the Mother Queen, watching the faces of the king and his father, the guards, and Denthold—observing everything with mask-like impassivity—Petra felt like throwing up.

It's not going to work. Someone will attack. Bowshot or firelance blast, it doesn't matter. Battle will be joined, and battle will become war, and even with Liberator, *we can't stop it!*

And then battle was indeed joined, but not by any of the forces arrayed in front of the smoking ruin of the Great Gate of City Primaxis.

From the mist north of the Nightdwellers, down the King's Way, galloped soldiers in the red-and-black livery of Prince Axel. In a moment of frozen clarity, Petra realized what fools they'd been not to consider Axel might have rein-forcements waiting near the city for his arrival. He hadn't been running away when he'd dashed into the forest. He'd been running to find his men. And by blasting the Great Gate to rubble, Petra had made it impossible for King Stobor's forces to meet them.

Axel couldn't be allowed to become king, couldn't be allowed to regain control of *Liberator* and all those firelances. He would seize the city, enslave the Priests, slaughter the Nightdwellers. Petra shoved the throttle forward, spun *Liberator* around, and raced back toward the Nightdwellers, who once again dived out of his way. With his right hand, he spun the aiming wheels until the firelance faced straight forward and down. As the galloping knights reached the wagons, Petra fired.

The blast ripped through a sunwagon. It exploded in a smoky fireball, tossing some firejars into the air and hurling others directly into the path of the oncoming horses. Mounts fell, armoured men crashed to the ground, lances and bones snapped. What had a moment before seemed an unstoppable charge fell apart in chaos, screams, and shouting.

With bits of chain still dangling from the manacles on his wrist, Axel wheeled his horse around to avoid the fallen animals blocking his path. He charged back in among his men, shouting orders. Well-trained, they regrouped quickly, but they had lost the element of surprise. Nightdwellers ran back through the wagons toward them with firelances in hand.

Petra slewed *Liberator* around once more and drove it back toward Primaxis.

67

BETRAYAL, BLOOD, AND BLADES

As the horsemen thundered down the King's Way, one of the Mother Queen's bodyguards reached down and scooped her up into the saddle with him. They galloped back toward the lines, the second bodyguard close behind.

Jin had to dive headlong to avoid the charging horses.

"Back to the city!" King Stobor cried as Jin clambered to his feet. But as Stobor and Pelidor turned to their horses, the guard holding the animals' reins released them. Already terrified, the freed horses galloped away.

The king stared after them, then glared at the guards. "Are you mad?" he bellowed.

In response, the guards drew their swords. "Long Live King Axel!" they cried and spurred their mounts. The horses' broad chests slammed into Stobor and Pelidor, knocking them to the ground. That fall saved them from the guards' blades, which whistled over their heads.

Jin whipped his own sword from its scabbard as the guards wheeled around. One guard reared his horse and tried to trample the king, but Stobor rolled, and the hooves thudded down scant inches from his head. The king scrambled to his feet and ran as the guard pulled at the reins. Stobor stumbled white-faced to a halt in front of Jin, staring at Jin's drawn sword.

Without a word, Jin tossed him the blade.

King Stobor caught it in mid-air. He spun just in time to block the guard's descending stroke, though the blow, with the weight of the horse behind it, drove him to the ground again. Jin ducked the guard's backslash and raised his head to see Petra's father running for the city, his blue robes flying. Jin jerked his head around to see the second guard spurring his horse toward the First Keeper. The guard would ride him down in seconds.

As the guard galloped past, Jin leaped. He slammed into the guard's side, and both of them thudded to the ground. Jin's breath whooshed out of him. The freed horse caught up to Petra's fleeing father, who flinched as he heard it approaching. But the horse galloped past him, frantic to escape the thunder crackling from the caravan as Night-dwellers turned their firelances on Axel's reinforcements.

Struggling to draw breath, Jin could only lie motionless and gasp like a grounded fish as the guard he had unhorsed struggled back to his feet. The soldier drew his dagger and started toward Jin, murder in his eyes.

"Hold!" shouted a voice.

The guard spun.

The First Keeper had returned. Grey-faced, he held one hand pressed tight to the left of his chest, which heaved as though he, like Jin, could not get enough air. "I cannot flee you," the First Keeper gasped to the guard. "I cannot fight you." He took a step toward the soldier. "But, my son, can you really strike down the First Keeper of the Temple of Vekrin? Will you really risk the God's wrath?"

Off to Jin's right, steel crashed. He turned his head. King Stobor battled his erstwhile bodyguard, whom he had somehow dragged from his horse so that they fought face to face.

Jin turned back again as the guard facing Pelidor snarled, "Vekrin? There is no Vekrin. The Gods are gone, and good riddance. We craft our own lives now." He stepped forward. "Except for you, old man. Your life is done."

Jin still did not have a full measure of air, but he had enough. He rolled over, gathered his legs under him, and just as the guard raised his dagger to strike the First Keeper down, he leaped. But Pelidor's eyes flicked toward him, and the guard spun, faster than Jin would have believed possible.

His dagger, cold as ice and yet hot as a brand, bit deep into Jin's left side.

Then Jin and the guard tumbled together again. Jin landed on his stomach, head turned to one side. He saw the king pull a bloody sword—Jin's sword—from the other guard's body. Jin tried to get up, but his left side burned like fire, and his limbs had no strength. He pressed his hand against the wound. Blood welled through his fingers; he couldn't stop it.

With enormous effort, he rolled onto his back.

The guard leaped to his feet, still holding his dagger, wet with Jin's blood. "Filthy savage! I'll gut you like a—"

And then both he and the world disappeared in a flash of light and a crack of thunder so loud it seemed to drive Jin deeper into the dirt. He blinked, dazed. Somehow his smoked-glass goggles seemed to have darkened; the light was fading all around him.

And then his senses fled.

68

GATHERING THE WOUNDED

Amlinn heard the thunder of hoofbeats and turned to see horsemen in red and black charging the rear of the Nightdweller army. Then she jerked her head back to the front again as Grandfather, suddenly galvanized, stood in his stirrups, raised his sword, and shouted, "With me, Freefolk! There's our real enemy! Lord Axel and the Mad Priest stole our sunscales and attacked our caravan! It's time to make them pay!" Grandfather spurred his horse toward the looming battle.

Shinnian and Ferrdri galloped after him. In that instant, *Liberator* roared, the sound echoing off the walls of Primaxis. As though its lighting-blast had broken a dam, the Freefolk shouted and charged after their clan leaders, riding to fight side by side with Nightdwellers, the creatures they had feared and battled for generations.

Amlinn stayed put, pressing her broken wrist to her aching side. She watched Grandfather until she lost him in the mist and confusion. Would she see him alive again?

When she turned to look back toward the Great Gate, she

gasped to see the king battling one of his own guards. The second guard galloped after the First Keeper. Like a hunting cat, Jin leaped at the soldier and knocked him from the saddle. The pair of them tumbled across the ground.

Pelidor halted his flight and stumbled back toward Jin and the embattled king.

Amlinn limped in his direction, though she was too far away to do anything to help. She saw the guard facing Pelidor draw his dagger, saw Jin stagger to his feet and leap at him, saw Jin crumple to the ground and the guard step toward him . . . and then another earth-shattering blast of Blue Fire from *Liberator*'s mighty firelance blotted away Jin's attacker. She flung a hand over her eyes and fell to her knees. Blinking to clear the streak of yellow *Liberator*'s lightning-stroke had left across her vision, she struggled to her feet and started forward again, side and wrist and ankle stabbing like knives with every step.

She arrived on the scene to see Petra's father, face pale as mist, cradling the fallen Nightdweller in his arms. A blue strip of blood-soaked cloth torn from the First Keeper's own robe wrapped Jin's chest. Pelidor raised a white face to Amlinn as she limped up to him. "He saved my life," he said, voice weak. "A Nightdweller, yet he saved the life of a Priest of Vekrin."

"He saved mine, as well," said King Stobor. "Ruler of his enemies." Blood soaked the king's left sleeve, and he leaned on a Nightdweller sword as though it were a cane. "Is he dead?"

"He lives," Pelidor said. Sweat glistened on his pale face. He gulped air before adding, "But barely, and not for long if we cannot get him to a Healer in the city . . ."

The king looked back at the walls. Soldiers were finally

trickling around the far corners of the wall, emerging through the small East and West Gates. "My men can take him to—"

"He would not survive your Healers," said a voice behind them. Amlinn turned to see Mother Queen Sayb—accompanied by Watchmaster Kar-Pur. "My Healer must attend him." She glanced over her shoulder. "The Freefolk have turned the tide. Axel's men are routed."

"And Axel?" growled King Stobor.

"I do not know. But even if he lives, he will not escape." She nodded to Kar-Pur. "Take Jin to Lir-Pur."

Kar-Pur knelt and picked Jin up as tenderly as if he were an infant. He turned and carried the boy toward the Night-dweller camp. Amlinn, still cradling her broken wrist, started to follow, and then heard a voice that made her heart leap.

"Father, are you all right?"

Amlinn spun. Petra knelt beside the First Keeper. She took a step toward him, but he didn't even look at her. All his attention was on his father. Pelidor had fallen on his side where he had knelt holding Jin. "No," he said faintly. "I think . . . it's my heart . . . I fear . . ."

Petra looked frantically around. "He needs—"

"Bring him," said Sayb. "Lir-Pur can help him too. The Scrolls of Ell have preserved much knowledge of Healing I do not think the Daydwellers possess."

"Can you walk?" Petra asked his father.

"I . . . think so."

With a tenderness that warmed Amlinn's heart, Petra helped his father to his feet.

"I must stay and take command," King Stobor said. He turned to look at his oncoming men. "We may have other traitors among us, but we won't have them for long." Then he glanced at Petra. "Please, let me know as soon as you can how your father and your young Nightdweller friend fare." He looked past Petra at the giant shape of *Liberator*. "And what about *that*?"

"That last blast exhausted its firejars," Petra said. "It can neither move nor fire again before tomorrow."

The king turned his gaze on Petra again. "I think," he said softly, "that it would be best if it could neither move nor fire again ever."

With his father's arm around his shoulder, Petra gave the king a long look, then nodded. Then, at last—at last!—he glanced at Amlinn.

Their eyes met. Petra said nothing. Amlinn opened her mouth to speak, but nothing came out. The silence seemed to stretch to infinity.

Then Sayb broke it by saying, "Let me help."

With a sense of wonder, Amlinn watched the Mother Queen of the Nightdwellers drape the arm of the First Keeper of Temple Primaxis over her shoulders, and together with the First Keeper's son, walk him toward the camp of the Nightdwellers.

As she limped after them, Amlinn's wonder faded to worry. A single question burned in her mind.

Does Petra hate me?

❧ 69 ❧

HEALING

Petra knew Amlinn was watching him, but at first, his attention was focused entirely on his father, and after, he realized he had nothing to say to her.

Not yet.

But the time came when his father was resting comfortably, his colour better, his breathing less laboured.

Jin lay in another wagon. Lir-Pur wore a grave look as he spoke to the Mother Queen about the young Nightdweller's condition, but they kept their voices too low for Petra to make out what was said. They would not let him see his friend, so Petra returned to the wagon where his father rested. He sat down on the ground with his back against the right front wheel. Around him, Nightdwellers, city guards, and Freefolk moved and mingled. He was so tired after the long journey south and the events of the day that what would have been unthinkable just days before hardly even seemed strange.

Burial parties were tending to the dead—so many, many dead. Healers tended to the injured. The smell of roasting meat and baking bread drifted across the camp from the cookwagons, where hot food and plenty of it was being prepared and distributed to all.

With his arms around his knees, Petra stared dully at his dusty boots. A second pair of boots, rather small, appeared in his field of vision. He blinked, then raised his eyes. Slender legs in calf-skin pants, torn at the knee and smudged with mud . . . a brown leather belt bearing a sheathed knife . . . a dusty green tunic . . . right arm bare, left in a sling . . . and above that, the face he had first seen in the mud outside the Temple Curtain. Years ago, it seemed. Blue eyes, framed by hair the colour of a raven's wing.

"Hello," Amlinn said softly. Her face, scratched and bruised and drawn with pain, seemed years older than the night he had first glimpsed it in the rain. He remembered seeing her tumble across the ground after her horse threw her, after he fired *Liberator*'s firelance into the ground in front of the Freefolk.

Both of them had attempted to stop the Freefolk from attacking the Nightdwellers, but she had put herself at far greater risk than he.

I could have killed her, he thought, feeling a little sick.

Of the three of them—Amlinn, Jin, and himself—only he remained unwounded after this day's events.

But then he remembered pulling the trigger to burn alive the guard threatening Jin, how a living man had exploded into red mist and black smoke in an instant. He remembered the feel of blood pouring down his side from the throat of Grido, the man Jin slew in the sunwagon the night Petra drew the salt-sigil. He remembered all those who had died because of his choices, his actions, and he realized he hadn't escaped being wounded after all.

Far from it.

Amlinn limped over to the wagon, put her back against the wheel, and slid down beside him. "I need to know, Petra," she said softly. "I need to know what you thought when you heard I'd escaped the Nightdwellers and rejoined the Freefolk."

"I thought you had betrayed us." Petra picked at the mud on the right knee of his trousers. "I thought you had gone to urge the Freefolk to attack us before we reached Primaxis."

"I went to the Freefolk to *stop* them from attacking," Amlinn said. "I wanted them to wait until the Nightdwellers reached the city, to see what happened when the Mother Queen and the king met, and then decide what should be done." She tugged a stem of grass from the ground and twisted it. "I didn't betray you. Or maybe I did, a little. But not the way you thought. I did it because—"

"Because you thought it was the only way to stop a war." Petra sighed. He felt more tired than he could ever remember feeling in his life, and his days-old bruises and the half-healed cut from Jin's blade were making their presence felt with renewed vigour. "All my life, I was taught that the highest virtue was loyalty. Loyalty to my vows, loyalty to the Priesthood, loyalty to Vekrin. But in the end, I broke my vows, betrayed the Priesthood, and spat in the face of Vekrin."

He turned his head toward the wagon where Jin lay. "Jin betrayed his ruler and his people's beliefs. And then you, we thought, betrayed us. But now it turns out your betrayal was for the same reasons as ours." He suddenly felt old, far older than sixteen years. He doubted he'd ever feel like a boy again. "We can hardly condemn you for that."

Amlinn smiled tentatively.

The sight went through Petra's heart like a crossbow bolt. He realized how much he'd missed that smile. How much he'd missed *her*.

"Thank you," Amlinn said softly. "I hoped that Samarrind and the other Wise Women could see they were wrong about the Nightdwellers. I thought they'd believe me when I told them I'd met them, lived with them, and knew they're not savage, ignorant beasts. But they wouldn't listen. Not even . . ." She swallowed. "Not even Samarrind. She accepted the word of Arrica over the word of . . . of me." Her face scrunched up; in grief, he thought for a moment, but then recognized it for what it really was: anger.

"The Gods have a lot to answer for," Amlinn said. "If they ever do come back, I'll . . ." She pulled the blade of grass in two. She stared down at it, and then her scowl dissolved into a grin. "Right. I'll just cut the Gods down to size." She laughed, then winced. "Ow. Cracked ribs and laughter don't go together."

It hurt Petra to laugh, too, but he did it anyway, and the smile she gave him eased the ache in his heart and body. "The Gods aren't coming back," he said at last. "And if they do, well, you and I and Jin managed to bring together Freefolk, Nightdwellers, and Citydwellers as allies." He nodded toward a nearby campfire, where one of each sat together talking, their tones cautious and curious, but certainly not hostile. Farther off, the Mother Queen sat with the Freefolk clan leaders and a Priest he recognized as Tepris, the Second Keeper. "That's more than the Gods managed. Maybe they should be scared of us!"

Amlinn laughed, grimaced, touched her side, and settled for a grin. Petra grinned back.

Lir-Pur popped into view from around the back of the wagon. "Quiet!" he said sternly. "Petra's father needs rest."

"Sorry," Petra said, instantly contrite.

"How is Jin?" Amlinn asked.

"I am cautiously optimistic," said the Healer. "He is young, and the blade did not damage any vital organs. But he lost a lot of blood. This night will tell the tale." He examined them narrowly. "I have Healer's orders for you two, as well. You both look exhausted. Get something to eat and get some sleep. You can do nothing for either the First Keeper or Jin waiting here."

Petra yawned, the depth of his exhaustion suddenly striking home. The shifting wind once more wafted the smell of roasting venison in their direction, and he realized he was also ravenously hungry. When had he last eaten? Yesterday? Or was it the day before that?

"Come on," he said to Amlinn. He got to his feet and held out his hand. She took it with her good one, and he pulled her to his feet. Looking at her smiling face, bruised and scratched though it was, he had a sudden urge to kiss her.

So, he did. For quite a long time.

He'd forgotten Lir-Pur until the Healer cleared his throat. "Rest, I said."

Amlinn blushed and then grinned at Lir-Pur. "Yes, Healer." She glanced at Petra.

"Yes, Healer," Petra said dutifully.

Hand in hand, they walked to the cookwagons.

A FIERY END

Jin came slowly awake, surfacing from a confused dream involving lightning and smoke and fire and blood. He ached all over, but one spot on his left side, in particular, hurt the most. His eyelids seemed sticky, but he managed to slide them open. He stared blearily up at a low wooden ceiling. A blurry face moved into view. He blinked hard a few times and finally recognized Lir-Pur.

"Good," said the Healer. "Here, drink this." He offered Jin a cup, putting one arm under his back to help him sit up.

Jin sipped the liquid. It was all he could do not to spit the sour, bitter fluid right back out again. "What is that?" he croaked, face scrunched in disgust.

"Something to ease your discomfort," said the Healer, and indeed, Jin could already feel his aches receding, the sharp pain in his side becoming duller.

"What—" *What happened?* Jin intended to say, but in a flash, he remembered it all—Axel's attack, King Stobor betrayed, the guards, the dagger, the blast of Blue Fire. "Who won?" he whispered instead.

"You're alive, aren't you?" said Lir-Pur. "Who do you think?" He took away the cup. "Everyone is friends now. Well, almost everyone. Lie still and concentrate on healing."

There came a knock on the door, and the Healer sighed. "Every five minutes," he said. He went to the door and opened it, letting in a flood of cool night air. "All right," he said. "He's awake. You can come in. But only for a short time."

Jin turned his head to see Petra and Amlinn crowding into the small space. "Hello," said Petra.

"Hi," said Amlinn.

Amlinn. Jin had been so sure she'd betrayed them all, right up until he had seen Amlinn ride out in front of her own grandfather to stop the Freefolk from attacking the Night-dwellers. Now he felt ashamed of his doubts. "Hello," he said.

The Healer made his exit, leaving the three of them alone.

Jin's eyes flicked down. Amlinn and Petra were holding hands. He looked up again at their faces. "Everyone is friends now?" he asked, repeating the Healer's words.

Petra grinned. "For the moment. I have seen things I never thought I'd see. Nightdwellers throwing dice with Freefolk. City guards singing drunken songs with them both."

"What about the rulers?"

Amlinn laughed. "Well, Sayb's not throwing dice with Grandfather or King Stobor, and I haven't heard any of them singing. But at least they're talking, not fighting."

Petra's smile faded. "There's a lot of work to do," he said. "Despite what has happened, it won't be easy to build a new way of governing Nevyana. There are Priests who will push back against my father."

"How is your father?" Jin said. "He looked ill—"

Petra nodded. "It was his heart, but not as serious as I feared. Lir does not believe his heart was damaged. He has given my father some potions that will help should he feel the heart-pain again, and others that will keep it beating strong and steady." He shook his head. "Lir has skills that no Healer of the Daydwellers could match, amazing knowledge of the inner workings of the body."

Jin said nothing, knowing some of that knowledge had come from the careful dissection of slain Daydwellers.

"I think we all have a lot to learn from each other," Amlinn said. "But Petra is right, it won't be easy. Many of the Freefolk remained with the Wise Women when we rode to City Primaxis. Samarrind won't . . . the Wise Women won't give up their vows to Arrica easily."

"There will be many of the Nightdwellers who resist the change, as well," Jin said. He smiled a little. "But the Mother Queen," he said softly, "is a force to be reckoned with."

"As is my father," said Petra.

"And my grandfather," said Amlinn.

They sat in silence for a moment, each lost in his or her thoughts.

"Actually," said Jin at last, "we're rather a force to be reckoned with ourselves."

The others laughed, and Jin laughed with them, even though it made his side hurt. From the expression on the others' faces, it made theirs hurt, too. He let his eyes flick to the joined hands of Petra and Amlinn. "And you two," he said, smiling without teeth. "Are you a mated pair yet?"

Their faces turned red, and Jin's grin widened. He never got tired of that strange Daydweller reaction.

Then Petra laughed. He looked down at Amlinn fondly. "Not yet," he said. "But maybe someday soon."

Amlinn smiled up at him. "Maybe," she said.

The door opened, and Lir-Pur looked in. "That's enough, you two," he growled. "Out. Let my patient rest."

"Will Jin be well enough to come outside at first light?" Petra asked the Healer.

"What's at first light?" said Jin.

"You'll see," said Amlinn.

The Healer sighed. "I suppose. But he must rest afterward."

"Agreed." Petra gave Jin a quick grin. "We'll come for you then." Still holding hands, he and Amlinn went out.

Jin thought that now he was awake, he would surely not need to sleep again for hours, but he was wrong. He closed his eyes after his friends left and woke to find them returning, opening the wagon door and letting in morning light that made him wince and squint.

"Come on," Petra said. "We'll help you up." He handed Jin his smoked goggles.

Jin pulled on the goggles gratefully. "I'm hungry," he complained. "In fact, I'm starving."

"We'll feed you before we bring you back to bed," said Amlinn. "But we all need to be out there for this."

"For what?" Jin asked, and again got no answer. His friends helped him up, and together they emerged from the wagon into the growing light of a new morning.

Unlike the day of the battle, this one dawned clear. The mountains in the west, snow-capped and forest-shrouded, looked close enough to reach out and touch. City Primaxis stood wide open, the ruin of its Great Gate mostly cleared away. The Nightdweller camp seemed to have tripled in size, and Jin wondered at that—until he realized that the Freefolk had moved their camp next to it.

Before the destroyed Great Gate, *Liberator* sat motionless where Petra had left it. Six guards stood around it, two Freefolk, two Citydwellers, and two Nightdwellers, all armed with firelances. That alone showed how much had been accomplished already.

Then Jin blinked in surprise. Denthold stood next to *Liberator*, unshackled and holding a lit torch. He wore ordinary clothing rather than his usual Priestly robes bearing the defaced symbol of Vekrin.

Nightdwellers, Citydwellers, and Freefolk thronged a little farther away, mingling freely for the most part, though here and there were large clumps of just one or the other, especially among the Citydwellers. Jin saw several Priests in bright blue. They mostly kept to themselves, all except one, who suddenly detached from the group and ran toward them, resolving into a tall, skinny boy with blond hair and freckles. "Petra!" he called.

Petra turned, and his face lit with an enormous grin.

"Cort!"

The two friends collided in a hug so fervent that Jin half-expected Amlinn to be jealous of it.

"I thought you were dead!" Cort said as they separated. "I couldn't believe it when you showed up driving that . . . that thing." He indicated *Liberator*.

"Where were you?"

"On the wall. Almost off the wall, when the Great Gate blew up. But I held on. I saw everything." He grinned. "You've been having adventures while I've been stuck in classes, haven't you?"

"One or two," Petra said. Amlinn cleared her throat. Petra glanced at her a little shamefacedly. "Cort, this is—"

"You'd better not say I'm one of your adventures," Amlinn said warningly.

Cort stared at her. "You've got a girlfriend? A Freefolk girlfriend?" He held out his hand to her. "Pleased to meet you. What do you see in him?" He jerked his thumb at Petra.

"Things," Amlinn said, smiling at Petra. "And stuff."

Petra's face turned red again.

Jin chuckled and then clutched his side. "Ow," he said. "Please don't make me laugh."

The Mother Queen, King Stobor, the three clan leaders of the Freefolk, and Petra's father—looking much better than the last time Jin had seen him—stood together facing *Liberator*. They seemed to be waiting for something, and it gave Jin a start when the rulers' heads turned in his direction, and he realized the something they were waiting for was them.

He, Petra, and Amlinn walked forward. Sayb nodded gravely. King Stobor said, "Greetings." Amlinn's grandfather smiled and said, "Good morning," and Shinnian and Ferrdri inclined their heads slightly.

But Petra's father broke ranks and came directly over to them. He held out his hand to Jin, who let go of Amlinn's arm to shake it. "You saved my life," Pelidor said. "And that of the king. And I'm told you have done the same for my son. You brought all the people of Nevyana together." He bowed, deeply, formally. "I am forever in your debt."

Jin felt horribly uncomfortable. He didn't know what to say, so he simply bowed his head in return.

The First Keeper returned to his place, and then all of them turned to face Denthold.

The Heretic was staring at the ground. Something glittered there, and Jin, following his gaze, saw a complex sigil in salt, the same sigil Petra had used to disable the firejars when the Nightdwellers launched their attack on Axel's men. The Heretic studied that sigil for a moment, then he took a deep breath, raised his head, and shouted, "My name is Denthold. You know me better as the Heretic or the Mad Priest." His voice rang through the still morning air to every corner of the crowd.

A stir rippled through the crowd as people suddenly recognized him. Denthold waited until the noise subsided before continuing.

"I broke with the Temple and betrayed my vows because I felt that the power of Blue Fire rightfully belonged to all the people of Nevyana, all except the Nightdwellers, whom I did not think were people at all.

"I made common cause with Lord Axel as a means to my own end, thinking that even if he seized power, he could not hold it once my own agents had spread the knowledge of Blue Fire everywhere.

"My plans were ill-conceived, and my vision half-formed. It took a young Priest-Apprentice to see that. A young Priest-Apprentice who looked beyond the lies of the so-called Gods and realized that everything we thought we knew about the Nightdwellers was wrong, that they, too, had to be a part of the better world I imagined.

"But it took a young Nightdweller and a Freefolk girl to drive that point home for me—for all of us—with their actions in yesterday's battle." He looked around the crowd. "My fate and my punishment lie in the hands of King Stobor, the First Keeper, the Mother Queen, and the clan leaders of the Freefolk. I have wronged all of their peoples in some way, and I accept whatever fate they decree for me.

"But I have requested, and they have granted me, permission for one final act as a free man. Blue Fire should work for us all. It can feed us, warm us, power wonders we can't even imagine. I knew all that, yet the first thing I did with it was to turn it into a horrible weapon.

"I called it *Liberator*, and it has played a role in our liberation, though not the one I intended. But it is still a monstrosity that should never have been built. And it must not continue to exist. And so . . ."

He turned and thrust the lit torch under the belly of the giant wagon.

There was a dull "whump!" and a puff of smoke, and then flames began to lick the edges of the wagon bed. Denthold stepped back and extinguished the torch by thrusting it into the ground. He moved to the ring of guards. Two of them took him by the arms and led him toward the city, but he walked with his head high, like a man at peace.

Jin watched him go and found, to his own surprise, he could not hate the Mad Priest despite the death and destruction he had caused. After all, Denthold spoke the truth. The three peoples of Nevyana would never have come together without his vision to begin the process, without his courage to risk the wrath of the Gods.

Jin turned back to look at *Liberator*. Flames surrounded it now, leaping ever higher. The bottom dropped out of the giant wagon. Firejars crashed to the ground, scorched. Liquid gushed out of them and instantly ignited, engulfing the entire wagon in leaping yellow flames so hot that Jin stepped back involuntarily. A column of grey smoke rose from the fire, towering higher and higher into the still air.

Jin gazed up at the smoke through his dark goggles, watching it curl and twist against the bright blue sky, the daylight sky that Nightdwellers would never again fear to see.

A final burnt offering to the Gods, he thought. *Ell, Arrica, Vekrin, whatever you were, wherever you went, we have moved beyond you.*

He turned to Petra. "So that's that," he said. "Now. What about breakfast?"

Petra and Amlinn grinned. "I hear the Freefolk fry up a lovely omelette," Petra said. "And it's particularly good with Nightdweller salt."

"The city guards have the best bread," Amlinn put in.

"Some of everything, then," said Jin.

Petra took Amlinn's hand, Amlinn took Jin's arm, and together they went in search of all that Freefolk, Night-dwellers, and Citydwellers had to offer.

THE END

E.C. BLAKE is the author of the *Masks of Aygrima* trilogy (DAW Books), *Masks*, *Shadows*, and *Faces*. E.C. Blake is a pseudonym for Edward Willett, the author of more than sixty books of science fiction, fantasy, and nonfiction for readers of all ages. His novel *Marseguro* (DAW Books) won the Aurora Award (honouring Canadian science fiction and fantasy) for Best Long-Form Work in English in 2009. His young adult fantasy *Spirit Singer* (recently rereleased by Shadowpaw Press) won the Regina Book Award for best book by a Regina author at the 2002 Saskatchewan Book Awards. Several other of his books have been shortlisted for those and other awards.

Ed's most recent novels are *Worldshaper*, *Master of the World*, and *The Moonlit World*, the first three books in the *Worldshapers* series (DAW Books). Other recent titles include *The Cityborn*, also from DAW; the *Peregrine Rising* duology (*Right to Know* and *Falcon's Egg*), originally published by Bundoran Press, and the five-book *Shards of Excalibur* young-adult fantasy series, originally published by Coteau Books. (Both series are now available from Shadowpaw Press.) His nonfiction runs the gamut from science books to biographies to history. He hosts *The Worldshapers* podcast (theworldshapers.com), winner of the Aurora Award for Best Fan Related Work, in which he talks to other science fiction and fantasy authors about their creative process.

Born in Silver City, New Mexico, Ed moved to Saskatchewan from Texas at the age of eight, and grew up in Weyburn, where his father taught at Western Christian College. He earned a BA in journalism from Harding University in Searcy, Arkansas, and returned to Weyburn to begin his career at the weekly *Weyburn Review*, first as a reporter/photographer/columnist/cartoonist, and eventually as news editor. He moved to Regina in 1988 as communications officer for the then-fledgling Saskatchewan Science Centre. He began writing full-time in 1993.

For most of two decades, Ed wrote a weekly science column that appeared in the *Regina LeaderPost* and other newspapers, and talked about science weekly on CBC Saskatchewan's *Afternoon Edition* radio program.

In addition to being a writer, Ed is a professional actor and singer who has performed in numerous plays, musicals, and operas, and sung in several auditioned choirs, including the Canadian Chamber Choir. He lives in Regina, Saskatchewan, with his wife, Margaret Anne Hodges, P. Eng., a past president of the Association of Professional Engineers and Geoscientists of Saskatchewan. They have one daughter, Alice, and a black Siberian cat, Shadowpaw.

You can find Ed online at www.edwardwillett.com.

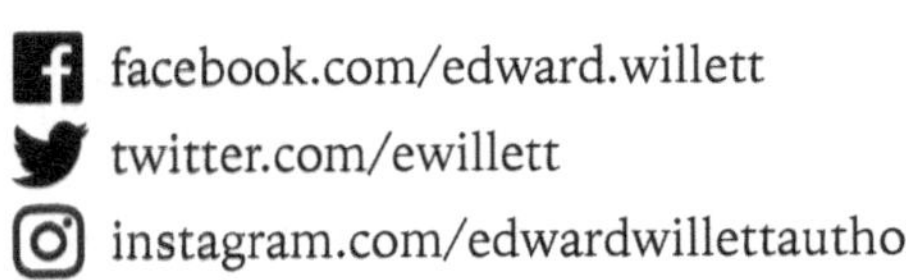

From Shadowpaw Press

Paths to the Stars

Spirit Singer

From the Street to the Stars

(Andy Nebula: Interstellar Rock Star, Book 1)

PEREGRINE RISING

Right to Know

Falcon's Egg

THE SHARDS OF EXCALIBUR

Song of the Sword

Twist of the Blade

Lake in the Clouds

Cave Beneath the Sea

Door into Faerie

From Your Nickel's Worth Publishing

I Tumble through the Diamond Dust:

A Collection of Fantastical Poems

www.ingramcontent.com/pod-product-compliance
Lightning Source LLC
Chambersburg PA
CBHW031734180726
48283CB00005B/1506